YA Series
8.99

PRAISE FOR THE
PALACE OF SPIES SERIES

★ "A rollicking spy caper in corsets. . . . This witty romp will delight fans of historical fiction as well as mystery lovers."—*Kirkus Reviews*, starred review

"This combination of willful heroine and royal backdrop will appeal to history buffs and readers who like their subterfuge accessorized by a few frills and ruffles." —*The Bulletin*

"The perfect balance of history and mystery, this novel is fantastic." —VOYA, 4Q 4P J S

"I was completely riveted by this tale of plots against the royal house, betrayal among friends, and unreliable spies!" —Tamora Pierce

"More thoroughly satisfying mischief and mayhem are afoot." —*Kirkus Reviews*

"Feisty, strong, and quick-witted, Peggy is a welcome change from vapid romance heroines." —*Booklist*

A PALACE OF SPIES NOVEL

Assassin's Masque

BEING A TRUE AND ACCURATE ACCOUNT OF THE
FURTHER ADVENTURES OF MARGARET PRESTON FITZROY,
MAID OF HONOR, CARDSHARPER, HOUSEBREAKER,
FORGER, THIEF OF PRIVATE CORRESPONDENCE,
SOMETIME CONSPIRATOR, AND
CONFIDENTIAL AGENT AT THE COURT OF
HIS MAJESTY, KING GEORGE I.

SARAH ZETTEL

HOUGHTON MIFFLIN HARCOURT
Boston   New York

www.hmhco.com

Text set in LTC Deepdene
Design by Christine Kettner

Library of Congress Cataloging-in-Publication Data is available
LCCN: 2015012289

ISBN: 978-0-544-07408-8 hardcover
ISBN: 978-0-544-81317-5 paperback

Manufactured in the United States of America
DOC 10 9 8 7 6 5 4 3 2 1
4500631540

Thanks to my agent, Shawna, and the
members of the Untitled Writers Group.

Prologue

IN WHICH OUR HEROINE MAKES A FEW SUMMARY REMARKS.

I trust those readers not yet familiar with these chronicles will permit me the liberty of making my own introduction. My name is Margaret Preston Fitzroy, though I am more familiarly known as Peggy. Publicly, I am the daughter of Jonathan and Elizabeth Fitzroy and a maid of honor to Her Royal Highness, Caroline, Princess of Wales. Privately (or at least, less publicly), I am a confidential agent in the service of the Crown.

Until recently, I was also an orphan. I lived with my dour uncle, Sir Oliver Trowbridge Preston Pierpont, and my less dour, but far more nervous, Aunt Pierpont, née Delphine Amilee Carlton. Fortunately for me, this uninviting pair was provided with a daughter of about my own age, Olivia, who became my best friend, despite her penchant for keeping flocks of small, fat, excessively fluffy dogs.

My residence with uncle, aunt, cousin, and dogs halted abruptly when I refused to honor the betrothal my uncle had contracted to a youth named Sebastian Sandford. I had intended to do my best by the arrangement until Mr. Sandford attempted to help himself to my virginity prior to our marriage, without my consent.

Presented with this information, my uncle displayed his sympathy for my plight by throwing me out into the street. This being an unpromising state of affairs for any young lady, it caused me some consternation. Fortunately, however, the gentleman who would become my patron and tutor in all matters related to the craft of the confidential agent and courtier had recently introduced himself. At that time he called himself Mr. Tinderflint. It was some time before I discovered that this overdressed, easily flustered, and apparently foolish "Mister's" right name and title were Hugh Thurlow Flintcross Gainsford, Earl Tierney.

Under the auspices of Mr. Tinderflint and Certain Other Persons, I found myself impersonating a maid of honor to Her Royal Highness, Princess Caroline. I discovered a forged letter, which led to a series of Nefarious Plots with Foreign Implications designed to topple the House of Hanover from the throne of England and set up the pretender James Edward Stuart as king.

It was very much the fashion among our English aristocrats to become out of sorts with the individuals who wore the crown of England. Therefore, on a regular basis, sundry persons would organize their armies with the intention of changing out one monarch for another. This happened to Charles the First, and after him the Lord Protector, and, more recently, James the Second. James, being more prudent, or perhaps just faster, than Charles, managed to get away to France before he was deprived of his head as well as his crown.

Once James the Second fled, William and Mary Stuart, and then Anne Stuart, took the throne. Anne did not leave any living heirs, so the English nobility was faced with a weighty decision: to allow the stubbornly unrepentant—and Catholic—James to resume the throne, or to find some entirely new (and Protestant) branch of the monarchy to fill his post. Opinions were expressed, plots were hatched, but all to no avail. It was decided that the ruling family of Hanover was close enough kin to the dying Queen Anne to fill the bill. So it was that the Elector of Hanover was offered the throne, which he accepted. In so doing, he became our current king, George.

As may be imagined, this turn of events left James Stuart (formerly James the Second) somewhat put out. He proceeded to express his displeasure through a series of (unsuccessful) invasions, which continued at regular intervals until he died. His son—the previously mentioned James Edward Stuart— proved himself a model of filial piety, and continued in the family tradition of attempting to seize the throne. As may be imagined, these efforts spawned an ongoing series of plots and plans on the part of those Stuart partisans who had by now come to be known as Jacobites. These plots happened to involve the Sandford family—most particularly Sebastian Sandford's father, Lord Lynnfield, and his older brother, Julius.

The plots also, much to my surprise, involved my dour Uncle Pierpont.

Rebellion, it must be understood, is an expensive business. It requires careful, discreet men to handle its money. And as Uncle Pierpont owned a private bank, the Sandfords and others funneled a great deal of money through that bank and into the Jacobite cause. This, while lucrative for the House of Pierpont, was also treasonous. This treason was compounded by Uncle Pierpont's acquiescing with the Sandfords' insistence that I honor my engagement to Sebastian Sandford.

It may be therefore understood that I experienced a great deal of satisfaction in exposing the Sandfords as Jacobite Plotters and Nefarious Persons. That satisfaction, however, arrived only after the Sandfords engaged in a spirited attempt to deprive me of my life.

Although I assure my readers my efforts were considerable, my survival was much aided by the abrupt and unexpected return of my father, Jonathan Fitzroy. He had not been in his grave as I'd thought. He had instead been in France, which some might declare to be worse. When I was still a child, a royal command had sent him to ferret out the plans of the would-be Stuart king, James III. While my father spied upon James and his allies, my mother, Elizabeth, also unbe-knownst to me, conducted similar investigations among Lon-don's drawing rooms and royal court.

Those few who knew my parents' profession considered it unnecessary to inform a small child her parents were spies. Therefore, I was left to conclude that my father had simply abandoned me. I was, of course, delighted to find this was not the case. At the same time, adjustment to the ownership of a father of any sort—let alone such a dashing and unpre-dictable character as Jonathan Fitzroy—was proving to be more complex than I would have imagined.

For a time, I was able to soothe this agitation by hap-pily looking forward to a future entirely devoid of Sandfords. The senior member of that clan did not survive his particular brush with Adventure. I confidently assumed the family's re-maining branches would be quickly pruned by the blade of the King's Justice. After all, the old lord had been a smuggler, traitor, kidnapper, murderer, and cad, and there could be no doubt that at least the elder son, Julius, partook of these de-lightful activities as well.

Julius, however, now held the title of Lord Lynnfield, and the possession of a minor title is a great shield and bar to prosecution, even when it comes to treason.

It was also the case that much of the proof against the Sandfords had been destroyed.

When Julius Sandford was taken to the palace to be questioned, Uncle Pierpont decided he did not wish to be arrested, charged, and hanged, with his goods and chattels confiscated while his wife and daughter were reduced to irredeemable disgrace and poverty.

This was the true and ultimate reason behind the house fire in St. James's Square, which, not coincidentally, started in the book room, where my uncle kept the majority of his private papers. He also kept himself there while it all burned to ash.

So it had come to pass that while I was poor and fatherless no longer, that coldest of states had fallen squarely upon my cousin, Olivia. Olivia responded to this reversal with all the grace and fortitude that I had so frequently observed in her throughout the years of our friendship.

That is to say that, by the day of her father's funeral, it was becoming increasingly evident that my dearest cousin was ready to explode.

CHAPTER ONE

London, October 1716

IN WHICH OUR HEROINE SUPERVISES A PERIOD
OF GENERAL MOURNING AND IS UNEXPECTEDLY
REUNITED WITH CERTAIN ACQUAINTANCES.

In order to place events before my readers in proper order, I fear I must begin at that most solemn of affairs — my uncle's funeral reception.

"How terrible it all is for you, poor child!" The latest woman in black to arrive in our parlor caught Olivia's face with her gloved hands and squeezed.

"Thank you for your sympathy," murmured Olivia as she extricated herself. Olivia and I had rehearsed this and other useful phrases that morning as we laced each other into our stiff black dresses.

"Oh, poor Delphine! He was such a good man! You must be prostrate with grief!" The black-clad matron proceeded to squeeze my Aunt Pierpont's hands with the same energy she had expended on Olivia's face.

Funeral Custom does not require people to keep a polite distance. It does require those receiving such vigorous sympathy to show appreciation. My aunt therefore murmured some response I assume was polite, if only because I'd never seen Aunt Pierpont be anything but polite.

She looked nothing less than shattered.

Standing beside her mother's chair, Olivia did not look shattered. Nor was she wan, drawn, or any other dolorous adjective generally deemed appropriate for such occasions. My cousin instead looked increasingly furious. I, therefore, wasted no time inserting myself into the conversation.

"May I offer you a cup of punch?" I kept my tone gentle and melancholy, leading the woman out of range of Olivia's razor-sharp tongue. This was my chief funereal function—to keep Olivia from making unscripted remarks to the guests. Secondarily, I was to ensure no mourner was left without brandy punch, cake, cold meats, or someone with whom to talk while we all waited for the men.

Custom dictated that bereaved women could not walk with the hearse or attend the burial. Therefore, my father —or indeed, any gentleman off the street—could accompany Uncle Pierpont's earthly remains from church to burying ground. However, my aunt, who was merely the one who had borne his children, managed his household, and stood by him through thick and thin, was required to sit in a parlor, dressed and veiled in unrelieved black to politely receive a crowd of ladies.

I set our most recent arrival milling among the others,

who all conversed decorously on such pious topics as the splendor of the coffin.

All, that is, except one. Unfortunately, this one happened to be my late uncle's mother.

"You've spent too much!" The Dowager Mrs. Pierpont stumped across the threshold from dining room to parlor, having consumed what was approximately her twentieth slice of ham. "And what is all this nonsense?" She swung her cane out and caught one of the lengths of plain black cloth that covered a mirror. The poor parlormaid, Dolcy, squeaked as if she'd been struck and ran to steady the looking glass.

I spared a selfish moment to be thankful that this woman was my grandfather's second wife. My mother, Elizabeth, had been born of his first. This meant that the apparition crossing the parlor was, blessedly, no blood relation of mine.

Aunt Pierpont had no such consolation. This woman was her late husband's mother, her own mother-in-law. She could not, therefore, be ordered off the premises or sent to bed without supper. My aunt's remaining option was to clutch her black handkerchief more tightly and murmur, "I only wanted to do what is decent."

Old Mother Pierpont snorted. "Decent? It's frippery! My son needed no fripperies in life! What's the point of throwing away good money on 'im now he's dead? Never a lick of sense in you, Delphine," she added, lowering herself carefully into the empty chair at my aunt's side.

"But, *dear* Grandmother," said Olivia from between

clenched teeth, "you know we paid for none of it. You should be pleased with Mother for managing such a significant savings."

Olivia's words might have been laced with as much vinegar as sugar, but they were also the truth. My father, Jonathan Fitzroy, had neglected to serve advance notice of intent to return to my life. He had, however, most considerately returned with plenty of money at his command. This granted him the ability to pay for a funeral service, coffin, carriages, plumes, gloves, announcements, several men of assorted stations in black coats, black draperies with which to adorn the reception rooms, and all other such trappings deemed necessary by Custom for conveying the box from parlor to church to burying ground.

Whatever reply Old Mother Pierpont meant to make to my cousin's rejoinder was cut off when the new footman opened the doors again. This time, he revealed a pair of richly but soberly clad young women whom I recognized—instantly and unexpectedly. In fact, had I been walking, I would have stopped in my tracks.

"Peggy," murmured Olivia. "Aren't those Molly Lepell and Sophy Howe?"

I nodded in mute response. Against all expectation, my sister maids of honor had arrived.

Molly, Sophy, and I were all ladies in waiting to Her Royal Highness, Caroline, Princess of Wales. Like myself, Molly was smallish and dark-haired with sloping shoulders and pale skin, making her the epitome of the maid-of-honor type. Together, Molly and I, along with Mary Bellenden, the fourth of our clan, might have been taken for sisters, or at least cousins.

This made sense in a rather unflattering way. Our chief function, after all, was to be ornaments to the court, and so we reflected the taste of those who selected the ornaments.

Sophy Howe was the exception to the type. She was the tallest of us by several inches and easily the thinnest, although thanks to expensive and well-constructed corsetry, she managed to appear well curved where it was considered to count the most. Her hair was quite golden. This shade, as near as I could tell, was entirely natural to her. The same could not be said for the pallor of her face. That exquisite mask of cosmetics and powder disguised a mind more calculating than any mathematician's.

Molly stepped up first to our little receiving line. "Hello, Peggy." She leaned in to brush her cheek against mine. "I couldn't stop her, so I thought I better come as well," she whispered as she let me go.

This was the final point of distinction between these two maids. Molly Lepell was my best friend at court. Sophy Howe may not have been my worst enemy, but she had applied for the post. Unfortunately, in these circumstances, I was almost as helpless to do anything about Sophy as my aunt was about her mother-in-law.

Almost, but not quite.

I stepped straight into Sophy's path so that I might at once embrace her and breathe words of sisterly welcome into her delicate ear.

"Make any sort of show, ask any inappropriate question, and I will pitch you out on your derrière."

Sophy hugged me back, hard. "Why, Margaret, one might believe something was not right here."

I smiled as I pulled away and answered only with my eyes. Had Sophy been able to read that message, she would not have been able to repeat it in polite company.

I turned to my aunt. "Aunt Pierpont, here are Molly Lepell and Sophy Howe. They are also in waiting to Princess Caroline. Molly, Sophy, may I introduce my aunt, Lady Delphine Pierpont, and her mother-in-law, Mrs. Amelia Pierpont. I believe you know my cousin, Olivia."

Aunt Pierpont glanced up. "So kind."

Molly smiled softly and curtsied to my aunt, then moved on to make similar gestures toward Olivia.

Sophy took Aunt Pierpont's hand. "Such a tragic accident. It must have been a horrible shock. How fortunate there were so few persons in the house at the time."

Old Mother Pierpont thumped her cane. "Ha! Sloth, that's what it was! Sloth and idleness. If those serving fools —not to mention these fool girls—had been home as they should, the thing would have been smothered in a trice! But oh, no! Our fine miss must be gadding about the town, getting up to who knows what fancy tricks!"

Sophy arched her perfectly plucked brows and turned

to Old Mother Pierpont, clearly fascinated by this succinct assessment of the family's misfortune.

"I'm sure Sir Oliver was a most diligent man," Sophy said to Mrs. Pierpont. "And that everyone did her best. A simple mistake with a candle, no doubt . . . ?"

"Ha!" Old Mother Pierpont snapped, and thumped. "Candle! Not likely! But you'll see." She nodded sagely. "You'll see what's what when it all comes down to it."

"Oh, I'm certain of *that*," replied Sophy. "The truth will out."

"We must take this as a lesson that life is brief and fragile," announced Molly in a pious and valiant attempt to end the conversation. "We can none of us know when the final blow will fall."

"I know where the first blow will fall," muttered Olivia.

"Oh, dear, Olivia, you have gone quite pale." I caught my cousin's elbow. "Come, let me get you your salts. It has all been too much . . ."

Spouting this and many other untruths, I dragged my cousin out of the parlor, up the stairs, and into her room.

"Ghouls!" Olivia cried as I slammed the door shut. She plumped herself down on the edge of her bed and folded her arms. "Can one disown a grandmother, Peggy? She has always been awful, but this is beyond the limits!"

I couldn't disagree with this sentiment. At the same time, it wasn't Mrs. Pierpont who was foremost in my thoughts. That position belonged to Sophy Howe.

When she'd walked in, I'd assumed Sophy had come both to gloat and to satisfy her unwholesome curiosity. Now, though, I was less certain. Just before Uncle Pierpont's death, Sophy had been trying to winkle out information about his private bank, and about me. Now here she was at the funeral, trying to draw out details about the fire from the spiteful Old Mother Pierpont.

Sophy had also recently taken up with my former be-trothed, Sebastian Sandford.

"Peggy?" said Olivia. "You've got that look on your face. You're worried about something."

I pulled my mind back to the present and did my best to wipe away "that look." "I'm just worried about your mother," I told her, which was true. "But it will be over soon. Dr. Wallingford will come back with the men. He'll say a prayer and we'll have supper, and then we'll be able to shove the whole pack of them out the door."

But even once that door closed, none of the agonizing complexities surrounding Uncle Pierpont's death would end. Not today, or for many months to come. Sophy's presence and her insinuating questions were grim proof that rumors regarding Uncle Pierpont and his business dealings already flew about the town.

Olivia screwed her face up tight with the effort to hold back the tears. But my cousin's strength deserted her, and she began to cry. I gathered her at once into my arms and held her close.

"I don't know what to do, Peggy," she wailed. "He was

my father . . . he was my father and he was a villain and I don't know what to do!"

Her words were garbled, but I understood her perfectly. We are told daily that a dutiful daughter loves her father without measure or question. Olivia did not love her father thus. Sir Oliver Pierpont had been a hard, taciturn, unpleasant man who would have gone to extremes to enforce his will upon his household. Arguments between father and daughter were frequent, and a few days before his death, Olivia had walked out of his house, intending never to return.

For all that, he remained her father. No sermon or homily yet written could make sense of the confusion between what one should feel and what one does feel upon such a loss of such a person.

"It's all right, Olivia," I murmured. "You don't need to do anything. Not right now."

"But Mother's all alone down there with those . . . those *creatures.*" Olivia pulled herself away and wiped at her eyes and nose with the heel of her hand. "And Grandmother. I have to—"

"I just told you—you don't have to do anything." I handed her the kerchief I had tucked up my sleeve against just such an emergency. "Stay here. Be prostrate for a while. I can keep the creatures at bay."

"Even Grandmother?"

"I shall turn upon her the full force of my maid-of-honor courtesies." I lifted my chin in the loftiest of fashions. "Should that fail, I'll get Templeton to pour gin into her punch—hers and Sophy's. Once they pass out, we can hide the bodies in the cellar."

This earned me a wan smile and a squeeze for my hand. "Thank you, Peggy."

I pressed Olivia's hand in return. Then I let her see how well I could assume an air of dignity before I glided slowly from the room.

CHAPTER TWO

In which a mysterious and expensive stranger arrives.

I was in a desperate hurry to get back downstairs so I could separate Sophy and Old Mother Pierpont before any more injudicious words were spoken. I told myself to be calm. The matter might well be taken care of. Molly was expert in all social settings. If anyone could elegantly and delicately drag them apart, it was that maid dubbed "The Treasure" by the fashionable press.

At first glance, this seemed to be the case. Sophy stood in the far corner of the dining room with Molly and two plump women I did not know. Old Mother Pierpont was still seated beside my aunt, alternately snorting and harrumphing at everything she saw. Between them, the milling, murmuring, sipping, and nibbling continued undisturbed.

This distance between Mrs. Pierpont and Sophy eased

my worries but did not erase them. Whatever Sophy's reason for being here, I knew there was nothing good behind it. I needed to get her out of this house, especially before anyone felt obligated to invite her and Molly, as my fellow courtiers, to stay for supper.

My mind was so much on this, I failed to be properly circumspect as I started across the parlor.

"And then there's this one!" Old Mother Pierpont waved her stick at me. "With her name always in the papers. Oh, yes, my gel. I read the papers!" She drew herself up, clearly proud of such literary accomplishments. "And you spend your time flaunting yourself among all those fancy Germans at court! As if any decent gel would want to see her name in print, except to get married or buried!"

Fortunately, I was much used to navigating crowds and so was able to slide quickly past that ancient and opinionated dame.

"Templeton," I whispered as I reached the maid where she stood beside the refreshment table. "Tell Dolcy to get Miss Howe's and Miss Lepell's cloaks, and then find out if there's any gin in the house."

Before she answered, I turned and sailed up to Sophy and Molly.

"Thank you both so much for coming," I said, making sure my words could be heard above the general murmur. "I know you must return to the princess, but it was very good of you all the same."

Molly caught my gist at once, as I knew she would. "Yes,

indeed. We were specifically enjoined by Her Royal Highness to convey her sympathies on your loss, but we must return to our duties. Come, Sophy, we cannot be late." Molly laced her arm right through Sophy's. If Sophy chose to object now, she'd just make herself look ridiculous, especially as every mourner in the room was watching our little scene with interest.

"Do let me walk you out." I put my hand on Sophy's shoulder for emphasis.

"I am so sorry not to have met your father while we were here, Margaret," Sophy began. "How delightful for you to have your parent back! Tell me —"

"Sophy," I interrupted, "if you want to taunt me, surely you can wait another few days. I've got too many other things to deal with. Thank you for coming, Molly," I added as we passed into the dark-paneled entrance hall, where Dolcy waited to help them into their cloaks. I beckoned to the footman. "Hayden, the ladies are ready to leave."

Hayden moved to the outer door. Before he could put his hand on it, however, there came a thud from the brass knocker on the other side. The rest of us jumped, even Dolcy. Hayden simply opened the door to bow in whoever had made the sound.

I looked up, my polite smile rising of its own accord. But when I saw the woman who entered, all thoughts of murder, gin, conspiracy, and Sophy Howe fled my mind.

This new arrival carried herself with the rigid composure of one who has spent years being tutored in the art of deportment. The black satin of her overskirt and gloves gleamed in the candlelight. Jet beads sparkled across the luxurious folds of her skirts and the full length of her sleeves. The part of me made mercenary by my time at court tried to calculate the cost of enough Spanish lace to make the veil that trailed from her head to her hems, and failed. The part of me that daily grew more accustomed to the arts of the spy noted that this profusion of riches made it impossible to clearly discern any feature of her face or person.

In defiance of all good sense, the apparition wore no bonnet or cloak. In defiance of all good manners, she swept straight past me without speaking a word.

"Molly," I murmured.

Molly touched my arm and stepped away. "Come along, Sophy."

Sophy, for a wonder, let Molly lead her away without protest. Before the door shut, I caught a glimpse of the Howe's face. Under all her perfectly laid-on paint, Sophy had gone white as a freshly laundered sheet.

I hurried back to the parlor as quickly as skirts and corsets allowed, but the veiled woman already stood in front of Aunt Pierpont's chair. My aunt gazed upon this expensive apparition from behind her much more modest veil of Irish lace, and she shuddered.

I stepped between them.

"Thank you so very much for coming, madame." I presented the veiled woman with my most precise and polite curtsy. "I pray you will excuse my inattention. I did not hear your name."

We stood close enough that I could just make out how this lady's eyes gleamed as hard as any of her black beads. "But you, I gather, are Miss Pierpont?" Her voice was high and rough, carrying the accent of the Midlands.

"Miss Pierpont is my cousin, madame. I am Margaret Fitzroy."

"Margaret Fitzroy? Yes. I should have known at once." The stranger spoke these words slowly, almost caressingly, but it was the caress of a well-honed blade against bare skin. "You look very much like your mother."

My *mother?* I could not have been more stunned had she thrown back her veil and danced a minuet. My mother had died when I was eight years old. Since then, I had met only one person outside the family who would admit to knowing her.

The veiled mystery took advantage of my shocked silence to reach out to Aunt Pierpont, but she didn't get far.

"Well, and here's another fine one!" cried Old Mother Pierpont. "With plenty more fripperies about her! No good there, I'll warrant. What have you to say for yourself?" She thumped her stick. "Speak up, madame!"

The apparition turned toward the withered and tart old woman, and when the stranger spoke, I heard the smile in her voice. "Good afternoon, Amelia. How delightful to see you again. I am only sorry as to the circumstances."

These gentle, polite words produced the most astonishing effect. Old Mother Pierpont positively and unmistakably shrank backwards in her chair.

Apparently satisfied with this as her answer, the woman bent down so close to Aunt Pierpont that their veils brushed together. It was only by straining my gaze sideways that I was able to see that she was pressing something silver into my aunt's hand.

When the stranger spoke, it was in a murmur. "Against that day when you will need your true friends."

A warning tremor ran down my spine as she straightened.

"Will you take some punch, madame?" I asked quickly.

"No, thank you, Miss Fitzroy." Again her tongue lingered about the syllables of my name. "I must away."

"Then let me see you to the door." I fell into step beside her and, whether she would have it so or not, walked with her into our cool, and quite empty, entrance hall. "Again, I thank you for coming in this sad time. Do let me once more beg your pardon for my terrible inattention." I faced her and smiled in what I hoped to be gentle befuddlement. "I still do not know your name."

The woman made no answer but took a step closer to me. She smelled strongly of musk and old roses. I could just make out the shape of her face beneath her veil. It was sharp, with hollow cheeks and, I thought, the marks of age.

"But I know you, Margaret Fitzroy," she said. "I know who you are and all that has been done to you."

She clearly meant to discomfort me with this. Unfortunately for her purposes, I had been intimidated by experts, some of whom were armed with far worse than words. "You are singularly well informed, madame, and evidently well acquainted with the Pierponts. Were you also acquainted with my mother?"

"Extremely well. You might say Elizabeth and I were birds of a feather." She may have smiled beneath her lace.

"And yet you won't tell me your name."

"Not yet, Miss Fitzroy. But that will come quite soon." Now I was sure she smiled. I could hear it coloring her voice. "Now that I have seen you, and seen Elizabeth in you, I shall know how to act."

She meant to turn her back and glide away. I could tell. It was, after all, a fine speech and would have answered very well for an exit. Alas—giddy maid that I am—I can be deeply inconsiderate when it comes to other people's dramatic turns.

"How is it any friend of my mother's should come to our house afraid to show her face?"

Movement caught the corner of my eye. It was Olivia, standing in the doorway from the parlor, pale but determined, and glowering. The apparition must have seen her too, but the appearance of a witness apparently gave her no pause.

"Very promptly spoken, Miss Fitzroy. In truth, it is my own fault. I was too slow and left too much in the charge of others. But I am here now, and we will be together again in due course." The veil turned toward Olivia. "Look to your family, both of you. Remember who you and yours truly are, and do not be dissuaded."

This time, the apparition did glide, right out the door and into the street, while we were left to stare.

❧❧❧

CHAPTER THREE

IN WHICH OUR HEROINE HAS SEVERAL
UNCOMFORTABLE CONVERSATIONS
AND MAKES A WELL-INTENTIONED,
BUT SOMEWHAT RASH, PROMISE.

The appearance of the veiled mourner had one lasting effect on the rest of the funeral day: it almost exactly replaced my attitude with Olivia's and vice versa. Olivia found the strength of purpose to stand by her mother's side, even to the point of ignoring every one of Old Mother Pierpont's vehement declarations. For my part, I found it nearly impossible to return my attention to funeral matters. My thoughts raked over the veiled woman, searching each detail of her form and voice for some clue as to her identity. I needed to know who she was and what had brought her to my treacherous uncle's funeral. More than that, I needed to know how she dared pretend an acquaintance with my mother.

Perhaps most importantly, I needed to know why she

had frightened not only Aunt Pierpont and Mrs. Pierpont, but the unflappable Sophy Howe.

Of course, I was also frantic to discover what she had given my aunt, but we were not afforded any fresh glimpse of the item. Not even when Aunt Pierpont stood to receive the gentlemen as they returned from the graveyard.

Being chief mourner and host, my father, Jonathan Fitz-roy, led the black-clad and wholly masculine crowd into the parlor. He bowed solemnly to Aunt Pierpont before he passed to me.

"All well, Peg?" he asked softly.

"As well as can be, sir," I murmured as I made my curtsy in greeting.

His dark gaze held mine for a long moment. I was still growing accustomed to having any sort of father, let alone one with such startling looks. Jonathan Fitzroy had a long, strong, angled face accentuated by a pointed beard and mus-taches. He wore the dark curling wig favored by the French. In his mourning clothes, he looked like the devil come dis-guised as a bank clerk, which is an unnerving comparison to make of one's parent.

I was certain he knew that something untoward had happened. Like me—and indeed, like my mother—Jonathan Fitzroy was both courtier and spy. I burned to tell him about the veiled mourner, but now was most decidedly not the time.

The rest of that long day passed with only the normal sorts of strain. The men circulated decorously among the women. Dr. Wallingford did indeed speak a solemn prayer. He also said an appropriate number of consoling words to Aunt Pierpont and Olivia. For the chief among the guests, a supper was in due course presented. Not once during that meal did my aunt look at me. Olivia mostly pushed the food on her plate about, and in an impressive show of self-restraint, she answered any remark addressed to her with a solemn shake of her head.

With Old Mother Pierpont we did not have to contend. Shortly after the men returned, she declared herself "done with this never-ending nonsense" and took herself up to her bedroom. I spent most of supper wondering if this declaration and her accompanying absence were related to that veiled, nameless, unwelcome woman.

When our new housekeeper, Mrs. Biddingswell, was finally able to shut the door behind the last of the departing mourners, all four of us let out sighs of relief. My father and Aunt Pierpont were scarcely less demonstrative about this than Olivia and myself.

Aunt Pierpont did dab at her eyes and take my father's hand. "Thank you, Fitzroy. For all you have done. I'm sorry . . . I'm so sorry . . ."

"Don't distress yourself, Delphine," he answered. "I'm glad to be able to return a little of the good you did for Peggy while I was abroad."

"Yes. Yes. Of course. Well. I am very tired. I think I'll go to my room . . . if . . . that is to say . . ."

I found myself looking at her hands, to see if I could catch some glimpse of that silver artifact the veiled woman had given her, but all I saw was her tightly crumpled kerchief.

Father patted her shoulder. "It's exactly what I was going to suggest. Anything else can wait for the morning." He bestowed upon me a significant glance. "Peg, Olivia's also looking tired. Why don't you girls go upstairs as well?"

With this, we, the distaff members of the household, all proceeded up to the second floor. On the way, I debated with myself. I knew what I wanted to do, and it was not right. It was, in fact, deeply inconsiderate. My aunt had just lost her husband. I should give her all possible time to grieve in peace.

We arrived at the door of Aunt Pierpont's room and she turned. "Good night, Peggy, Olivia. My dears, I . . . you are both very good girls."

I swallowed. "Are you certain you're all right, Aunt? You have everything you need?"

"Of course, dear. Fitzroy—your father, that is—has been so very kind."

Olivia watched me closely. My conscience dug in its heels. For better or worse, however, I'd become adept at ignoring such internal inconveniences. "I'm worried that woman upset you."

My aunt blinked her big, watery eyes up at me. "Which . . . oh, *that* woman." Her gaze darted between us. "She was only an old friend of my . . . of Sir Oliver's, and his family," she added with more haste than such a statement would seem to warrant. "She's been abroad a great deal in recent years, so I suppose she's acquired some foreign manners. Foreigners can be so dramatic, as I'm sure you know, Peggy."

"She told us she was acquainted with Peggy's mother," said Olivia.

"Did she?" Aunt Pierpont blinked. "She may have been. She knew all the Pierponts at one time, I believe, and when Elizabeth still lived with us, we all were used to going out a good deal. We met many people."

"She never said her name," Olivia pointed out. "That seems . . . odd for a friend of the family."

Aunt Pierpont blanched at this. My conscience took an unusually firm hold and squeezed, but not quite hard enough.

"I know so few of my mother's friends," I said. "I would like to correspond with her, if I could."

"Oh. Ah. Let me see." Aunt Pierpont twisted her handkerchief. "When I knew her, she was Eleanor Wall, I think. Yes, Eleanor Wall. She married when she went abroad. That would make her . . . let me see . . . something with an O . . . I'm sorry, Peggy—I simply don't remember."

Disbelief tightened my stomach. This could not be happening. It was not possible that mild, nervous Aunt Pierpont was lying to my face.

"But what did she give you?" I asked. This startled Olivia, who had not been there for that particular exchange, but she recollected herself enough to remain silent.

"A little memento, some trivial thing. I've already

forgotten where I put it." Aunt Pierpont looked around herself in mild confusion, as if the trinket might have fallen to the carpet.

Olivia, with that presence of mind that is so particularly hers, stepped forward. "I'm sure it will turn up in the morning." She kissed her mother's cheek, fondly but quickly, and grabbed my arm firmly. "We'll just say good night now."

"Yes, thank you. I am very tired. Olivia . . . Olivia, I'm so sorry, about everything."

"Don't, Mother," Olivia whispered. "None of this is your fault."

Without waiting for her mother's reply, Olivia pulled me into our room, shut the door, and locked it. Then she sat me down on the edge of the bed and grasped both my hands.

"Tell me everything." She must have understood something of the look on my face because she added quickly, "And don't you even think of trying to shelter me. If this is about my father, I have every right to know what consequences are coming to us."

What protest could I possibly make against that? I took a deep breath, and I told her what I had seen.

"You're sure it could not have been simply a keepsake?" she asked. I knew from Olivia's knitted brows and hardened jaw that she was already considering whether to storm out and demand answers of her mother. Hopefully, my cousin would decide against it. I didn't feel quite up to tackling her from behind.

"What sort of memento could it possibly be?" I asked

her, and myself. "And why bring it now? And why would she be so careful to disguise herself? If she'd had one more inch of lace about her person, she could have opened a milliner's shop." I could have gone on. For instance, if this mysterious Eleanor, who might also be "Mrs. O," was a friend of my mother's, why wait to make herself known until Mother was eight years dead?

But then, she'd never said she had been Mother's *friend*. She said they were "birds of a feather." Mother had been yet another member of the Fitzroy firm of confidential agents, so that phrase could mean many things, some of which were less than benign.

Olivia frowned at the fire, at the door, and at me. "You should tell your . . . that is, Uncle Fitzroy." She stumbled over the designation that was even newer for her than it was for me. "He's still acting as a confidential agent for the Crown, isn't he?"

"I think he is. He has not said otherwise." Not that we'd had many opportunities for private conversation. When a person dies, there is a great deal to be done, even when the necessity of finding a new house and facing inquiries from various magistrates, lordships, bankers, royalty, and a spy master or two are not involved.

I saw the unavoidable importance of laying matters before my father. But reluctance crept over me, which was as strange as it was ridiculous. If some new Adventure was about to seek me out, I should be glad to have Father's protection, not to mention his staunch and experienced assistance.

Despite this, I did not move, at least not toward the door.

"Let me get out of these weeds first." I shook out my black skirts. "I can barely think for the itching."

If Olivia realized I was delaying, she said nothing. We helped each other out of our heavy mourning and into lighter housedresses and wrappers, caps, wool stockings, and slippers. The house my father had taken was of older, half-timber construction, and the late October drafts had not only gained easy entrance but now chased one another merrily about the floor.

And I still hesitated.

"Do you want to come with me?" I asked Olivia, and hoped it did not sound too much like a plea.

Olivia shook her head. "No, I think you should talk to him alone. You can tell me all about it later. I really am tired." I remembered again it was her father we buried today. Such a thing was wearing, even for someone of Olivia's energetic and dramatic temperament.

I took up a candle. I swallowed and brushed at my wrapper. Olivia smiled.

"Come now, Margaret Fitzroy." She opened the door and stepped back. "You've faced swords and pistols. You can face your own father."

This was most likely true, and I was entirely out of delaying tactics. There was nothing to do but set off into the dark, old house and hope to find Jonathan Fitzroy in a communicative mood.

CHAPTER FOUR

IN WHICH THERE IS A FRANK

EXCHANGE OF VIEWS.

The gleam of firelight from underneath the closed parlor door told me where my father might be found. I hesitated, lifted my hand, hesitated, chided myself, hesitated, blushed, hesitated, and knocked.

"Come in."

I obeyed.

Father had drawn a tapestry chair up close to the fire and sat with his stockinged feet on the brass fender. In one hand he held a long white clay pipe. All the attendant paraphernalia of tobacco pouch, knife, and tamping tools had been laid out on the table at his elbow, along with a pewter tankard of what I supposed to be beer. He'd left off his dark wig. In truth, he hardly needed it. His own black curls tumbled almost to his shoulders. He'd evidently been scratching at his chin, because his previously pointed beard now closely resembled a squirrel's nest.

Father gestured to the empty seat on the other side of the hearth while still managing to tuck a fresh wad of Virginia leaf into his pipe. "I hope you've no particular dislike of tobacco," he said. "I acquired the habit on my travels. I suspect it may not be entirely wholesome, but it does help a man think."

"Pray do not stop on my account," I murmured as I put my candle on the mantel and took my seat on the other side of the hearth.

He nodded his thanks, lit a spill from the fire, and applied the flame to the pipe. I watched this operation in uncertain silence. I wanted to talk with him, to grow to know him, and I wanted him to know me. But I wanted different circumstances. Different settings. Perhaps what I truly wanted were different emotions.

When Father had his pipe going to his satisfaction, he settled back in the chair and blew out a long, fragrant plume.

"Well, Peg, it has been a long day."

"It has," I agreed.

"Your aunt says you've been a great help and comfort."

"I did what I could. She has always been kind to me."

There then followed a labyrinthine silence, the sort where you desperately want to find a way out, but cannot.

It was my father who provided the exit. "Have you made up your mind yet?"

"On what point?"

Father regarded me through the twisting veil of his smoke. "Whether or not I'm to be trusted, I think," he said at last.

I felt a fresh blush. "I wish that I could make up my . . . not my mind, exactly." The words tumbled out of their own accord. "My heart? I want things to be right between us, but I can't see what right is, and I am trying. Truly, I am."

My father reached out and took gentle hold of my shoulder. This close I could see the lines about his eyes and the shadows beneath them. "It's all right, Peg. We have been apart for a long time. We should neither of us be afraid if the breach takes more than a day or two to mend." He offered me a smile. This I accepted, and returned one of my own. "There, that's better, my pretty little Peggy-O." He chuckled.

"If I may be so bold as to ask a favor of you, sir?" I murmured.

"Why, of course. Anything you need."

"I need you to never call me that in public."

That drew a sharp bark of laughter from him. "You have my word on it." He laid his hand over his heart.

Something in me eased. If we could laugh with each other, surely we would not remain distant for long.

"Will you tell me what happened today?" Father asked as he settled back in his chair. "Was it something to do with Olivia?"

"No. Not entirely." I took a deep breath to try to wash the pique from my tone and told him of the veiled woman. I did not omit our exchange in the entrance hall.

"She said she knew my mother. She said . . . that they were birds of a feather."

Father made no answer. He only puffed away at irregular intervals, like a blocked chimney.

"Did you hear me, sir?"

"You may be very sure that I did. But you have not finished yet, I think."

This startled me a bit. But it was accurate, so I told him of the much briefer conversation when Olivia and I had accompanied Aunt Pierpont up to her room.

"She lied?" His eloquent brows arched. "You're certain?"

"I've learned to identify the phenomenon." I believe I may have lifted my nose in the air a trifle.

"Of that I have no doubt. Well." He took another long and thoughtful draw on his pipe. "It is not at all what I'd expect of Delphine."

"She must be at least somewhat aware of Uncle Pierpont's involvement with the Jacobites."

"I'd be surprised if she wasn't. But did she agree with the involvement?"

"She's far too conventional, and too nervous. She'd never take a rebellious stand, not even out of loyalty to Uncle Pierpont."

"Quite true." Father puffed a few more times on his pipe. "Probably she's trying to protect you, and Olivia, of course."

"From what?"

"That is the question." He removed the pipe stem from his mouth. "She gave you no name for this veiled woman?"

"Not an entire one. She said she'd known the woman once as Eleanor Wall, and that the woman might have married some man whose name begins with O."

My father dropped his pipe.

The clay shattered on the hearthstones, scattering ash and sparks in every direction. Father and I both shot to our feet, he with a rather greater abundance of exclamations. There followed a period of madly brushing and stomping at the sparks, with the tankard of beer being sacrificed to douse the infant flame that sprang up on the edge of the new Turkey carpet.

When all the sparks had been extinguished, my father and I stood staring at each other, breathless.

There was a knocking and the door opened. "Is everything all right, sir?" asked Mrs. Biddingswell.

"Yes," answered Father calmly. "A trifling accident. You needn't wait up. It can be cleared away in the morning."

"Yes, sir." Mrs. Biddingswell clearly didn't believe this, but she did withdraw.

When the door shut, I said mildly, "I take it you also know this mysterious Mrs. O?"

Father shook his head and shook it again. I watched him considering whether to lie, and how much. I prepared myself to be angry.

"You know I was sent to Paris to spy on the Stuart court in exile at Saint-Germain. You also know I was betrayed and sent to the Bastille." Father stopped. It was a long time before he started again. "I heard, much later, that the letter revealing my mission and identity was written by one Mrs. Eleanor Oglethorpe."

"Oglethorpe?" Mysterious veiled women at funerals should not be named Oglethorpe. DuMonde. Veracruz. Fierenza, certainly. Oglethorpe entirely lacked dramatic grandeur.

I opened my mouth, but Father held up his hand.

"We don't know," he said firmly. "We know absolutely nothing. We can, however, surmise that this Swedish plot you so recently uncovered is part and parcel of some larger effort."

I was sitting again. "I might observe, sir," I said with rather exaggerated calm, "that a woman—whatever her name—who would betray you to the Stuarts and the French should not be publicly parading about my uncle's funeral claiming close acquaintance with my mother."

"That concerns me greatly. I do not like conspirators— whoever they may be—who are not afraid to make a grand show. They tend toward other dramatic gestures of the more dangerous variety." This cool understatement sent a chill through me.

"But if she is this Mrs. Oglethorpe, and is a Jacobite . . . do you think she really knew my mother?"

He was a long time answering. "She may have." He picked up the largest pieces of his broken pipe and laid them carefully on the table. "Elizabeth, your mother, was at court when several of our most important treaties with the French were signed, not to mention during at least one of the attempts by the Pretender to return at the head of his own army. Even I do not know how many plots she may have overturned by her work. Lord Tierney never found all her letters, and he is a very thorough man. She may have burned them, of course."

"Or they may have been stolen."

He nodded in agreement as he settled back into his chair. "Because of that, I cannot say for certain why this is happening now, but I will find out. No one has the right to use Elizabeth's memory to play their petty games against us. When are you due back at court?" he asked abruptly.

"That is not fixed. Her Royal Highness told me I should take as much time as I needed."

This made him chuckle. "When the Princess of Wales says one should take as much time as one needs, Peg, it is as well not to presume too heavily on the statement. But more importantly, I dislike this veiled mourner, whether or not she is Mrs. Oglethorpe. I think we need to inform Lord Tierney of her appearance. He should be able to give us good information in return, as he's been spending these past several days delving into Sir Oliver's affairs." This did not surprise me. "You should also be there at court to hear at once when anything new occurs," he added.

Despite its many inconveniences, I liked my court life. I should therefore have been quite relieved that my father showed no inclination to insist that I retire from it to the shelter of his house, there to live anonymously, not to mention stainless and pure, until he found me a suitable bridegroom.

I could not, however, help but find Jonathan Fitzroy's easy acceptance of my circumstances perplexing. After all, when we'd found each other, we'd come within an inch of being killed. One would think that might have earned me a protective gesture of some sort.

Father must have realized something of my confusion. "While I was imprisoned, I thought of you and your mother, Peg," he said softly. "But the only picture my mind carried of you was the little girl who rode on my shoulders. When I saw you—the real you—I saw an extraordinary young lady who had earned her life, and her place. I could not be more proud, but I don't know how to be a father to that lady." He lifted his face toward mine. "I very much want to be someone you trust. I want . . . I want you to feel you can talk with me, and I want you to know that I will help you however I can." I noted how his hand shook where it rested on his knee.

"There is another reason I should perhaps return to court," I said, more to break the fresh silence than anything else.

"What is that?"

"When the veiled mourner arrived, there was another girl here, Sophy Howe. She clearly recognized the woman and might be talking with her. Sophy is not above slander, or blackmail, if she feels it might gain her some advantage." I paused. "Also, just before I . . . left . . . she'd taken up with Sebastian Sandford."

"Did she, now? I've heard about Sebastian Sandford's conduct toward you." Father's tone made me look at him again. He was speaking to the fire, but his face had hardened. His body had gone stiff and still. I knew that attitude. It was the posture of a man readying for a fight.

Had I wanted some protective measure? Here it was.

Father relaxed again, but only slowly. He also eventually managed a smile. "No more of this uneasy talk. You look exhausted. Get you to bed, young lady."

"And what of you, sir? Should you not also retire?"

"I shall assume the privilege of my age and station and not answer that. Go, my girl. Look after yourself and your cousin. I will see you in the morning."

I stood and bobbed a respectful curtsy as I had been taught. "Sir, I must extract one solemn promise from you before I go."

My father looked up at me. "Whatever it is, you already have it."

"Then swear to me, upon your immortal soul, you will get Old Mother Pierpont out of this house before someone —I will not say who—is driven to violence."

Father chuckled, but his face remained stern. "Leave Amelia Pierpont to me." There was a soft undertone to these words, a cross between a purr and a growl. I did not like it at all. Father seemed to notice my discomfort. "And I equally promise, Peg, I shall be responsible for the protection of Delphine and Olivia, no matter what happens."

He spoke firmly. He wanted me to believe him, and so did I.

-ᴼ᷈ᷓᴗ᷌·᷐᷌ᴗ᷌ᴼ-

IN WHICH OUR HEROINE PLOTS HER
RETURN TO COURT, WITH FRIPPERIES.

One does not, of course, simply walk back into the Palace of St. James. This is true even if one is nominally in residence there or has important, clandestine information to communicate to certain royal personages. As with all momentous events, letters must be written first.

My initial letter addressed my mistress, Her Royal Highness, Caroline, Princess of Wales, and humbly requested her leave to return to my duties. As I was reasonably sure permission would be granted, I also wrote to my maid, Nell Libby. I'd had to depart so suddenly that there had been no time to put my belongings in any sort of order. Therefore, I'd left Libby at St. James with instructions to look after things there. Libby was a tiny girl of about my own age. Her intellect was so sharp, I was sure sooner or later one of us would be cut by it. She had, however, proved quite willing to put her wits, as well as her skills as a hairdresser and compounder of cosmetics, to work on my behalf. For my part, I rewarded her as far as my purse allowed. Thus far we were both satisfied with the arrangement.

Then, of course, I had to write Mr. Tinderflint to inform him of my impending resumption of post and place. I did not set down any description of the curious events from the funeral day. Letters have a nasty habit of going astray, especially when one is being watched by veiled women and known blackmailers.

Then there was one other letter. This last took longer to compose and suffered from several false starts. This note was to Matthew Reade.

Matthew Reade had begun life as the son of an apothecary. His family, recognizing some spark of genius, or possibly mischief, had caused him to be apprenticed to the celebrated artist James Thornhill. Matthew's chief work in the service of this great man was to assist in the management and operations of the Academy for the Improvement of Art and Artists in Great Queen Street.

He was also tall and lean and possessed a head of dark red hair, fine gray eyes, and a smile of devastating sweetness.

At the time of this writing, Matthew and I—and I am forced to admit this against the dictates of a nature my readers will have observed to be generally cautious and circumspect—had fallen head over heels in love.

I did attempt to hide the strength of my feeling for a while. This façade, however, had proved impossible to maintain. I loved Matthew Reade. I loved his humor, his intelligence, his kindness, and yes, shallow thing that I am, his handsome face and fine form.

But I still knew fear. It came most strongly during the times when it seemed that the turmoil of my life would never settle. I had dragged Matthew into very real danger not once but twice, and I now possessed unquestionable evidence that fresh dangers waited just over the horizon. That was a great deal to ask a lover to endure. How much should I confide in him? How much more would he accept and still stand beside me?

I stared at the fresh sheet of paper in front of me. It was so tempting to close my desk without finishing the letter. Surely the veiled Mrs. O's appearance would amount to nothing. Everyone who mattered already knew my uncle had been involved with Jacobites. It was only to be expected that one of them would show up at his funeral. Jacobites loved dramatic gestures: from loud toasts to bonfires on certain birthdays to attempted invasions at regular intervals. Also, common sense told me there was any number of perfectly incongruous reasons Mrs. O could have dredged up my mother's name, and unnerved my aunt, and quieted Mrs. Pierpont, and turned Sophy Howe pale. If I gave myself enough time, I could surely assemble a complete list. There was no need to inform Matthew of such trifles.

Yet, if I evaded the truth and he found out, things would surely be the worse for us both.

I was taking far too long about this. Olivia had already gone down to breakfast and I had promised to join her. Probably she supposed I meant sometime before noon.

I dipped my quill into the ink and laid down the words with an uncertain hand.

My Dearest Matthew:

You asked once that I not hold anything back from you when it comes to any business I might have with Mr. T. Unfortunately, it seems I will have to keep that promise sooner than I had hoped. Be assured, I am well and looked after, but I am most likely returning to court sometime during the next s'en night. When I do, I will bring more of that business with me. Write to me there and I will reply as soon as I can.

I miss you and I love you. Please write soon.

Yrs. ever,

Peggy Mostly

I sanded, folded, and sealed the letter as quickly as I could so my coward's heart would have less time to change the work of my rather more conscientious hand.

As I applied my seal, a knock sounded at the door.

"Come in," I called, picking up my quill to write the direction. The knock was soft enough that I assumed it was our new footman come for the letters.

But when I turned, Aunt Pierpont was standing at the threshold. "I hope I'm not interrupting, Peggy."

She still wore her heavy black dress, as she would for a while yet. She clutched her black handkerchief, but her eyes were dry and there was an unexpected air of resolution about her.

"No, of course you're not interrupting," I said quickly, dropping my quill back into its stand. I was somewhat surprised, however. My aunt usually spent her mornings abed, resting her nerves. Since for once those nerves had sound and objective reason to feel strained, I had assumed we would not hear from her until well into the afternoon.

"Fitzroy—that is, your father—tells me you are to return to court soon." She advanced a few steps into the room.

"I hope to. It all depends on Her Royal Highness."

"Yes, of course." Aunt Pierpont fiddled with her handkerchief. "I do not wish to impose, but . . . do you think there is any way you could bring Olivia with you? She is eating her heart out here. I am afraid she will make herself ill."

I found myself staring in surprise. "Are you sure, Aunt Pierpont? That is, I would think you and she needed some time to . . ."

But my aunt just shook her head. "I might need some time, but Olivia needs distraction, and, well . . ." She swallowed. "She is not betrothed yet, of course, and I am no longer—that is, I no longer move in the right circles . . ."

With that, all things became clear. My aunt was asking me to take Olivia to court so she could catch herself a husband. For once, something in my life had a perfectly conventional explanation, and I found myself rather appalled.

"But would you be all right here, alone?" True, my father was currently in residence, as it was his house. However, he had a bad habit of disappearing on short notice. Then there was the specter of Mrs. O to be considered.

"Oh, I shall be perfectly well," replied my aunt with forced cheerfulness. "In fact, I had thought once Olivia is safe with you that I might go away for a bit."

Had I been startled before? Now I was dealt a resounding blow. Aunt Pierpont had never once before spoken of leaving London's immediate environs. Indeed, for her to go from St. James to Mayfair was an undertaking that involved every servant in the house, not to mention all the wraps, shawls, and smelling salts.

Aunt Pierpont took note of my undisguised shock and lifted her quivering chin. "I have some family of my own. In Colchester. I have not seen any of them in such a long time. Mrs. Pierpont will want to return to her own home soon, I think." *I hope.* It was not difficult to hear these words under the others. "She will feel easier if she has someone more than just a maid to help her. If all goes well, I mean to travel with her to Norwich and then go on to my own people."

"Are you sure, Aunt Pierpont? Maybe you should take a little more time to recover . . ."

My aunt just shook her head. "I believe that when all other things are taken into account, it is best if I am away from London for a bit. I find myself in need of a respite from this difficult business, and, well, especially as my home is gone. I'm leaving all my business in your father's hands." She twisted her handkerchief. "It is not precisely as my husband would have wished, of course." This was putting things mildly indeed. Had Uncle Pierpont been more than a handful of ashes, he would have reared up out of his coffin. "But Fitz-roy was always good to me, and your mother loved him so. I am certain he will do what is right for me and Olivia."

I was almost certain he would mean to, but he'd left his family alone once before, for eight years. It might have been longer if I hadn't stumbled over him during my own adven-tures. How much could we really count on him for mundane details such as paying the household bills?

And what would he think when he heard that Aunt Pier-pont planned to leave town in the company of her mother-in-law? As I considered it, I wondered if there might have been more than the hope of a marriage behind her desire to get Olivia out of the house.

I found myself looking at my aunt with fresh eyes, and I did not at all like what I saw.

Stop this, I ordered myself. *You are inventing fears. Haven't you enough real ones?* I rallied my spirits and conjured up a smile. "I will, of course, do everything I can to help."

"Thank you, Peggy." Aunt Pierpont gave her much-abused handkerchief an extra twist. "I knew we could count on you."

"Will you come down and tell Olivia?"

"Oh, no, no. I'm still quite worn, and you know I cannot bear the smell of food before one of the clock. I will go to my room and rest for a while, and then there will be so many let-ters to write, I'm sure you understand."

I did not. I did not understand one thing that was going on. I said I did, however, and accordingly wished her good morning. Aunt Pierpont closed the door, leaving me alone with my rapidly growing sense of disquiet. Which was ri-diculous. Aunt Pierpont had nothing to do with Jacobites or veiled women, or court, or anything of the kind.

But her husband had, and her mother-in-law might, and my deceased mother, who was once my aunt's close friend, most decidedly had.

This was entirely too much to contemplate before breakfast.

I hurried downstairs, determinedly keeping my thoughts fixed on food and coffee. But as I reached the dining room door, I heard a shrill voice shiver through the thick oak planks.

". . . Oh, I see through you. You're thinking, 'I'm clever. I'm a modern, educated gel, and my father is dead. I can slip out of all this easy enough.'"

I clamped my mouth shut around a most heartfelt groan. That was something I had failed to take into account. Aunt Pierpont might not take breakfast, but Old Mother Pierpont most definitely did.

"Really, Grandmother—are you talking of family, or a hangman's noose?"

"Ask yourself this, my gel," said that sagacious dame. "Where's all this ready money come from so sudden, eh?" I could not make out Olivia's reply, but it did not mollify Old Mother Pierpont. "You're a fool ten times over, Miss Olivia. What is stolen from one Pierpont is stolen from all."

"If you think for one moment I'm going to listen to your calumnies, you old—"

This seemed a prudent time to rattle the doorknob and sail into the dining room.

"Good morning, Mrs. Pierpont, Olivia." I breezed over to the sideboard, where breakfast was laid out in covered porcelain dishes. "How do I find you today?"

"Hmmph." Mrs. Pierpont stared a fine set of daggers at me as I helped myself to cake and jam along with a ragout of root vegetables and the previous night's roast beef. Olivia's look—somewhere between alarm and relief—was far more disturbing.

I joined Olivia and Old Mother Pierpont at the foot of the table. That grand dame immediately leaned over my plate and sniffed. "What sort of mess is that, I'd like to know? Stuffing your face with them slurries and sugars!" She had a small bowl of watery porridge in front of her, accompanied by nothing but the salt cellar. "I suppose that's a fashion you picked up among all your fancy friends at the court. You think that complexion of yours will last forever? Well—"

"Just so, Mrs. Pierpont," said my father.

Father had entered a good deal more quietly than I had. He made his bow to our little assembly and passed to the sideboard. There, he removed the cover on one of the tureens and helped himself to nothing less than gray, watery porridge before settling at the head of the table. "In addition to the expense, a luxurious breakfast is extremely hazardous to the digestion. If I may trouble you for the salt, Peg?"

I passed the salt. I also exchanged a meaningful glance with Olivia before we two returned to ruining complexion and digestion with plum cake and ragout.

Mrs. Pierpont narrowed her eyes at Father. "Are you mocking me, sir?"

"I am agreeing with you, Mrs. Pierpont." Father tucked into the thin mess he'd selected with apparent relish. "There's no excuse for wasting money on something so ruinous to one's health. Unfortunately, with the unavoidable necessity of entertaining so many guests, extra provisioning had to be brought in, and the house is not yet ordered entirely as I would wish it. As waste is the more grievous sin, the food must be eaten somehow."

"You needn't trouble yourself with any more flattery, Mr. Fitzroy. Oh, yes, I know flattery when I hear it." Mother Pierpont nodded. "Your daughter is proof of your genuine views—nothing but meringue and mischief picked up from them Germans at this new court."

Father cast me a careful look that, if short on meringue, certainly held a fine dose of mischief.

"Nothing like the court of the good old queen," he murmured, shaking his head.

"Exactly! These trumped-up foreigners and their lackeys

and their women with these ideas and fancy French talk. How could any man allow his daughter to mingle with such corruption?"

"Profit," he said.

Mrs. Pierpont's mouth shut like a box lid.

"As little as I like it—being entirely of your opinion about the hazard these foreigners represent to the heart and soul of our nation—there is only one way to wring the cash of England out of the German hands that hold it, and that is from within their ranks."

He looked toward me again, and I dropped my gaze modestly and exerted all my powers to raise a blush in my cheeks.

"Dutiful daughter that she is, Margaret returns among them to be the eyes and ears of the Fitzroy family." He paused and turned his dark, knowing gaze upon Mrs. Pierpont. "I very much hope she will continue as the eyes of the Pierpont family as well." His fresh pause was so pregnant with significance, I expected it to burst all across the breakfast table. "To that point, if you have finished your meal, there are one or two matters I think it important we discuss. The children do not need to be involved in such business." He rose and extended his hand. "May I see you settled into the back parlor? I've given orders that the fire in there be banked for the morning. A warm house is unsettling to the humors, not to mention a waste of fuel, especially after a heavy meal."

Whatever foes Mrs. Pierpont had faced in her life, she clearly had never known such an assault of agreeable shrewdness. Mute with what I presumed to be wonder, she extended her arm to let my father walk her solicitously from the room.

The door closed behind them.

"Did that just happen?" asked Olivia.

"It did," I replied. "I will thank him later."

"We both will." She raised her cup to me, and we clinked our rims.

"What was she going on about when I came in?" I asked as I turned back to my coffee and cake.

"I barely remember. I'm sure it was family, family, and more family."

This I did not entirely believe, but I also recognized that mulish gleam in Olivia's eyes and knew I would get nothing further from her at this moment. "On the subject of family, Olivia." I pushed some cake crumbs about my plate with my fork. "Your mother came to see me."

"She got up before one?"

"She did, and it was to ask me to speak with the princess on your behalf, to see if you might come to court."

Olivia sat back and blinked at me. "Mother suggested this?"

"She says she wants to go back to her people in Colchester and that she wants you to stay with me." I left out the bit about it being a husband-catching expedition. There was no reason to set off that particular explosion before we'd finished breakfast.

Olivia looked past me to the door and said nothing. Silence from Olivia was never a good sign. Her mind worked so quickly, any of a hundred things might have been happening in there simultaneously.

Then her face lit up in a brilliant smile. "It's perfect!" she cried. "We'll be able to work together to unveil our mysterious mourner!"

"Olivia," I said as sternly as I could manage. "Clearly we need to uncover what's happening, but we can't go charging about like angry bulls or mad playwrights."

"Of course not!" Her reply held an astonishing amount of indignation. "But isn't this exactly what we wanted, even before this disaster began? We'll be pursuing your work, both of us together, and we'll be free, really free, for the first time in our lives!"

She seized my hands, obviously overjoyed, and yet there was a determination underneath that joy that caught at me like a thorn against skin.

"Only if you're sure, Olivia."

"I'm entirely sure. Everything is working out for the best."

Since "everything" included her father's demise and her mother's heretofore-undiscovered talents at deception, this was not an entirely reassuring statement. "Olivia Pierpont, you are not a normal sort of girl."

"That, Margaret Fitzroy, is the pot calling the kettle sooty. When do we go?"

CHAPTER SIX

IN WHICH OUR HEROINE RETURNS AMIDST

MUCH COMMOTION ONLY TO RECEIVE

A VERY SMALL — AND FLUFFY — PRESENT.

The first reply to my flurry of correspondence came from Her Royal Highness and arrived in grand style: carried by a messenger in a red coat with blue cuffs and gold braid. The princess's letter indicated approval of my plan to return and suggested I should do so in time for the levee the following morning.

Thus do we learn that making requests of princesses can be a hazardous business. I had thought to have at least another day or two to complete my arrangements.

With these orders came a second missive, not, as I expected, from Mr. Tinderflint, nor, as I had hoped, from Matthew. This one was scrawled in a childish hand and filled with suspect spelling.

Dear Miss Fitsroy,

I trust this find you well. I wish you to know that you puppie, Isold, is well and grows every day. It is my wish that you should come see me and Izolde as soon as is convenyent.

Yrs.,

Anne, Princess Royal

I had to smile at this. Six-year-old Anne was the eldest of the three daughters of the Prince and Princess of Wales and was what is generally described as a precocious child. This meant she understood her own mind, and her own power, far better than anyone was comfortable with. She had attached herself to me largely because I had been instrumental in her acquiring her flock of lap dogs. Much to my consternation, my reward for this was to be gifted with the smallest member of the recent litter.

The next letter came with the regular post from my maid, Nell Libby. It informed me that all was in order for my return. I waited the entire day, but no further missives arrived, not from Mr. Tinderflint, nor from Matthew. The first worried me. The second left me with a wish to give in to an attack of the vapors.

Unfortunately, being under royal command left no time for vapors or waiting about for delinquent correspondence. There were persons to inform, transportation to arrange, and, unavoidably, clothes to select.

The next morning, only Father and Olivia came onto the

stoop to see me off in the chill and fog. Aunt Pierpont was keeping to her room to rest her nerves. Old Mother Pierpont was holding solitary state at the breakfast table.

"Tender my greetings to Mr. Tinderflint, and don't worry. I've things well in hand here." Father kissed my damp brow and resettled my cloak's gray hood. He also eyed the waiting sedan chair and its slouching attendants. "And I promise you, this is the last time you'll be traveling by chair."

These separate declarations did surprisingly little to lighten my mood, especially when it is remembered that I very much wanted to return to the palace and I loathed sedan chairs. I could not, however, shed my worries about what would happen with Father and Mrs. Pierpont and Olivia once I left the house. Still, I managed to smile at Father before I turned to Olivia, kissed her cheek, and whispered in her ear. "Do no violence against your grandmother, and keep an eye on your mother. Write if anything happens."

Olivia took my hand in affectionate farewell. She also pressed something into it. When we drew apart, I was holding a wad of paper tight against my palm. Olivia leveled at me a look of such significance it could have been seen from Paris, let alone my father's vantage point. I tucked the paper up my sleeve and tried very hard not to meet his eye as I clambered into the waiting chair.

A sedan chair is, in its essence, a cabinet with a seat built into it. If one is lucky, that seat is padded. If one is even luckier, that padding is of some recent vintage. This cabinet is attached to two long poles, which are lifted by two strong men, one in front and one behind. These chair men then proceed to run, or at least waddle, through the streets, carrying the cabinet's occupant to her destination.

During the pauses in the chair's twisting, tipping, and jolting progress, I managed to extricate Olivia's note from my sleeve. With only a few indelicate phrases to accompany the effort, I was also able to undo its multiple folds and (eventually) read the following:

> Silver medallion, about the width of my palm and
> as thick as a sovereign coin. Designs on both sides.
> One side: large horse trampling down a house, noble
> lady (Britannia?) holds crying baby and weeps.
> Reverse: a man holding crown and scepter raises
> hand (in blessing?) to crowd of people reaching out
> (beseeching?), separated by waves. Edge engraved
> (stamped?) with NOBILIS EST IRA LEONIS.

"Olivia, you are hopeless." I returned the note to my sleeve, striving to remain appropriately appalled by Olivia's unfeeling behavior. Clearly, my cousin had not lost a moment in resuming her self-appointed station as my assistant in spy work. At some point during the night, Olivia must have rifled through her mourning mother's possessions to find the memento.

The fact that her observations might prove useful made this show of proper feeling difficult.

"Hopeless," I muttered again as I stared out the window at London wobbling past. "All of us."

London made no answer at all.

St. James's Palace is famous across Europe. Unfortunately, its fame derives largely from being low, cramped, labyrinthine, and in general unsuited as a home for the rulers of Great Britain. These inadequacies extend to its four great courtyards. On any given day, even the largest of them is filled to the brim with a monumental uproar of persons, carts, and livestock. On the day of my return, the madness had reached a fever pitch. The Prince of Wales's birthday celebrations were almost upon us. Following the grand fête, His Royal Highness would begin a tour of the southern counties, and somewhere among these festivities, there should also occur the much-anticipated birth of a new member of the royal household. Such a confluence of great affairs required extra deliveries of supplies and a greater than usual influx of persons of all stations and sorts, from provisioners and additional cooks to the men who would stage and manage the fireworks and theatricals.

Despite this swelling flood of human activity, my arrival in the Color Court did not go entirely unnoticed.

"Peggy!" A small girl wearing a blue velvet cloak and carrying a covered basket barreled out the nearest door, cutting a chaotic path between porters, carters, and a flock of highly annoyed geese. This bit of expensively dressed enthusiasm was followed by two individuals made extraordinary by their contrast to each other. The first was Lady Portland, the most senior of the royal governesses. A tall, thin apparition in black, she wobbled along on wooden pattens in a futile attempt to keep up with the girl. The second, shorter personage was my patron, Hugh Thurlow Flintcross Gainsford, Earl Tierney, or, as he was privately known to me, Mr. Tinderflint.

"Your Highness!" shrieked Lady Portland. "Your manners! Your *shoes!*"

The immediate result of this explosion was that all persons within earshot, regardless of station, were forced to stop whatever they might have been doing and make their reverences, for the minute and exuberant individual in blue was none other than Her Highness, Anne, Princess Royal.

"Lord Tierney said you'd come back today!" Princess Anne bounced to a halt in front of me, entirely ignoring that she did so in a mud puddle. "Thank you for telling me, Lord Tierney," she added as he came puffing up behind her. She spoke with the lofty, lisping courtesy she was capable of assuming at the drop of a hat or turn of a whim.

"It was my pleasure, Your Highness." He bowed, still puffing.

I have labored to find the exact words to fit Mr. Tinderflint. *Portly* barely begins to describe his girth. *Splendid* possibly does justice to his elaborate dress. *Dry* suits his humor, and his manners are the epitome of *courtly*. What remains beyond description, however, is the shrewd and sometimes ruthless mind beneath the surface of the short, round, beribboned, bejeweled, and excessively refined individual.

Princess Anne's moment of courtesy vanished as quickly as it had arrived. "The dogs have missed you so much! And look! I brought you Isolde!" Her Highness thrust the covered basket forward. "She can stay in your rooms now, but you must bring her back to play with the others every day!"

I kept my smile fixed as I peered into the basket. A fluffy white puppy, small enough to fit in my cupped hands, peered back at me with eyes of demon-bright intelligence.

"Of course, Your Highness. I am looking forward to it." This was not true, but it is difficult to confess that one holds no fondness for dogs, especially to royal girls giving them out as gifts. I reached out and attempted to pat the little creature's head. I was experienced enough in the ways of the royal lap dogs, however, that I was able to snatch my hand back before the overfluffed ingrate snapped her sharp little teeth around my index finger. Lady Portland looked disappointed. She and I had never agreed, even before I became responsible for her nursery being saddled with Isolde's large, loud family. Sometimes I got the feeling Lady Portland itched to see me turned out with all of the dogs in my luggage. Fortunately, my rank in the court, as well as the favor I was held in by royals large and small, limited her ability to injure me to the occasional sharp glower, such as the one she used now.

Mr. Tinderflint, as usual, accurately read both Lady Portland's glare and my urge to say something we might all later regret. He gave a delicate cough. "Tiny pups can become

chilled so easily. It would be advisable, I think, for Miss
Fitzroy to take Isolde inside before her pillow grows damp."

"Oh, yes, of course." Princess Anne deposited the basket
into my hands so that I was forced to juggle it and my band-
box. The basket's occupant growled.

"Oh, don't worry, Izzy!" The princess went up on tiptoe to rub the puppy's ears. "Miss Fitzroy will bring you to
play often! You promise, don't you, Miss Fitzroy? No matter
what?"

"No matter what, Your Highness." I hoped Princess
Anne did not notice my smile straining around the edges.

The princess nodded, a surprisingly adult gesture that
emphasized her resemblance to her mother. "I shall expect
you shortly, then."

"After lessons, Your Highness," prompted Lady Portland. "Which you will soon be late for."

Princess Anne rolled her eyes, sighed, and flounced away
with an attitude of righteous tolerance. Lady Portland also
departed, but not without one more backward glower.

Isolde, for her part, gave me another sharp growl and
burrowed back down into the depths of her basket. I felt a
surprising amount of sympathy with this act.

"How very good it is to see you, Peggy, my dear!" Mr.
Tinderflint said as he helpfully relieved me of my box so I
could wrap both arms around the basket.

"And you, sir!" I gave him the curtsy I had neglected
before. This caused the basket to joggle, which in turn

caused Isolde to yip in outrage. "But isn't the hour a bit early for you?"

"It is, it is." He nodded, setting all his chins wagging. "But I could not deny myself the pleasure of seeing you as soon as possible."

"And the chance to remind Princess Anne of our friendship was merely pleasant coincidence."

"Naturally." Mr. Tinderflint winked heavily. "For no man of proper feeling would attempt to ingratiate himself to a mere child, no matter how highly born." He extended his arm. "May I claim the privilege, the very great privilege, of escorting you and your new charge to your apartment?"

"You are all kindness, sir." I cradled the basket in one arm so I could lay my hand on my patron's blue silk sleeve. "We must talk," I murmured.

Mr. Tinderflint made no direct answer but bestowed upon me a swift and owlish glance to indicate he had heard. "Yes, yes. Come along, my dear, do come along. Her Royal Highness has not been feeling very patient of late."

With this ominous declaration, my patron led me inside to the place that, for better or worse, had become my home.

"Welcome back, miss," said Libby as I entered my rooms. The fire was going, the candles were lit, and I felt myself relaxing as familiar walls and furnishings surrounded me. I could even regard with some good humor the way Libby halted in midstride when she heard my basket growl.

"Oh, no," she said.

"Oh, yes." I deposited the basket on the hearth. "We'll need some rags, and a bowl of milk, and some towels."

"I expect so, miss," Libby muttered. "And some more towels after that. I'm going to need extra coin for the laundry women."

"Yes, Libby," I said obediently as I allowed myself to be divested of cloak, gloves, pattens, reticule, scarf, and all other such outdoor trappings, which Libby whisked away into the dressing closet. Libby, among other things, suspected I did not take my responsibilities toward my worldly goods seriously enough.

As soon as Libby was out of sight, I deposited Olivia's note into my writing desk. Mr. Tinderflint watched this with great interest and arched brows. I shook my head and mouthed, *Later.*

"You seem to have kept everything in excellent order," I called to Libby to cover the noise as I locked the desk. Libby murmured her thanks. She came out of my closet to glance sharply around at the room's relatively simple furnishings of bed, chairs, writing desk, and stool. I wondered what was missing, or had been missing until recently. Libby I trusted, but she kept some company among the palace servants of which I was less certain.

"Well, now, my dear, I must leave you in your maid's most capable hands," Mr. Tinderflint said regretfully as he gave me another of his courtly bows. "I am, alas, alas, not able to accompany you to this morning's gathering."

"Why not? Surely nothing's wrong." I said this with a smile and a very strong awareness of Libby's bustling presence and attentive ears.

"Oh, no, no. It's a mere matter of business. If you will permit, I will wait on you following the levee." It was not strictly proper that I should receive Mr. Tinderflint in my apartment. I was an unmarried maid, after all, and he an unmarried man. But Libby's presence combined with the general belief that he and I were related in some not-entirely-understood way would give us a fig leaf of propriety.

Isolde chose this moment to scramble out of her basket and tumble onto the hearthstones. She immediately set about establishing her rank and status by barking furiously at them. I watched, overcome by the sinking feeling that I would never know a sound night's sleep again. "Please do come after the levee," I said grimly. "You may be needed to help hide the corpse."

"Now, now, my dear, when you are with others you may pretend you do not understand the advantages of being godmother to the royal lap dogs. But with me?" He laid one bejeweled hand on his expansive chest and assumed a doleful air. "We know each other better than that. Oh, ah, yes, and you might find these useful." He made a great show of patting his pockets before drawing out a wooden box to hand me. I lifted the lid to reveal a small store of anise biscuits.

Mr. Tinderflint winked, bowed, and took his leave. Isolde followed dangerously close to his high heels, barking as if she were personally chasing him out the door. As soon as she was denied Mr. Tinderflint's heels to molest, she immediately turned and began barking at my toes.

While I had hoped for at least one or two fluff-free days, I had known I would not be able to put off assuming responsibility for Isolde for long. I had therefore recently entered into correspondence with St. James's Master of the Hounds—a bandy-legged, irascible, tobacco-spitting man who seemed highly amused to be discussing a creature that would never hunt anything bigger than a silk ribbon. Nonetheless, he had provided me with some sound advice regarding the tendencies of canines in general, which I hoped to combine with my knowledge of the royal lap dogs.

There was one particular trait that all the members of Isolde's family shared. They would do anything, follow anyone, if they thought there might be food at the end of the journey.

I snapped one of the biscuits in two. "Isolde, shh! Can you keep a secret?"

She stopped her barking in confusion. I dropped the biscuit. "Secret!"

Isolde pounced on the tidbit with alacrity and silence. I watched, a whole set of unaccustomed ideas filling my mind. Not that I had time to put any of them into play. Libby stood at the threshold of my closet, tapping her foot. From this I deduced that I was, as usual, in danger of being late to wait upon Her Royal Highness.

In short order, Libby had stripped me down to my

chemise and pushed me into the dressing table chair so she could begin work on my face. Isolde decided to investigate the closet. She apparently took exception to my clothing and dove at my fresh hems with a growl.

This time, I was prepared.

"Secret!" I dropped the other half of the biscuit. Isolde was diverted, my hems were spared her displeasure, and Libby was able to wield her brushes and pomades in peace.

A good hour — and four more of Mr. Tinderflint's biscuits — later, my maid pronounced me fit to be seen. By this time, Isolde was stretched out in her basket in front of the fire, her swollen belly emitting ominous rumbles and indelicate, anise-scented vapors. I was therefore able to collect my fan and leave the room entirely unscolded and even unnoticed.

The Princess of Wales's apartments were not difficult to find. The corridor was brightly lit, and teemed with well-dressed persons. If this was not indication enough that august personages waited behind the double doors, there were also a pair of footmen and four yeoman, not only on duty, but at attention.

I gave myself a final moment to smooth my skirts and touch my pomaded hair. As ready as I could be, I snapped open my black and lavender lace fan and nodded to the right-hand footman. He nodded back solemnly and drew in a great breath.

"Miss Margaret Preston Fitzroy!" he cried, and flung back the doors.

CHAPTER SEVEN

IN WHICH OUR HEROINE REESTABLISHES
HERSELF IN FAMILIAR TERRITORY, THERE TO
FIND THE GAMES VERY MUCH IN PROGRESS.

Every head turned. Every eye fixed itself on my progress through the princess's antechamber and into the brimming drawing room. My shoulder blades twitched, as did one particular spot beneath my corset, corresponding with a recent bruise. I did not permit myself to hesitate. Instead, I walked straight through that assemblage of the glittering and the great.

It had taken more than the usual level of fuss and bother to get my wardrobe even somewhat prepared for my return. That cruel dictator, Custom, commands those of us who suffer the loss of any near relation to attire ourselves accordingly for lengths of time that vary depending upon our proximity to the dead. This leads me to suspect that the powers behind Custom's throne consist largely of mantua makers and handkerchief merchants.

I, as a mere niece, was not expected to wear unrelieved black for a year like my aunt and cousin, but I did need to dress somberly for several weeks at least. I (and Libby) chose to honor this particular collision of Fashion and Custom with a black skirt and white underskirt accompanied by a bodice and stomacher of plum and gray. I felt very much like a twilight shadow as I crossed between persons arrayed in rainbow hues and trimmed with quantities of sparkling gold and silver.

I saw Molly Lepell standing at the center of the crowd with Mrs. Howard, one of the women of the bedchamber. Mary Bellenden, our sister maid of honor, was in the corner talking and laughing with several evidently captivated men. Her previous favorite, Lord Blakeney, was not among them. Had poor Blakeney fallen in that maid's fickle estimations? As if she guessed my thoughts, Mary looked at me over all their heads and winked with her usual careless humor.

The person I did not see was Sophy Howe, who should have been front and center at this gathering. I could not ask anyone about this unexpected absence, however, for no one among the gathering could officially acknowledge my arrival until I had made my greetings to the princess.

"And here you are, Miss Fitzroy," Her Royal Highness, Caroline, Princess of Wales, remarked as I dropped my deepest and most respectful curtsy. The royal dressing table had been moved from the bedchamber to the drawing room for the levee. The princess reclined on a comfortable couch, with her slippered feet resting on a cushioned stool. Her corsets had been loosened to their fullest extent to make room for her great rounded belly.

As with many ceremonies, the levee has its origins in the French court. There, the nobles would assemble to watch the royalty getting bathed and dressed. Why France's rulers felt the need for their courtiers to see them wearing naught but what the Lord blessed them with at birth remained beyond my powers of comprehension. Thankfully, the levee as practiced in Great Britain did not involve viewing royalty in their most natural state. At this time, for example, Princess Caroline was almost entirely dressed, missing only a few details, such as her rings, the ribbon for her throat, and her shoes.

"You see, Lord Amesbury, I told you Margaret would not disappoint." The princess beamed slyly at a thin man in a full-bottomed wig and a coat of shimmering aquamarine satin. "I must warn you, though, that you are only one among the crowd asking after her. Margaret, I had not realized you achieved quite so many conquests during your brief time with us."

There was only one answer to that, and it involved the fluttering of my freshly painted eyelids and a demure murmur. "I'm sure I don't know what you mean, Your Highness."

The princess laughed, but I couldn't help hearing that the sound was strained. "Well, perhaps they simply wish to recoup their losses from gaming tables. Is this the case, Lord Amesbury? Have you lost money to our Margaret?" The princess tilted her chin up to him flirtatiously. I didn't know who Amesbury was, but if my mistress was taking so much trouble to charm him, I needed to find out.

"Heavy pride and a light purse are indeed a fearsome combination, madame," quipped that worthy. "But neither drives a man so hard as the prospect of spending time in charming company."

We all laughed at this elegant phrasing, as did the few persons within earshot. It was expected that we maids would partner with the gentlemen, play cards, laugh charmingly, and lose prettily. However, as the stakes at these games ranged from the merely high to the utterly ruinous, I had become rather good at, let us say, clandestinely controlling the flow of the game. I do assure my readers this was purely out of self-defense.

"Lord Amesbury is certainly welcome to try his luck, if he thinks it has turned," I said. "But I believe I may swear off cards."

"Why is that?" asked the princess.

"The sight of how terribly crestfallen the gentlemen become when they lose is far too much for my delicate nerves."

This earned me a round of raised eyebrows and "oho's" from our bystanders. The princess smiled and nodded her approval.

"We cannot have you risking your health on any account, Margaret. My daughter Anne will never forgive me." Her tone caused me to risk a glance at my royal mistress, one that was closer to direct than was strictly allowed by the twin forces of Rank and Custom. For my pains, I got an unpleasant shock. Princess Caroline was smiling and laughing, but not a trace of this sparkling humor reached her clear blue eyes. Those remained cold and hard as glass.

Fortunately, I was not called upon to make further reply. "Now, Margaret, I release you to the room and Lord Amesbury to his luck." Her Highness waved her fan in a broad gesture that ended with her beckoning to her chief women of the bedchamber, Mrs. Titchbourne and Mrs. Claybourne.

Dismissed and unsettled, I withdrew. I needed to speak with Molly Lepell. At once.

The art of navigating a crowd necessitates a great deal of vague smiling and waving in combination with determined forward motion. At last I reached Molly's side and we were able to clasp hands and brush cheeks.

"Hello, Peggy," said Molly. "I see you've lost none of your edge for being away." She nodded at Lord Amesbury, who had joined a cluster of men and women at the far side of the room, but who was nonetheless watching us with speculative attention.

"Welcome back, Miss Fitzroy." Mrs. Howard gave me a kiss in greeting. "It is good to have you with us once again."

Mrs. Howard had the dubious distinction of being much admired, much talked about, much married, and much in the favor of the Prince of Wales all at once. Unlike some others, she did not relish her notorious and complicated status. Also unlike some others, she had an astoundingly steady nature.

"Thank you, Mrs. Howard. It is good to be back." It was surprising to not just say those words but to realize how much I meant them. "I'm afraid, however, I have a favor to ask. Could you inquire as to whether I might be allowed a private word with Her Royal Highness?"

There is a hierarchy to communication with the sovereign, even for those of us who have royal regard. When one plans to ask for favors, it is prudent to observe all the protocols.

Another woman, especially one so highly placed, might have mentioned that it was a bit soon for me to be trespassing on Princess Caroline's time, or her own. Unlike many of the other ladies and women of the bedchamber, though, Mrs. Howard was fairly well disposed toward me. "I'll see what can be done." She gave me a smile that did not reach her grave eyes and slipped away easily through the crowd, leaving me and Molly as alone as two people can be in a room filled to bursting with servants, courtiers, nobles, and royals.

The ability to carry on a private conversation in the middle of such a crowd is yet another skill that those desiring a successful career at court must cultivate. When I spoke to Molly, I made sure to keep my tone light, lest I attract undue attention to the words.

"Her Highness seems in poor humor today. Is anything amiss?"

"You mean anything beyond your recent discovery of funds for the plot to return the Stuarts to the throne?" Molly smiled over my head at someone and nodded toward someone else. "If anyone knows, no one's telling, not even Mrs. Howard."

And I had just sent her to ask for some of the princess's time so I could beg a favor. My chances of achieving my aims seemed to shrink precipitously.

Molly, for her part, wasted no time in changing the subject. "I confess, Peggy, I did not expect you back quite so soon. Not that I'm sorry. It's been positively dull here without you."

I smiled and waved my fan vaguely toward some of my own acquaintances. "Surely Sophy's been at pains to provide you all with entertainment. Where is she, by the by?"

"I couldn't say." Molly searched the crowd briefly and shook her head. "She asked permission to withdraw shortly before you arrived."

"Really? Am I so terrifying that the Howe must flee? She was bold enough to meet me at my father's house." Molly's mouth twisted tight and I dropped my voice to a murmur. "You said she was fairly insistent about coming to the funeral."

"She was. Although I can't tell for certain whether the idea came from her or her Mr. Sandford."

That spot beneath my corset twitched again. I do not lightly label anyone an enemy, but the members of the Sandford family were all enemies to me, most especially Sebastian and his older brother, Julius. These were not simply the snippy, annoying antagonists such as a maid might be expected to develop at court. Clan Sandford dealt in life and death.

"The papers have been full of Sophy and Sebastian's exploits at the card tables," I ventured. "They seem to be permanent partners these days."

Molly nodded. "And it's getting worse. One begins to wonder if they have some special need for all that money."

"Perhaps they mean to flee the court. Or the country."

Molly laughed. "Hold tight to hope, Peggy. You may need it later. Ah!" she cried, raising her voice to a volume meant to be heard. "Now there stands Lord Amesbury, all alone. I'm sure Her Highness told you he has been *most* persistent in his requests to make your better acquaintance, Margaret. As have about a dozen others." Then she added, sotto voce, as she looped her arm through mine, "Are we ready?"

"We are," I replied, and with that, Molly and I plunged into the crowd.

CHAPTER EIGHT

IN WHICH ONE MYSTERY IS SWIFTLY
EXCHANGED FOR ANOTHER.

All during the hours of the levee, the doors opened at irregular intervals, either to admit newcomers to the gathering or to allow those who had business elsewhere to depart. Despite the demands on my attention, I kept a close eye on these comings and goings. But none of the newcomers was Sebastian Sandford, and Sophy Howe didn't seem to be returning.

Where were they? What were they up to? I had no answers and no way to find any. Until the levee ended, duty and protocol demanded I remain here, helping to amuse Her Highness's guests.

There are things in this world about which one cannot properly complain. One of these is an excess of attention.

Any attempt to moan over the fatigue generated by hours of receiving compliments from richly dressed men or invitations to parties and the theater from a bevy of wives and widows is far less likely to generate sympathy than dismissive laughter.

I attempted not to lose sight of the fact that none of these flattering attentions resulted from my own charm or effort. They came because I stood in good stead with Her Royal Highness. The lords and gentlemen who smiled and flirted, as well as the women and wives with whom I exchanged witty barbs, all wanted one thing — to move that much closer to the center of power. At the same time, I could not help but relish the compliments, the congratulations, and the requests for my opinion on various questions, much the way one relishes a fleeting patch of sunlight on a rainy day.

But why should it be fleeting? murmured an insinuating voice in my mind. *You have well-placed friends. You have a father now, and he has money. You have the princess's good will, and she's given you a task and trust for which you cannot easily be replaced. Why shouldn't this be your life for as long as you wish it?*

It may be seen by this that there are some small, still voices inside us that have nothing to do with conscience.

By the time the levee ended, my memory was stuffed with names and invitations. Molly had already given me several warning taps with her fan, probably because she detected in me symptoms indicative of a severe spinning of the head. The last tap was actually a hard poke in the ribs. When I turned to stare indignantly, Molly jerked her chin toward

Mrs. Howard, who stood beside the princess and beckoned me over.

"You wished for a private word, Margaret?" said the princess as I made my curtsy. Although the footmen were closing the doors behind the last of the guests, we were, of course, not alone. That never happened. The ladies of the bedchamber remained arrayed about us. They were all politely doing something else, however, such as standing and talking with one another or directing the servants to move various displaced furnishings back to their proper locations.

"Yes, madame. I do not wish to presume . . ."

Her Highness dipped her chin and gave me a Quelling Look. Princess Caroline hated false courtesy, including any declaration that one was not doing the thing one was clearly about to do.

I started again. "With Your Highness's permission, I would like to bring my cousin, Olivia, to stay with me for a little time." Being at court essentially meant one was a permanent houseguest. One could do very little without the host's direct permission.

"This would be the cousin we met so recently? The breeder of Princess Anne's puppies?"

"Yes, madame."

"She is also, I believe, the daughter of Sir Oliver Pierpont?"

"Yes, madame." I tried to keep my tone matter-of-fact, but this was exactly what I had feared. The accusations against Uncle Pierpont had already come home to roost for Olivia.

"Margaret, it is imperative that you understand our situation is extremely delicate." The princess's demeanor had changed. Gone was the warm and witty lady of the levee. Before me now was the clear-eyed and calculating mistress of palace and court. "No matter what the upheavals of your personal life, I need you here and I need your attention fixed on the matters that have been entrusted to you."

"Yes, Your Highness, I do understand. Because of that, I feel I should mention that Olivia was of great help to me when it came to the recent discoveries."

"And you will vouch for your cousin's conduct?"

"Yes, Your Highness, without hesitation."

There is no silence so sharp as that belonging to a princess, and Princess Caroline could wield her silences like a carving knife. I knew I should go on to explain that Olivia had no part in her father's doings, that she was not only my cousin but my firm and fast friend. But the words would not come. I kept remembering Olivia's heedless cheer at the chance to turn courtier and spy. Perhaps it would not be so terrible if permission to come to court was delayed a little — just until Olivia's temper had time to settle and I knew more of what was going on.

I had no opportunity for speaking at all just then, because the drawing room doors opened and the footmen snapped to abrupt attention.

"His Royal Highness, the Prince of Wales!"

All persons in the room stopped whatever they were doing. Those who were seated rose, including Princess Caroline, with Mrs. Howard's assistance. We likewise all dropped into grave and respectful curtsies, our eyes directed modestly downward.

I was, of course, forbidden to straighten, or even look up, until granted permission, but I could hear a whole clattering crowd of men's hard-heeled shoes crossing the floor. I strained my gaze to its limits, but all I could make out was a flock of decorated shoes, white silk stockings, and parti-colored coat hems. There was, I noted, one pair of black stockings among them, matched with a pair of plain black shoes.

Prince George and his retinue came to a halt in front of the princess. There then issued forth a loud rustle of stiff silk brocades and starched linen to indicate they were all bowing.

"Good morning, madame!" cried the prince in his hearty, German-accented French. "I apologize that our business kept us so long that we could not join your levee, but these gentlemen wished very much to make their duty known to you."

He gestured to the room at large, permitting all of us to straighten. I took the opportunity to raise my eyes a little.

On all occasions to which I had been witness, George Augustus, Prince of Wales, affected the character of a bluff and hearty gentleman, filled with lavish praise for all things English. This last habit especially endeared him to many, which was why he did it. In physical terms, His Highness was a medium-size man, inclined to a certain thickness about the middle, who preferred to dress as if he were about to go riding or shooting.

Today he wore a dark blue coat with black cuffs and only a modicum of gold braid. His white breeches were stout cloth rather than velvet. In contrast, the half a dozen gentlemen currently in his train had mostly donned jewel-colored silk coats with full skirts and bright buttons. One, however, dressed in the unrelieved black of deepest mourning.

Cool, poised, and proud as a black cat stood Julius Sandford, Lord Lynnfield.

First I froze. Then I staggered. How had I not known Julius Sandford was here? I should have felt it in the creeping of my skin. I'm sure I would have, but for one small fact: his presence was impossible.

Julius Sandford could not be standing with Prince George. His Royal Highness might appear shallow, but he was no fool, and he had a knack for spotting his enemies. He could not have been taken in by a man whose father had been an avowed and proven Jacobite.

Who less than a fortnight ago had tried to murder me.

Lord Lynnfield also could not be here because Mr. Tinderflint would have known it, and Mr. Tinderflint would not have concealed such vital information from me. Of this I was certain, or mostly so.

Julius Sandford's eyes—that is to say, Lord Lynnfield's eyes—flickered in my direction, no doubt taking in my sudden pallor. His younger brother would have smiled to see it. Lord Lynnfield did not betray any such malicious expression, or indeed any expression at all.

I became aware that Mrs. Howard had grabbed my elbow and pinched hard. She was not the only one among the ladies who noticed my discomfort. Her Royal Highness nodded regally toward me. "You may go, Miss Fitzroy. You have my permission to speak with the Lord Chamberlain about your cousin's accommodation. When she is settled, send word and I will receive her."

"Thank you, Your Highness," I murmured, and curtsied again. All the gentlemen, save the prince, bowed while I made my departure. I felt Lynnfield's gaze like a leaden weight.

It took a year to cross the princess's drawing room, and then there was the antechamber and the gallery. It was another year before I rounded a corner into an empty room and was finally able to collapse against the wall, pressing my hands against my stomacher and dragging in the deepest possible breaths. Spots danced in front of my eyes. I squeezed them shut and fought for calm, but calm would not come. My mind was too full of the memories of roaring water. I saw Julius Sandford's blank blue eyes as he raised his cane high, ready to strike. I saw his father toppling into the Thames and vanishing beneath the waves. I heard the crack of gunfire and felt the ball strike my midriff. I felt the icy Thames drag me down.

"Oh!" cried a woman's voice. "I *knew* I heard something."

Oh no. My eyes flew open. *It can't be her.*

I lifted my head. I was right. It wasn't *her.* It was *them.*

Sophy Howe stood in the doorway, poised and perfect in a gown of blue and cream with fountains of white lace at the throat and sleeves. A man's silhouette lurked in the corridor behind her. I could not see him clearly, but I knew to the depths of my soul who this shadow was.

"Look, Mr. Sandford, it's our Miss Fitzroy." Sophy Howe beckoned Sebastian to her side. "And she seems to be in some distress."

"I do believe you are right, Miss Howe." He folded his arms and lounged against the threshold, elegantly, of course. "Whatever is the matter, Miss Fitzroy?"

Sebastian Sandford smiled contemptuously at me from his place beside Sophy Howe. The golden pair stood almost touching and gazed down at me with false concern and genuine triumph.

It required a massive effort of will, but I pushed myself away from the wall. These two were not permitted to look down on me. I hardened my stomach muscles, blessed my corsets, which helped me to stand up straight, and looked them both in their sparkling, predacious eyes. I might have been afraid, but I would not be cowed, not by them. Not ever.

"It is nothing at all." I flipped open my fan and fluttered it energetically. "A momentary faintness, no doubt brought on by the excitement and heat of the levee." I took my time looking them up and down. Sophy and Sebastian were well matched in many ways. Both were tall, blond, and possessed of good looks that could be used to dazzle, if you knew nothing about the characters beneath. Like his brother, Sebastian dressed in all black, down to his stockings and polished shoes.

"I had expected to be able to greet you there," I went on, forcing a casual tone into place. "Your absence was much remarked upon. There was even some idle speculation that you might be finding a cold welcome at . . . certain tables, shall we say."

"Idle speculation?" Sebastian's smile rivaled Sophy's own for brilliance and danger. "Can it be we are becoming talked about, Miss Howe?"

Sophy laughed. "Don't be silly, Mr. Sandford. Miss Fitzroy is teasing, naughty thing that she is. But I do think I might hear just a trace of jealousy in her voice. Perhaps she misses you."

"Jealous? Oh, dear me, no, Sophy. You two deserve each other. In fact, I feel I should congratulate you. You must exert a most extraordinary fascination over your gentlemen. Mr. Sandford is not known for his constancy."

"Some women inspire man's constancy by their actions," replied Sebastian. "As others do contempt."

I had to make myself think. I needed to get past the bile and the fear and, if I could, steer this most unwelcome conversation into a direction that might yield useful information. To this end, I managed a small laugh. "Lud, Mr. Sandford, if that's a sample of your conversation these days, It's a wonder your brother lets you out of the house at all."

Sebastian stiffened. Unlike Julius, Sebastian possessed a temper, and when it was set off, his discretion crumbled. This could be a dangerous game, though, as the darkness behind his eyes reminded me. When Sebastian lashed out, it was not just with words. "You'd best beware how you toss about my brother's name, Miss Fitzroy. You may find yourself on the receiving end of more attention than you wish for."

"How is that, Mr. Sandford?" I strove to maintain a sunny tone. I fear I managed only to achieve vaguely overcast. "Don't tell me you and Lord Lynnfield will be staying on at court? That will be a change. Your father always displayed such splendid disregard for palaces and princes."

At last, I had scored a touch. Sebastian's face flushed an arresting shade of scarlet and he moved to push past Sophy.

"Don't, Sebastian." Sophy touched Sebastian's arm, which spasmed as if he wished to snatch it away. "She's just trying to draw you out."

Much to my annoyance, this intervention had its intended effect. Sebastian visibly reined in his temper. "Still playing your games, are you, Peggy? You should be careful. You're not nearly so well protected as you think."

I forced my gaze to drift past his shoulder, as if unutterably bored by this remark. Inside, I fought the urge to shout at his threat, to demand to know what he and his brother were up to.

Sebastian took Sophy's hand and raised it. "As delight-ful as this has been, Sophy and I have places to be. You will excuse us, Miss Fitzroy?" He bowed to me.

"I'm so sorry, Margaret." Sophy sighed. "But I must delay the pleasure of further conversation, and I did have something I particularly wanted to mention to you."

"Sophy, we spoke on this subject." Sebastian tugged at her hand, but she ignored him and kept smiling at me. This close, I could see two of her lower teeth had begun to turn gray.

"Indeed, I stopped by your rooms earlier, but they were much occupied. I had no idea you had so many gentlemen friends to entertain."

Gentlemen? Plural?

"Enough, Sophy," said Sebastian with a credible air of command. "We need to be elsewhere. You are *quite* finished with Miss Fitzroy."

Evidently, Sophy heard some extra note of warning in the words, because she turned her back on me and looped her arm through Sebastian's. "Goodbye, Margaret. Do give my best to all your diverse gentlemen."

In perfect step with each other, Sebastian and Sophy strolled away into the gallery. Neither of them looked back to see how closely I watched them go.

※ ❧

CHAPTER NINE

IN WHICH ANOTHER REUNION IS UNEXPECTEDLY
ACHIEVED, AND OUR HEROINE RECEIVES FRESH
AND NOT ENTIRELY WELCOME INSTRUCTIONS.

When I finally reached my rooms, my first sight was of Mr. Tinderflint rising from the chair at my hearthside. Considering his girth and style of dress, he did tend to draw one's gaze, especially in a small space. He nearly eclipsed Libby, who sat on a stool in the chimney corner, sewing and eyeing me sourly.

The flood of emotion I felt at seeing my friend and patron after so many unpleasant shocks threatened to overwhelm my delicate maiden's sensibilities.

"Why didn't you warn me!" I demanded as I slammed the door shut. "I just had to—"

Mr. Tinderflint coughed and nodded over his shoulder. I whipped around to see a much younger, much slimmer, and infinitely more welcome person standing beside my closet door.

"Matthew!"

My paramour made his bow and turned upon me the particular smile that melted my heart and mind as surely as a sunbeam melts snow. "Hello, Peggy Mostly."

Mr. Tinderflint had become intensely interested in poking up the fire. This provided Matthew and me a moment to exchange our private greetings, or it would have if Isolde had not scrambled from her basket and scampered over to me, barking and wagging mightily. Fortunately, Mr. Tinderflint had provided himself with more anise biscuits and was able to lure the puppy away.

I allowed myself to luxuriate in Matthew's embrace, an experience doubly welcome after my unsettling encounter with Sebastian and Sophy. Being encircled by his arms was wonderfully relaxing and yet filled me with a kind of warm agitation. It was, I decided, the clash of these two sensations that enticed. Well, that, and the glow in Matthew's gray eyes. And the way the light caught in his copper-colored hair. And his smile, of course, especially when taken in combination with the press of his hands on my lower back as he kissed me.

I had not in any way finished reacquainting myself with the lengthy list of Matthew's unique virtues before he broke our kiss.

"I believe you were about to chastise Mr. Tinderflint,"

he murmured with a regretful nod toward that individual's broad back.

I sighed and rested my forehead against Matthew's shoulder, after which I had to brush a wealth of face powder off his good jacket. "I'm afraid it's a matter that cannot wait."

Matthew, clearly uncertain whether to be amused or worried, stepped back and swept out his hand, indicating that the path was clear. I turned to my patron.

"Thank you, sir, for bringing Matthew," I said with my best air of lofty dignity. Matthew's station as an artist's apprentice did not allow him general access to the palace. It was also, of course, against the rules of conduct for any solitary young man to enter the private apartments of a maid of honor, at least when anyone might see.

"Not at all, not at all." Mr. Tinderflint settled himself slowly and heavily into the tapestry chair. Isolde growled uneasily at his golden shoe buckles. I picked her up as I sat on the cushioned stool. I also covered her, and a bit of biscuit, with my kerchief.

"Secrets," I said. Isolde hushed and gnawed. Mr. Tinderflint looked surprised.

"I suspected you and Mr. Reade had not had much of a chance to see each other these past few days." Mr. Tinderflint smoothed down the lace ruffles that adorned his shirt from neck to waistcoat. Isolde could not see and so for once did not bark at the movement of my patron's hands or his lace. "Now, I expect you wish to know why I did not inform you that the brothers Sandford were also at St. James today?"

"Why, Mr. Tinderflint, however did you guess?"

He bowed his head. "It is a reproach I deserve, yes, I do. Because, you see, I did not know myself."

"Do you expect me to believe that?"

"I'm rather afraid you'll have to, my dear, for it is the truth."

"It is, Peggy," said Matthew unexpectedly. He had helped me more than once in my affairs as a confidential agent, indeed had saved my life, but these adventures had left him with a deep disquiet where Mr. Tinderflint was concerned.

"Did he tell you?"

Matthew shook his head. "While we were waiting for you, Sophy Howe turned up at the door."

"I thought so. I met her in the gallery. She all but said she'd already been peering through keyholes."

"Knocking on doors, to be precise," said Mr. Tinderflint. "Fortunately, your excellent Libby"—he nodded to my maid at the fireside, who was pretending in equal parts to mend a stocking and ignore this conversation—"rose admirably to the occasion."

"Libby answered the door and received the message," translated Matthew. "While we hid in your dressing closet."

"I shall be trusting entirely to your discretion in this matter, Mr. Reade, yes, entirely." Was Mr. Tinderflint actually blushing? It was a sight entirely without precedence. "For a dashing young fellow such as yourself, hiding in a lady's closet is a humorous anecdote. For a man of my age and, ahem, girth, it descends rather quickly to low farce."

The picture of Mr. Tinderflint and Matthew jostling for position in my small dressing closet required me to stifle what I hoped would be taken for a series of short, sharp coughs.

"I regret you were put to any trouble," I said when I could speak again. "Especially since it doesn't seem to have worked. Sophy accused me of having multiple gentlemen in my rooms, although that might just have been one of her ordinary slanders." I paused. "What was her message?"

"That you should be careful where you stepped," said Matthew. "Because Lord Lynnfield was with the Prince of Wales today."

"It was," Mr. Tinderflint said, sighing, "something of a shock."

"Something of a shock!" My patience, which had made a brief appearance, departed abruptly for parts unknown. "How could you not know this!"

Isolde poked her head out from under my kerchief and growled at my patron.

"Secrets." I patted her and she ducked back under the kerchief, looking for biscuit crumbs.

Mr. Tinderflint bore my shout and Isolde's growl without so much as wincing. "You will recall, my dear, that I also have been away from the palace on business. I had thought myself well informed on all pertinent matters, but it seems I was mistaken."

There was something particularly dreadful about the idea

that the Sandfords had been able to slip past Mr. Tinderflint. Since we were alone, or practically so, Matthew was able to put his arm about my shoulders.

"Do you have any idea why Sophy would want to warn you about Lynnfield?" he asked.

I shook my head. "When we met just now, she seemed to want to talk with me, but Sebastian was with her . . ."

"Was he, b'God?" murmured Matthew. Matthew's opinion of Sebastian was even lower than mine, if such a thing was possible. Sometimes I feared he might act on that opinion and then have to flee the country. Sebastian, for all his gross and obvious faults, was the son of a titled family, whereas Matthew was the son of an apothecary. When it came to the law, blame, like Newton's apple, tended to fall to the lowest possible point.

"He was," I said. I laid a hand on Matthew's arm and endeavored to show a calm demeanor. "And he was unusually opposed to Sophy and me communicating."

"Now, that is interesting—yes, yes, very interesting indeed." Mr. Tinderflint's eyebrows arched up to the line of his periwig. "Mr. Sandford and Miss Howe have been quite close since you've been gone, or at least as close as they've been permitted to be."

"I believe the expression you're looking for is 'hand in glove,'" I said tartly. "Although for them 'hand in pocket' might be more accurate. I've already heard that news. Several people at the levee went out of their way to further acquaint me with it, in fact." I frowned. "What I can't work out is why Lynnfield would permit them to be together at all. It's not as if Sophy has any money she hasn't won off some unfortunate gamester." But I wondered then if she might have other connections. Once again it occurred to me how very little I actually knew about Sophy Howe.

"Will you seek her out?" asked Mr. Tinderflint.

"Between this and the funeral, I don't see how I can avoid it."

"The funeral?" echoed Matthew. "What happened at the funeral?"

I did not answer at once. Instead, I picked Isolde up off my lap and deposited her in her basket. "Libby, would you take Isolde for a walk down in the Color Court? Or the gardens?"

Libby curtsied, the very picture of demure obedience. She then took the basket as if it held something vicious, or at least malodorous. Which only proved that my maid also had direct experience with the royal lap dogs.

Once we'd closed the door behind Libby and Isolde, I told Matthew and Mr. Tinderflint about "Mrs. O," the veiled mourner, and her brief but noticeable effect on the senior Pierpont ladies and Sophy Howe. I told them how carefully Mrs. O had passed her memento to my aunt. Finally, I took Olivia's note describing the object from my desk and handed it to Mr. Tinderflint.

"Well, well," murmured Mr. Tinderflint as he read. He must have found this phrase either instructive or comforting, because he repeated it several more times. "This 'memento' is surely a commemorative medal. You noted the symbols? The white horse stands for Hanover, and it is trampling a good English home. Here on the reverse we clearly have the King over the Water, James himself. And in case anyone missed the message, we have"—he ran his fat index finger under the Latin words Olivia had said were stamped on the medal's edge—"*Nobilis est ira leonis,* which is the motto of the Stuart House."

"'The roar of the lion is noble,'" translated Matthew promptly.

"Yes, yes, very good, Mr. Reade." Mr. Tinderflint turned the paper over, presumably to see if there was anything on its back, and then turned it over again. "Such medals are given out as keepsakes by persons attached to the Pretender's court. Sometimes it is in thanks for some service, other times simply as largess to keep the loyalty of those they need and to show they are prosperous enough to give gifts."

"Then it isn't anything important," said Matthew stoutly. "We know that Sir Oliver was moving money about for the Jacobites. This is their thanks."

"Except," Mr. Tinderflint said with a sigh, "we also know, or rather my friends know, that this particular design was struck in Saint-Germain, to be given out only by the hand of the Pretender himself."

I opened my mouth. I closed it again. "It still doesn't have to mean anything. This . . . Mrs. Oglethorpe was probably supposed to give the medal to Uncle Pierpont as thanks for his role in the Swedish plot. When she found out he was dead, she decided to tender the thanks to his widow."

In reply to this hopeful speech, Mr. Tinderflint gave me one of his most owlish looks. "Your aunt, I believe you told us, recognized the lady, despite her veils, and was much disconcerted."

"Everything disconcerts Aunt Pierpont."

Mr. Tinderflint sighed again. "But I also believe you said it was after she received this that Lady Delphine asked you to bring your cousin to court?"

I made no answer. I did lean a little closer to Matthew.

"Has the princess agreed to let Olivia stay?" asked my patron.

I nodded. "And she made sure both the prince and Lord Lynnfield heard her do it."

"Did she indeed?" Mr. Tinderflint turned Olivia's note over again. "Now, that is also interesting. Yes, yes, most interesting."

I knotted my fingers together. I did not like the path down which I was being led. "My father says it was a woman named Oglethorpe who caused him to be arrested while he was in France."

"It could have been, yes, yes," said Mr. Tinderflint. "The Oglethorpe family has been conspiring for the Stuarts for decades. Their matriarch, Eleanor, is called the Old Fury because of her righteous temper. Of her six children, her namesake daughter, the Young Fury, is married to the Marquis de Mézières and currently lives in Paris. A second daughter, Anne, remains with the mother and acts as her private secretary. If any one of these uncovered your father's identity and mission, she could have made a great deal of mischief."

"Mrs. O also said she knew my mother."

"She did," Mr. Tinderflint answered, and when he saw the shock on my face, he smiled gently. "My dear, the Oglethorpes form a line of communication between the Pretender and his friends in England. Your mother got hold of that line and brought what she learned from them to me."

A pang of loneliness shot through me. When I was a child, it had seemed to me that my father's departure had also taken away my mother. She went out almost every night and did not return until the small hours of the morning. I would sometimes keep myself awake in the hopes of catching a glimpse of her on the stair. Then, I hadn't known what she was doing. I did now, for I was engaged in exactly the same work.

Why didn't this make me feel any better about those lonely nights?

Matthew snapped his fingers and I jumped. "Now I know where I heard that name," he declared. "Wasn't there some rumor or the other in the broadsheets that a Mrs. Oglethorpe is the Pretender's real mother?"

"What?" I exclaimed with more than a bit of feigned disbelief. "She's the warming pan?" One of the most repeated rumors about James, the would-be Third, was that he was not actually the son of James, the formerly Second. They said his mother had falsified her pregnancy and arranged for a baby to be smuggled into the birthing chamber inside the pan normally used to carry coals to warm the royal bed.

Mr. Tinderflint chuckled. "Not a warming pan, no, no, no. But Eleanor Oglethorpe did give birth to a son named James about the time James the Pretender was born. The story goes that Mrs. Oglethorpe was one of old James the Second's mistresses and that her son was fathered by James the Second. The legitimate James Stuart is supposed to have died of a fever some five weeks after being born. After this, the illegitimate James Oglethorpe was secretly brought in to take his place."

I sat silent for a long moment, attempting to untangle this knotty thread of Jameses. "When I am in charge, I am going to require that all fathers give their sons distinct names."

"When you are in charge, I will heartily support the motion," agreed Mr. Tinderflint. "What this rumor shows us, however, is how very close the Oglethorpe family is to the Stuarts." He paused. "And now we appear to have a line from the Pretender to the Oglethorpes to the Pierponts. Does that line also extend to the Sandfords, and from there to Miss Howe?"

"You can't believe Sophy Howe has turned into a genuine Jacobite?" said Matthew. "She's vicious, but she's nobody's conspirator, at least not in politics."

"I'm not sure I like your becoming an expert in court machinations, Matthew," I told him lightly. "It might remove the blush of your innocence."

This earned me a smile that was most decidedly not innocent. "Sometime I'll tell you all about the backstabbing that goes on between artists, especially when there's money on the table."

Mr. Tinderflint turned Olivia's note over in his fingers several more times. "Whatever Miss Howe's game, Peggy, you must take extreme care when your cousin arrives in court. Both Miss Howe and Mr. Sandford will be very interested in her presence here. There may be others as well."

I shifted in my chair and tried not to show it. "If Olivia is with me, then everyone will know that unlike her father, she is part of the princess's circle and a Hanoverian. That will keep the Jacobites at a distance."

"Will it?" asked Mr. Tinderflint. "Or will it bring them swarming around, seeking her assistance and her loyalty to their cause?"

"What if it does?" I replied stoutly. "If they're foolish enough to think there's any good to be gotten from talking to Olivia, that's to our advantage. It's my job to bring such people to light, after all." But even as I spoke these words, a chill rushed through me. I didn't doubt Olivia's ability to take all such maneuvers in stride. Hadn't I joked from the beginning that she was the one who should be the spy? But I had just suggested we use her presence to draw the Jacobites out. That felt less like allowing my dear cousin to assist my spying and more like using her as bait.

Mr. Tinderflint's reply, when it came, offered no reassurance. "We are entering a serious time. We must approach it in a serious manner." He paused and shook out the lace on his cuffs. "Word has reached King George in Hanover regarding the Swedish plot and Peggy's discovery of it. My correspondents tell me His Majesty is severely displeased regarding the Prince of Wales's management of his affairs and so is hastening back. His early return will change the calculations of all sorts of schemers at court, and it may push the Jacobites into some hasty action."

I said nothing. I realized I'd once again leaned close to Matthew only when I felt the fabric of his shirt brushing against my cheek.

Mr. Tinderflint adjusted several of his rings. "If you decide you wish to leave your post, my dear, I will not blame you for it. Oh no, far, far from it, especially now that your cousin might become involved. But if you do want to go, you should do so now. Otherwise, you may not be able to leave at all."

In that moment, it was not Olivia's face I saw, but Old Mother Pierpont's, and I could hear her sly, cracked voice intoning, *You're thinking, "I'm clever . . . I can slip out of all this easy enough."*

I hadn't told Mr. Tinderflint about that conversation. I was used to dangers coming from outside my family, but to sense such danger under the vicious words of an old woman inside my family bounds . . . I didn't like it, and I didn't like myself for becoming the sort of person who would suspect it. That was probably why I did not mention the exchange to him now.

Besides, since Mrs. Pierpont was leaving London, it didn't matter. At least, it wouldn't have mattered, save for the fact that Aunt Pierpont was defying habit and good sense to go with her. Aunt Pierpont, who had recognized Mrs. Oglethorpe as surely as her mother-in-law had.

A soft scratching sounded at the door. It took me a moment to realize Libby wasn't here and that I must get up to answer it. Before I reached the door, however, something small and white shot across the floor.

It proved to be a scrap of folded paper. Mr. Tinderflint, whose grasp of manners varied wildly according to circumstances, leaned forward to watch as I unfolded it. Matthew looked over my shoulder, which was much more distracting.

The note was terse and to the point.

MY ROOMS. BEFORE WAITING TOMORROW.

There was no signature, but none was needed. I recognized Sophy's hand.

"I have to stay on," I said as I folded the note back up. "There's far too much to be done." What I did not say was that if I scuttled away now I'd never find out what was behind Sophy's extraordinary behavior. I'd also be handing her, and the Sandfords, a victory. May Heaven help and forgive me, but that was more than I could stomach. I suspected that both men with me now knew this without my saying it. But Mr. Tinderflint only nodded.

"Excellent, and exactly what I'd expect to hear from the daughter of Elizabeth and Jonathan Fitzroy." But Mr. Tinderflint wasn't looking directly at me. He was looking over my shoulder, at Matthew. Coward that I was, I did not look at Matthew. I did not want to see his face just then. Instead, I took his hand from where it rested on my shoulder. "I'm sorry."

"I expected nothing less," he replied.

This was not the same as saying he agreed or that he understood. I felt a small but distinct crumbling underneath my heart, and there was nothing at all I could do about it.

CHAPTER TEN

In which Our Heroine enters the
lioness's den, where the subsequent
roaring is rather less than noble.

My dreams that night were not comfortable. They featured churning water and fire, not to mention the ghosts of the dead reaching out to welcome my grinning uncle. This culminated in something cold, wet, and horribly real touching my nose, which led me to scream and flail at the bedclothes, which, in turn, raised a furious yipping. Only then did I realize it was not my old ghosts coming for me, but my new puppy.

I fell back on the bolsters. Isolde scrambled up my chest and burrowed under the covers at my right hand.

"Secrets," I murmured to her, and to myself. "Secrets."

The direct result of all this private drama was that Libby had no reason to scold when she came in to light my candles and fire. Despite the unusually early hour, I scrambled out of my bed and dressed as quickly as humanly possible. The sooner I could go down to meet Matthew, the sooner his presence would wipe away the last of my nightmares.

Before he'd left me the night before, Matthew had insisted on coming to my rendezvous with Sophy.

"She might have Sebastian with her," he reminded me grimly. "And I am not letting you near him alone."

"I swear upon the Holy Bible that I'll take Libby with me." I took his hand to emphasize my point. I may also have looked into his eyes in a pleading manner. "She'll be watching every instant."

"No."

"Then will you at least—"

"No." This time he kissed me in what I choose to believe was an apology for his obstinacy rather than a blatant attempt to disorder my wits.

Whatever Matthew's ultimate intention may have been, I admitted defeat. This earned me another kiss, proving that the time-honored strategy of calculated retreat has its merits.

The morning was a cold one. Frost filmed the mud puddles and rimed the cobbles of the Friar's Court. Isolde, whom I'd brought out to save at least a few towels, stepped gingerly as we, along with Libby, emerged from one of St. James's many side doors. Fortunately, Matthew had already arrived and needed no more signal than my raising my hand to hurry across the yard to us.

"They'll be missing you at the academy," I remarked after we'd finished our lengthy personal salutations. Libby discreetly took Isolde off to attend to her individual business. Matthew was wearing his good jacket again, I noted. This was not a surprise. He owned only the one. But even in the dim light of St. James's back stairs, I could see that the jacket was quite rumpled. Normally, Matthew took good care to brush it out and fold it neatly.

"I'm expected to be at the palace daily until His Royal Highness's birthday masque."

"Are you?" I drew back. "How very . . . convenient."

"I'm helping to paint the stage scenery. With all the other news yesterday, I forgot to tell you. Mr. Tinderflint arranged it." He paused to take note of the confusion in my expression, as well as the distance I put between us. "I thought you'd be pleased. We'll be able to see each other every day."

"Of course I'm pleased. Still, you must have risen very early."

It was then I noticed that the slight smudge of face powder I had left upon his shoulder was still there. "Oh, *lud*, Matthew, you never left last night, did you?" My sweetheart greeted this accusation with a shrug. "Are you mad? Staying out all night, and turning up late today! You'll lose your place with Mr. Thornhill!"

"Well, what of it? It's better than you losing . . . than losing you."

My patience bridled at this. There was so much uproar

in my life, I desperately needed Matthew to keep a level head. "You can't really believe I'm in any danger from Sophy."

"What should I believe, then?"

There were a hundred answers to this, but I couldn't find even one of them. I was entirely confident I could meet and match whatever hand Sophy Howe chose to play. But there was Sebastian Sandford lurking in the shadows, as well as his far more dangerous brother, Lord Lynnfield, who couldn't be bothered with lurking and had come right out into the open.

Lacking a cogent argument, I fell back on sentiment. "You should believe that I love you."

"And I love you," Matthew replied solemnly. "Which is why you're not going to see that harridan and her bully boys alone."

I tipped my face up so he could see me smile. "One day, Matthew Reade, I'm going to push you too far."

"Probably, but it's not today." There was not as much warmth in this answer as I might have wished. I told myself that it was the combination of the late night and the early hour of this meeting.

There was not quite as much confidence in this conclusion as I would have wished either.

Matthew and I followed Libby into the world known as "the back stairs," a snarl of poorly illuminated stairs and sooty corridors, all of which were continually full to overflowing with the army of servants and officials who kept the palace in working order, as well as by anybody who didn't want to be seen by the world in general.

We collectively ignored the muttered complaints of those we pushed past, until we emerged into the gallery where we maids of honor were lodged. We first returned an affronted Isolde to my hearth-side and from there continued on to Sophy's chamber.

To my surprise, it wasn't Sophy's maid who opened her door wide to release a stifling cloud of heat and perfume. It was Sophy herself.

"Ah, Margaret. There you are. I'd quite given up on you." Sophy let her gaze wander over both Matthew and Libby. "Your artist may wait outside. What I have to say is for your ears, and, as you can see, I have no one concealed in my apartment."

Today. But I did not say that aloud. I just turned toward Matthew. I was very afraid he might argue, which was not an event I wanted Sophy to witness. Matthew, however, simply nodded, although I could tell he was not in any way happy. I could also tell he was going to keep watch on this door until Libby and I emerged.

I wished I could kiss him, or at least tell him once more there was nothing to worry about, but Sophy's presence as an excessively hostile witness limited me to a small smile.

Walking into Sophy's apartment was like stepping into a treasure trove or a pawnbroker's shop. Every available surface (and there were plenty of these) was covered in trinkets. There were elaborate jewelry and snuffboxes of enamel, gilt, and silver. There were silk scarves that would make a sultan blush for their richness, fans with silver staves, mirrors with gilded frames. Painted porcelain figurines of well-frilled shepherds and shepherdesses decorated the mantel and most of the carved and painted tables.

Libby retired at once to the chimney corner, her sharp eyes shifting left and right to take in the scene from under her modestly lowered lids, quite probably adding up the worth of all these movables. I edged into the stifling chamber, trying to avoid knocking something over or being set on fire by one of the many candles.

"Tell me, Margaret, was it your artist who delayed you so?" Sophy took her seat at an elaborately inlaid writing desk with painted enamel panels and gilt trim.

"Sophy, you and I can exchange barbs at any hour, anywhere in the palace. If you have something important to say, please do get on with it." I looked about for some place to sit where I would not dislodge a scarf or crush a shepherdess. Finding none, I remained standing.

Sophy glared at me but seemed to decide that delivering her message was more important than giving me yet another dressing-down. "I have information for you, or perhaps I should say for your master."

"I have no idea to whom you are referring."

Sophy rolled her eyes. "We can also lie to each other at

any other place and time, Margaret. Do you want to know what I have learned?"

"Would I be here otherwise?"

"Very well. I know the name of that woman who came in disguise to Sir Oliver's funeral. I also know what she wanted there. I can give you this information, and more, but none of it for free."

This sounded much more like the Sophy with whom I was acquainted. It instantly raised every suspicion I possessed. "Why would you give me any information at all?"

"Does it matter?"

"Yes. You might be spinning me a story for profit—yours and Sebastian's. Not that he was exactly eager for us to be holding more conversation." *Or you might once again be planning to make a fool of me in front of Her Royal Highness.*

"Mr. Sandford does not always know what is best for him." Sophy spoke with a soft regret I had never before heard from her. Either she was plumbing fresh depths of her acting abilities, or I had struck a rare vein of genuine feeling.

"I think that's largely his brother's fault," I ventured. "And their father's."

"You are right in that. What a surprise." The drawling insult had the feel of a reflexive response, and I let it pass.

"What is it you want in exchange for your information?" I asked.

Sophy took a deep breath and mustered her considerable nerve. "I want your help— yours and your master's." I opened my mouth to remind her how little I cared for that phrasing, but her next words stunned me into silence. "I need to get Sebastian away from his family, but he refuses to go."

It was a long time before my power of speech returned. The eventual result was not at all shrewd or even witty. "I don't understand."

Sophy laughed. "You understand perfectly. Lord Lynnfield is in neck deep with the Jacobites, just as his father was. One would have thought the deaths of both a near relation and their principal banker would serve as warning, but no. They are pressing ahead with their plans."

This was not happening. I was not sitting here in this dragon's cave of a room hearing vain, clever, shallow Sophy Howe calmly discuss high treason.

"Why bother with me?" I croaked. "You're a maid of honor; you have the princess's ear. You could tell her what you know and take the credit for whatever discoveries come of it."

When Sophy spoke again, it was with her eyes directed at the arrangement of porcelain sheep and shepherdesses on the nearest marquetry table. Sophy could have sold off this treasure trove and lived like a queen for years. Yet as she cast her glance across her hoard, Sophy looked neither proud nor covetous. She looked fearful.

"If you expose the Sandford family and their plans, Sebastian will think nothing of it. If he discovers I am the one who betrayed them, he will turn from me."

Why on earth was she still keeping company with Sebastian Sandford if she intended to sabotage his standing with his family? It made no sense. Either the Sandfords had some hold over her, or Sebastian was a far more useful co-conspirator than I had initially realized, or . . .

Or Sophy and Sebastian were playing for larger stakes.

If the current Lord Lynnfield was taken up for high treason, that would leave Sebastian heir to the Lynnfield title, lands, money, houses, and all other aristocratic perquisites. If Sophy then married Sebastian, she would trade this over-crowded room for a house, an income, and lands and title besides.

Now, *that* made sense. What was more, it was very like the Sophy Howe I knew. "Well then, do tell me, Sophy, who is this lady, and why did she come to bother us? Would her name be Oglethorpe, by any chance?" Sophy blanched, and that was answer enough. "I take it you've also discovered some connection between the Oglethorpes and the Sandfords?" *And the Pierponts*, I thought, but I didn't say that out loud. I didn't trust my voice not to stumble.

Sophy could have a remarkably steady gaze when she wanted, and she used it now. "Mrs. Oglethorpe and Lord Lynnfield will both be in attendance at the prince's birthday masque. I will lead you to them, and you will expose their plans to the Crown and all the world."

She might do it. Sophy had always been willing to use every weapon in her considerable arsenal to get what she wanted. If the truth could serve, she would use that. If enemies could serve, she would use them just as quickly.

"Well, Margaret? What is your answer? Are we agreed?"

Agreed? How could I agree with Sophy Howe, who had set herself against me from the start? She had forged letters and seduced men she believed to be my favorites. In fact, she had tried every possible trick to ruin my reputation. If I did as she asked, I would elevate Sebastian Sandford to a title and hand Sophy prosperity and nobility.

But I could not forget that my principal business was to unearth the Jacobites at court, and Sophy was offering to help. If she was telling the truth, I would not only be serving my king, I would be sending Lord Lynnfield to the Tower.

My thoughts had no time to range further. From outside the door came a man's shout, followed fast by the distinctive thud of a fist against flesh.

CHAPTER ELEVEN

IN WHICH A DISAGREEMENT BETWEEN
GALLANTS IS CUT SHORT.

Forgetting for a heartbeat all our quarrels, Sophy and I together rushed into the gallery. There we were treated to a dramatic tableau formed by Matthew and Sebastian. The pose did not do Sebastian a great deal of credit. He was pressed against the wall with Matthew's forearm across his throat. His blue eyes bulged in their sockets as he struggled to get some purchase on Matthew's arm while at the same time trying to reach the dress sword dangling at his side.

"You will *not* go near her," said Matthew from between gritted teeth. "You will *never* go near her!"

Sophy charged forward. I suppose I was expecting her to do something useless like beat on Matthew's back, or I promise I would have moved much more quickly than I did.

Instead, she kicked Matthew's ankle with one slippered foot, which would not have done much good on its own, but she also grabbed his ear and twisted, hard.

Matthew cried out and staggered. I darted forward. I aimed to grab Sophy's hand, but hearing the ring of steel as Sebastian finally managed to draw his sword dislodged that plan. I swung both my fists under the blade and into Sebastian's solar plexus. He grunted hard and doubled over, and I snatched his sword from his grip. Matthew grabbed my arm and hauled me backwards.

"I'm fine," he panted, before I could so much as open my mouth. "He wanted to go in. I informed him he could not. We disagreed. That's all."

"That looks to have been quite enough," drawled a new voice.

We all turned. At least, the three of us did. Sebastian just groaned and clutched his midriff, trying to breathe.

"Really, Peggy!" Mary Bellenden laughed as she sauntered into the gallery. Apparently her wits were so rattled by the scene before her, she forgot she was still wearing nothing but an insubstantial nightdress. "You do keep managing to find the most entertaining gentlemen! Hello, Sophy. I must say yours is not looking half so well as Peggy's."

"This is none of your business, Mary," snapped Sophy.

"If you want to keep your quarrels private, you shouldn't stage them in the gallery." This tart comment was not from Mary, but from Molly Lepell, who had also emerged from her rooms. Unlike Mary, Molly had remembered to cover herself with a silk wrapper and had the sense not to flounce into the middle of our little gathering. "Peggy, what are you doing?"

I glanced at Matthew and at the slender dress sword in my hand. Matthew took the blade from me and walked up to Sebastian. He handed that worthy the rapier, hilt first. Sebastian glowered but managed to straighten up enough to reclaim his property and sheathe it.

"I will kill you, you low-bred son of a bitch." Pure hatred rang in Sebastian's voice and showed in the terrible scowl of his twisted mouth. Matthew met his gaze, utterly impassive. I had seen Matthew look like this only a handful of times, and I never knew what to feel. Matthew did not fight for sport. When he fought, it was in deadly earnest, and he would do whatever it took to lay his opponent low. This frightened me a little. Not because I feared Matthew himself, but because I did not know this part of him—not where it came from nor where it might lead.

Mary laughed and applauded. "Oh, bravo, all of you! Sophy, is this your new scheme? You've gone from winning at cards to staging high farce? Will you play in Drury Lane?"

"Mary," said Sophy without taking her attention from Sebastian or Matthew. "If you don't close your prattling mouth, I will put on a show from which you will never recover."

Mary let her eyes and mouth go round in mock horror. "Heavens, Sophy! You know better than to mind me. Besides, it's too cold to be standing about watching your dramas. Good morning to you, Peggy. I look forward to hearing the whole story." She gave a skipping turn, making sure she flashed one bare shoulder toward Matthew before she disappeared back into her own rooms.

Sebastian had finally managed to push himself away from the wall, and he looked set to start stalking toward Matthew, probably so he could more conveniently utter his threats. Matthew stood ready to receive them, implacable, immovable. Sophy, thankfully, grabbed Sebastian's arm. The look she bestowed upon him had nothing to do with concern for his well-being, but it did successfully divert him from his planned confrontation with Matthew. Head and chin held high, Sophy all but dragged her paramour into her rooms.

A moment later, Libby stumbled out into the gallery so fast, I realized she had been shoved from behind. My maid gathered her dignity quickly and glowered at me.

"She owes us for our candle she's keeping in there," Libby announced as she brushed past us. I saw a suspicious bulge under her skirt where her pocket hung and wondered if Sophy might find herself short a snuffbox or two.

Matthew looked at me. I looked at Molly Lepell, who had maintained her station on her threshold throughout this exchange. I touched Matthew's fingers in a silent request for him to remain where he was while I walked over to her.

"Her Highness will not be happy when she hears about this," Molly said. Her face had darkened perceptibly and I found myself wondering if she was considering the wisdom of remaining my friend. But what she said was something quite different. "Poor Sophy. She never could shield her heart as she ought."

I choked. "*Sophy!* Sophy has a *heart?*"

"I rather thought you'd be surprised. But then, you haven't seen her much except to make an enemy of her." Molly's mouth quirked into a melancholy smile. "Sophy falls in love with the same men she's trying to use. Her heart has been broken more times than a parliamentarian's word, and yet she keeps hoping that this time, this plan, this scheme, will be the one that binds Mr. or Lord Whomever to her forever." Molly shook her head.

"That's . . ." *Incredible. Impossible. Not the girl I know.* "That's quite sad."

"Yes. But predictable. We all fall in love with men we should not—for power or flattery or simply because we are so tired of having to pretend to love them all." Molly's gaze strayed to Matthew, who was diligently feigning interest in the details of the gallery plasterwork. "I envy you, Peggy, with your heart so occupied by your artist. Has he a brother at home, do you think?"

"Not that I know of," I murmured.

"Ah, well." Mary shook her head. "I'll leave you, then. It would be good if one of us was on time to wait upon Her Highness."

Molly closed her door. I glanced at Matthew, who was gesturing that it was time to make our departure. I very much wanted to, but I did not move. More important than intelligent retreat was the chance to find out what the pair inside

Sophy's rooms was saying. I mouthed apology to Matthew, then crouched down and did that thing of which I had been so often accused—I put my ear to the keyhole.

Matthew slapped his hand against his mouth, smothering either a laugh or an oath of frustration. Despite this, he positioned himself close by, watching over me in the most literal sense.

Listening at keyholes is another of those techniques that works best on stage, where the participants have trained voices pitched to carry to the audience. Actors also seem to make rather less noise as they move about. Sophy and Sebastian most inconsiderately kept themselves well away from the door and spoke in croaks and whispers, and their movements all produced great creakings, rustlings, and rattlings, which meant I could catch only about one word in three.

". . . cannot trust the . . . her! She will use . . . danger . . ." railed Sebastian.

". . . simpleton . . . use her and save . . . your brother . . ." answered Sophy sternly.

There followed a fine explosion of verbiage from Sebastian. I would have drawn back to preserve my delicate maiden's sensibilities, had I not been afraid that my movement might be heard.

Then there was more rustling, a bang, and a tinkling clatter. From the sound of it, Sophy was now shy a table full of shepherdesses.

"What are we to do, then?" Sophy asked, her voice low and clearer than it had been. I could picture Sebastian as he spoke: the flush across his hollow cheeks, the cold and contemptuous light in his eyes.

"We win at the tables, and we keep on winning. Those silken buffoons want to make use of us . . . cannot live without . . . gambling; they can pay for the privilege and keep on . . . until they have nothing . . . we will break them. Then we will have all the money we want, and we are owned by no one."

"How does this help us against your brother?"

"Stop it, Sophy!" Something slammed against something. Any number of somethings rattled in response. "There's nothing we can do except stay out of his way. Otherwise, we make targets of ourselves, and I warn you, he has very good aim."

"But he's made himself vulnerable! He's playing too high, Sebastian."

"He isn't . . . at all, don't you see that? This *isn't* too high for him . . . doesn't stand a chance. This . . ." Sebastian's next words were lost under yet more rustling and rattling. Now it was my turn to curse. I did so within the privacy of my thoughts as I pressed closer to the keyhole, which seemed to have developed some unpleasant ridges that dug into my ear and cheek.

Matthew laid his hand on my shoulder. This touch brought to me no warmth, for it was not for comfort or reassurance. This was a warning.

I felt it then—an actual pricking in my thumbs, or at least in my fingers' ends. My skin crept across my bones. I turned. I knew who would be there before my eyes lifted.

Julius Sandford, Lord Lynnfield, stood behind us.

I got to my feet as smoothly as I could manage. Matthew did not move. He was taking the man's measure, carefully, thoroughly.

"Have you some business here?" Matthew inquired. "My lord?"

Lynnfield ignored him. His attention remained fixed entirely on me. "By your presence here, Miss Fitzroy, may I assume I have found Miss Howe's door, and my brother's current whereabouts?"

"I could not say, sir," I replied calmly, although my heart hammered so hard it set my ribs aching. "Whatever games your brother and Miss Howe may be getting up to do not interest me in the slightest."

"Strange to hear you say so, considering you have in the past won those games quite handily." The admiration in his voice was entirely unfeigned, and it raised goose bumps all down my back. "You've done great credit to your family, especially your late mother."

Anger rushed through me, carrying away all my paralysis and a certain amount of my good sense. "You have no right to even *mention* my mother."

This made him smile, but his eyes remained terribly cold. He hadn't blinked, I realized. Not even once. "There you are wrong. But you will have ample opportunity to discover that for yourself in these coming days."

"Speak plainly, sir!"

"You would not believe me even if I did. Oh." He held up one hand to forestall comment. "I do not blame you, considering how badly all things have gone between us. Therefore, I shall leave the plain speaking to other voices and other pens. As you have demonstrated, you are astoundingly clever; you may yet be brought to understand the truth of your position and your parentage. Now, if you will excuse me, I must go speak with my brother."

He bowed, walked past us quite coolly, and turned Sophy's doorknob. Evidently, in her agitation, she had neglected to close the bolt. As the door opened, I had a fine glimpse of both Sophy and Sebastian turning to stare in shock before Lord Lynnfield calmly shut the door behind him.

I stood, my fists and teeth clenched in fury, and one terrible part of my brain thinking I should again crouch at the keyhole.

Matthew took hold of my arm. "Let's get out of here, Peggy."

We returned to my rooms, and I did remember to lock the door behind us. Libby was in the dressing closet. I knew this not because she had left the door open, but because of the ostentatious banging and thudding that she made, attempting to remind me of the lateness of the hour and my current state of unreadiness to assume my post.

Matthew slumped beside the hearth. "Should I even ask if you're all right?"

"Should I say that you were entirely right, and thank you for being there?"

This drew a small smile from him. "I think that you should, yes."

"Then do consider it said. Add that I am sorry and I hope . . . I hope . . ." I couldn't finish my thought. My mind and wits were far too disordered by all I had seen and heard.

"What did Sophy say to you?" Matthew asked. "Does she know anything?"

"She does . . . she knows . . ." I made myself stop and take as deep a breath as allowed by corsetry. Slowly, I was able to set aside the sight of Lord Lynnfield and concentrate on all that Sophy had said and all that had happened afterward.

"Sophy Howe said more than she realized," I told him, with a certain grim satisfaction. "She has handed us the Sandfords, and this time we're going to finish them off."

CHAPTER TWELVE

IN WHICH THERE IS AN UNFORESEEN
AND INCONVENIENT REVERSAL.

Molly, as usual, was right in every important particular: Her Royal Highness did find out about the Drama of the Maid's Gallery, and she was very much less than pleased.

My summons to Her Highness's closet—the chamber that for more ordinary persons is known as the bedroom—came during the time set aside for nuncheon. It was served up by hand by Mrs. Howard, who, unusually, would not give me the least hint as to the princess's mood or purpose. This in and of itself spoke volumes, and by the time I made my curtsy to the princess in her close and well-appointed bedchamber, my knees were trembling.

Princess Caroline sat in her favorite chair with her feet up on the padded stool and her chambermaid hovering close behind. Her two sternest and closest ladies, Mrs. Titch-bourne and Mrs. Claybourne, were on duty, but Mrs. How-ard stopped at the threshold of the antechamber. This did nothing to ease the sinking sensation under my ribs. Nor did the fact that Princess Caroline looked more worn and tired than I had seen her previously. I tried to tell myself this was surely the fatigue of her approaching accouchement, but that effort did not survive longer than the time it took her to look me over in protracted and disapproving silence.

"I hope, Margaret, that this scene involving a duel be-tween your paramour and Mr. Sandford in a gallery of my home was to some good purpose?" She spoke in German, something she did when we needed to be as private as pos-sible. I was one of the few maids at court who was fluent in the language.

"I . . . I hope that it was, Your Highness." I did not say it had not been a duel. The princess's frown told me she was not in a mood to bear contradiction patiently.

"Dare I hope it was in regard to that particular business with which you have been charged?"

"That was my intention, madame."

"And were you successful?"

My tongue pressed against the roof of my mouth. Was I successful? That depended entirely on whether I could trust Sophy's word. If she was lying, if this was another of her attempts to discredit me in the eyes of our mistress, I was doomed.

I couldn't trust Sophy. Not an inch. I could trust Sebastian even less. But I could, and I did, trust Molly Lepell, and it was Molly's assessment of Sophy that gave me my answer.

I squared my shoulders. "Your Highness, I believe the Sandford brothers are plotting to continue their father's treasonous activities. Exactly what that plot is or how it has progressed, I do not yet know, but I suspect it will reach a turning point at the prince's birthday masque."

The princess made no reply. I was forbidden by protocol to so much as shift my weight, but all the sinews of my body tightened until I was sure my bones would snap.

At last, she said, "You can bring me proof of this?"

"Not yet, madame." I thought of telling her about Sophy's involvement, but what did I really suspect her of? It would have been easier if I still thought she might be hand in hand with the Jacobites, but since talking with Molly, I couldn't honestly accuse her of anything worse than wanting a rich marriage. There was her cheating at cards, but if my mistress didn't know about that already, she was deaf and blind, and I knew from hard experience Princess Caroline was not deaf. "I . . . I can tell you what I have overheard; that is all."

"No." The princess shook her head slowly. "That will not do. Not anymore." She paused. "You may have heard His Majesty the King has cut short his visit to Hanover."

"Yes, Your Highness." It had, in fact, been the talk of the drawing room that morning. Some people speculated that his abrupt return was meant to put an end to the rumor that

His Majesty did not actually care about his British kingdoms. Some suggested it was to get more money out of Parliament to fund his German wars.

Not one of those speculating persons said to me what the princess did now. "His return and the Sandfords' rise are both entirely your fault, you know, Margaret."

This pronouncement so startled me, I barely remembered to keep my gaze properly downcast. "I . . . I don't understand, madame." Mr. Tinderflint had said the king had planned to return early because of the Swedish plot, and that discovery was mine. But how could I possibly be blamed for the prince favoring Lord Lynnfield?

"The details of the Swedish plot you uncovered were forwarded to His Majesty, as is to be expected. Now he is most concerned about how affairs in his kingdoms are being managed." She looked down at her hand where it lay upon her rounded belly. When she spoke again, it was softly and with a regret such as I seldom heard from her. "My husband is perhaps being a little hasty in his attempts to solidify our separate influence before his father's return. He is accepting help from . . . sources he might not otherwise."

There it was. Lord Lynnfield had positioned himself as the prince's ally, using some combination of lies, flattery, chicanery, and good plain English bribery. Plus, of course, adroitly shifting blame for his treasons to his dead father. The princess, with her keen eyes, saw through him. The prince, angling to undercut his father's power, did not.

Regret never lasted long with Princess Caroline,

however. She was a woman of determined action, even when action must be concealed under a smile and a laugh. "You understand, therefore, that proof of Lynnfield's doings is vital. It cannot be a matter of my telling someone something that one of my maids, however trustworthy, overheard."

"Yes, Your Highness. I do understand."

"And what will you do?"

I bit my lip and hastily released it. "There is someone I need to speak with, madame. Once I have, I will know better how to proceed."

"Then do so as soon as possible, Margaret. We do not have much time. Will you need to be excused from your rehearsals to do this thing?"

"I very much wish I did, madame, but no."

For the first time since I had entered her chamber, the princess smiled. "Then go, Margaret. And please inform your artist he is not to threaten any more of the English nobility in the palace."

"Yes, madame." I made my curtsy and began my withdrawal, but her next words stopped me.

"A great deal depends on this, Margaret. You and I may believe the Swedish plot was only one strand of the web, but I must have something indisputable to convince His Royal Highness."

There was only one answer to this.

"I will make sure of it, Your Highness."

❧ ❧ ❧

I confess that I made my way toward the lower hall, and the appointed dance rehearsals, with something less than ordinary enthusiasm.

The lower hall of St. James was normally used as a kind of secondary banqueting area or ballroom. Currently, however, it was given over to preparations for the prince's birthday celebrations and resembled nothing so much as a warehouse. Lumber, wicker frames, crates, barrels, and dozens of workmen filled the great space. The stale air reeked with paint, sawdust, and mineral spirits and tallow. Everywhere rose a mighty clamor of hammering and sawing and the shouts of all those craftsmen and their laborers.

Even amid this huge and variegated crowd, I was at once able to spy Matthew. He knelt on the floor, plying his brush on a pink cherub that was decorating a section of board probably destined to be a festive archway. I caught his eye, and we shared a grimace. Matthew and cherubs had an uneasy history. Unfortunately, I had no time for further commiseration, as I had to hasten to stand with my sister maids in front of the Master of the Revels.

With such a title, one might have expected Garrick Wolverton, Lord Beckenstile, to be of a cheerful and exuberant personality. Instead, he was a severe, dumpling-shaped individual with a great red nose and a pair of the smallest eyes I have yet beheld on a human face. Those eyes, however, proved to be as sharp as any when it came to calling out the faults of his newly recruited players.

"Now, pay attention, if you can!" he bellowed. "This X"—here he slammed his cane against the floor—"is the entrance to the bridge, over which the seasons will cross. That is the four of you. Following this line here"—again the cane slammed down—"each of you will stop at this X"—whack! —"to make your bow to His Royal Highness and then recite your speech. You have memorized your speeches, have you not?" His little eyes glared at us and we all nodded in solemn affirmation. I suspected that Mary Bellenden, at least, was lying. I certainly was. "Once your speech is completed, you will then proceed to this X, where you will wait, smiling, in your row. Then, upon the signal thus"—he swung the cane up—"you will all begin the dance of the seasons, following this line, which indicates the path across the green, to this X . . ."

"It does make one wonder what the letter X has done to merit such treatment," I murmured to Mary.

"If you have some edifying remark, Miss Fitzroy, you may address it to the whole of the assembly!" snapped Lord Beckenstile. "Now, to the dance of the seasons itself. You will follow this line . . ."

We certainly tried. Unfortunately, four sets of hems and slippers turned those elaborate chalk lines into colorful blurs long before the movements of the dance impressed themselves into our minds. This caused our steps to wander, which caused Lord Beckenstile to bounce up and down on his toes in frustration, which caused Mary Bellenden to laugh out loud, which caused her to be singled out to walk through her routine in front of the rest of us.

Which left me standing beside Sophy, hands neatly folded, pretending to watch Mary's trial with undivided attention. Molly Lepell, sensibly, managed to keep herself well out of earshot.

"I see you have arranged for your artist to be here as well," murmured Sophy to me. "Do you fear some imminent attack? Or perhaps you simply don't trust him out of your sight?"

"He's working for Lord Beckenstile," I muttered back.

"Of course he is. Really, Margaret, I had not thought you to be quite so transparent."

I had any number of replies available for this. I decided not to waste my time with them. Mary actually seemed to be making some progress, and our moment for communication would soon be over. "Sophy, I've thought on our earlier conversation. I will be able to do as you asked."

"Oh, that," Sophy murmured, apparently intent on watching Mary turn in a graceful circle. "Thank you, Margaret, but you won't be needed after all."

"*What?*" I exclaimed before I could catch myself. Lord Beckenstile hollered. I did not hear a word that he said. "I . . . but . . . you told me . . ."

"Whatever I may have said, and I confess I truly cannot recall much of what it was, it has all changed." Sophy's gaze never wavered as Mary stepped down the line that was the bridge, paused in the center, and raised one hand to strike her pose. "Our misunderstandings are cleared away, and Lord Lynnfield and Sebastian and I are in perfect charity with one another. So much so that Sebastian has gone home."

Lord Beckenstile gestured furiously toward us. Sophy lifted her chin and glided forward. She made the required reverence on what I assumed to be the required X, because Lord Beckenstile only glared at her. He was rather more voluble with me as I, quite literally, tripped along the same path. I could not remember the first thing about where to put my feet. Sophy's reversal had driven what little I knew of our dance out of my head.

Sophy and Sebastian both in perfect charity with his brother? I didn't believe it. It was impossible. The Sandford brothers had never displayed any emotion for each other beyond contempt.

What could Lord Lynnfield have possibly said to change Sophy's outlook so entirely? And where was Sebastian? He could not have really just gone home.

These questions so fully occupied me for the rest of the rehearsal, I was a little surprised to find myself outside my chamber door. I did not remember anything of walking here, let alone whom I had passed or what they may have said to me.

"Libby?" I called as I let myself inside. I received no answer, which was surprising and a little aggravating, as I needed yet another change of clothing to prepare for that evening's concert. There was no sign of Isolde either, so I assumed Libby had taken the pup out to the courtyard to tend to her own particular business.

What did catch my eye was a letter laid neatly on top of my locked writing desk.

The paper was thick and of excellent quality. There was no direction on it, only my name written in a bold and flowing hand. Its seal was plain brown wax.

My immediate thought was that some overheated swain among the court had sent me a love note. This happened on occasion. But I didn't recall seeing any new moonstruck youth or smitten venerable among the gentlemen. I settled myself at my desk and broke the seal.

The initial paper inside was blank, but it had been folded around a second sheet. This inner page was much thinner, stained with both damp and age. I unfolded it carefully and squinted at the neat, small words written in fading ink.

My Dearest Mrs. Righthandwall,

I received your last letter, and I am all in astonishment. The news is too wonderful. Are you certain of it? The arrival is set? And he's to come in full state and good company? Your daughter has indeed written we are assured of our good uncle's help?

You must think your young friend very foolish for writing with such show of nerves, but this waiting has been such a long and difficult business, I can barely believe all our hopes are soon to be realized and he is to come safe to us after all.

Write as soon as you can and let me know what I can do to help with the preparations.

Yr. Loving Friend,
Mrs. Tinderflint

12578091 039185 387109
440295 652011 330912 670076
1149018 884019 743090

MRS. *Tinderflint?*

I read the signature again, and yet again. What on earth was this? When had Mr. Tinderflint been married? True, I knew little of his personal life, but still, one would think a wife, living or dead, might have come up in conversation.

Of course, Tinderflint was not and had never been my patron's real name. Up until this moment, I had believed Lord Tierney had adopted the pseudonym of Tinderflint at the beginning of our association. But this letter looked quite old. Could Mrs. Tinderflint be a nom de guerre for his mother, or perhaps a sister? Spying ran in families, as I had reason to know.

Or could my patron have adopted a female persona in order to further deceive any unauthorized person who might happen across these lines?

But the most important question was *why?* Why would such a letter come to me now? Lord Lynnfield had said he would leave the task of persuading me to other voices and other pens. This must be what he meant.

A cold shudder ran up my spine. I closed the letter swiftly and turned to unlock my desk. As I did, my fingertip snagged against a jagged edge of the metal plate. I gasped in surprise and snatched my hand back. Then, slowly, reluctantly, I bent closer to look at the desk's lock. The keyhole was set in a small, decorative plate shaped like a blooming rose. I touched it again. The place was scratched and, in one place, sharply gouged. Had those scratches always been there? Possibly. It was a piece of furnishing given to me when I took up residence here, and I'd never looked closely at it. But that gouge, at least, and the accompanying snag — those were new.

Someone had tried to force the lock.

CHAPTER THIRTEEN

IN WHICH LETTERS ARE ENDANGERED, SUSPICIONS ARE STACKED, AND CERTAIN INDIVIDUALS ORGANIZE AN OVERLY HASTY DEPARTURE.

I spent the next hour combing through my letters and possessions, trying frantically to determine if anything had been stolen or interfered with.

I spent the hour after that trying to decide if there was anything I should burn. For a long, uncertain moment, several of my most prized letters from Matthew were in distinct jeopardy.

At some point during this process, Libby returned with Isolde. At once, I launched into a barrage of questions about whom she had seen, when she had left, and how long she had been gone.

The result of these operations was twofold. First, Libby dropped Isolde into my lap and locked herself in my dressing closet until I apologized for suggesting there might have been some neglect on her part. It also meant a sleepless night, one during which I didn't scold Isolde for barking at every little noise, for fear one of those noises might be the return of my burglar.

One thing, at least, seemed absolutely clear as I stared into the darkness: This intrigue had gone beyond my powers to understand. If I wanted to unravel its mysteries before the masque, I would need help.

My ultimate decision to remain at the palace for the next three days was one of the most difficult I had ever undertaken. But the arrival of the letter and the attempted burglary of my desk came too soon after Sophy's revelation that Sebastian had gone home for me to believe the incidents were unconnected. I had to find out, if possible, why Sebastian had really left and where he had really gone.

To this end, I kept myself constantly at the ready as I waited at the levees, the drawing rooms, the reception for the Venetian ambassador, and the public dining. I searched every cranny and corner of the palace for any word or glimpse of Sebastian or, better yet, Lord Lynnfield. I strained to overhear as many conversations as possible. I asked all the leading questions I could think of at the card tables, especially when the gentlemen had finished their third or fourth bottle of wine. All that I received for my pains, however, was laughter and sweet remarks about how concern with politics would surely ruin my pretty face.

It will not come as a surprise to those readers who have

most closely followed these memoirs that the gentlemen who said such things tended to lose rather heavily afterward.

But all this work and waiting yielded me exactly nothing. Not even the cabinet members such as Mr. Walpole could tell me more than that Lord Lynnfield had accompanied his brother back to their country estate with no word as to when they would return.

Sophy was the only person who might possibly have known more, but she appeared to be studiously avoiding me. I was reduced to the uncertain course of enlisting Libby and her confederates to watch Sophy's correspondence. Either no letters came from the Sandfords, or Sophy and her confederates were better at concealment than Libby and her confederates were at spying, or I needed to pay my allies better. It was difficult to tell.

These days tasked my professional abilities at waiting to the utmost. I lost track of the number of times I began writing to Mr. Tinderflint to tell him about the attempted burglary, as well as the strange and secretly delivered letter signed "Mrs. Tinderflint." An equal number of times, I reminded myself that I would be seeing him shortly. The attack on my innocent desk was fresh proof that letters were not a safe means of communication.

I attempted to keep myself occupied by attending to my own affairs. For instance, I taught Isolde three new commands. I also took her to visit her family and Princess Anne every day, as I had promised. I wrote to Father, Olivia, Mr.

Tinderflint, and Matthew asking them all to be at Father's house on Wednesday afternoon *"so that we may say a proper farewell to Aunt Pierpont before she travels to her family and Olivia comes to stay with me at the palace,"* although my intentions went far beyond bidding adieu to Aunt Pierpont. I did not reveal any more in writing. I did, however, remind Mr. Tinderflint that despite my open invitation, he should take the precaution of not arriving until the late afternoon so we could be certain that he and Aunt Pierpont did not cross paths. They had met once, long ago, under circumstances that involved my uncle losing the majority of his money. As mild a person as she was, Aunt Pierpont might conceivably harbor some resentment on this point.

Then there were also more interminable rehearsals of our part in the prince's birthday masque. I mostly spent these being shouted at by the Master of the Revels for inattention to my dance steps. This was inevitably followed by enduring Sophy's smirks and Mary's not-so-hidden laughter as I dutifully moved through those steps on my own so that Lord Beckenstile could more thoroughly criticize me. He was lucky it was only a wet paintbrush Matthew left on his chair. Such action was, of course, childish, and I'm certain I upbraided my sweetheart soundly for it during one of our stolen moments.

While in waiting, we maids are expected to be on duty at all hours. We are also, however, regularly allotted a half day to spend as we choose. By the time my half day arrived and

I climbed into the shining new coach my father sent, I was more than ready to follow my aunt's example and dissolve into nervous spasms.

I'd had exactly one good piece of news in the past few days, and that had been from Olivia. Old Mother Pierpont, it seemed, had decided there was no point in wasting further money and time hanging about in "the foul smoke" and undertook for her and my aunt to leave London a full day early. This meant there was no chance at all of Aunt Pierpont and Mr. Tinderflint actually meeting.

Which turned out well, because it seemed Mr. Tinderflint had decided to entirely ignore my instructions as to the timing of his arrival. When I reached my father's rather sprawling half-timbered house in Lincoln's Inn Fields, Mr. Tinderflint's enormous blue and gilt conveyance was pulling up at the front door. My pique at being so disregarded was only a tiny bit soothed when the carriage door opened and Matthew climbed down.

I scrambled out of my own coach, barely remembering to take Isolde's basket with me. Bringing Isolde was a decision of the last possible moment. This was not because I had developed any sentimental attachment to the overfluffed animal, but because against all expectations, she proved to have her uses. Also, if I did leave her behind and she was harmed by any nefarious person trying to invade my rooms, Princess Anne would never forgive me.

Matthew smiled as I hurried to his side. He limited his

salutation to a bow and a regretful glance toward the stoop. Olivia stood ready to greet us all, with my father directly beside her.

I grimaced at this overly prompt appearance of my relations and turned to curtsy at Mr. Tinderflint. "Thank you so much for bringing Matthew, sir, but you are rather earlier than I expected."

"Not at all, not at all." My patron bowed. He did not, however, appear to have heard the second part of my little speech, because rather than addressing it, he brushed past me to mount the shallow stoop. There, he returned brief but polite greetings to my parent and my cousin.

"But where is Lady Delphine?" Mr. Tinderflint peered past the open doorway as if he might catch a glimpse of my aunt in the hall. "I cannot imagine she is looking forward to renewing our acquaintance, but I was very much hoping for an opportunity to speak with her."

His words brought me up short. I'm sure my surprise must have showed, but he was not at this point paying any attention to me.

"I'm afraid you've come too late, sir," Father said. "Lady Delphine left yesterday."

"Indeed?" Mr. Tinderflint murmured. "That is . . . that is disappointing, yes. Well. Still. I do not suppose it could be helped."

My patron and my father were regarding each other carefully, without any blinking or shifting of weight. Matthew glanced at me in inquiry as we mounted the steps, and I in turn looked to Olivia. She just shook her head and mouthed, *Must talk.*

My father's kiss of greeting was as calm and noncommittal as his words to Mr. Tinderflint. Olivia exclaimed over Isolde, although a combination of too many biscuits and the rhythm of the carriage had put the tiny dog to sleep. For my own part, I drew myself up a little straighter and gripped my cousin's hand as I watched Matthew make his bow to Father. They had met before, but not formally. Perhaps Father, who turned out to be rich enough to afford a house, servants, and coaches, had reconsidered the advisability of my liaison with the son of an apothecary. Perhaps he would decide to exercise paternal prerogative in my choice of companions. Perhaps . . .

But Father just smiled and shook Matthew by the hand. I did my best to muffle my heartfelt sigh of relief. In this, I was not entirely successful.

"Shall we go in?" Father winked and held out his arm to me. "I've had coffee laid in the parlor."

The rich scent that filled the parlor when we entered told me it was very good coffee. I noticed that Dolcy, who was setting out the bone china cups, wore a new black dress and spotless apron. I also noticed that although the sun was well up and the day remarkably fine for October, the parlor curtains remained closed.

"Thank you, Dolcy—that will be all," said Father as I set down Isolde's basket by the hearth. "Peg, you won't mind playing hostess for us?"

"Not at all, sir." I at once began pouring out coffee and handing around cups. They were extremely delicate, as were the dainty silver spoons for stirring in the sugar and cream, and I had not seen any of them before. There was cake as well, and a further battalion of silver utensils to eat it with.

Whatever else had been happening these past few days, my father had been spending freely.

Olivia, with all due ceremony and many Significant Glances, bolted the door. Only afterward did she accept her cup of sweet, milky coffee and choose a place on the new tapestry sofa beside Matthew, thus saving me from having to deliberately avoid sitting there.

Mr. Tinderflint, by right of rank and stature, claimed the largest chair in the room. He watched my father from behind his raised coffee cup as if taking his measure for the first time. "Tell me, Fitzroy. Did Lady Delphine give any reason for her early departure?"

"Travel preparations came to fruition a day or so early," Father answered. "Delphine and Mrs. Pierpont decided not to delay and perhaps waste the dry weather."

"I did not realize this was a matter of concern to you, Mr. Tinderflint, or I would have informed you myself," I said with a studied casualness as I poured my own coffee.

"Oh, it's of no matter." My patron, equally casual, waved one hand. "No matter at all."

At this, Olivia rolled her eyes and made a strangled noise. "I appreciate that I am in a den of spies," she announced. "But could we agree to speak plainly for these next five minutes? What was it you wanted to say to my mother, Mr. Tinderflint?"

For a moment I thought Mr. Tinderflint might actually answer. So, to all appearances, did my father, for he set his coffee down in anticipation.

Mr. Tinderflint, however, was not to be rattled, even by something so unexpected as a direct question. He sipped his coffee and then produced a lace handkerchief so large it might easily have served as a tablecloth, with which he delicately blotted his lips. "I do think that, considering our time is so very limited, we should let Peggy speak her piece." He turned toward me. "I gather from your demeanor, my dear, that the reason you brought us together here is quite grave. Is it more to do with Lord Lynnfield?"

Father looked as though he was about to protest. I came close to letting him. Whatever might lurk between him and my patron, I wanted it out in the open. Unfortunately, Mr. Tinderflint was right: we had a scant few hours for this meeting. I did have a great deal to explain, and I expected to hear a great deal in response.

I took a deep breath and began recounting my conversation with Sophy, complete with her offer to reveal the name and motives of the veiled mourner.

"Then it *was* her?" Father interrupted angrily. "It was definitely the Old Fury?"

"Sophy confirmed as much."

Father got to his feet and strode to the window. "In my

house," he muttered to the closed draperies. "That woman had the gall to walk into *my* house."

"I understand your feeling, Fitzroy," began Mr. Tinderflint.

"I doubt that." Father gripped the dark velvet as if he meant to tear the curtains down. "I doubt that very much."

Mr. Tinderflint gave a seated bow in acknowledgment of this. "But perhaps we should let Peggy finish?"

Father grunted. He did not turn around, nor did he release his stranglehold on the inoffensive drapery.

I explained Sophy's original proposal to use me to upset the fortunes of Clan Sandford. I glossed over how Sebastian had put an end to that conversation. Matthew rewarded me for this small discretion with a wry grin. I told of Lynnfield's arrival and then of Sophy's seemingly complete reversal of opinion and intention.

That finally got Father to face our little meeting again. "What do you suspect, Peg?"

"I believe Sophy and Sebastian are playing for the Lynnfield title." It was the first time I had voiced this thought aloud, and it sounded even colder than it had in my mind. "If I can work that out, so can Lynnfield. What if he made them an offer in return for their mutual silence? He agrees to their marriage and promises to remain single. If Lynnfield never fathers a legitimate heir, all Sophy and Sebastian have to do is stay alive and they eventually inherit everything—land, title, and money."

Silence fell as my audience considered this unpleasant possibility for several long moments.

Mr. Tinderflint cleared his throat. "Forgive me, Peggy, but why should Lynnfield bother keeping Sophy quiet at all? Her only connection to the business is Sebastian, and Lynnfield can control him without resorting to outside help."

"Because Lynnfield's afraid of Peggy," said Matthew. "He knows if Sophy brings Peggy into the matter, she stands a good chance of overturning his plans."

Absurdly, I felt a blush of pride rising in my cheeks at this.

"Yes, yes." Mr. Tinderflint nodded with his usual vigor. "That would make excellent sense. Peggy has proved to be such an obstacle to his plans before this . . ."

"Afraid!" cried Father. "Have you lost your mind, Tierney? This whole thing, it's sloppy. Careless. Worse: it's *obvious!*" He spat the word like a curse. "Can't any of you see? Peg is being used!"

Apparently, we did not see, or at least not sufficiently. Father threw out his hands, appealing to Heaven for patience. "Lynnfield could have spoken to Sophy at any time, but he made sure Peg saw him do it. He had to know she'd come straight to me—to us—with anything she learned. I've seen what Lynnfield gets up to in his own country. It's impossible he could be so thoughtless. He *wanted* her to tell us what she'd seen."

"I wonder, Uncle Fitzroy"—Olivia turned her mildest expression on my father—"what it is that Lord Lynnfield gets up to in his own country. You've quite neglected to mention it."

Father paused, clearly considering how much he should say. I watched his hesitation with a growing mix of anger and concern.

"The barony of Lynnfield includes a stretch of the Great Romney Marsh," he said finally. "In addition to being a home for disease and a graveyard for the unwary, vast marshes have always been the haunt of smugglers."

"What do they smuggle?" asked Olivia eagerly. "Weapons for the Jacobites? Secret messages? Or spies?"

Father smiled. "Tea, mostly."

"Oh." Olivia flopped back. "How dull."

"Dull, but profitable." Tea was abominably expensive stuff and carried high tariffs as well. "In the past, Lynnfield's barons have allowed the smugglers to pass unmolested across their lands, as long as they receive a share of the money, of course."

"What's changed?" asked Matthew.

Father's mouth twisted. "The late baron, old Augustus, and his eldest son are more ambitious than their Sandford predecessors. They started pressing the individual smugglers into a larger gang. Better organization means more contraband can be moved and more money can be made. And, of course, a higher percentage of that money can be skimmed off by Lynnfield."

"It's a wonder the smugglers tolerate the interference," said Matthew, which just made Father shake his head.

"You know that I lived for some time in disguise as a servant in that house. I saw Lynnfield's recruiting tactics. If someone doesn't want to work directly for the baron, boats are smashed and men are beaten. Some have simply vanished."

"So whatever it is the Sandfords plan to get up to at the masque, it might have nothing to do with the Jacobites," I said. "It might be related to their smuggling ring."

"But the two things are tightly linked—yes, tightly." Mr. Tinderflint shook his head. "It has long been known, for instance, that the Oglethorpes use the smugglers in the Romney Marsh to carry letters, or people, to and from France. If Lynnfield is indeed taking over the Romney Marsh smuggling trade, the Oglethorpes must now deal with him directly."

I was glad Father chose this moment to peer out at the street from around the edge of the curtain. I did not want him to see my face as I considered a very unpleasant confluence of facts.

It was Olivia who broke our mutual reverie. "So with the Sandfords, it's all about the money. They don't care who is actually on the throne."

Mr. Tinderflint smiled at this display of charming innocence. "Perhaps, perhaps not. Under one king, a family might be simple country barons. Under another, they might rise to be marquises, or dukes, even. They might be given offices in the Inland Revenue, where the pickings are lush and friendship and patronage are richly rewarded. If Lord Lynnfield helps Prince George now, the Lynnfields might stand to gain when the prince becomes King George."

"Or if James Stuart makes a successful return to the throne, and if the Lynnfields helped him on his way, they stand to gain from that . . ." I paused, amazed by the audacity. "They're playing both sides against each other. They win no matter which way the cards fall."

"Exactly, Peg, and you've just proved my point." My father cast the most significant sort of glower at Mr. Tinderflint. "A man like Lynnfield, who is capable of playing such a double game, is never careless. Lynnfield wanted Peg to see what he was doing, and he wanted it because Mrs. Oglethorpe wanted it. There is one explanation: she is using Lynnfield to get to Peggy, and to me. She hopes to drive me to some rash action to save my daughter."

This seemed like a further leap than the facts warranted, but Matthew spoke before I could.

"Then, Mr. Fitzroy, you think Sophy's request for Peggy's help was all part of the Sandfords' game?"

"Oglethorpe's game," Father corrected him firmly. "And I certainly think it's more likely than Miss Howe's coming up with the idea of using her sworn enemy on her own."

"But you're wrong, Uncle Fitzroy," said Olivia.

"I beg your pardon?"

"There's nothing simpler and more natural than Sophy taking Lord Lynnfield's part." Olivia looked about at all our stunned expressions. "Good gracious, do none of you see it?

It's as obvious as the reason no one has seen nor heard from Sebastian Sandford."

"And what reason might that be, Miss Pierpont?" inquired Mr. Tinderflint.

Olivia rolled her eyes. "Because, Mr. Tinderflint, Sebastian Sandford is dead!"

❧❦❧

CHAPTER FOURTEEN

IN WHICH OUR HEROINE DISCOVERS
THAT ALLIANCES ARE — BY THEIR TRAGIC
NATURES — FRAGILE THINGS.

As accustomed as I was to my cousin's outrageous pronouncements, this one stunned me into silence for a full minute. And not just me. The only noises in the parlor came from Matthew choking on a mouthful of coffee and Father thumping him hard between the shoulders.

Even when I found my voice again, I could do little more than sputter. "You don't mean . . . you can't possibly think . . . that Sophy . . ."

"Good gracious, no, Peggy!" cried Olivia. "Lynnfield did the actual deed, probably somewhere in the marshes. Sophy only keeps the secret." She paused, considering. "I am surprised they didn't send a few letters in Sebastian's hand for Libby to find and throw you off the scent. Now, that was indeed careless."

"It's impossible!" I cried. "I know it sounds preposterous, but Sophy does love Sebastian."

"Peggy," said Olivia with exaggerated patience, "Sophy wants to make an advantageous marriage. Why should she bother with the younger son if the older makes himself available?"

My jaw dropped.

"Lynnfield proposed marriage to Sophy Howe, in return for her promise to keep silent about the fate of his younger brother?" said Matthew slowly.

Olivia spread her hands, indicating the simplicity of the plan. "Sebastian is a liability to any subtle plan, because his pride and his temper are at odds with his reason. Lynnfield knows that. The deeper the game, the greater a drag Sebastian would be. Therefore comes the necessity that he should be disposed of. Lynnfield wouldn't need to extract any prom-ise of silence from Sophy either. Her self-interest will en-sure her silence as soon as the marriage occurs. Of course, Lynnfield probably hasn't told Sophy he's already murdered Sebastian. That might be a bit much for even Sophy's level of sang-froid. He probably just said Sebastian was being packed off to Barbados in an attempt to recover the family fortunes there."

"But Miss Howe is surely intelligent enough to realize Lord Lynnfield is not the most reliable of patrons," murmured Mr. Tinderflint. "Would she trust his proposal?"

I wished profoundly my friends would stop talking. I'd been so sure I knew what was happening. Now my head was spinning to the point where I could barely remember my own name.

Was it possible Olivia was correct? Could Lynnfield have murdered Sebastian and then kept Sophy from asking questions by proposing marriage?

"I need to get back to the palace." I blurted the words out. Never mind my mysterious letter. Never mind the attempted burglary. I needed to find proof, whatever it might be, of Lynnfield's treasonous intent before he had the prince too tightly ensnared.

I also needed to find Sebastian, and find him alive.

I did not care that this was ironic in the extreme. I'd heartily wished Sebastian to the devil any number of times, but my soul actively rebelled at the possibility that Sophy Howe was complicit in murder. Olivia might believe Lynnfield had kept the truth from Sophy, but I had nothing like so much faith in him, or her. If Sebastian had been killed, Sophy would have found out. And that meant she was deliberately keeping silent. If her silence had been bought for the money and advancement Lord Lynnfield could provide, what was to stop her from conspiring in the murder of other persons? Including me, or Matthew, or Olivia?

Including the prince himself?

"I'll have Robbins bring the coach." Father moved to ring the silver bell on his table.

"Oh, there's no need, no need at all." Mr. Tinderflint carefully wiped his fingers on his handkerchief. "I can easily accommodate our young friends in my conveyance, as well as

Miss Pierpont's luggage." Personally, I thought it probable that Mr. Tinderflint's coach could have accommodated us, the luggage, and any elephants that might pass by, but I did not say so. I was distracted by the way Father narrowed his dark eyes at Mr. Tinderflint's bland and casual tone.

"I should not wish you to be put to any trouble, sir," Father said. "There's also some advantage in the court becoming used to seeing Peg come and go in my conveyance. That way, should she need to leave suddenly, it will be assumed she is only returning to this house."

"A very good thought, sir. Yes, yes." Mr. Tinderflint nodded rapidly. "Peggy, what is your opinion? Which do you think prudent?"

I thought it prudent to keep my mouth shut for a count of ten, lest I express my impatience with them both. "Thank you for your offer, Mr. Tinderflint. I'm sure we're all grateful." I bowed my head to hide my gritted teeth. "I think your coach will be most convenient."

"Very well, sir," my father said. "We will leave matters in your hands." His tone remained entirely amiable, but his face darkened with a mixture of anger and concern.

I met my father's gaze. I tried with all my might to convey to him that I was not choosing sides between him and Mr. Tinderflint.

But Father had already turned away.

Nothing involving Olivia could be a simple matter, especially if it necessitated any sort of packing. My cousin spent the next two hours flying upstairs and down again, remembering a dozen last-minute items that had to be stuffed into trunks already full to bursting. Isolde, of course, had to investigate everything, and she was nearly trampled underfoot. She also seemed to have forgotten every command I'd taught her, and I found myself wondering if my assessment of her elevated intelligence had been premature.

All this fuss did, however, allow me to unearth the letter from Isolde's basket and tuck it up my sleeve with none being the wiser, not even the ever-observant Mr. Tinderflint.

At last, Olivia's boxes were lashed to the coach; cloaks, coats, and hats were fetched, and Father stood in the entrance hall to say his farewells to us. He took Matthew's hand first and leaned close to say something I could not make out, due to the combination of Isolde's growling in her basket because I'd forgotten her biscuit and Olivia's squeezing my arm eagerly, in case I missed the significance of my father and my sweetheart parting on friendly terms.

Mr. Tinderflint, from his position by the door, certainly did not miss it. In that moment, the mask slipped. I was no longer looking at the clownish sophisticate who fluttered and stuttered and charmed. This was the calculating man who would risk any life to achieve his ends. Including his own.

Including mine.

"Now, Peg, you needn't look so grave." My father smiled as he stepped up to me. "I've been on my own before."

"I know." I took both his hands and pressed them earnestly. "But I shall miss you."

It is difficult to pass a paper from a sleeve to one's own hand and from one's own hand to another's hand without it being seen. It may be managed, however, if one has sufficient practice. My father's fingers closed over the paper as it slid from my hand to his.

"You will write to me?" I said as I moved back. I did not glance toward Mr. Tinderflint to see if he had noticed the surreptitious exchange.

"Of course I will write, you goose." Father pinched my chin. "We are in this business together, after all, and we need to see it through."

We smiled at each other. He kissed my brow and I kissed his cheek. Then I took Olivia's arm and together we paraded out past both Matthew and Mr. Tinderflint without so much as a backwards glance.

I had never been in such a conveyance as Mr. Tinderflint's coach. Pulled by a team of no fewer than six horses, it moved as ponderously as a whale through the streets. At the same time, it was so well sprung that all of the usual jolting from the London cobbles was reduced to a gentle roll. There were shelves, storage boxes, and all manner of appurtenances, and Mr. Tinderflint himself direct us all on how to make ourselves most comfortable.

"Now, Mr. Reade, my good sir, if you'll just help Peggy adjust her rug. Miss Pierpont, is that foot warmer still hot? Excellent. If you would be so kind as to hand me that muff you'll find at the bottom of the box, we will all be quite snug." He tucked his plump arms up to the elbows into an enormous draping of rabbit fur. "Are you all warm enough?" he asked, every inch the anxious host.

"Very, thank you." In fact, I was near to perspiring.

"Excellent. Excellent." Mr. Tinderflint nodded several times. "I do confess, Mr. Reade, Miss Pierpont, I am very glad—yes, very—you are in the palace to help look after Peggy. Especially you, Mr. Reade, as you have proved yourself so many times to be the gallant chevalier. The extent and nature of this conspiracy is grave, yes, most grave."

Matthew inclined his head in acknowledgment of this flattery. Whatever mood gripped Mr. Tinderflint, it had not engendered subtlety. I wondered if he imagined Matthew to be naive, a thought that left me as out of sorts as Isolde deprived of a biscuit.

Olivia had taken Isolde's travel basket on her own lap and now rubbed my puppy's ears thoughtfully. "My question is, who is the true master of this conspiracy? Is it really Lord Lynnfield? Or could it be Mrs. Oglethorpe? I saw her only for a moment, of course, but she struck me as the sort who could direct whole armies."

"She certainly has that reputation," Mr. Tinderflint agreed. "Still, we must consider that the Sandfords have been involved in this particular aspect of Jacobite affairs since the beginning, but the Oglethorpes—while venerable conspirators in their own right—are only now making their presence known. That speaks not to long involvement but to a recent alliance, if an alliance there is."

Having the Oglethorpes and the Sandfords plotting separately did not make me feel any easier. Rather, it was like being caught in the jaws of an unpleasant and dramatic sort of vise.

"But Mr. Fitzroy was servant and spy in the Sandfords' country house," Matthew reminded Mr. Tinderflint. "He surely knows who Lord Lynnfield's friends are, and he believes their alliance with the Oglethorpes to be of long standing."

Mr. Tinderflint watched the crowds outside the window picking their way across the cobbles and stone walkways and, incidentally, all traveling more quickly than his coach. "I have the greatest respect for Fitzroy and his abilities — yes, yes, I do," he said softly. "But I must also ask myself how I would feel if I returned from prison only to discover that my beloved wife had died. Then there comes into my home this woman who perhaps knew my wife, who perhaps caused me to be imprisoned while my wife languished and died and my daughter was left to the indifferent care of virtual strangers." His words trickled through my mind, as cold and slow as melting ice. "It could interfere with a man's thinking. It could make him wish for revenge, no matter what else might be happening around him."

He spoke softly and with deep sympathy in his voice. Despite the heat of the coach, understanding left me chilled. My father was a man of passions. He had lived among ruffians and was ready and able to do violence. I had seen it. If he believed his wife had been wronged, could he leave the matter unaddressed? Even if those responsible had nothing to do with the conspiracies nesting in the palace?

"You think Father wants an excuse to go after Mrs. Oglethorpe directly."

"It would take one of the Almighty's saints not to long for revenge under such circumstances as Fitzroy finds himself in. Even should it . . . distract from more pressing business."

"Do you suggest, sir, that my father would act independently and against the interests of his king or his country?" I demanded. "After all he has been through on their behalf?"

Mr. Tinderflint paused, seemingly uncertain. I could not tell whether this was genuine feeling or yet more play-acting. "Peggy, we have not talked much about your mother." He said this in such a low voice I had to lean closer to hear him over the creak and rattle of the carriage. "That has been a mistake on my part, I think. She was so very talented, so adept at what she did. And magnificent. I'd never seen a woman who could walk into a room and catch every eye as she did . . ." He stopped. "You see, that's my problem. I knew Elizabeth as a talented agent who did great good service to . . . well . . . various causes, and to her queen, of course. But to your father, she was his world." Mr. Tinderflint let his gaze touch each of us in turn. "I think it is very important we are mindful of this as we confer about our actions, and Fitzroy's actions, from here on after."

I had no name for the feeling that rushed through me at

these words. This man, my patron, had saved me from the worst possible assault. He had brought me into a life where I had friends, rank, and purpose. Now, for the best and most urgent reasons, of course, he asked me to inform against my father. My father, who might, perfectly understandably—yes, yes, quite understandably—have become confused between his duty to his country and his desire for vengeance. Of course, I would do this without letting my father know who had urged me to find the information. All in the best interests of myself, and my father, and my friends, and my king and country, of course. Yes, yes, of course.

Mr. Tinderflint wanted this of me, and he didn't even show me the respect of asking me directly.

"You may be assured, Mr. Tinderflint," I said without blinking, "I will do all that I can."

CHAPTER FIFTEEN

IN WHICH BOTH IDENTITIES AND LOYALTIES
ARE SERIOUSLY QUESTIONED AND CERTAIN
IRREVOCABLE WORDS ARE SPOKEN.

Despite the coach's stately progress, we did eventually reach the palace and the Color Court. As Matthew helped me down, the cold wind whipped hard into my eyes and I had to grab my cloak's hood to keep it from being blown back.

Mr. Tinderflint busied himself with giving orders—not only to his men, but to several passing porters as well—on the disposition of Olivia's trunks. Olivia, of course, could not be left out of a task with which she was so intimately connected. She shoved Isolde's basket into my hands, hiked up her hems, and waded into the fray.

This left me facing Matthew. My sweetheart sighed and jammed his hands into his coat pockets. "I should get down to the hall," he said. "I've been gone too long already, and Lord Beckenstile wants more cherubs for the Arch of Prosperity."

We were back on our manners. One day, I promised myself, we would end this. One day, I would be able to take his hand and kiss his cheek and not care who saw. That this change of circumstance would necessarily involve the two of us making an extra visit to church one morning was something I decided not to think about too much.

Instead, I returned what I knew to be a weak smile. "I would never choose for you to endure more cherubs, not even for my sake."

"Duty requires so many sacrifices from us all." He smiled and bowed. "I'll come find you later," he breathed.

I nodded my acknowledgment as I curtsied. We already had a great deal to talk about, and I suspected Olivia would furnish yet more subjects for conversation as soon as we were alone.

Her attitude from the instant I entered my rooms certainly appeared to bear this out. She stopped her work of pawing through an open trunk to grab me by both hands and drag me to sit beside her on the bed.

"Oh, Peggy, you can't imagine what I've seen since you've been gone! I'm bursting to tell you!"

Unfortunately for us both, this breathless prologue was followed by a knock at the door. Not the scratch of a maid, but a firm knock.

"Matthew?" I jumped up and hurried to answer it ahead

of Libby. But instead of Matthew, there was a bearded man wearing a long white smock and worn boots. He held a corded trunk in his gnarled hands. It wasn't until he lifted his face and allowed me a glimpse beneath the brim of his slouch hat that I recognized my father.

"Last box for the lady," he said gruffly.

There are times when my cousin proves her inherent worth. While I stepped back, struck absolutely dumb, Olivia leapt to her feet and snatched up her purse. "Libby, take this down to Mr. Tinderflint's coach and make sure the porters have all gotten their tips. Then go find Mr. Reade in the lower hall and tell him he needs to come up here as soon as may be. Oh, and then you can wait for the cart and my maid Templeton to arrive and show her up."

Normally, Libby would have hesitated, but she had a good eye and could tell by my unguarded expression that our new arrival was nothing so simple as a porter.

"Yes, miss." My maid hurried from the room, and Olivia, true to her dramatic instincts as well as her intelligence, bolted the door.

"Why are you here, sir?" I cried. "You said you cannot be seen at court."

"As myself, it's unwise. But as some anonymous porter, I think I may be safe." Father set the box down on top of a stack of similar crates. Isolde scampered up to his boots and nosed at them. Displeased with what she saw, she growled. Father nudged her aside gently so he would not tread upon her as he came over to me.

"This letter, Peg." He pulled out the much-folded paper I had passed him. "Where did you get this?"

"Letter!" cried Olivia. "You had a letter and did not tell me!"

I ignored her. "It was delivered here anonymously. I saw the signature, the Mrs. Tinderflint . . ." Olivia gasped. I ignored her again. "Do you know what it means, sir?"

"No," Father croaked. "Not entirely. I . . . I do know this is Elizabeth's—your mother's—handwriting."

Olivia, evidently deciding she had been left out of the conversation long enough, snatched the letter out of Father's hands. He started. I squeaked. Olivia paid us no attention but flipped open the fragile paper and scanned its contents. Father shrugged, resigning himself to the inevitable, as one tended to do with Olivia. "Have there been any others?" he asked me.

"No."

"Yes," said Olivia.

My father and I both stared at her.

"I haven't received them, but . . ." Olivia swallowed, suddenly hesitant as she refolded the paper. Hesitation, however, seldom lasted with my cousin. She dropped the letter onto my desk, hurried to one of her many boxes, and began wrestling with the cordage.

Father tossed his hat aside and drew a wicked-looking knife from his belt. Swiftly and efficiently, he sliced the ropes. This allowed Olivia to snap the trunk's latches. She raised the lid, lifted out several trays, laid several skirts on the bed, and rummaged so deeply in the bottom I feared she might fall in like a child into a well. Eventually, however, she came up for air, clutching a badly embroidered pink workbag. This she dumped out unceremoniously onto the bed to reveal, among other things, a battered notebook. I was all but ready to scream as she flipped through the pages. It is fortunate for us all that in that moment, she apparently found the correct memorandum.

"'My Dear Mrs. Righthandwall,'" Olivia read. "'I received your description of the proposed outing with great attention. Needless to say, I am overjoyed with the scheme! It is perfect in every detail. I have discussed it with our friends here, and you may be sure we will be able to make the journey to Godalming in good time so that we may all together travel on to the Firth of Forth for the fifteenth. I can only pray the weather remains kind to us and all our good friends!' It was signed 'Mrs. Tinderflint,' and then there were these numbers." She held it out to Father. "Just like on Peggy's letter."

Father all but tore the book from her hands. "Olivia, where did you get this?"

"The letter was in Mother's papers," said Olivia, without a trace of shame or apology. "I was helping her pack and I, well, I found a great box full of letters that I'm sure I'd never seen before." She stared at both of us, as if daring us to challenge this version of events. "I would have copied more, if I'd had the time. Those numbers are a code, aren't they?"

"A cipher, yes." Father peered closely at the page. "Yes, they most certainly are."

"Mother is a spy." Olivia spoke the words gingerly, as if something might break if she said them too loudly. "My. Mother. Is. A. Spy. She's Mrs. Righthandwall!"

"You're jumping to conclusions," muttered Father.

"What other explanation is there?" Olivia demanded. When Father did not answer, she turned to me. "We know your mother and mine were close friends when they were younger. We also know my mother spoke with Mr. Tinderflint when he found out Father worked for the Jacobites during the first uprising. Maybe that meeting wasn't really about Father's affairs. Maybe it was about *hers*."

"It can't be," I said. Surely it was against the laws of nature and nature's God that my foolish, nervous, quivering aunt was a member of Mr. Tinderflint's harem of drawing-room spies.

"Who else could Mrs. Righthandwall be?" demanded Olivia.

"Mrs. Oglethorpe." The words burst out of my mouth, followed more slowly by the appropriate memory. "Mrs. Oglethorpe, who was born Eleanor Wall."

"She also has a house in Godalming," said Father. He reached again for the other letter, the one I'd received, and flipped it open so he could compare the two.

"Oh." Olivia pouted. But then: "Oh!" she cried, as fresh light dawned. "If Mrs. Oglethorpe is Mrs. Righthandwall, that means . . ."

That "Mrs. Tinderflint" was my mother. And it meant that, despite what Mr. Tinderflint said, this was not Mrs.

Oglethorpe's first appearance in our mystery. It also meant that Mrs. Oglethorpe could very well have been the one who sent me the original letter.

Unless, of course, it was Aunt Pierpont, who, for some unaccountable reason, had a store of Mother's old letters.

Isolde had set to barking again. "Secrets, Isolde." I scooped her up, sat down on the tapestry stool, and covered her with my handkerchief. She circled about in my lap looking for biscuits. This operation gave me time enough to find my voice once more. "Father, did you bundle Aunt Pierpont out of the house early? To keep her from talking to Mr. Tinderflint?"

"Eh?" Father held the book and the letter in front of him, one in each hand, as if weighing them against each other. "No. Of course not."

The puppy in my lap wriggled and yipped. Olivia frowned at me, scooped Isolde out from under my kerchief, and set her down on the floor. It was then that my cousin saw the distressed turn of my countenance and took both of my hands. Hers, I noted, had gone very cold.

Father had drifted over to the hearth. For a minute, I wondered if he meant to throw Olivia's notebook into it. The look on his face said he very much wanted to. In the end, however, he only snapped it shut.

"This is it." He held up the book. "These letters are why Tierney wanted to speak with Delphine today. They must be."

"But what do they mean?" asked Olivia.

"I don't know yet, and I won't until we get these letters deciphered." He paused. "When is the prince's birthday celebration?"

"In two days."

He nodded. "Very well. That should be just time enough, if I leave at once—"

"Leave!" I cried. "Where could you have to go at such a time!"

I trust my readers will forgive this unfilial, and somewhat shrill, outburst when it is remembered that the last time my father left me, it had been for a rather extended period.

"I'm only going as far as Oxford." Father laid his hand on my shoulder and gave me what I'm sure was meant to be a reassuring squeeze. "There's a man there, name of Willis. If anybody can break this cipher, he's the one. I will be back in time for the masque. Don't worry, Peg." He squeezed my shoulder again, and even had the nerve to smile. "I'll find my way in and I'll find you—you may depend on it."

I eyed him coldly. Yes, the cipher had to be broken. Of course it did. But there must be a way that did not involve him abandoning me again, especially when we couldn't be sure as to the extent of the dangers around us. When I wasn't even certain I could trust Mr. Tinderflint anymore.

When Mr. Tinderflint wasn't sure any of us should be trusting my father anymore.

Father picked up his hat off the stack of boxes. He did not place it on his head, but stood there with the battered object in his hands, looking more like a servant or a petitioner than he should. Isolde decided she'd had quite enough of his boots and lunged for the toes.

Father reached down, grabbed her by the scruff of her neck, and held her in front of his face. "However did you come by this extraordinary creature?"

"Royal decree." I took the pup from him and handed her to Olivia. "Sir, let me be plain: if you are to go, please go. I have to change, and find some sort of room for Olivia in this chaos, and dine, and dress, and not be late for the drawing room so that Her Royal Highness will not be further upset with me. I *cannot* play the spy right now!"

"Can you play the daughter?"

"I'm trying!" I cried. Could he not see? I was trying so desperately to trust him and his judgment, even when my patron said I should not, and my father was giving me no help whatsoever.

The door opened once more and Matthew darted inside, followed more slowly by Libby. Matthew recognized the man in front of us and pulled up short.

My father stared at Matthew, and Olivia, and at last at me.

He nodded once. "I'd best go," he said. "There's no need for more suspicions to be raised."

He started for the door. Matthew stepped back.

"Wait." I moved to Father. He was a tall man. I felt small looking up at him—small, young, and very uncertain. I saw the stranger I did not know if I should trust, and I saw the father I missed. Just as clearly, I saw the grieving widower whose questions ate at his heart.

"I owe Mr. Tinderflint a great deal," I said, unsure of where the words were coming from or which might be the next to arrive. "Almost everything since Uncle Pierpont threw me out, and even a little before that."

"I know, Peg. I—"

"I may owe him my life, but my loyalty is not so unconditional, and I don't owe him . . . I don't owe him . . ." I had to stop. "I will not let him stand between me and those nearest me."

My father smiled, and a warmth spread through me, but also a yearning, because nothing had changed, not even with that smile. He was still leaving.

"I'll see you in one day's time, Peg. Two at the very most." He winked. Once again assuming his posture as the careless adventurer, he made a sweeping bow and left us.

I was a long time staring at the door. My breath strained against my stays. I raised my fist and I set it against the door's surface. I pounded, once.

Matthew was behind me. I smelled his distinct scent of paint and fresh air. "It's all right, Peggy Mostly."

I shook my head hard. "It isn't! What in God's name am I supposed to do with two of them!" I cried, indifferent to blasphemy and to the shock on Olivia's face. "It's bad enough to have a master, and a mistress, and princes and kings, all insisting I be loyal to them and confess to them and spy for them, but now I've got a father in on the game!"

"What do you want to do?" Matthew asked.

"What do *we* want to do?" Olivia corrected him tartly. "She's not entirely alone, you know."

I did know. I also knew my heart strained as badly as my breath. Sailors speak of the worst possible place as being caught between the devil and the deep blue sea. They, clearly, had never been caught between a new father and an old spy.

My father and Mr. Tinderflint. Neither of them was entirely wrong but neither was entirely right, and now they were at odds and each wanted me on his side. Who was I to believe?

There was only one answer. I was to believe myself.

"We do what we must," I told the door firmly.

"Wonderful!" said Olivia. "What is that?"

"We go to the masque," Matthew answered for me. "We find Sophy Howe, and this Oglethorpe woman if she's there, and we follow them. Perhaps we find the Sandfords, or," he added as Olivia opened her mouth, "at least some sign of their genuine whereabouts."

"Exactly." I turned around. Decision made everything better. Of course, anything would be an improvement on tangled questions of love, loyalty, and brimming loss. "If we catch them in some act, that's all to the good. But we see whom they talk with and what they do. Matthew . . ." I met his gaze. "Matthew . . ." I hated what I saw there. I hated myself. One day, we often joked, I would push him too far.

He folded his arms and sighed. My heart plummeted. "Peggy, Olivia . . . it's time we started thinking about something. Why us? And by that I mean, why Peggy?"

It took me a moment, but I caught the gist of his question. "You mean why did Mr. Tinderflint seek me out? Why did he concoct this fantastical scheme of substitution to start me at court on a lie and a prayer, after the last girl he planted there failed rather spectacularly?"

"You mean she died," said Matthew flatly. "There had to have been others he could have chosen, but none of them would have called your father out of hiding. No one else would have led him to Sir Oliver *and* Lady Delphine, not to mention this Mrs. Oglethorpe."

"Bait," I whispered. "I'm bait."

"Or the Judas goat," whispered Olivia.

Matthew nodded grimly. "I don't know if it's true, but we have to find out."

Before one of us went too far. Before one of us died as that other girl had. As my uncle had, and maybe even Sebastian had.

I stared up at Matthew. I couldn't do this. I couldn't drag him in any further. With Olivia, it was one thing. Her blood kindred was involved in this mess. I couldn't ask Matthew to risk himself for me, for us, again. Not when I knew so little about what was happening. Not when he'd already risked so much. Not when he'd almost been killed . . .

"Oh, dear! Isolde's gotten into the closet! Come back, naughty thing!" Olivia called, which only made Isolde howl. Olivia ran into the dressing chamber after her and slammed the door.

I couldn't move. I couldn't even look away as Matthew reached out and took my hands. "Please, Peggy. You have to trust me."

"I do trust you!" I cried, but he only shook his head.

"No, you don't. You think I don't see who you really are."

"You don't understand, Matthew . . ."

"This is what I mean!" he shouted. "Just what is it that I don't know? For the love of God, Peggy! I was *there*! I kept your secrets while you were impersonating a lady! I helped you break into a blasted palace and cheat a baron at cards in front of the Prince of Wales! I've seen you charm half the court while lying through your teeth to the other half. You're brave, you're mad, you're magnificent, and you're always wondering"—he cupped his palm around the back of my head—"when I'm going to get tired, or afraid, or simply fed up and leave you. After everything we've been through, you still don't trust me to make up my own mind about what it is I'm doing!"

"You deserve someone who isn't constantly running you into danger. Someone who can be a helpmeet and . . ." *A wife. A normal girl who will make you a normal wife.*

"I deserve you," he said, giving me the mildest of shakes. "At least, I want to. I'm not innocent, Peggy. I've had the chance to fall in love with other girls. Artists, even just 'prentices, if they like women at all, there's plenty . . . Well, never mind. The point is, not one of them touched me, not the way you did from the first." He lifted his other hand to cradle my chin. His calluses rasped against my bare skin and his heat bled straight into my heart. "I love you, Peggy Mostly. Not halfway—not until it becomes too difficult or dangerous. But always, and wherever it may lead." He paused, anguish rising in his bright gray eyes. "Peggy, if you can't trust that I am speaking the truth, then tell me so and do it now. Because that is the only thing that could ever make me leave you."

I couldn't breathe. I should say it. I knew that. I should save his life and his heart and say that I did not believe him. That I did not trust him. I should send him back to . . . to whoever those other girls had been and let him choose again, choose better, choose normalcy, choose safety.

But I had never once been able to lie to Matthew Reade.

"I do trust you, Matthew, and I always will."

We kissed, of course. We kissed for a rather long time.

CHAPTER SIXTEEN

In which Our Heroine makes
a spectacle of herself.

It was only natural that when the time for His Royal Highness's masque finally arrived, it should bring with it a last-minute storm of deliveries, activities, and raised voices.

"Hold still!" cried Libby as she balanced on her toes atop a stool, where she wielded her entire arsenal of hairpins.

"OW!" I cried in heartfelt response.

"I *told* you to hold still!"

This elevated exchange was caused by Libby attempting to fix some complex ornamentation onto my head. This would not be unusual, save that the headdress in question was composed of waving golden wires adorned with bits of green ribbon meant to simulate willow leaves. It was a lavish, ungainly arrangement, and its sole purpose seemed to be to topple to the floor the instant I stood up. It was also the crowning glory of the costume assigned to me as the representation of summer for the maids' "dance of the seasons."

Probably it would be healthier for all of us if the Master of the Revels remained out of arm's reach for the duration of the masquerade.

Given all this rattling and rustling and running about, it was a blessing that we had no need to worry about Isolde tonight. Princess Anne had determined that since this was a celebration, the whole lap dog clan should be reunited for the evening, and my puppy was in the bosom of her family, no doubt being spoiled half to death.

This was also fortunate because Libby was attempting to get me ready out in my main bedchamber. Olivia had commandeered the dressing closet a full hour ago and showed no intention of relinquishing it. She had not even allowed her maid, the long-suffering Templeton, to peek inside.

On a certain level, Olivia's introduction to court life had gone quite smoothly. As promised, Princess Caroline had received my cousin politely and pleasantly at the drawing room. A number of the grand personages present remembered her last sojourn into their midst and were glad to welcome her back, especially as she carried with her the glow of royal favor. The gentlemen were, of course, pleased because she was a pretty face.

On her side, Olivia was over the moon because I was able to introduce her to the poets Mr. Pope and Mr. Gay. Her only disappointment was that neither "Mad" Dean Swift nor the writer Daniel Defoe had been able to attend that evening.

On another, more private level, however, I was beginning to feel the shortcomings of this scheme. I had humbly, on all-but-bended knee, made inquiry of the Lord Chamberlain about arranging apartments large enough to adequately accommodate both myself and my cousin. I mentioned most tactfully that Her Royal Highness had given her blessing to this increase in living space. The Lord Chamberlain responded by blithely telling me that all would be arranged as soon as possible. As matters stood, Olivia and I slept in one bed just as we had when we were children, and in general we lived in each other's pockets. My love for my cousin was without bounds, but my tolerance for having to wait my turn to get at my own closet was showing distinct signs of wear.

"Olivia, what on earth are you doing in there!"

My cousin's reply was predictably amiable and informative. "I will be out sooner if you don't keep shouting—*ow!*—at me."

I could have borne all these strains with greater patience if it were not for one grave occurrence. Perhaps I should say the *absence* of an occurrence. We had arrived at the time of the masquerade without receiving any word from my father. I'd sent Norris, one of my usual errand runners, to the house twice, only to have him be told, and I quote here exactly, "Mr. Fitzroy ain't home, so no good you hangin' about."

At first, this news angered me. How could Father

disappear like this when so much was at stake? That anger proved thin and insubstantial, however, when compared to the fear that formed behind it. Had something happened to him? If it had, how would I even know? I had no way to send for him and no knowledge of where he might have gone, apart from the very general destination of Oxford and the name Willis.

Another pin grazed my scalp. I felt Libby lift her hands away. "Try it now, miss."

I swallowed, and amid a veritable cacophony of rustling emerald ribbons and rattling wires, I stood. The headdress did not immediately fall off, for which I was grateful, I supposed.

"Can you walk?" It was one of the few times I'd heard Libby sound anxious. She did take her handiwork seriously, even when that handiwork was me.

I walked across the room slowly. The slim gray dress I wore was in the "Grecian style." It was also two steps from indecent, being exceedingly thin and light. The skirt had no hoop beneath it and precious little in the way of petticoats. You could almost see the outline of my legs. It was also unexpectedly comfortable, despite the winding sash of bright green vines adorned with little purple bundles that, I think, were meant to represent grapes.

I might, in fact, have felt quite stunning were it not for the ludicrous headdress. As it was, any appreciation I had for my gown was overwhelmed by my straining neck and abused scalp. I wasn't even going to need the sparkling mask that lay on the table at Libby's right hand. No one would be able to see my face through this absurd forest of glimmering antennae.

I reached the door and turned. I considered shaking my head, quite accidentally, to knock the hideous thing off. I refrained only because I would also have had to quite accidentally trample it underfoot. I might have attempted it, if I hadn't seen one last yard-long pin clutched in Libby's tiny fist.

"Try a dance step," my maid commanded.

I (badly) executed one sliding skip-hop. The headdress wobbled and it rattled, but my maid had done her work too well and it stayed firmly put.

"You are a wonder, Libby," I said.

"Thank you, miss," she replied with a most unprecedented trace of modesty.

"Merciful heavens, Peggy!" came Olivia's voice. "What is that on your head?"

I lifted my chin carefully. "It is the representation of summer, the season of warmth, grace, and plenty as symbolized by the graceful willow tree." I turned, even more carefully, toward her. I stopped. I was suddenly grateful for my veil of false branches, because it prevented Olivia from seeing my eyes attempt to start out of my skull.

This was not my cousin. Oh, my cousin had indeed gone into the dressing closet; she had simply failed to come out of it. Olivia was the flower of English maidenhood. Her gold and rose beauty filled youths, and any number of older men, with thoughts of love.

This person might well have been one of those youths. "He" was a dashing blade dressed in a coat of blue satin, embroidered with silver and trimmed with Irish lace. One white-gloved hand held a ribboned walking stick. A gold-handled dress sword hung from his left hip. He wore a blue and white feathered mask with a hooked nose meant, I think, to simulate a poll parrot. A blue hat with trailing feathers perched on his full-bottomed wig, and he sported a single round patch on his right cheek.

"Good evening, Miss Fitzroy." The dashing blade executed a perfect bow.

It took several tries before I was able to gasp out, "*Olivia?*"

The dashing blade grinned. "Ah! I fear that lady has returned home. My name is Orlando Preston, and I am your devoted servant." He bowed again.

"I don't . . . I can't . . . Olivia!"

Grinning in delight at her triumph, Olivia held out her arm. "Shall we go, cousin? I believe you are expected in the lower hall."

Completely bemused, I took "his" arm and let myself be led out into the corridor. My headdress shifted and clattered with each movement, but it was not just my false branches that were making movement awkward. The lightness of my skirts made walking unexpectedly hazardous. If I moved too quickly, the flimsy, unshaped fabric flew upward, allowing all the world to glimpse my ankles or even — oh for shame to confess it! — my shins.

"Now," I murmured to Olivia as we made our careful way through the galleries and down the stairs. "You remember — you are to meet Matthew in the Ambassador Court, not the Color Court. That will be a madhouse. Well, I expect it will all be a madhouse, but you can ask any of the yeomen for directions, and —"

"And then we are to take up our positions by the Arch of Prosperity," Olivia recited dutifully. "From there, we will be able to spy what Sophy does and whom she talks to as she leaves the stage. Once you are released from the processional, we will each pick a direction and circulate about the party. When the bells strike midnight, we will rendezvous at the arch again and compare notes. Should any dire emergency occur, we are to find Mr. Tinderflint's private pavilion by the park pond and plead for his presence promptly, Peggy." She paused to see if I was astonished at all by her alliterative alacrity.

I wasn't. "And if you really want anyone to take you for 'Orlando Preston,' remember to keep your voice down and don't giggle." There may have been a hint of peevishness in these words, but it must be remembered that I had rather a lot to manage at this point, both internally and externally. "And don't be late for Matthew; otherwise we'll never find each other."

Despite my stern admonishment, Olivia giggled. "As if there were any earthly possibility we'd lose you while you're wearing those branches. Peggy, promise me this thing was not your idea."

"That, cousin, I can and do promise most faithfully."

The anniversary of a royal birth must of necessity be celebrated in royal style. St. James's Palace might not be ideally situated for favorite royal pastimes like water parties, but it was still conveniently placed next to a broad green parkland that was perfect for grand illuminations, fireworks, and processions of decorative ladies.

Although the scenery and much of the scaffolding had been moved to the various stages erected in the gardens and parklands, the lower hall was still full of bustling persons of various professions and rank. Lord Beckenstile was naturally in the thick of it, shouting orders to workmen and servants as they darted or stomped back and forth. This, of course, did not prevent that gimlet-eyed man from taking full note of my arrival.

"So kind of you to join us, Miss Fitzroy," he drawled loudly as Olivia and I came through the doors. "Will you take your place? Or am I to inform His Royal Highness we must all await your convenience?"

"I'm so sorry, Lord Beckenstile," I murmured as I made my way through a somewhat disorganized crowd of youths impressed into the role of torchbearers. These attendants were dressed in black, blue, and white, meant to symbolize the broad heavens, I think. Those I could see through my combination of mask and branches looked as unhappy in their costumes as I in mine.

We maids were, of course, meant to represent the four seasons. Molly Lepell, all in shades of green, pink, and primrose yellow, was spring. Mary Bellenden, in darker greens, reds, and golds, was autumn. Both of them, I noted, were allowed to wear perfectly reasonable wreaths of trailing vines and blossoms in their neatly dressed hair.

"And who is this?" cried Mary as "Orlando" led me, rattling, to my spot in the line. "Don't tell me Mr. Reade has a rival!" She then proceeded to bat her eyes at my escort in such a show of flirtation that I could not tell whether she was having a joke or if she'd been truly taken in.

"Certainly not," I said loftily. "This is my cousin, Mr. Orlando Preston." At this, Olivia bowed in a flurry of broad gestures and flourishes of lace that would have done Mr. Tinderflint proud. I found a moment to enjoy the extreme consternation on Sophy's face.

"Yet another one?" Sophy murmured. "Be careful, Mary. The members of Miss Fitzroy's family tend to be rather more than they first seem."

Sophy was the representation of winter, and I must admit she wore the part well. Her costume included a considerable acreage of pure white silk and figured blue gauze, not to mention cascading silver lace and a glittering blue and silver stomacher.

I wanted to be closer to her. I wanted to see whether

her pallor was the result of too much face powder or because Sebastian was still missing. I had made all the inquiries I could. No one had seen Sebastian, or his brother, for days. Given that Sophy did not do nearly as well at the card tables without her partner, few of those I spoke with seemed discomforted by the absence.

It did, however, leave me in the impossible situation of being worried about Sebastian's fate and of what lines Sophy might have crossed to help bring it about.

"Well, Mr. Preston, what do you say?" Mary tilted her head just so, in order to peer mischievously at Olivia/Orlando. "Are you here to deceive us as well?"

"Is that not the point of a masquerade?" inquired Olivia. "Not that I stand the slightest chance at deceiving such sagacious ladies as yourselves."

"Ooooh!" Mary clapped her hands. "I think I like this new cousin of yours, Peggy. Promise me we will see more of him later."

"Yes, do, Peggy," said Olivia.

Mary laughed brightly. Molly turned her face away and pressed her fingertips over her mouth. Sophy frowned hard.

Lord Beckenstile cleared his throat, loudly. He also thumped his white staff for emphasis.

"But I have overstayed my time." Olivia made one more bow. "I will see you anon, Peggy." She capped this performance off by winking at Mary before she sauntered away, wobbling only slightly in her unfamiliar shoes.

Lord Beckenstile sniffed irritably. "If you are quite

finished exhibiting your relations for Miss Bellenden's approval, Miss Fitzroy, you might exert yourself to find your place in line."

I curtsied humbly, assumed my right station between Mary and Molly, and took my decorative brass lantern from the serving man who stood ready. At that same moment, a page came running hotfoot into the hall to bow to the master.

"His Royal Highness has arrived!" boomed Lord Beckenstile. "Places! It begins!"

I have endured much in my service to the Crown. I have stood for hours without complaint. I have been cornered and pawed by assorted "gentlemen." I have gracefully lost ridiculous sums at the card tables to flatter those whom my mistress wished to keep in good humor. I've been kidnapped, shot, threatened at sword-point, and almost drowned. But nothing will ever equal the horror that was my performance as the Summer Willow.

I ask my readers to imagine being led out of doors by a double file of torchbearers into a high, cold wind, holding a flickering lantern in one hand and their hems in the other. Then come the rickety stairs to be mounted to a vast and equally rickety stage decorated in a manner meant to suggest the whole of not just England, but Scotland, Ireland, and the Germanies. These fanciful bits of scenery sway in the wind nearly as violently as the lantern flames. Once arrived in this agreeable location, the dancer must try not to appear as if her gaze is riveted on the faint chalk line at her feet as she hops, slides, turns, turns again, skips, tries to find the dreaded Xs, weaves in a grand hay, crosses creaking scenery bridges, and crosses them again, all to the confused music of fife, flute, horn, and drum, which can barely be heard because of the rattling headdress.

I trod on Molly's hem. Mary's hot brass lantern brushed my bare arm twice during one of the more complicated turns. I kicked Sophy's ankle.

Yes, for once, entirely by accident.

The only good I can say is that it did not rain.

Somehow, though, we succeeded in navigating our hazardous pathways mostly unscathed and even successfully found our final Xs. That Molly Lepell had to cough loudly to signal me to my proper place is a scurrilous rumor. We did raise our lanterns high with something approaching easy grace as the musicians brought their final crescendo to a triumphant close.

Not that anyone was watching us at that moment. Everyone's attention was fixed on the stand where the royal family sat, and more particularly on the prince and princess, waiting to see how they would respond.

The prince rose to his feet and brought his hands together.

"Bravo!" he cried.

Now that it was safe, cheers and applause rose around us. Princess Caroline was also on her feet, as were the three little princesses, all making an appreciative uproar. Distance and the dancing shadows prevented me from reading my mistress's expression. This bothered me. I'd had no opportunity to converse with her since my return with Olivia and so had been unable to determine how things stood between Lord Lynnfield and the prince.

I tried to wrench my mind back to more immediate concerns. Such as how the Master of the Revels stepped to the fore to make his bow and lead us off in reverse order, which meant I was watching Mary and Sophy precede me. Sophy moved with her usual controlled perfection. Whatever activity she had planned with or without Mrs. Oglethorpe, who might, or might not, be here this evening, Sophy did not permit it to affect her deportment.

Perhaps there was nothing. Perhaps the plans had been changed during that same conversation that had changed her mind about Lord Lynnfield. Perhaps Sebastian had simply been sent home to keep him out of trouble. Perhaps Lynnfield had left because, after all, smuggling gangs in the Great Romney Marsh could not be trusted to manage their own affairs. Perhaps Mr. Tinderflint, and my father, and the princess were all wrong, and the Swedish plot really had been the beginning and the end of matters.

Perhaps I would be crowned Queen of the French tonight.

We returned to the Ambassador Court, which was thronging with well-wishers. Ladies and gentlemen, friends and family, as well as idlers and the simply curious, cheered and clapped as we maids filed entered the court. As Olivia had predicted, my ungainly headdress served to make me highly visible, and I endured only a brief moment of twisting and turning before I spotted my cousin sauntering toward me with Matthew beside her.

I nodded to them both and backed to the edge of the swirling mob. Now that I knew my friends had seen me, there was only one question left.

Where had Sophy gotten herself to?

The courtyard was little more than a shifting sea of backs and shoulders. I held my pathetic lantern as high as I could reach. I strained to stand on my toes on the uneven cobbles. I may also have used the cover of so many voices to utter a few new expressions I had learned from certain disreputable persons. Had I lost her? Could she have already slipped away?

No. Sophy had only separated herself from the crowd. Her glittering white dress stood out sharply against the darker backdrop of the palace's brick walls. Most unusually, she stood alone, her own decorative lantern held high. Like me, Sophy Howe sought someone in particular.

That someone was not long in coming.

I shoved my branches back with my free hand. Now that I was looking in the correct direction, I could make out a man dressed all in solemn black—a wide-plumed black hat, black mask, and black gauntlets, holding a black and silver walking stick. A tall lady, elegantly dressed in similar unrelieved midnight shades, walked at his side. Both were moving deliberately through the crowd toward the beacon that was Sophy Howe.

"Here, Peggy, you're going to ignite something."

I jumped. I'd become so engrossed in watching Sophy, I'd missed Olivia and Matthew's arrival.

Matthew took my lantern and blew out the candle inside. In contrast to Olivia's dashing blade, Matthew was dressed as a scholar. He wore a black velvet cap, a white mask, and a dark red robe. A magnifying glass dangled on a chain about his neck, and he tucked a huge leather-bound (false) book under his elbow.

"What are you staring at, Peggy?" asked Olivia, pushing back her hat brim and peering about. "Oh!"

She had spotted the Howe. The pair in black had reached Sophy, and proceeded to make their bows. The lady, I could now see, was masquerading as a Spanish *duenna* in a black velvet gown with a high comb in her hair and a veil fashioned from yards of black lace.

Black lace like I had seen so recently before.

"Is that Lynnfield all in black there?" Olivia was saying. "That could be the cane he takes with him everywhere. Who's the woman? You don't suppose that's his *mother*, do you?"

"Does he even have a mother?" muttered Matthew. "I've never heard anyone so much as mention a Lady Lynnfield."

"Be quiet, both of you," I ordered. My brain was spinning and I needed to right it quickly. Because Sophy had been telling the truth that day she had tried to recruit me to her cause, and despite all my hopes those plans had not changed.

The woman on the cavalier's arm was none other than Mrs. Oglethorpe.

CHAPTER SEVENTEEN

IN WHICH BOTH IDENTITIES AND
MOTIVATIONS MIGHT WELL BE MISTAKEN.

The realization that we were all staring at Mrs.
Oglethorpe brought an avalanche of smaller realizations. The
first was that we had no time to waste.

"Get this thing off me!" I croaked.

"Which thing, Peggy?" said Olivia. "You're wearing
rather a—"

Matthew, always quick to understand, dropped his book
into Olivia's hands. "Hold this, and keep an eye on Sophy."

He immediately set to work finding the multiplicity of
pins Libby had concealed in my hair. I once again cursed fashion, masquerades, and my duty. Here I was, with the man I
loved running his fingers through my hair, and I couldn't actually enjoy the moment because I was in public and because

I had to worry about a trio of Jacobite conspirators getting away.

"What do you see?" I hissed at Olivia. I couldn't see anything for myself, as I was busy grappling with my slipping branches. Matthew yanked out another pin.

"They're chatting. Some people are coming up and bowing and . . . Oh, get out of the way, can't you!" She stretched up onto tiptoe. "They're turning, they're walking. Hurry, Peg!"

Fortunately, at that moment, Matthew found the crucial pin. The hated headdress tumbled free and slithered to the ground. At long last, I was able to kick it aside, with only the smallest twinge of guilt at the waste and expense.

"Matthew, Olivia . . ." I began.

"Well!" cried a new voice. "Here we are again, Mr. Preston!"

The three of us spun about. Like a fairy appearing in the morning mists, Mary Bellenden in her autumnal garb slid gracefully through the crowd. With a swift and much-practiced movement, she threaded her arm through Olivia's.

"Peggy, do loan me your cousin for a bit. I've a thousand friends who will be delighted to meet such a charming gentleman." Mary sucked in a deep breath and batted her eyes at Olivia. "You *must* agree, Mr. Preston. I am quite prepared to stand here all night and argue until I carry my point. I beg you, please spare me that trouble and come along quietly!"

I motioned frantically for Olivia to refuse. Olivia,

however, appeared to decide that this was an excellent moment to lose her mind.

"Of course," she said, in a credible imitation of a gentleman's booming agreement. "I will accompany you wherever you wish. How could I possibly refuse? You will excuse me, cousin? Mr. Reade?"

Mary laughed and dragged Olivia into the crowd. I could do nothing at all but stand and stare.

"What does she think she's doing?" I demanded of Matthew.

"Getting Mary out of the way before we lose Sophy and whomever that is she's with," he replied calmly. "And circulating to spy on the gathering, like we're supposed to."

"Oh." I would have to apologize to Olivia later for the several horrid thoughts I had momentarily entertained.

Sophy, in the meantime, was making her curtsy to the couple in black. The man in cavalier garb separated from the duenna. Clearly they were getting ready to head off, and in different directions.

I bit my lip and made a rapid decision.

"If anyone goes to the palace, I'll follow. You stay with those who head into the park. If you have to make a choice, follow the Oglethorpe."

"You're not—"

"I have to. If I'm seen, I have a thousand good reasons to be roaming about the palace. You don't." I was straining like a horse against the bit. The cavalier was listening as the duenna spoke another few words. He'd move away any instant.

"In fact, it will go the worse for us both if I'm found wandering in the dark with you."

There was something more I did not say: I was certain Mrs. Oglethorpe wanted me to see her. Why else would she wear her distinctive lace veil? There was no telling if the idea had come from her or Lynnfield, who surely must be the midnight cavalier. It hardly mattered. I had no intention of being so easily lured into the dark with them.

The cavalier gripped his stick and headed for the nearest door into the palace. Sophy and the presumed Mrs. Oglethorpe set off in the opposite direction.

Matthew squeezed my hand once. Then he drew the hood of his red robe over his cap and set off after them.

I hurried into the palace, almost instantly regretting the loss of my decorative lantern. The gardens and yards might have been lavishly illuminated, but no such expense had been wasted on St. James's near-empty corridors. I had to move with the tiniest steps, one hand grabbing my light hems out of the way, one stretching out to feel for the walls.

The man I followed seemed to have no such troubles. He moved with confidence through the darkened corridors, walking with a deliberate, comfortable pace. He not only knew where he was going, he belonged here. That attitude, even more than the black and silver stick, convinced me Olivia had been right. This must be Lord Lynnfield.

But where was he going? Was he meeting someone? Was he intent on stealing something? Now would be the time. The vast majority of the palace population was in the parks and gardens, enjoying the festivities. I and my midnight cavalier had the palace almost to ourselves.

The silence and the dark together made it maddeningly difficult to follow at a safe distance. He moved quietly, and there were one or two turns where only the faint rustling of his costume told me which way to go.

The cavalier vanished around another corner. I stopped and held my breath. There was a soft scraping of metal on metal, the unmistakable sound of a key being fitted into a lock.

Slowly, with my heart thumping like Lord Beckenstile's staff, I peered around the corner. It was a short, wide gallery papered in dark silk, which told me we were in one of the newer segments of the palace. Given the dark and how intently I had been concentrating on the cavalier, this was all I could say for certain about my location. The yellow glow of candlelight surrounded the cavalier as he pushed open a pair of doors in the left-hand wall. He stepped through and silently closed them, leaving me once again in the dark.

A second set of doors waited on the right-hand side of the gallery. I slipped up to these as quickly as I could and tried the handle. To my relief, the doors opened easily, and I was able to dart inside. The chamber in which I found myself was dark, windowless, and populated by a series of anonymous black blobs that were probably furniture. I held the door open just a hairbreadth and crouched down so that the glittering trim of my costume would be less likely to catch the light from whatever candle might come along next.

In this attitude, with my eye pressed against the crack between the doors, I waited.

It felt like a very long time. Long enough to become grateful for my shocking costume with its lack of heavy hoops or constricting stomacher. It was certainly long enough to wonder how Lord Lynnfield, a country noble whose father had so recently and dramatically been involved in a plot against the throne, had gotten hold of one of the keys to the palace. Surely the prince had not gone that far in trusting him. Had he?

Of course, it didn't have to be the prince who had gotten him the keys. It could easily have been Sophy.

Which led me to wonder what was happening to Matthew, not to mention Olivia. Had it gone on midnight yet? This deep in the palace, I might not hear the bells that signaled the time of our next rendezvous. Was my delinquent father out among the revelers searching for me? It would serve him right if he was. In fact, I desperately hoped it to be the case.

And what of Mr. Tinderflint? At least I knew he was here. My patron had told me in detail how he intended to station himself in a striped tent beside the pond, there to entertain his "particular friends." Numerous such pavilions were set up around the park by those who could afford to create private parties within the larger public celebrations. It was also, of course, a base of operations for the men in ordinary dress he had scattered about the party.

"I'm a rather recognizable figure," he'd confessed,

smoothing his waistcoat over his considerable paunch. "Mask or no. It will not hurt to have a few extra eyes and ears about, in case there is any mischief afoot."

He'd nodded significantly. I hadn't told him what I'd planned with Matthew and Olivia. I was still piqued at him for his remarks about my father and his murky motivations. Except now that Father had failed to appear as he'd promised, I was beginning to wonder if I had been mistaken, again. Perhaps my patron remained the one I should trust. Surely if I'd told him what had happened, Mr. Tinderflint could have found out where Father was and gotten him help if he'd needed it.

At exactly the moment my legs began to cramp from crouching so long in one position, I heard the scrape of the lock. I eased myself back on my heels and waited. The cavalier emerged from the other room, locked the door behind him, and walked unhurriedly out of the gallery and around the corridor.

He actually swung his cane and whistled as he did so.

I clapped my hand over my mouth to muffle my startled gasp. I knew that careless gait and attitude. This wasn't Lord Lynnfield. He'd never give away a whistle, and he'd certainly never swing his stick that way.

I'd been following Sebastian.

I tried to shoot to my feet. In this I failed, collapsing backwards in an undignified pouf of silk and grape leaves.

When I finally gathered myself up and scrambled back

out into the gallery, my first thought was how deeply disappointed Olivia would be to have her murder plot discredited. My second was that I must get into that locked room.

I crept toward the corridor, straining eyes and ears to their limit to be sure that Cavalier Sebastian was nowhere nearby. Then I caught up my flimsy skirts and ran out into the hallway, toward the brightest patch of light I could see.

As I had hoped, light indicated the presence of persons. In this case, much to my delight, those persons were a group of footmen lighting candles in the wall sconces set about the stairwell, in preparation, I supposed, for the return of the palace's more celebrated inhabitants.

Here I had an advantage Sebastian Sandford could not match. He might pretend to belong to the palace, but I actually did.

"Hullo there," I called to the nearest man, whipping off my mask so that I might be better recognized and understood. "Who would have the keys to the rooms off the short gallery there?" I pointed behind me.

"I'm sure I don't know, m'lady," said the nearest of the men. Of course, I wasn't officially a "m'lady," but I did not bother to correct him.

"Can you find out?" I dug into my grapevine sash and came out with a silver half crown. This was another habit I'd acquired since I'd begun my career as courtier. I always kept a coin or two tucked in sash, or glove, or wherever else I could find a place. Sometimes this was a challenge. That Master of

Fashion who decreed women had no need of pockets would receive a stern lecture as soon as I learned his name.

The footman eyed his compatriots. The one up on the ladder shrugged. The shorter one, who held the lantern and tapers, rubbed his fingers together in a universal sign of approval and greed. My man bowed. "If you'll wait but a moment, m'—"

"Miss Fitzroy." I laid the coin in his hand, and he strode away with a commendable turn of speed.

The other two went back to their business of bringing light to the darkness. I desperately wanted to go back outside. I needed to know where my father was, where my friends were, and most importantly, where my enemies were. I wanted to find Matthew, Olivia, and Mr. Tinderflint. I wanted to find Mrs. Oglethorpe before she got away and before she met with her own compatriots to finish whatever plan had brought them here.

Footsteps clattered on floorboards and I jumped. It was the third of the work party returning with a ring of keys. I suppressed my nervousness long enough to lead him to the short gallery and the double doors.

I took charge of the candle while the man sorted through the keys. He seemed to find it necessary to peer closely at each one in order to determine which belonged to the doors in front of us.

I gritted my teeth until I felt they might break. How much longer? It was surely past midnight now. Why had I let

Sebastian distract me? If Mrs. Oglethorpe wanted me to find her, I should have obliged.

At last, the man found the key, fitted it to the lock, turned it, and pushed open the door.

It was a book room, and I needn't have bothered with the candle. A small brass lantern flickered on a round marble-topped table.

Next to this table, arrayed in her magnificent white silks, stood Sophy Howe.

CHAPTER EIGHTEEN

IN WHICH OUR HEROINE ACQUIRES THE LOW
HABIT OF READING OTHERS' CORRESPONDENCE.

What are you doing here?" And how had she gotten into the room without my seeing her? I had a brief, fantastical vision of her swapping costumes with the midnight
cavalier. A glance at her dirtied white hems showed the more
likely scenario: she must have come up the back stairs to meet
Sebastian.

But if there was a back-stairs route to this room, why
had Sebastian used the public ways?

"Her Royal Highness sent me to retrieve a book she
wanted." Sophy had long ago mastered the trick of lifting
her chin while at the same time looking down her nose. She
put this skill into practice now as she pulled a volume from
the shelf.

"In the middle of the prince's birthday party?"

Sophy shrugged. "To settle a bet. Something regarding a quotation. I'm sure I don't know, but we all must do as we're told, mustn't we? And what were you doing here?"

"Looking for someone." I attempted to force a tone of flirtation into my voice, but the result was sadly limp and inadequate.

Sophy laughed at it, and at me. "In a locked room? Peggy, you are always so original. What on earth do we find to talk about when you are not with us?" She flashed me one of her brilliant smiles and brushed past me. As she did, she breathed, "Find me when you know the favor I've done you."

Favor?

But she was already gone, leaving us both staring—me at the door Sophy let close behind her, and the footman at me.

"Thank you," I said to the footman. "You can go." I was sure Sophy and Sebastian had wanted something in this room or had left something behind for others to find. I needed privacy to conduct a search.

"But I'll have to lock up, Miss Fitzroy."

"I'll do that, and my maid will return the keys." I had every faith Libby would know to whom such items should be sent.

The man didn't like it, and I didn't blame him. I silently vowed I would send another coin along with the keys as an apology.

Somewhat at a loss for where to begin my search, I studied the shelves in front of me. There was a great deal to examine. Our former queen, Anne, had not been a great one for reading, but her sister, Mary, had loved learning and built up the palace libraries with great attention and energy. This single room contained dozens of volumes, perhaps as many as a hundred. All were shelved so close together, it was easy to see the gap left by the one Sophy had removed. As I bent closer, I saw that the book to the right of that gap had been placed on the shelf upside down. It was a newer volume, with a bright green cover and fresh dark lettering stamped upon it: *Histoires ou contes du temps passé,* by one Monsieur Charles Perrault. From the page indicating the contents, it appeared to be a collection of stories, some with truly odd titles—there was "Little Red Riding Hood," something called "Cendrillon," and "The Master Cat, or Puss in Boots."

I riffled through the book and shook out the pages. No convenient letter fluttered down. I set that aside and pulled out the book on the left-hand side, another volume by this M. Perrault, who appeared to be a busy scrivener, and subjected this tome to similar treatment with similar result.

I blew out a sigh in lieu of the curse I wished to mutter. My candle was burning dangerously low, and I had no notion how long I had been here. Matthew and Olivia would surely be worried. Sophy might well be toying with me or deliberately delaying me. I quickly moved to replace the books, telling myself that I had not entirely wasted my time. We now knew that Sebastian was alive and that he and Sophy and the Oglethorpe were all working together. Perhaps with his brother's knowledge, but perhaps without it.

This thought gave me pause. What if Sebastian had fled from his brother? What if the reason Lynnfield had left the palace was to try to find him? I could never imagine Sebastian outsmarting the cold, calculating Lord Lynnfield, but Sophy was another story.

That was when I saw the loose panel.

Had it been replaced properly, I never would have noticed it at all. As it was, whoever had last laid hand to the square of dark wood had been hasty or sloppy, and it was crooked. Even so, the shadows from my guttering candle all but obscured it.

It took a moment's nervous scrabbling to pry the little panel loose. Goose pimples prickled my thinly clad arms, quite at odds with the flush in my cheeks and the pounding of my heart.

At last, the thin square of wood came away in my hands. What lay on the other side wasn't a proper hole, but just a patch of brick, little wider than the span of my hand. I sucked in a breath, disappointed. Once again, I had found absolutely nothing.

Lingering stubbornness, though, combined with a deep respect of Sophy Howe's talent for connivance, drove me to pick up my candle and bend closer. There. In the central seam of the brickwork, the mortar had been cut away, leaving a narrow slit. And in that slit, I could see the edge of a paper.

I picked at it with my fingernails until I was at last able to grasp the paper and pull it free. It had been folded into a tight square, wrapped once with plain blue ribbon, and sealed in plain blue wax. I had seen ribbons and seals of this sort before—all on Jacobite letters.

I bit my lip and glanced at the door, which remained shut, and at my candle, which flickered fitfully. There was no way to tell if it was Sophy or someone else who had planted this letter, let alone who was expected to receive it. If I broke the seal to read it now, whoever that other person was would know it had been read. If I took it away and didn't have it back before it was missed, the person would know the letter had been found. In either case, if the letter contained plans, those plans would be changed at once.

But if I left the letter here and Sophy's co-conspirators came to retrieve it, we would lose all chance to know what it contained or who any additional conspirators might be.

Nearly shaking with my uncertainties, I tucked the letter into my bosom. I replaced the panel and the books, making sure the *Histoires ou contes du temps passé* was upside down as I had found it.

I took up my candle and the keys and hurried from the room.

Contrary to my fears, midnight had not passed while I was in the palace with Sebastian and Sophy. The bells began to peal that portentous hour almost exactly as I entered the Ambassador Court. Counting my blessings, I made my way toward the Arch of Prosperity. Matthew was there ahead of me. He had his red hood down and his white mask pushed up high on his forehead, and he watched the crowd intently.

Under the convenient cover of the general revelry, I all but fell into his arms.

"Are you all right, Peggy?" he cried. "What happened?"

"I found Sebastian, and Sophy, and a secret letter."

Matthew blinked but did not waste his breath on exclamations. "I'd say your time was better used than mine, then. I must have made two full circuits of the park following that duenna."

"Whom did she talk to? What did she do?"

"No one and nothing, in that order." He frowned. "Could we have the wrong woman?"

"I don't know. I don't know anything at this point." I craned my neck to see among the celebrants. "There's Olivia!"

My cousin, taking full advantage of her male garb, strode speedily across the grounds. But when she reached my side, I could see she was flushed with far more than exertion.

"Peggy! What do you think has happened!" she cried. "I've been challenged to a duel!"

"WHAT!" I cried, appropriately aghast. My normally sober paramour, on the other hand, responded to this pronouncement by doubling over, clutching at his stomach and making a series of alarming choking noises.

"Stop that!" cried Olivia. "It is not in the least funny!"

"Yes . . . it . . . is," whooped Matthew. "Who was it? Prince George himself?"

"As a matter of fact, it was Lord Blakeney," Olivia said, sniffing. "He came upon me—that is, Orlando—and Mary Bellenden, and . . ."

I turned to Matthew, who still seemed to be finding my cousin's inappropriate, not to mention time-wasting, antics a matter for general hilarity. "Mr. Reade, will you take Mr. Preston up to my rooms before someone murders him?" Upon recognizing the touch of my very sharpest glare, Matthew struggled manfully against this unworthy and unfeeling display and promised to do as I asked.

Olivia, for her part, promised to go quietly. I had no choice but to believe them, because I needed to find Mr. Tinderflint at once.

The mood of the crowd had grown noticeably more raucous since I'd entered St. James. A good many of the persons I elbowed my way between held whole bottles of drink and were loudly engaged in pulling off one another's masks, and occasionally other things.

I averted my eyes and went on.

I kept thinking I might finally see my father in this great stew, but I did not. Nor did I see Sebastian, or Sophy, or Mrs. Oglethorpe. I comforted myself with vague hopes that they might be standing in a circle somewhere, wasting their mutual breath with accusations about what might have happened to the letter I now carried.

When I reached Mr. Tinderflint's pavilion, I found him engaged in distributing wine and other strong drink to a whole crowd of merry personages. I had not seen his chosen costume before this, and looking on it gave me a very long pause. Mr. Tinderflint was dressed in the red robes and full-bottomed wig of a high-court judge. But not just any judge. He had on the black velvet cap of a judge ready to sentence a man to death.

I had not taken more than one step into the pavilion before he glanced up and saw me. Mr. Tinderflint needed no sign or signal. He did not even bother to set down his wine bottle; with many bows and grand gestures, he made his way to my side. In my turn, I brought out the letter with its blue seal.

Mr. Tinderflint met my gaze, nodded once, and gestured for me to lead on, which I did as swiftly as I could.

In my rooms, Olivia and Matthew had divested themselves of masks and hats and, in Olivia's case, her dress sword. Libby was brewing a fresh pot from my precious stash of tea. Norris stood stiffly by the door. I suspected that Norris and Libby had been enjoying the quiet together before being so rudely interrupted, but there was neither time nor reason to remark on this.

Mr. Tinderflint certainly did not seem to find anything untoward in the scene. Quite the opposite, in fact.

"Excellent! Excellent!" he cried. "Libby and Norris, the very persons. I have a particular task for you. You are to take this bottle"—he handed Norris the wine bottle he'd carried all this way—"and go to the juncture of the gallery. You are not to drink, mind you, but pass it back and forth as if you were. Should anyone—and I do mean any man, woman, or child—come by, drop the bottle. You may take a scolding, but be sure, it will be worth your while."

Libby was eyeing the velvet that trimmed my patron's robe and the rings that sparkled on every plump finger. Norris was probably doing the same, but he managed to be less obvious about it. They did both make their bows and slip away into the gallery. This time, I was the one who bolted the door.

"Now then, Peggy, may I see this letter?" Mr. Tinderflint lowered himself into the chair by my writing desk. It creaked ominously. "How did you come by it?"

"Another letter?" cried Olivia. "Peggy! You never tell me anything!"

I laid the sealed paper in front of Mr. Tinderflint and described my adventure in the darkened palace. Mr. Tinderflint rubbed the paper between his blunt fingers and ran them over the ribbon. He carefully held the letter up to a candle and peered at it. He brought it to his bulbous nose and sniffed the sealing wax.

"Hmm. Hmm. Interesting. Yes. Well. I think we need to have this opened." He held the letter again to the light, so close, in fact, that I had to restrain myself from crying out that he would surely burn it.

"Yes," he said again, finally. "Have you paper and pen in this desk, Peggy, my dear?"

"I have something." Matthew dug into the inner pocket

of his coat and pulled out a small notebook, along with several sharpened pencils.

"Excellent, Mr. Reade!" cried Mr. Tinderflint. "And you, Miss Pierpont—I believe your cousin says you are a great writer? Yes? We'll require your help as well."

I got out a blank piece of paper for Olivia and found a book she could use as a writing surface. Thus armed, Matthew and Olivia flanked Mr. Tinderflint.

"Once I've removed ribbon and seal, Peggy will open the letter. Then you, Mr. Reade and Miss Pierpont, will note down what you read as quickly as possible." While he spoke, Mr. Tinderflint folded another sheet of paper until it was the exact size of the sealed letter. Then he brought out a slender knife sheath. From this, he drew the thinnest, most delicate blade I had ever seen and held it over the candle flame. "Mr. Reade, if there are any sigils, signs, or drawings, it will be your task to reproduce them while Miss Pierpont concentrates on whatever text there may be. Is that understood?" We nodded. Mr. Tinderflint nodded back and turned the blade over to make sure it was evenly heated.

"This is an operation much beloved of our finer playwrights," he went on in a calm and conversational tone. "I fear it is seldom as simple as they make it out to be. If not done with care and precision, the seal is marred and traces of the tampering are left on the paper. Those who write secret letters are ever alert for these little signs. Yes." He gently touched one side of the blade. "Now."

Mr. Tinderflint's fingers were built on a scale with the

rest of him—that is to say, they were noticeably short and thick. This made the delicacy with which they now moved astounding. Ignoring the insistent tick of the mantelpiece clock telling us time was flying on, he patiently worked that thin, hot knife beneath the blue seal. With infinite care, he lifted the blade and the seal. His free hand teased the letter out from its loop of ribbon. He handed the note to me. "Now," he said again.

I flipped the letter open and jumped back. Olivia and Matthew bent over the page, eyes darting back and forth, pencils scribbling madly. While they worked, Mr. Tinderflint occupied himself by sliding the folded blank paper into the ribbon loop and lowering the seal onto it.

I opened my mouth to question this, but Mr. Tinderflint held one finger to his lips and nodded toward the copyists.

"I have it, I think," said Olivia. "But what—"

"Mr. Reade?" Mr. Tinderflint cut her off.

"A moment . . . Finished."

"Excellent." Mr. Tinderflint now reversed the previous procedure, reheating the knife, lifting the seal again, teasing out the blank page.

"The blank helps preserve the integrity of the sealing wax," he said, anticipating my question. "It also ensures no telltale stain is left on the ribbon. Again, it is these little things that are the difference between success and failure for such an operation. The letter, please, Peggy."

I had it ready, folded again along the original lines. Mr. Tinderflint slid the letter back into the ribbon. Taking his lower lip between his teeth, he turned the blade ever so slightly, lining the seal up precisely with the stain on the paper.

"There," he said with a sigh of satisfaction, as if he'd just finished an excellent meal. "We will let that cool and hopefully return it to its place with no man being the wiser. Matthew, Olivia, may I see the copies, please . . . Thank you."

Mr. Tinderflint claimed Matthew's notebook and Olivia's paper and laid them out side by side on my desk. Neither of them watched him. Both stared at me. In answer, my throat tightened. Wishing I could simply avert my eyes, I tiptoed closer and peered over Mr. Tinderflint's round, red-clad shoulder.

Olivia's paper contained nothing but long strings of numbers and dashes.

891241 3773-25 89-5624 12-12-97 85 . . . and on. Six lines of number sets formed a perfect square in the center of the page.

"Is it a cipher?" she asked.

"It certainly appears to be," said Mr. Tinderflint. It was as well he was busy examining the copies in front of him. That way he didn't see me struggle to keep my countenance under Olivia's steady regard. She was waiting for me to speak. I must be the one to decide whether to inform Mr. Tinderflint we'd seen numbers like this before, in those other letters signed "Mrs. Tinderflint" that I had failed to tell him about.

"This, Mr. Reade, is very good work." Mr. Tinderflint

raised Matthew's notebook closer to his eyes. "Unfortunately, it tells us we should be concerned about what we've found —yes, very concerned."

Matthew had also copied out the numbers, but a corner of his copy was decorated with a sketch of three fleurs-de-lis on a dark shield. This shield was surmounted by a crown, and the whole image surrounded by a chain of some sort.

"It's a seal?" I guessed. "A French seal?"

"That, my dear Peggy, is the seal of the House of Orléans, the house of the current Regent—that is to say, the ruler—of France."

A coded letter from the Regent of France? Sealed in Jacobite blue and hidden in the palace? I felt the blood drain from my face.

Since this latest phase of my adventures had begun, I had imagined many dire conclusions—from disgrace for Olivia all the way up to assassination attempts. Until this moment, however, I had also been able to tell myself these were mere imaginings. That comfort was now stripped away. The ruler of France had sent a coded message into the Sandfords' hands. The Sandfords', and Sophy Howe's. With this letter I could finish them all.

Triumph, I was fairly certain, should not make one feel ill. Nonetheless, I found myself pressing my hand against my stomach. Because if this letter did come from Versailles, what did that say about Aunt Pierpont, who had letters bearing a similar cipher in her possession?

And she was not the only one. I thought of the letter

that had been sent so surreptitiously to me and was even now in my father's hands, wherever my father's hands had gone.

"Now, we must not be hasty." Mr. Tinderflint patted my shoulder. "Seals, like so many other things, can be forged. We know from your previous encounters that Miss Howe is a keen amateur in that line. But there are other details . . ." He pursed his lips, considering. "I think, Peggy, that you and I will need to go visit my very good friend Mr. Willis."

"Willis? But—" I clamped my mouth shut, but it was too late. Mr. Tinderflint turned. The chair creaked. Olivia pressed her hand over her mouth.

"May I take it you've heard the name, Peggy?" inquired Mr. Tinderflint mildly.

"Yes. Perhaps." I twisted my fingers together and tried to think of some covering story, but my wits were far too disordered. "Father told me he was going to Oxford to speak with a man named Willis."

Mr. Tinderflint's eyebrows lifted. "Did he indeed? Do you know why?"

"He did not say."

Mr. Tinderflint held my gaze for rather longer than was necessary. "I fear your father has wasted a journey," he said finally. "Mr. Willis, if indeed we mean the same man, is not in Oxford just now. He's come down to London, at my particular request."

My heart constricted underneath my ribs. If this Mr. Willis was in London, where was my father? He surely would not have lingered in Oxford once he knew his man was no longer there. He would have turned right around and come home. Wouldn't he?

"Who is this Willis fellow?" asked Matthew, probably because he saw I had passed beyond rational speech.

My patron paused before replying. "Mr. Willis is one of our foremost code breakers. If there's anyone in England who can determine whether this" — he waved his hand at the papers in front of him — "is the genuine article and decipher its meaning, Willis —"

Outside there was a muffled crash. A dropped bottle, broken glass.

Someone was coming.

CHAPTER NINETEEN

IN WHICH OUR HEROINE
IS DISCOVERED IN COMPROMISING CIRCUMSTANCES
AND A CERTAIN GENTLEMAN
MAY BE SEEN TO FAIL IN HIS AIMS.

Mr. Tinderflint froze. So did the rest of us. Together, we listened to the mumbles of apology out in the gallery, and then a man's angry reply.

"Matthew." I grabbed his arm. Matthew dropped his pencil into his pocket and followed closely. At the door I turned quickly to face him, grabbed both his hands, and shoved his fingers into my hair. At almost the same moment, I went onto my toes and kissed him, hard.

As aware as I was that I was being stared at and that I must hurry, the intensity with which Matthew answered that kiss caused me to linger perhaps a little longer than was wise. I broke away as quickly as I could manage. Even so, I had only a heartbeat to see the confusion and delight in

Matthew's face before I turned, undid the bolt, and eased the door open the narrowest crack.

"Well. Half the world is looking for you and this is all you're up to," said Sebastian from the other side. His grin was odious, and I fairly itched to wipe it off his face. I also noted, however, that his cavalier's hat was askew and he had abandoned his black mask at some point, which made it easy to see that his face was red, as if he was angry, or drunk.

Or simply in some tremendous hurry.

"Hello, Miss Fitzroy," Sebastian continued, with that particular sneering amiability at which he was so expert. Matthew crowded close behind me, effectively blocking what little view Sebastian might have otherwise had of the room. "I thought I might find you hiding here. Aren't you supposed to be downstairs waiting on things?" He gestured down the gallery.

"What business is it of yours where I am?" I snapped, largely to cover the rustling behind me as Mr. Tinderflint and Olivia cleared away evidence of our recent clerical activities.

"None at all." He shrugged. "But you should know, your absence has been remarked upon."

"By you and Sophy, yes, I'm sure it was." I attempted to sound utterly bored by this, but inside, fresh worry blossomed.

"Not just by us. I'm deadly serious about this, Margaret Fitzroy." Sebastian stepped closer until only the width of the door separated us. He had whiskey on his breath and a wild, worried glint in his blue eyes. "You need to come with me, or there will be trouble."

Matthew closed his hand around mine. I did not move. "Trouble for me or for you?" I asked Sebastian.

"For you. There is someone very particular looking for you. *Very* particular."

The rustling behind us had stopped. Matthew squeezed my hand. I chose to take it as a signal that the various papers had been appropriately concealed and we could put an end to this strange and uncomfortable scene. There were, however, one or two points yet to be covered. "If we are to speak of persons who are missing, Mr. Sandford, I might ask where you've been. And what of your brother?"

Sebastian sighed sharply. "Oh, Julius is somewhere about his business. As you should be about yours."

For a heartbeat, I actually considered going with him, in hopes of finding out who had sent him and why. But the most likely reason for his presence was that he was to take me on a wild-goose chase about the grounds while some confederate attempted to retrieve the Jacobite letter. *Find me when you know the favor I've done you*, Sophy had said. It hit me she might very well be playing a double game, taking whatever Lynnfield offered with the one hand while attempting to expose his treasons with the other.

"Do thank whoever sent you for their concern," I told Sebastian. "You may assure them that I will rejoin the celebrations shortly."

With this, I shut the door. I was pleased to note that I had, for once, come away from an encounter with Sebastian without the slightest tremor in my hands.

"You are to be congratulated, my dear." Mr. Tinderflint climbed ponderously to his feet. "That was excellent work, and very quick thinking, very quick indeed."

His words warmed me, but not enough to take away the chill of what had just happened.

"They know the letter's missing," said Olivia. "And they know we've got it."

"Yes, I'm afraid that may well be the case." Mr. Tinderflint shook his head with gentle sorrow, as if he'd just heard it would rain on a day when he had an excursion planned.

"It also means it's genuine," said Matthew. "Whatever else it is, that letter really is from Versailles and the Regent."

"It increases the probability," admitted Mr. Tinderflint. "But we can say nothing for certain until Willis has had a look at it."

"But if it is genuine . . ." I couldn't finish. If it was genuine, it meant invasion by the French, maybe with the Spanish thrown in for good measure. It meant war and conquest and vengeance. I reached out and found Matthew's hand.

Olivia had drifted to the hearth. She lifted a lump of coal from the scuttle, turned it over in her fingers, and tossed it into the flames. It fell with a loud crackle, and a fresh flame leapt up. Her expression was entirely still and closed, but I knew what she was thinking. She was thinking how the letter's authenticity could also show some direct and unmistakable connection between her mother and the Jacobites.

When she turned around again, her features were set in her most terrifyingly determined expression. "Peggy, you have to tell the princess, and you have to tell her *everything*."

I bit my lip. No. It was not my duty to condemn my aunt to a traitor's fate and my cousin to disgrace and poverty. It could not be. France, Spain, Stuart, and Hanover could all go hang themselves. Nothing was worth the loss of those I held dearest.

"I see your feeling, Peggy," said Mr. Tinderflint. "And I understand it, yes, I do. But Olivia is correct. We have reached one of those rare moments when the truth is what will serve us best."

He didn't understand, though. Not really, because he didn't know about the connection between the enciphered letters and Aunt Pierpont. Because I hadn't told him.

"I can't do it tonight." I hated that I sounded like I was pleading. "There will be no way to speak to Her Highness alone. In fact, she might have already retired. It will have to be in the morning."

Olivia hadn't moved from her spot in front of the fireplace. I suddenly wished Isolde were here. Then my cousin would have something to hold on to, something that wasn't about to destroy what little of her family she had left.

It was Matthew who went to her. He put a hand on

her arm, as a brother might. She glanced up with a look of sorrow and gratitude.

I couldn't move. My mind was awash with a thousand different feelings, none of them clear or easy.

"You are not without friends, my dear," said Mr. Tinderflint to Olivia. "You will be protected, whatever comes of this."

My cousin shrugged with one shoulder and said nothing.

Faced with Olivia's most unusual silence, Mr. Tinderflint turned brisk. "Now, I am sorry to leave you in such a moment, but I have preparations and inquiries of my own to make." He picked up the letter and tucked it into his judge's robe. "As it has already been discovered missing, I will keep the original of this letter. It will need to be examined carefully. After you have spoken to the princess, Peggy, please send for me. We will go together to see Willis. Assuming that I am left in charge of this matter, which I think I can arrange. Yes, yes, yes."

I made my curtsy to Mr. Tinderflint without looking up at him. I did not want to risk him seeing the hard and hated questions in my gaze. Why me? Why *us*? Was this — the exposure of Aunt Pierpont, along with her husband, the Oglethorpes, and the Sandfords — the result Mr. Tinderflint had desired from the first?

He paused for a minute in his bow, as if there was something more to add. He never spoke, however — only let himself out of the room and closed the door.

"You can stop looking like that, Peggy," Olivia said. "It's not as if we didn't know this was coming. I've known Mother was involved from the moment I found those letters among her things. As did your father," she added.

I shook myself. Standing and staring like a stunned sheep would do nothing for any of us.

"You don't have to do this, Olivia. This isn't a drama and—"

"How *dare* you!" she snapped, her voice low and dangerous. "Stop treating me like a child! I know what is happening as well as any of you! She betrayed me!"

"No, Olivia, you mustn't think that," said Matthew.

Olivia turned on him, both literally and figuratively. "Then what am I to think? Tell me!" She flung her arms wide. "She helped him! She kept his secrets even after he was dead, and then, when it looked like she might be discovered, she ran away and left me alone! I hope she is caught!" Olivia shouted. "I hope she is hanged! She and Grandmother both, and then they can all be dead and done together and I can get on with my life!"

Another girl would have broken down sobbing after such an outburst, but Olivia stood up straight, proud and absolutely unashamed. I had known something boiled beneath my cousin's skin. Not even Mary Bellenden could have been as insouciant regarding her family's troubles as Olivia had appeared to be. Now here it was, and I had not the first idea how to answer it.

Except with one slim possibility. "What if your mother is innocent?" I asked softly.

Olivia's glower was beyond contemptuous. It was positively murderous. "How could she be? Are you *blind*?" Olivia stabbed a finger toward the door. "She has the coded letters. Even if she isn't 'Mrs. Tinderflint,' she kept those letters for a reason!"

"Yes, I agree—Aunt Pierpont knows more than she's said." I walked toward Olivia, one cautious step at a time. "But so does Mr. Tinderflint, and so does my father."

"So do we," said Olivia. Something in her tone set me wondering again what had happened those days I'd been away from the house. I opened my mouth to ask, but Matthew spoke first.

"And that's the real reason Peggy needs to tell the princess what's happened. No one else can force them all—*us* all —to speak the truth."

Olivia's face twisted up again, this time with fear and with strain. "I thought it would be over tonight," she whispered. "I really did. I thought we'd find . . . whoever it is, whatever they're doing. We'd unmask them and it would all be over. Bring down the curtain. But all we've got is more questions." She turned her gaze to me. "Is being a spy always like this, Peggy?"

Her hand shook as she reached out, and I seized it tightly. "I'm sorry, Olivia, but it is. There are always more questions and more conspirators. I don't think it's ever really going to be over."

"But we will find out what my parents—and yours—did. We can find out about our families."

"Yes," I said to her, and to Matthew. "We will find out what they've done to all of us in the name of kings and crowns. This much I do swear."

CHAPTER TWENTY

Wherein Our Heroine is given
her final instructions.

It was nearly dawn by the time I walked Matthew down to the Color Court. Despite the freezing air and the unseasonable hour, revelers still filled the yard. Many of them would likely be carried away by wheelbarrow once the sun rose.

"I wouldn't leave if there were a choice." Matthew's breath steamed in the light of the dying flambeaux. I wore my dark traveling cloak, and he had pulled up the hood of his scholar's robe. This made us as close to anonymous as two persons could be in such a gathering. "My work here is supposed to be done, and I have to at least make an appearance at the academy today."

"Matthew . . ." I risked a step closer. Surely there were things I had left unsaid. I would think of them all in a moment.

"I will be back as soon as I can." He kissed me lightly. "If there's any delay, I'll send word."

I murmured farewell and watched him thread his way through the crowd. Only when he had vanished through the open gates did I turn and walk the long, cold way back to my rooms.

As tired as I was, two very strong factors argued against actually going to bed. The first was that Princess Caroline was a habitually early riser, and my best opportunity to speak with her would be before the court's formal day began. The second was that Olivia very clearly needed to talk more than she needed to rest.

So it was that I spent the time between Matthew's departure and the day's dawning curled up in my chair by the fire listening to Olivia. Olivia, for her part, alternated between sitting on my stool with her hands clasped together and feverishly pacing as she talked. She did not say much of consequence, but I let her meander on, occasionally contributing an affirmative or sympathetic sound. What other comfort could I give? Some little time after the clock struck seven, I was able to persuade (and bribe) a drowsing Libby to try the kitchens for rolls and chocolate while Templeton laced Olivia and me into acceptable gowns and made sure we were pomaded and painted well enough to hide any dark circles that might have formed beneath our eyes.

"Olivia, why don't you go to Princess Anne this morning?" I ventured as I poured some chocolate into her cup.

"You know she always welcomes your company walking the dogs."

"Yes, and Lady Portland is always so glad to see me," Olivia muttered around a bite of roll. "Almost as glad as she is to see you."

We both rolled our eyes in acknowledgment of this. "You need to fetch Isolde back, in any case." I had an ulterior motive for this suggestion. A morning with a young princess and puppies would distract Olivia while I was closeted with Her Royal Highness. "I'm also giving Libby a note for Molly Lepell. We can trust her. You haven't got a post, but if you're with Molly, you can still attend all the public events. That way you can keep an eye on Sophy Howe while I'm off fetching Father."

We assumed that once Her Royal Highness heard what we had discovered, she would send for all the parties involved. This assumption was accompanied by the hope that she would give me leave to go directly to my father's house. If I did not find him at home, I would beg, bully, and badger all the servants until I learned where he was meant to be. Wandering freely about the countryside was no longer an option for any of us.

Because he was still wandering. I had to believe that. Even the simplest alternatives were too much to bear.

"I'll give you a full report." A determined gleam showed in Olivia's eye. As surprising as it might seem, I was relieved to see it. It meant Olivia's natural spirits were reasserting themselves, even under the weight of all that had happened and must still happen.

"Thank you," I said, striving for calm. "And for Heaven's sake, remember to tell Mary that Orlando Preston has fled the country." My cousin looked mulish at this but agreed. We toasted each other with the last of the chocolate, and then I got to my feet. What came next, I must do alone.

There was no protocol for this. In fact, it was in direct contravention of all rules of palace behavior. I was the princess's servant and agent, but not her intimate. My access to her presence was not unfettered or casual. And yet, alone, uninvited, and empty-handed, I had to present myself at the doorway of Her Royal Highness's antechamber. There, I lied to the drowsy yeomen, saying I'd been summoned. I told the same lie to the footmen in the drawing room.

At the far end of the drawing room waited the private parlor. This, normally, was occupied by the women and ladies of the bedchamber who did not have other duties. As I crossed into it, it was quite empty.

The other set of doors in the parlor led to the royal closet. These were firmly closed. I glanced at the footman who had accompanied me this far. Another pair of men, similarly attired in full livery and curled white wigs, looked down at me.

"I'm sorry, madame," said the right hand of the pair. "There is no admittance."

I had to do this, and I had to do it now. There was no choice. I faced them both.

"I must speak with Her Royal Highness at once!" I shouted. "It is a matter of the utmost urgency!"

There was a slow susurration of cloth and blankets from inside the closet.

"Keep your voice down, you little fool!" growled the right-hand man. "I'll have the yeomen throw you out!"

"I am Margaret Fitzroy and I am on Her Highness's business!" I shouted back. "I must see her, *now!*"

"What is all this!" cried a voice from the other side of the doors. A man's voice.

It was, in fact, the groggy, annoyed, and highly recognizable voice of the Prince of Wales.

This particular understanding took a long time to penetrate my frozen mind. So long, in fact, that the doors flew open before I remembered to bend my knees into a curtsy.

I saw a pair of slippered feet stomp up to me. I saw a pair of bandy legs encased in white woolen stockings and a flapping shirt hem.

"It's Miss Fitzroy, ain't it?" he boomed. "What in God's name is the meaning of this, Miss Fitzroy? Eh? Disturbing my wife at this hour?"

"I'm so sorry, Your Highness," I gasped. "Truly, I would not, if it was not urgent. I . . ."

"Let her come in, sir," called the princess's voice, also groggy and also entirely unmistakable. "I will get to the bottom of this. If you will, you may send the man for Mrs. Claybourne and I think Mrs. Howard."

"Hmmph." The prince snorted. "Well? Do as Her Highness says, girl—get in there." Probably there was a gesture to accompany this, but I was too terrified to lift my eyes. "And remember you're presuming a great deal on your special status here."

"Yes, sir," I murmured. "I'm sorry, sir. I'll . . . with your permission, that is . . . I . . ."

It is forbidden to turn one's back on royalty. Nor can one approach royalty backwards. But I had royalty on opposite sides, both already distinctly annoyed with me, and I had to move from one to the next. The result was a sort of sideways scuttle combined with a desperate attempt at respectful reverence that I hope I shall never have to repeat.

A single candle burned in the princess's bedroom. The draperies were all closed. My mistress sat up in the huge, scarlet-canopied bed, propped on bolsters, with a plain white shawl wrapped around her shoulders and a nightcap trimmed with lace and blue ribbons on her head. It made for a surprisingly domestic scene, especially with her pregnant belly showing clearly under the quilts.

"Close the door," she said sharply. "There is no point in either of us catching cold."

I did as I was ordered and went to stand at the foot of the bed.

The princess sighed. "Well? Speak, girl. Tell me what occasions this extraordinary behavior."

I licked my lips and framed my reply in German. "Your Highness, I beg you must excuse me. The investigations you set me on have taken a bad turn."

"You will explain," she snapped. She gave no indication that I should sit. She made no motion for me to come closer. Therefore, I stayed where I was, drew a deep breath, and began.

I told her of Mrs. Oglethorpe's appearance at my uncle's funeral and her connection to the Jacobites and my father. I told her of the arrival in my room of the first Mrs. Tinderflint letter and its cipher and of how my cousin had found other letters with similarly enciphered lines. I told her about Lord Lynnfield's flattery and Sebastian's treachery and the attempt to burgle my writing desk. My story exhausted the whole of my German vocabulary, but I did not permit myself to hesitate or stumble. I told her about Sophy Howe. I told her about Aunt Pierpont.

Lastly, I told her about following Sebastian and finding Sophy and the hidden letter sealed in Jacobite blue and bearing the seal of the House of Orléans.

Princess Caroline did not once interrupt my recitation. She did not ask a single question, nor did she give any indication of what she thought or felt as I poured out my words.

It was only when I finally fell silent that she looked away from me, as if contemplating the burning candle at her bedside. I did not know what she saw, but I could be fairly certain it was not the clear yellow flame. That simple sight could never engender such bitterness or contempt as clouded her pale and dignified countenance.

"Yes," she said finally. "Yes, it all fits."

"I don't understand." I could not seem to raise my voice above a whisper.

The princess turned her face toward me again. I dropped my gaze at once, partly out of protocol, partly out of fear of what I might see.

"What you have told me fits very well with certain other pieces of information that have recently been relayed to His Royal Highness." Her voice was studiously neutral, almost bland. "You should have come to me before, Margaret."

"I know it, Your Highness. I was afraid, for myself and my cousin, and my aunt." There. I'd said it. I'd confessed to one of the most powerful personages in the land that I believed Aunt Pierpont capable of duplicity on the grandest scale. "She's a good woman, truly, madame. She was always as kind to me as she could be. She . . . whatever she's doing, I'm certain she believes it to be out of loyalty to her late husband, not . . ." Not because she really wanted the House of Hanover thrown down. Not because she meant harm to my mistress and her family, or anyone's family.

"I have heard you, Margaret," the princess replied. "It will all be taken into account." I longed to be able to ask what information the prince had been given and where it had come from. There had to be some sort of reassurance I could take back to Olivia. Despite her angry words, she could not really wish Aunt Pierpont taken up for her crimes, whatever they might be.

Princess Caroline sighed and shifted uneasily on her bolsters. "Knowing you, Margaret, you have come here with some plan in mind."

"Yes, madame," I said. "You see, the letter . . ."

"Is with Lord Tierney—yes, that is to be expected." She spoke this last bit softly, almost regretfully. "You will not concern yourself with it further, Margaret. It will be taken care of by the proper persons."

Not concern myself with it? How could I not? But I swallowed this question and took my thoughts all firmly in hand. "Yes, madame, but I thought it might be best to bring my father to the palace. He has additional information about this Mrs. Oglethorpe and the Sandfords that might prove useful."

"And you want to be the one to fetch him, do you not?" I had seldom heard such weary skepticism from her.

"If Your Highness will permit it. And I thought . . . again, with your permission . . . if I was away on that errand, Olivia might accompany Molly Lepell to waiting today."

"Yes, yes." The princess waved her hand. "It would be for the best. You may make the arrangement, if you have not done so already. Is there anything else you would have of me?"

To say that this last question was pointed would be a gross and unprecedented level of understatement. "No, madame. I'm so sorry to have intruded. Should I go now?" There was a shameful note of strained hope in those last words.

"In a moment, Margaret." The silence that stretched out

after this was long and as hard to bear as her cold words had been. "I would not have you believe it is you I am angry at," she said at last. "I am angry at the world, and its necessities, and how our paths at times all cross those of the wrong men." She shook her head slowly. "Once you bring your father here, you are done with this work."

"*Done?*" I cried. I could not help it. "But—"

"You have accomplished the task you were given. From now on, these matters are in the hands of others. You are one of my waiting maids, and nothing more."

My mind reeled. My mistress surely could not expect me to just assume the persona of one more frivolous courtier and leave my family's fate in the hands of others.

And yet she did. She'd laid the order down, and I had no more say in the matter than Libby.

"Yes, madame," I whispered, because it was the only answer available to me.

"Good. This one"—she touched her belly—"will be making its appearance in the next few days. I will need your steady nerve and your skills at language with me."

"Yes, madame," I said again. "I . . . I will not fail you," I added.

"I will hold you to that, Margaret." There was a scratching at the door behind me. "Enter," she called in French, and then in German she said to me, "Go get this father of yours. I feel certain what he has to say will prove most instructive."

Light spilled in from the parlor, along with a draft of chilly air. Mrs. Claybourne and Mrs. Howard stepped up to the foot of the bed and curtsied, but this did not prevent either of them from looking askance at me.

"He . . ." I swallowed. "He has said he should not be seen at the palace."

"Well, that was before." The princess closed her eyes. "I am very tired of all this, Margaret. You will go now."

"Yes, madame." I made my reverence. "I am sorry, ma dame."

She did not even open her eyes as I took my hurried leave. It was not until I was halfway across the drawing room that I dared lift my hand to wipe the damp from my cheeks.

CHAPTER TWENTY-ONE

IN WHICH OUR HEROINE RECEIVES
A MORNING CALLER IN SUSPECT CIRCUMSTANCES.

Y ou must know something!"

It is a mark of refinement, not to mention good sense, to speak politely to housekeepers and all other persons charged with the task of making sure one's life and home function smoothly. Unfortunately, by the time I reached my father's house, my good sense had apparently packed up and gone on holiday.

"I'm sorry, Miss Fitzroy." Father's housekeeper, Mrs. Biddingswell, folded her hands and turned on me a show of patience that would have done Libby proud. "He went alone, on horseback, and left no instructions beyond that we were to keep the house ready against his return. If he said nothing more to you, it is hardly my fault."

In this, I was forced reluctantly to agree with her. "Have there been visitors of any sort since he left?"

"Besides that . . . person you sent from the palace?" If it is possible to look down your nose at someone who is not present, Mrs. Biddingswell did so. "Some tradesmen with bills or deliveries, but otherwise no one."

"Any letters?" I tried hopefully.

"The letters are placed in the book room, miss. Will there be anything else?"

Dismissed by the housekeeper as firmly as I ever had been by the princess, I bowed my head. "Not at this time, thank you."

As soon as Mrs. Biddingswell was out of sight, I boldly and without hesitation walked into my father's book room. If he was not going to leave me any useful information, I had no choice but to go looking for it.

Despite the lack of windows, the room would be cozy once there was a fire in the hearth. My father had been busy with his shopping. The carpet under the desk was fine and new, as were the two stout armchairs and the tapestry footstool. The mantel held a beautiful gilt clock, as well as several porcelain jars for tobacco and tea. The carved bookcases held a host of volumes, mostly new, but several looked quite old. The elaborate parquet floor added an elegance that made up for the plain, dark paneling and the old-fashioned whitewashed walls. So did several landscape paintings, which, thanks to my association with Matthew, I recognized to be of the Dutch school.

The broad oak desk, however, was empty except for stacks of bills, a ledger, and a small pile of unopened letters. I sorted through these, trying to convince my conscience that considering the circumstances, I was fully justified in breaking the seals and reading them all.

But if I found nothing, what then? Should I follow Olivia's example and search Father's bedroom? Or should I first search Aunt Pierpont's, to see if she had left anything informative behind?

The thought of my aunt made me look through the letters again.

"Nothing," I murmured. Aunt Pierpont had always been a most dutiful writer of letters. She used to deliver us regular lectures on the importance of punctuality in all forms of correspondence. How was it possible she hadn't written to Father, or to her own daughter? The journey to Norwich was not accomplished in a single day. She would have been able to send a letter from whatever inn or house they had stopped at for the night.

She would have written first thing to say they'd already arrived safely and remained in good health. But I saw no trace of my aunt's spidery handwriting on the sealed packets. "Aunt, has something happened to you?"

"That's what I wondered."

I screamed. I also jumped. Letters flew in every direction. When I came down again, I saw my father standing beside the chimneypiece, having seemingly appeared out of thin air.

"WHAT IN HEAVEN'S NAME ARE YOU PLAY-
ING AT?" I inquired.

"I'm sorry, Peg, truly." He did not sound sorry. In fact, he
sounded as if he might have been trying not to smile. "If I'd
known you were here, I would have been back sooner. Why
are you here, by the way?"

"I'm looking for you!" I informed him, mildly, of course.
"Should I have looked up the chimney?"

"No, under the carpet." He gestured to the floor beside
the hearth. I must have stared blankly at him, because he
clicked his tongue in admonishment and bent down to lift
away a section of the parquet floor. It was a trapdoor. Underneath, I now saw, was a ladder to the cellar.

"There's a tunnel under this room," he told me. "Leads
to the stables. Probably dug during Cromwell's time. There
are more of these around the town than anyone knows. Smugglers use them now, mostly. It's the reason I chose this house.
Sometimes a man needs to come and go without being seen."

He seemed to be waiting for me to make some exclamation of surprise and possibly of admiration. A truly filial
daughter probably would have obliged. I, however, had a
few other things on my mind.

"How long have you been back? I've been out of my mind
with worry about you!"

It finally seemed to occur to my fond parent that I might
have some sort of genuine grievance with his conduct. "I'm
sorry," he said. "That business in Oxford took longer than I
thought it would."

I stopped and let his words play over again in my mind. Yes, he had said it, and he'd looked me in the eye as he had done so. I returned his steady gaze. "But Mr. Willis isn't in Oxford."

That caught him off-guard, although just for an instant. "No, as it happens. But how did you come to know it?"

"Mr. Tinderflint told me. We found a letter at the palace containing a cipher. He said Mr. Willis is a code breaker."

Father blanched. "What letter? Where?" His pause was a long one. I lifted my chin. "Why are you here, Peg?"

"The princess has ordered you to come to the palace."

He didn't answer this right away, but when he did, his voice was soft and serious. "What's happened? What has Lord Tierney done now?" Instead of waiting for my reply, he whirled abruptly toward the door. "Damn."

With this highly informative, not to mention polite, exclamation, Father strode from the room. I grabbed up my hems and followed him down the hall and into the parlor. I'm sorry to report that both of us ignored Mrs. Biddingswell's startled shriek at finding her master so abruptly returned.

As before, the parlor drapes were tightly drawn. My father stole to the window and lifted the edge of one heavy curtain with his finger. "I thought as much."

He gestured for me to come stand beside him so I could also see. Outside was the general bustle of Lincoln's Inn Field. All the persons in the broad, rutted street, whether they were on foot or horseback or riding in coach or chair, clearly had someplace else to be. All, that is, save for whoever was in the small, low-slung, black coach with its pair of unremark-able chestnut bay horses. The driver, in his plain brown coat, leaned his elbows onto his knees and watched the passersby.

"Now, if I told you this was the second time in as many days that that coach has shown up here, who would you guess was inside?"

The coach's curtains were tightly drawn, but as the whole of it was as black as any hearse, it was impossible not to form certain associations.

"I'd say it was Mrs. Oglethorpe. She seems to love black."

He nodded. "Do you have any idea what she might want?" His tone was a little too carefully neutral and made me look at him a second time.

"I don't," I said. "But she wanted to speak to me enough that she donned her black veil at the masquerade and made herself as obvious as possible."

"Did she, b'God?" he murmured. "Well, well. I won-der if she, or whoever it might be, wants to speak with you badly enough to come into the house?"

I bit my lip, profoundly uncertain. We did not have time for this. My mission was to bring my father to the palace. I had, in fact, been specifically enjoined from ever again engag-ing in any more clandestine activities. At the same time, I was painfully aware that this might be my last opportunity to gain even one answer to my vast store of questions and suspicions.

"What should I do?" I asked him.

The pride in my father's smile was mixed with a generous dollop of mischief. "Go out and talk with her. Do everything you can to persuade her inside. Bring her into my book room. I'll be waiting." He touched the side of his nose.

I nodded. I also squared my shoulders and, with an effort, set my anger aside. This might be my last bit of spying, but it was hardly the last conversation I would have with my father about it, not by a long chalk.

With Mrs. Biddingswell sputtering behind me, I walked from parlor to front hall and out into the public street without cloak, hat, or pattens. I felt for the housekeeper. Surely she had not taken the position with the expectation that her master would appear at random intervals like a conjurer. I would explain matters to her one day when we both had more leisure, and I'd assure her she would receive a good character reference if she decided to seek less exciting employment.

I picked my way across the rutted street, avoiding the puddles as best I could. When I reached the coach, the driver turned his head to look at me, then leaned over the side and spat a large wad of tobacco into the street. Clearly, I was not considered a matter of immediate concern.

I decided to address myself directly to the curtained windows. "It is considered polite to send written notice of an intent to visit," I told them.

The curtains did not move, not even about the edges. Nonetheless, a voice emerged. "That would have been unwise."

She might have been keeping her face hidden, but her voice remained as distinctive as her veil had been.

"Mrs. Oglethorpe," I said. "What do you want?"

"To see that you are well, Miss Fitzroy." She betrayed no surprise at all that I had learned her name. "I feared for your safety."

Of all the things I might have expected to hear, this was not on the list. "My *safety?*"

I heard the sound of the coach door being unlatched. That door opened to reveal a shadowed but apparently well-upholstered interior. Mrs. Oglethorpe had arrived in her customary veiled state and beckoned to me now with one black-gloved hand. "Please get in. It is urgent that we speak."

Was it possible the woman believed me fool enough to climb inside her coach? Even if I hadn't been intent on getting her into the house, to step happily into such a conveyance with the horses harnessed and the driver ready to take up the reins would have required an entirely unprecedented sort of naiveté.

Fortunately, my hours spent adorning public events had taught me to quickly adapt to shifts in conversation. Mrs. Oglethorpe had mentioned my safety; I latched on to that now.

"I daren't," I breathed, glancing behind me for good measure.

"Are you watched?" She leaned forward. "I can help you, if you will but trust me."

I bit my lip and glanced behind myself again. In my mind,

I heard Olivia warning me not to overplay my scene.

"You must come into the house," I said quickly. "Father is still in Oxford. I thought he'd be back by now. I thought . . ." Mrs. Oglethorpe reached out as if she meant to touch my hand, and I knew I'd made the right choice of conversational strategies. "You can tell your man to take the coach into the mews around back."

"Impossible. The servants will have already seen too much."

I twisted my hands. "But there's nowhere else, and I'm expected back at the palace soon. There's so much happening now . . . I don't know when I'll be able to find you again."

It was a performance worthy of the Drury Lane theater, and it seemed to have the desired effect. Mrs. Oglethorpe nodded solemnly, closed her door, and signaled to her coach-man. I picked up my skirts and hurried back to the house.

"No questions, please, Mrs. Biddingswell," I said as I once again brushed past the housekeeper. "Just clear the staff from the first floor. I'm going to be bringing a lady into the book room who does not wish to be seen."

Mrs. Biddingswell looked at me, shock and disapproval plain on her usually stolid face. Being the mistress of a house is a useful thing, however, and our servant did not question or argue. I hurried to the back door, but I made one stop, and that was at the parlor. I noticed my father's smoking tools were laid out on the hearth-side table. I snatched up the little hooked knife used for cleaning the bowl of pipes and tucked it, carefully, into my sleeve.

Father presumably had stationed himself directly beneath his trapdoor in order to hear whatever conversation might occur without his weighty presence impeding a full and free exchange of views. However, recent events had taught me that one never knew what a spy might attempt, and it was better to be prepared.

When I opened the back door the hairbreadth requisite to demonstrate fear of discovery, it was to see the black coach already there. Mrs. Oglethorpe clambered down at once and darted inside far more nimbly than I would have given her credit for, considering her age and voluminous skirts. I made sure my eyes were wide with worry as I beckoned for her to follow me.

Once we reached the book room, I locked the door. There was no hint of Father anywhere. Everything in that windowless room was exactly as it had been. I found myself glancing about nervously, as if I expected him to poke his head out from a desk drawer.

I very carefully and deliberately did not glance toward the floor.

Fortunately, my companion took this show of nerves in stride. She lifted back her dramatic veil and I got my first full look at Eleanor Oglethorpe.

She was a sharp woman. Her cheekbones were high and slanting, making hollows out of her sallow cheeks. This, in combination with a pointed chin, made her face resemble nothing so much as a doleful hatchet. Her thick hair had gone entirely gray, but given the pale shade of her skin, I suspected it had once been fair. Her eyes were unusually large and startlingly blue. These, along with the well-curved figure beneath her black dress, hinted that she must have been a beauty in her youth. Her appearance now combined with her bearing to give her an air of decided elegance. That elegance had a hard edge, though, and was filled to the brim with suspicion.

Nonetheless, she made a valiant attempt at softening her hatchet face as she gazed at me.

"What happened to you at the masque?" she asked, as if she had every right to know my doings. "I searched everywhere for you but could find no trace. We feared the worst."

I had been right. That veil was no true disguise. She had meant for me to find her. Why hadn't Sophy, or Sebastian, told her where I was and what had happened regarding the letter? Perhaps they had. Mrs. Oglethorpe was a liar, I reminded myself. She might be lying right now in order to draw me out.

The wisdom of the ages informs us that what is sauce for the goose is sauce for the gander.

I decided to flutter. It was something I did a great deal on various occasions, and I had gotten rather good at it. "I know you were looking . . . that is . . . I thought I knew . . . but I was afraid."

"Of course you were." The smile Mrs. Oglethorpe returned was thin, but it seemed to be genuine. She reached out and touched my hand. I had to make an effort not to pull away. "Your father has no doubt told you that our family was responsible for his arrest and many other heinous acts besides."

I did not let my gaze drop to the floor or turn toward the hearth. I most decidedly did not check to see if Father had properly closed his trapdoor. I swallowed. Mrs. Oglethorpe entirely mistook the reason for my uneasiness (I hoped) and pressed my hand.

"Miss Fitzroy—Margaret—I have done you great wrong. We all have. I can only hope in time you will be able to forgive us."

Now I did draw back. "Which wrong is that?"

"I should have come to you as soon as I learned of your mother's fate. I should have taken you into my own home, where you could have learned the honest truth of your heritage." She paced away, circling the desk with its ledger and letters in plain view. I gritted my teeth. She might be here to make some strange show of apology, but apparently Mrs. Oglethorpe was too much the spy to leave an enemy's papers unexamined.

"Why should you care about me?" I croaked, grateful that I'd chosen to put on a show of nerves at the beginning of this conversation.

"Because, Margaret, your mother—Elizabeth—was the dearest friend of my life."

CHAPTER TWENTY-TWO

IN WHICH HEAVY WORDS MAY BE SEEN
TO BE LIGHTLY THROWN.

Mrs. Oglethorpe's declaration hung in the air for an inordinately long moment, and yet I could make no immediate answer. I was in a state of shock. It was not possible she was going to try this move against me. "A great many people have claimed to be my mother's friends since I came to the palace," I said. It was only at the last moment I remembered to make some sort of fluttery gesture with my hands.

"Have any of them offered you proof? You read the letter I left you?"

"I did. I . . . well . . ." I twisted my fingers together. "I have seen falsified letters before."

Mrs. Oglethorpe reached into the reticule hanging from her wrist and drew out not one, but two more letters. These were as old and as creased as the other had been. I did not have to force the furrows into my brow as I took the letters from her.

My Dearest Mrs. Righthandwall, (I read)

>*Oh, how very much I miss you. Do promise me you will be returning soon. If it were not for my little mischief Margaret, I should be running quite distracted with boredom. How on earth shall I endure another drawing room or supper party without you to help me laugh at them all?*
>
>*You say you are pursued by a most troublesome suitor. And you, a married woman! Do write and tell me more of this bold gentleman. Does he really mean to importune you for your connections there? How very rude and saucy of him! Give me but a hint of who his people are here and I shall tell you all I can of his circumstances that you may know better how to act.*
>
>>*Yr. Faithful,*
>>*Mrs. Tinderflint*

My hands trembled. Memory surged across me, of my mother's voice filled with mock outrage. "Margaret! You little mischief! Come back here right now!" And laughter. Mother had had the loudest, longest, most beautiful laugh. I blinked hard to clear my vision.

I remembered I must ask a question. I must pretend ignorance and bewilderment. "You . . . Is . . . is my *mother* Mrs. Tinderflint?"

Mrs. Oglethorpe nodded. "And I am Mrs. Righthandwall. We had adopted the pseudonyms as something of a joke when we were still girls, but as our work continued, it became prudent not to correspond under our right names."

Her face had fallen into lines of gentle concern. My stomach twisted badly, and it suddenly felt easier to open the second missive than look at her any longer.

The handwriting in this next letter definitely belonged to the same person, but it was less clear and much more blotched, as if the words had been laid down by a trembling hand.

> Mrs. R:
>
> I cannot tell you what a relief it is to hear from you that this "suitor" of yours has been removed elsewhere by our good and loyal friends. I am breathing so much easier now. I have, I confess, been very concerned on your behalf since you told me he had found you out, not in the least because he might learn of our particular connection. But now I may continue forward with a . . . [here I had to stop because the next few words had been so badly smeared I could not make them out] . . . calm mind. Little Mischief is growing every day. You have talked of her future, and the futures of J & S. Yes, of course, it is a wonderful idea that our families should be united in law as we are in our cause, but my daughter is such an infant yet, I cannot think that far ahead . . .

There was more, but I couldn't make myself read it. This could not possibly be genuine. And yet, I'd been told by someone—Father? Mr. Tinderflint? I couldn't remember —that not all my mother's letters had been found.

Which meant someone had searched for them. Which meant someone had a reason to want to know what they contained and to keep others from seeing them.

But this letter was not real. It could not be real.

. . . You have talked of her future, and the futures of J & S. Yes, of course, it is a wonderful idea that our families should be united in law as we are in our cause . . .

I raised my eyes. Mrs. Oglethorpe stood as tall and triumphant as any queen.

"Yes, Margaret. It was your mother and I together who realized that the best thing for you would be to marry into the Sandford family. Initially, you were intended for Julius, but he balked, despite everything." She sighed with every appearance of deep and heartfelt regret. "We all of us so sadly underestimated you. I promise you, that also is finished."

"What . . . how . . . why," I sputtered in a most shameful fashion. "Why on earth would my mother want me married to any Sandford!"

"Is it not yet clear to you, Margaret?" Mrs. Oglethorpe moved closer. I could smell the damp London air on her, and that perfume of old roses. "Elizabeth's cause and mine are the same."

"That's impossible. My mother was for Queen Anne." And Hanover.

Mrs. Oglethorpe shook her head slowly, sadly. "That is the lie told to you by her enemies. I am sorry to cause you yet more pain and confusion, Margaret. But I cannot stand by and let Elizabeth's daughter remain so deluded."

"You mean you cannot risk me interfering with your plans." The words were out before I could remember I was supposed to be fluttering.

"You are being forced to interfere with the return of England's rightful king," she corrected me firmly. "You are being deceived by the clever lies told by his enemies, and yours."

"Including my father?"

"Yes, Margaret. I'm afraid so. Jonathan Fitzroy was the suitor in that letter." She touched the paper I still held. "I was only partly instrumental in his arrest. It was your mother who furnished me with the necessary information to complete his conviction in King Louis's courts."

No. No. I stiffened every sinew in my body against the extremes of anger coursing through me. This woman was a liar. The worst of all possible liars. She was making use of a dead woman for her vicious, scheming slanders. These letters meant nothing. They proved nothing. Mother was a spy. There could be a thousand double meanings hidden in these pages.

"Why do you think Sir Oliver, Elizabeth's *brother*, wanted you to marry into the Sandford family?" Mrs. Oglethorpe asked. "It was because in Lynnfield you would at last be safe and able to follow your mother's path. But we were too slow, and her enemies reached you first."

I turned my gaze away, my cheeks burning. I had to act

as if I accepted this blatant untruth. But it would be only pretense, because I knew she was telling me falsehoods. My mother had not helped this woman condemn my father, her husband, to the Bastille, because to have done so would mean my mother—my beautiful, loving, laughing mother, whom I still missed with all my heart—had been an unfeeling monster.

When I could speak again, I said, "It was not Mother's enemies who made me refuse my betrothal."

"I cannot tell you what a disappointment Sebastian has proved to be. I have shed many tears over him. Yes, I, who have not cried since the exile. I tried repeatedly to correct him. We all did, to no avail. Now I can only promise you he will not cause you any further trouble."

Slowly, I felt my thoughts resurface from the current of anger that threatened to drown them.

"What have you done?" This was madness. I could not be standing here actually worried about Sebastian's fate at the hands of this callous and vicious traitor.

"Only what was necessary, nothing more, I promise." But as she spoke these words, that softness she had attempted to assume vanished entirely. "In fact, his position will be much improved once the king is restored to his throne."

"That might not be for a very long time."

"No." Mrs. Oglethorpe's smile blazed with the light of pure triumph. "The time is almost upon us, and you, Margaret, though you did not realize it, have helped us greatly. Your discoveries urged some of our more cautious friends to action. That is why I am here. I must get you to the safety of my house before the storm breaks."

The room had grown intensely cold. I watched this woman with her long, delicate hands as if I thought she meant to strike some blow against me. I almost wished that she would. Then I could strike back. The little knife I had concealed burned against my skin. I could wipe the sorrow and righteousness from her face. I already knew what she would say next. I knew it as I knew my name. She had been leading me along this path, carefully constructing a maze of falsehoods so heinous, I was amazed she was not struck dead for it.

"You are going to tell me Lord Tierney murdered my mother," I said.

For once I had proved myself an apt pupil. My regal teacher bowed her head. "You have seen him kill, Margaret," she reminded me. "You saw him murder your Mr. Peele in cold blood not so long ago. Oh, yes, we know about that," she said before I could make any reply. "We have our loyal people in place even in the heart of the Hanoverians' court."

I closed my eyes. I did not wish to look at this creature anymore.

"It was poison, of course," she went on. "Just as he used on Lady Francesca."

I said nothing.

"Who else but Lord Tierney has been holding the reins of all your troubles and steering your footsteps as he wishes them to go? He planted your father in the Sandfords' house.

He sent you among the usurpers under false colors. He has used you as his pet and his pawn. He even enlisted your cousin and your lover to ensure your loyalty."

Why Peggy? Matthew had once asked, when none of us expected it to be Mrs. Oglethorpe providing an answer.

"I don't believe you," I said, and I said it firmly, even fiercely. "I don't believe you."

"Your father does."

"What?"

"He has been combing the streets for two days solid, even to the point of calling upon former servants and taking them out drinking to encourage them to talk. Why would he be doing so if he did not wish to learn the truth behind his wife's actions those long years ago?"

"My father was — is — in Oxford." I felt distantly pleased with the way my voice quavered around these words. I could not have done better had I tried.

"That may be what he told you, but my friends have been keeping watch on him since his return, and I promise you that is not where he is now."

No. Where he is now is under the floorboards listening to every word you are speaking. Tell your friends they need to be more careful.

This evidence of her fallibility restored me to my right senses. I took a deep breath and held it. I took another. This lying, scheming woman had dealt me a blow, but I did not fall.

"You should go," I said to her. "I am expected back."

"You don't have to return to the palace, Margaret," she said urgently. "You can leave now, with me. I will take you to my house and to safety."

"Are you planning to kidnap me as well?" I retorted. My patience and my invention were too sorely strained. "The Sandfords tried that recently and in the end decided murder would suit better."

"No, Margaret, no! Never that. My orders were specific and direct. They were only to spirit you away. Your life is in no danger from us. If anyone told you otherwise, it was a lie!"

It seemed no one had told her how old Augustus Sandford had shot at me. This was not surprising. Save for Father and myself, all the witnesses to that particular act were dead.

"I can't . . . I . . ." What excuse would this woman accept for my refusal to accompany her? "My cousin." The words came out in a rush. "Olivia is at the palace. If what you say is true, I must warn her."

For a moment I thought she would argue, but from all she had said so far, I knew Mrs. Oglethorpe believed in the bonds of family loyalty. She took my hand and held it. I wanted so badly to strike, to break and to cut. But I only smiled weakly.

"Things may be very unpleasant upon your return," she told me earnestly. "You must prepare yourself. The instant you have made arrangements for your cousin, send word to me here." She pulled another paper from her reticule and handed it to me. I noted the address and then, almost as a reflex, I tucked it up my sleeve. "Direct the message to Mrs. Right-handwall. I will know from whom it was sent. I will fetch you myself and we will go at once to Godalming."

"I . . . I cannot promise anything."

"You will." She spoke with confidence. That same confidence showed in her wide blue eyes. Those eyes stirred memories, but I could not understand why. "After today, you will understand that your path and place lie with us."

She sailed from the room and I stayed where I was. My mind remained an absolute blank. After all I'd heard, it seemed I could summon no new thought.

I don't know how long it was before I heard the soft scrape beneath the floorboards and saw the trapdoor swing open.

My father climbed up to stand beside me. His breathing was harsh, as if he'd run miles to reach this place.

"I promise you, Peg . . ."

"Not one word." I held up my hand. "Not one. I am under orders to fetch you back to the palace, and you are coming with me this minute."

"You're angry . . ."

I rounded on him. "Of course I'm angry! Do you know why? Because you're *lying* to me. All of you are lying! You, this Oglethorpe woman, Mr. Tinderflint, my aunt, my mother, all of you! And I don't know why, or whom to believe, because every time I think I've found the bottom of this disaster, it only turns out to be another great pile of lies!" I was shaking, but I could not help it. "To make matters worse, that woman thinks I'm a complete idiot!"

Father closed his mouth abruptly.

"Good Lord!" I threw up my hands. "You as well! Do you think after all those nights at court I don't know when I'm being toyed with? Of course Mr. Tinderflint didn't murder Mother! The Oglethorpe just wants me frightened and friendless."

Father had the decency to look ashamed. He also seemed to recognize that now was not the moment to attempt an explanation, even if there had been one adequate to the situation.

"I can't go in my everyday clothes," he said. "Those friends of the Old Fury's may be still watching the house. I'll borrow the coachman's coat and hat and drive you."

"Whatever you choose," I said. "So long as we leave now."

Father proved to be a skilled and efficient driver, but by the time we neared the palace, I was as exhausted as if I'd sprinted the entire way in my court clothes. My encounter with Mrs. Oglethorpe had left me badly disturbed. I knew that the vast majority of what she had said to me was lies. She meant to confuse me and plant suspicions. But some of what she said might be true. It was this that dug into my heart and would not be ignored.

London traffic is a fearsome thing, but we were lucky in

our timing and able to drive relatively unimpeded through the streets. As we turned the corner onto Cleveland Row, however, we came upon a massive crowd of persons, coaches, and horses, all crammed together in a solid barricade.

"What's happening there?" cried Father to the yeomen clustered by the palace wall.

"It's an arrest," answered one. "They've caught a spy, right in the middle of the palace. You can't go through this way—you'll have to go 'round."

What? I reacted more from instinct than thought. "No! You must let me through." I pushed open the carriage door and leapt down into the street. "I'm Margaret Fitzroy, maid of honor to Her Royal Highness. If there's danger, my place is with her!" I am ashamed at what I did next. I can only plead extremities of circumstance. I held my breath, thrust out my chest, and bit the inside of my cheek, hard, so that tears of pain glittered in my eyes. "Please! Please! You must let me through!"

The yeoman looked at my eyes, and my bosom. "All right," he muttered, glancing at his compatriot in a warning to keep quiet. "But just you—your man waits here with the coach."

"Thank you, oh, thank you!" I cried, which, if laying it on a bit thick, was at least heartfelt. I hiked up my hems and hurried, in the tiny steps that would allow me to move at some semblance of speed without losing my balance. Even then, I wobbled dangerously on my pattens.

Was it Sophy being arrested? Sebastian?

Olivia?

The Color Court's gates were closed. The yeomen stood with their pikes lowered to bar the way. I recognized one of the men, although I did not know his name.

I pulled on my desperate and persuasive airs again as I rushed up to him. "Please, sir, I must get to Her Royal Highness!"

The guard whose face I knew looked down at me and sneered. "Oh, no, not you. You can just wait out here with the rest of 'em."

But his comrade waved and shrugged. "Ah, let her through. They'll know what to do with her in there."

My blood was ice. I was shaking. I watched the yeoman unlock the smaller postern gate and step back. What did it mean? What *could* it mean?

Could it really be Olivia?

No. It can't be. It is not *Olivia.* I hurried through the gate and into the courtyard. Despite my pattens, mud splashed my hems and my stockings. The courtyard was crammed with bodies. I could see no one I knew, just a crush of backs and shoulders and heads and hats.

"Please!" I cried. "Please, I must get through!" I shoved and elbowed and stepped on not a few toes. I broke through the crowd in time to hear the fresh murmurs and see a square of yeomen marching toward a closed black coach with their prisoner in the center.

I stood, and I stared. The prisoner turned and looked at me, and nodded once. His hands were shackled, his wig was gone from his head. He was very bald.

He was Mr. Tinderflint.

CHAPTER TWENTY-THREE

IN WHICH FAR MORE QUESTIONS ARE ASKED
THAN ANSWERED AND AN IMPROBABLE OFFER
IS GRATEFULLY RECEIVED.

As I stared with the rest of the crowd, the yeomen prodded and pushed Mr. Tinderflint into the coach. It was, I noted absently, almost as large as his own gaudy conveyance. But that one had no lock to turn and no bars on its window, nor any contingent of men with swords and pole arms. And Mr. Tinderflint's coach took only six horses to pull it, not eight.

A hand closed about my shoulder. I didn't even flinch. I knew who it was.

"Is this your doing?" I asked my father.

"No. Whatever's happened to Tierney, it's no work of mine."

"Then what have you been about all this time?"

"Trying to find out what happened to your aunt!" he

cried. "D'you remember her, Peg? That lady who never left London in her life but who suddenly packed off with her mother-in-law, and who since seems to have fallen off the face of the earth? I've been trawling through Pierpont's old business and his old friends and even our old household to try to find out what she really did know and if that might have gotten her into trouble!"

Oddly, it was his exasperation that made me believe him. It also seemed to break my paralysis. As explanations would only add unnecessary delays, I simply seized Father's hand and dragged him to the nearest cluster of yeomen.

"This man is summoned by Her Royal Highness to speak with her immediately." I pushed him into their arms. I did not wait for their sputtering questions but instead waded as quickly as I could through the crowded yard and into the palace. I had to make sure Olivia was all right. Then I had to find Molly and hear the whole story of what had happened to Mr. Tinderflint. Then . . .

I made it no farther before the yeomen blocked my path. "Seems you're summoned for questioning as well, Miss Fitzroy," one said. "You're to come with us now."

And so I did.

It was not either of Their Royal Highnesses who questioned me in the broad, empty salon to which I was taken. Rather, it was a parade of different men—high clerks and royal confidants and assorted Lords of This and That. Some of them I knew because I'd played cards or danced with them. Some I knew only by name and reputation. Several pretended kindness. Others shouted or tried to browbeat me. As large as it was, the salon they used for this exercise had no chair. I think that was meant to cause discomfort. Apparently they neglected to consider that as a maid of honor, I was quite accustomed to standing for six or eight hours at a time.

I took care to adopt a uniform attitude of humility, complete with downcast eyes and folded hands. These men might be mere servants of the Crown as I was, but they also had the power to have me held in close confinement. At the same time, I was angry to the point of petulance. I needed answers, and they gave me nothing more than false sympathy, condescension, and a headache.

So it was that I replied to all their questions, but I did no more. Not one of them asked where I'd been that afternoon. Not one of them asked what had occurred at my father's house. Therefore, not one of them learned about Mrs. Oglethorpe's visit, much less what that lady and I had said to each other.

I hoped against hope that the princess might send word and release me from these gentlemen and their badgering, but no word came. Eventually, I was told I might return to my rooms. By then, I was thirsty and hungry and worried in the extreme. I opened my door, thinking only that I would send Libby at once to the kitchens, and then to find out where Princess Caroline and her retinue were so I could make my appearance as quickly and decently as possible and hear all the news there.

It was the sight of Olivia standing amid a sea of ruin that drove all such worthy thoughts out of my mind.

My chamber looked as if it had been picked up and shaken. I could only assume it had been searched, but those who had done the work had not had much care for how it was done. My desk had been stripped clean and all its draw-ers left open. What few ornaments I owned had been up-ended, including my clock. My tea had been spilled from its jars and strewn out across the hearth. All of Olivia's trunks had been opened, a number of them overturned. My closet door was open. I did not have the nerve to see what had been done to my wardrobe, my jewel boxes, my cosmetics.

I was so stunned, I barely remembered to shut the door. Isolde poked her head out from under her blanket by the hearth and bared her tiny teeth at me.

"Olivia . . ." I began, but Olivia was too busy diving for her overturned trunks.

"My notebooks!" she cried. She groped among the scat-tered, empty boxes. "They took my notebooks! Those fiends, those Philistines! Those . . . those . . ."

What followed was a string of exclamations, none of which belonged in the vocabulary of a gently reared young lady. For my part, I drifted over to my empty desk. I knew I should have been sharing Olivia's outrage. Those notebooks were her prized possessions. More than diaries, they were the notes and musings she had written down throughout her life to turn into the plays and poetry with which she be-lieved she would one day make her fortune.

Fear, however, has a way of transforming one into an entirely selfish being. While Olivia raged over her lost books, all I could think was that everything that had been in this desk was now in the hands of those unforgiving men who had questioned me.

"They took the letters." The letters filled to the brim with (possibly) French ciphers and spies' cant. The next knock on the door would surely be the yeomen of the guard. Would they, I wondered idly, house me near Mr. Tinderflint when I was taken to the Tower?

"What?" snapped Olivia. "The letters? Of course they didn't take them. Do you think I'm completely witless?"

Slowly, and with very little intent on my part, my body turned, and my eyes stared. In response, my cousin left her plundered trunks and stomped over to Isolde's bed. She expertly lifted the outraged puppy and yanked several papers out from under the cushion.

They were, of course, the Mrs. Tinderflint letters, both the one I'd been sent by Mrs. Oglethorpe and the one Olivia had copied from her mother's papers. There was also the description of the commemorative medal and, most importantly and blessedly, the copy she'd made of the enciphered letter with the House of Orléans seal.

I gaped. Olivia folded her arms. "I'll expect you to remember this the next time you're tempted to scold me for dramatics."

"You are the best and bravest of cousins!" We embraced and held on for a very long time. This gesture reassured Isolde enough that she trotted up to nose at my ankles and tug at my hems.

"Secrets, Izzy, secrets." Some of her biscuits had been scattered across my nightstand. I broke one in half and tossed it to her.

Isolde thus placated, I sat on the edge of my bed, which had been stripped of its covers. "Tell me what happened," I said to Olivia.

She righted my desk chair and sat down, uncharacteristically wringing her hands. "I barely know, Peggy. Everyone at the nuncheon was busy marveling over the fact that Sophy Howe has gone home—"

"What!"

"I don't believe it either, but that's the story, and she certainly wasn't in evidence at court this morning. All the ladies were busy speculating on whether she'd finally gotten herself into an indelicate condition. Except Molly, of course. Oh, Peggy, I like her. She's got an excellent wit."

"And the steadiest head you'll find at court. What did Molly say?" Isolde finished her biscuit and proceeded to burrow under my hems looking for more.

"She thinks Sophy's up and run off with Sebastian Sandford. He hasn't been seen for several days either."

"Then his appearance at the masquerade wasn't generally known. When did Sophy leave?"

"Yesterday, apparently. It was quite sudden. According to your maid, Libby—wherever did you find her, Peg? I've never known such a piece of work!"

I suppressed the urge to scream at my cousin's tangents. "She is, and an expensive one. But what did she say?"

"She says that Sophy's rooms have not been properly packed up, but her maid has gone off with her."

I thought on Sophy's personal treasure trove, and I shivered. Sophy would leave behind her worldly goods only if she expected to return, and return soon. And yet those apartments, and those worldly goods, came from her post, the one she would not be able to resume if she had actually run off with Sebastian. First and foremost, maids of honor need to be, well, maids. At least, they must appear to be.

Did Sophy love and trust Sebastian enough to give up her place at court for him? If Lord Lynnfield had blessed their betrothal, she might. She might also give it up if it was Lynnfield she meant to marry.

But when she'd told me to come find her, she surely hadn't meant I should look out in the countryside. Something had changed since the masque.

I shivered again. Lord Lynnfield clearing his brother out of court. Mr. Tinderflint taken to the Tower. Aunt Pierpont not writing her daughter. Any one of these would have been a momentous event, but all of them together? It felt as if the world was coming apart at its seams, and this was even without considering all of Mrs. Oglethorpe's brazen lies about Mr. Tinderflint and my mother.

"Tell me quickly, Olivia—what happened to Mr. Tinderflint? And to you?"

"It was all terribly confused." Olivia shook her head.

"We'd been dismissed from waiting. Molly offered to show me some of the principal rooms of the palace, to help me learn my way about. We were just beginning when a shout went up from the hall, and a whole troop of yeomen marched through, clearing the way. If it weren't for his, well, size, I'm not sure I would even have recognized Mr. Tinderflint. I'd only just caught my breath from that realization when a footman found me and took me to some salon or the other. Several very grand and long-winded men came in and asked all manner of outrageous questions."

"Did you tell them anything?"

A flush rose in Olivia's cheeks. "What could I possibly have told them?" Evidently, the look on my face reminded my cousin she had recently expressed a wish to lead both her mother and grandmother to the gallows. But she remained defiant. "If I am to condemn my family, it will not be to men who leer at my bosom while demanding to know whom I've been carrying letters for!"

A knock sounded at the door. "Come in," I called. Olivia looked horrified. I shrugged. If it was the palace yeomen, calling "I'm not at home" would be of no help.

But it was not the yeomen. It was my father. Wherever he had been, he looked no worse for it. Not that driving through London all morning had left him in particularly good repair.

When he saw the state of my apartment, Father exclaimed a phrase in French I probably should not have understood.

"I thought something like this might have happened." He came over to take my hand. "I'm sorry for it. Are you all right, Olivia?"

Olivia lifted her chin. "We've seen worse, you know."

"I do, and you have my deepest respect for it." Despite his coachman's garb, Father gave her a most courtly bow.

"Have you news about Mr. Tinderflint?" I asked.

Father shook his head. "I have a message for you from Their Royal Highnesses, though. Your princess, I find, is every bit as intelligent as she's said to be, and I'd not bet against the prince in any hurry either, for all he has reputation as a fool. They both, by the by, speak very highly of you, Peg." I blushed at this, but Father did not smile or make any joke. "Indeed, you may be the only reason I'm still at liberty. They were not pleased with my reluctance to present myself before this."

"What did you tell Their Highnesses?"

"What I could. That there is a long-standing plot with a probable invasion at the end of it. Its participants think it is close to bearing fruit. I gave them what names I am certain of, and did affirm that my late brother-in-law was involved. As to Lord Tierney's entanglements, I could not speculate." He looked at me directly as he said this. "I said I believed my daughter had placed substantial trust in him and that he had done great good service to the Crown."

"Thank you." I paused. "Did you . . . did you tell them about Mrs. Oglethorpe?"

"Not yet. But one of us will have to soon."

At this, Olivia could no longer contain herself. "Have you heard from my mother?"

He glanced sideways at me. "No, Olivia. I'm sorry. I'm sure you were questioned as well. Did you tell them about her? About the letters? Or anything else? No one will blame you if you did," he added.

I noted that my cousin looked unusually awkward at this, and I wondered at it. "Olivia didn't have to tell anyone about the letters," I said quickly. "I told the princess about them this morning. I also told her about Aunt Pierpont and Mrs. Oglethorpe."

I did not imagine the way my father swayed on his feet or the pallor that touched his face. But I did not have time to inquire what caused this extreme of feeling.

"I have to talk to Mr. Tinderflint," I told them both. "How—"

My father interrupted. "Princess Caroline anticipated you, Peg. She has given permission for you to go to him. Over, may I say, the objections of a certain Mr. Walpole. You are, however, strictly enjoined to be present at the drawing room this evening so no one may have further cause to speculate about your . . . involvement, I believe was the word she chose, with Lord Tierney."

This injunction left me very little time. My stomach rumbled loudly, reminding me I hadn't eaten since before sunrise. Which in turn reminded me that I didn't even know where Libby was.

But these concerns must be laid aside. The clock lying

sideways on my mantel would chime four in a handful of minutes. To be ready in time for the drawing room, I would have to be back in the palace before eight. How far was it to the Tower and back? How was it I did not know this important fact?

"Olivia, I need you to write to Matthew and tell him everything, only make sure it's Libby's Norris who takes the letter and no one else. Will you?"

To my surprise, Olivia acquiesced after only the briefest of pauses. I would, of course, be quizzed closely about every aspect of the place I intended to visit, but I considered this a fair price to pay for being allowed to make a swift exit.

Father offered no objection to these instructions either, but instead uttered such a declaration as no good English father had ever before spoken to his daughter.

"Come on, then, Peg—I'll take you to the Tower myself."

CHAPTER TWENTY-FOUR

The Tower.

It is a long, grim way into the Tower of London. There is a drawbridge to cross, and not one, but two portcullises with iron spikes—one at either end of a dark stone tunnel. The quiet green square at the end comes as something of a surprise.

There is a smell of cold stone, iron, and rot that not even late October's relentless rain can wash away.

The Tower ravens watch. They are large, healthy, and quite well fed, and their black beaks glisten. They croak like courtiers commenting unfavorably on your apparel when you pass them. The Tower guards also watch. These are not slouching palace yeomen who scratch and leer and would like as not abandon their post for a drink or a piss without a second thought. These are sharp-eyed men, and the blades on their pole arms glisten like the ravens' beaks. They are the ones who lead you inside the central building of this venerable fortress, up winding stairs and down narrow corridors to be met by the jailer, who has all the appearance of a bank clerk with his black coat, full-bottomed wig, and soft hands.

It is impossible not to stare at his great iron ring of keys that clang and rattle as he leads you up more stone stairs. Other than this noise, the place is eerily silent. I should have been grateful, I suppose. Part of me had expected screaming.

The Tower is not a well-appointed place; neither is it very dry. There is straw on the stone floors, but I still had to lift my hems to avoid trailing them through the filthy puddles. What few slit windows looked out from the corridor had no glass, so there was nothing to block the icy wind, nor that particular stench that was the Tower itself.

At last we came to an oaken door, practically black with age. It had an iron grill and was banded with yet more iron. The yeoman lifted the great bar from its brackets, and the gentleman jailer fitted his iron key into an iron lock that clattered as it turned.

The chamber on the other side was larger than I expected. There was even a hearth, although it had no fire, so the place was fiercely cold.

Mr. Tinderflint sat in a small wooden chair by the window, which was, thankfully, glazed. He had been stripped of his wig and much of his jewelry and ribbons. Even the buckles of his shoes were gone. I had laughed behind my hand at Mr. Tinderflint's appearance on any number of occasions.

Now I regretted that frivolity. In this cold, bare chamber, he looked diminished—deflated, even.

Mr. Tinderflint levered himself to his feet and held out both hands toward me. "Peggy, my dear."

I rushed toward him and seized his frigid hands. Doubt did not cease to swirl through my heart, but this man remained my friend and patron. In this instant, that seemed to be what truly mattered.

Behind me, the cell door creaked on its hinges and slammed shut. I heard the noise of keys and lock and the scrape of the bar being slid back into its iron bracket, announcing that I too had been locked into the Tower.

"Now, now, I know this looks very bad." Mr. Tinderflint spoke quickly and urgently, with much bobbing of his head and wagging of his chins. "But you mustn't worry for me—no, no, you mustn't. I'm to be allowed fire, as soon as it can be arranged, and a message has already gone back to my people that I stand in need of some movables and clothing. Those lodged here may pay the keeper for extra comforts, and I have more than enough money for all such. I will be made snug—perfectly snug, I do assure you—in short order."

I gaped at him. He was in the Tower of London, where kings and queens—never mind portly, overdressed, conspiratorial earls—lost their heads, and he thought I worried about whether he was comfortable!

The window had a narrow ledge, and I propped myself up on it so I could lean close as he sat back down.

"Tell me this is a plan," I whispered urgently. "This is

part of one of your schemes, isn't it? Just nod, or pat my hand, if you can't say it out loud. Please."

But Mr. Tinderflint did neither; he simply hung his head. My throat closed around my breath.

"Then who is responsible? Who betrayed you?"

He glanced over my shoulder at the closed door with its iron grille and shook his head minutely. I knew what he meant. We were not really alone. Someone was out there listening.

"You should not have come," he murmured to me. "It will make you look complicit. I'm surprised your father permitted it." He paused. "He did give you permission, didn't he?"

"The princess did, but Father drove me here."

"Did she? Now, that is interesting. Still, for appearance's sake, it is very bad, very bad indeed."

"I don't care how I look! I—"

"Keep your voice down, Peggy." Mr. Tinderflint dropped his own to the lightest whisper, and with a significant nod, he switched from English to Greek. "You must care how you look; you must care deeply."

Ready to strangle on my own impatience, I also turned to what limping Greek I possessed. "Or what will happen? I'll lose my place?"

"You'll lose your chance to bring the Sandfords and the Oglethorpes to this so-pleasant place," Mr. Tinderflint said. I had to strain to hear him. "I have followed the Jacobites for many years, Peggy, longer than you or your father has lived. Not once have they dared move against me directly. Something is different this time."

"But how did this even happen?"

"The enciphered letter," he breathed. "The one you took from the palace library. It was found in my desk."

"That's not possible!" Mr. Tinderflint would never have been so careless as to leave a coded letter with the House of Orléans seal on it in his desk. He had been trapped because he had taken a letter from my hand without thinking about it.

Because out of all the people in this mad business, he had trusted me.

I saw the truth then, and it was as cold as the approaching winter outside. I had not been the one they were after. I was the tool, the little girl spy simpering about the court. Why would they worry about me when they could ensnare my patron: the subtle, scheming man who had thwarted them across a decade or more?

Almost crying from the effort of it, I dropped my voice back to a whisper. "She—the veiled woman—when she came to me, she said plans were close to completion," I breathed. "She said she wanted to get me away before the storm broke."

My patron, as always, proved very quick on the uptake. "The Old Fury returned? You spoke with her?"

I nodded. "She had letters. She said that my mother . . . that Mother was a friend of hers and that she was the one who wanted me to marry a Sandford, so I could be part of their household and . . ." I choked on the words.

"You saw these letters?"

I nodded. "They were not the first." I paused, then said, "She said you poisoned my mother."

Had I ever seen my patron angry before? I couldn't remember, but if I had, it surely hadn't been like this. He jerked to his feet. He snatched up his chair and swung it high over his head. In one swift movement, he brought it crashing down against the floor. Wood splintered everywhere. I flung my arm up to cover my face and stumbled backwards.

I doubt Mr. Tinderflint even noticed. He stood there staring at the ruin of the room's only chair. His whole body shook and his mouth was moving, a string of silent oaths.

The lock rattled and the door creaked open. We both looked up to see the jailer standing there, with a yeoman of the guard right behind him.

"None of that, my lord," said the jailer calmly. "It'll be added to your bill."

"Of course," Mr. Tinderflint replied. "I do apologize for the inconvenience."

This seemed to satisfy the jailer, because he pulled the door shut once more.

Mr. Tinderflint returned to contemplating the wreckage he'd made of an innocent piece of furniture. He reached down and deliberately plucked one of the broken rails from the pile of wood.

"I'm sorry, Peggy," he said. "That was quite unforgivable of me."

"It's all right," I answered, because I had no idea what else to say. "I expect you've had a trying day."

"Yes, yes, I have, I'm afraid." Mr. Tinderflint laid the broken chair rail on the windowsill. "What else has happened?

"Sophy's left the palace," I told him. "Sebastian too. Lynnfield, of course, was gone days ago."

Mr. Tinderflint rested his hands on the sill right next to the chair rail. He stared out at the high walls and unforgiving October. The sun was setting, filling the room with twilight. There were no candles. Soon, it would be too dark to see.

"Dear God," he breathed. "Dear God in Heaven, it's happening. This time it's real." He closed his empty fists. "And I'm in here. All these years, all my plans, all my people in place, and when the moment at last arrives, I. Am. In. Here!" He clenched those fists until they shook and the knuckles turned white. "Did Mrs. Oglethorpe say where?" The words rasped in his throat. "Did she give you any hint at all as to where the landing will take place and who is backing this?"

I could only shake my head. "I'll go to Their Highnesses," I said, a little desperately. "I'll plead your case."

"It would take an order from the Prince of Wales, Peggy, and he signed the warrant that brought me here."

I looked into his watery eyes and saw a mixture of fury and helplessness that struck straight to my heart. Cold wrapped around me like the deepening twilight. "What should I do?"

Mr. Tinderflint looked over my shoulder again. His chins trembled. Slowly, he opened one of his fists. Just as slowly, he reached forward and took my hand. I felt a warm weight slide into my palm. The heft and shape told me I held a key.

I closed my hand around it.

My patron let his head droop as if in abject despair. When he spoke, it was in German and in the barest breath of a whisper. "There is a room above the Cocoa Tree in Pall Mall," he murmured dolefully. "In the desk are some letters that must be sent at once. The directions are already in place. These will serve to remind certain highly placed gentlemen of past matters that might still affect the present situation."

Blackmail. I did not say the word, but Mr. Tinderflint saw it written across my expression. He nodded.

"I have never been a nice man, Peggy. And this business we are about . . ." He sighed and evidently felt no need to finish that particular sentence. "Those letters constitute my surest route out of this cell, and it is vital that I am freed as soon as possible."

"I'll do my best." I did not forget that I had been forbidden to have anything more to do with clandestine activities. But how could I refuse?

I folded my hands together and twisted my fingers nervously, which, incidentally, provided some covering motion for the fact that I tucked the key into my sleeve. "What will happen to you while I'm gone?" I then slowly asked another question, hating myself for doing it. "Is . . . is there anyone to whom I should write? A Lady Tierney, perhaps?" A Mrs. Tinderflint. "You never said . . ."

His smile was faint. "Alas, there is no Lady Tierney. My sisters are dead, as is my mother, and to her eternal sorrow, I never entered the married state." He shook his head.

"Therefore, no. But if things stay . . . as they are . . . we may safely assume we have a few days at least before anything drastic occurs. I am still Earl Tierney, after all, and it takes time to try and convict such a man as myself. In the meantime, we must make use of those lessons you have learned so well." He wagged his chins at me. "Appearances, Peggy, must be preserved."

I met his solemn gaze. His eyes flickered once toward the door, with its listening jailer on the other side. He took a deep breath. I understood and let him see that I was ready.

Mr. Tinderflint gave me the faintest ghost of a smile. Then I took my own deep breath and leapt backwards.

"I will not hear you, sir!" I shouted at the top of my lungs, in good plain English. "I will not listen to another word!"

Mr. Tinderflint surged toward me. "Ungrateful slattern! After all that I have done for you!"

"Done for me! You have done nothing from the first but lie and deceive!"

"Have a care! I put you in your place—I can remove you from it just as easily!"

I drew myself up. My cheeks flushed, which was convenient in case we were being watched as well as overheard. "I am maid of honor to Her Royal Highness Caroline, Princess of Wales. I serve at her pleasure, not yours!"

"Think again, my fine miss!" Mr. Tinderflint pointed one fat finger at me and shook it vigorously.

"I have thought again, sir! Our association is done — *done!* I will not be drawn into your plots. I wash my hands of you and all your friends!"

Mr. Tinderflint looked at me. I looked at him. I bit my tongue and then spat on the floor at his feet.

I turned away, drawing my skirts in close to my body, as if I wanted to be certain my hems would not brush against him. I thought, perhaps, I saw a twinkle of approval in Mr. Tinderflint's eye as I sailed to the door in the haughtiest of fashions and banged on it with my fist. "Jailer!" I cried, and did not have to force the break into my voice. "Jailer!"

The man arrived with suspicious speed to open that portal to let me out. I was in no way surprised, especially not when I saw the corner of a book peeking from the pocket of his black coat. He'd not only been listening, he'd been taking notes.

I found I was not surprised about that, either.

I said not a word to my father when I emerged from the Tower. He was still in his coachman's coat, of course, and he seemed determined to keep up the part. He touched his hat brim to me as he held open the door so I could climb inside the conveyance. As he closed the door, I peered up at the Tower walls. I could not see over them to tell if there were lights showing inside. I could not tell if the jailer had remembered to bring Mr. Tinderflint a candle or if he still sat in the dark, waiting for me to free him.

Father climbed onto the box and touched up the horses. The coach rocked as they started forward. It was now far too dark to see well, so I listened to the creak and the jingle of the harnesses, the clop of hooves, and all the other sounds of travel. Even if I succeeded in freeing Mr. Tinderflint, my mistress was right. Matters had all gone far, far beyond me.

The coach slowed and stopped. My head jerked up. I looked past the curtains but saw mostly darkness and a few looming shapes, nothing like the illumination of the palace. From outside came the clatter and thump of Father climbing off the box. Somewhat absurdly, he knocked at the coach door. I undid the latch and let him clamber inside.

"It's best we talk before there's anyone to overhear," he told me. "How is Lord Tierney?"

I wanted to cry. I wanted to beg my father to turn the horses' heads away from the city and take us someplace, anyplace, where we would never hear the words *spy* and *Jacobite* again.

"Did he say how he came to be imprisoned?" Father asked. He spoke the words carefully, almost hesitantly, and I felt a strange sensation, as if I'd caught an odor I could not identify.

"He said an incriminating letter was found in his desk." I meant to go on to tell the story of how it got there, but something made my tongue stumble over the words. "It had the seal of the House of Orléans on it," I said finally.

My father shook his head slowly. My father, who had

spent all those years in France, spying on the courts at Saint-Germain and Versailles. "It happens. The best and most careful of men can make that little mistake at the wrong time. Did he ask anything of you? Give you any instructions?"

My father, who could disguise himself as any lowly person. Who could, I had reason to know, slip in and out of the palace unnoticed. Who had been absent from the masquerade even though he had promised me faithfully he would attend.

Who had served the Sandfords and who distrusted Lord Tierney.

My father, who'd supposedly been in prison for years, and in service after that, and yet still had money enough to set himself up in a fine house, one with a smugglers' tunnel. He'd left his money with friends, he said. Despite all such forethought on his own behalf, he'd never bothered to make arrangements with any such friend to watch over my situation, or to pass on any sum for my use, or indeed to make any provision for his family while he was gone.

That seemed odd for such a careful man, one who had known his life was in real danger.

I had been trying to sort out loyalties and grand schemes. Mrs. Oglethorpe did what she did out of the belief that God had somehow decided He wanted James on the throne after all. Mr. Tinderflint did his work out of belief as well, although his belief was that he knew which of the available kings was best for him, and us. But belief was not the only thing that motivated the confidential agent. The smuggling

Sandfords were, to all appearances, in the game for wealth and power.

Spies could also become quite wealthy. They could be paid well for their work. They could be paid better to change sides, and to change them back. Or not.

My father had a fine house, and a coach, horses, and servants, all since he'd come back from France.

"Peg?" Father's voice broke my reverie. "Did Tierney ask anything of you? Are you to get him anything or to take any sort of message? You're supposed to be back for the drawing room and we haven't much time."

"No," I said. "There was nothing."

CHAPTER TWENTY-FIVE

IN WHICH DISGUISES ARE ONCE MORE DONNED AND
MISTAKES, AS WELL AS DISCOVERIES, ARE MADE.

I had been ordered to be in place for the drawing room.
I had further been ordered to cease my clandestine activities.
Therefore, I had only one choice.

I would have to sneak out.

Olivia wanted me to dress as a boy for this particular
enterprise. I refused. My cousin might have developed an enthusiasm for it, but I did not favor male clothing. Besides, I
had no wish to be mistaken for Orlando Preston by the still-
fuming Lord Blakeney. As a result, Olivia had to be content
with my borrowing Libby's second dress, apron, and cap. I,
of course, paid for that privilege.

Olivia also had to be content with sitting up in my
rooms with Isolde, in order to tell anyone who might appear

at my door that I had a headache and could not be disturbed, rather than coming along to the Cocoa Tree. This took rather more persuading, but I gained the day by pointing out that if anyone tried to come into our rooms at this time of night, we very much needed to know about it.

I did not mention that if I got caught at this, the last of my credibility with Their Highnesses would fly away, and we would be shipped back to whatever welcome waited in my father's house.

Leaving Olivia on watch at the palace did not mean I planned to go out alone. Even at my most daring I was not prepared to wander the streets of London without an escort. I took Matthew with me. Despite my patron's warnings about the need for secrecy, I was sure Mr. Tinderflint would not have minded my sweetheart's inclusion. Besides, Matthew, rather unexpectedly, knew where the Cocoa Tree was.

My departure from the palace proceeded smoothly. Her High-ness had kept me at her side throughout the course of the drawing room, but she grew fatigued rather more early than usual and had the bedchamber women take her to her rooms. This engendered a great deal of speculation about her time being upon her, which I did not stay to listen to. Instead, I slipped back to my own rooms and let Olivia help me out of my court clothes and into my maid's disguise. With Libby once more playing the guide, I navigated the crowded back stairs down to the Ambassador Court. From there, I crept out into Cleveland Row, where Matthew waited, lounging against the side of a house and whistling in fine imitation of a lazy wastrel up to no good.

The Cocoa Tree might be a coffee and chocolate house, but we arrived to find its environs as loud and frenetic as any tavern. Even in the small hours of that wintery night, the place was so full its patrons spilled out into the streets. Apparently oblivious to the first flakes of snow drifting down around them, they sat on benches waving pipes at one another and arguing. Some, for variety's sake, crowded up to the newspapers posted on the walls and argued. Some of them even held cups of what I supposed to be coffee, pointing and gesticulating hard enough to splash the beverages over the sides.

Fortunately, the men were so engrossed in the arguments, their papers, their pipes, and their drinks that I in my cap and plain skirt was scarcely noticed. One lively wit did wink at me and slap his knee in the universal language that invited me to sit down. Matthew stepped between us, ready to take umbrage as needed, but the fellow just grinned and went back to his argument.

We ducked into the narrow, dingy doorway on the side of the house to find ourselves at the foot of an equally narrow, dingy stairway. Other than a little torch light filtering in from outside, the only illumination was the candlelight that glimmered under and around a few of the doors.

The stairs creaked dangerously as we climbed. The

smells of coffee and bitter chocolate mixed with those of mildew and filth. I tried to imagine my fastidious, spherical patron mounting this staircase, and failed.

One door at the far end of the hall had neither light nor noise coming from behind it and therefore seemed our best choice. After a certain amount of groping about, I was able to fit the key into the lock. It took a nervous moment of rattling and heartfelt pleading with the world at large before key and lock agreed to cooperate. The door's rusted hinges groaned in protest, but at last we stepped into Mr. Tinderflint's rooms.

Room and hearth were both as cold as his cell had been. By this time our vision had adapted to the dark, and we were able to make out the candle and tinderbox that had been placed in readiness on a rickety table by the door. While I shut the door and struggled once more with the lock, Matthew struck a spark and kindled us a light.

The chamber itself was much cleaner than the hallway outside. The walls looked as though they'd been white-washed at some point in the past few years. Two armchairs of antique vintage but considerable width and depth had been drawn up in front of the dark fireplace, where the hearth-stones were swept clean, the coal scuttle filled, and sticks laid in the grate, ready to be lit. A dusty bottle and a pair of glasses waited on the mantel. There was even a thin rug on the floor.

"Should we risk a fire?" asked Matthew, and his breath steamed white.

Reluctantly, I shook my head. "We've no time."

A plain writing desk stood underneath the window. It had two drawers on the side and one at the center, which proved to be locked. I admit to uttering a few mild curses at this. The side drawers contained leather-bound books filled with so many columns of closely written numbers that they might have been ledgers. I thought of the enciphered letter that had been Mr. Tinderflint's downfall. What codes were these, and who waited at the end of them?

I couldn't afford to linger over the question. There were no sealed letters in either of the drawers, and no amount of leafing through or shaking of the ledger-style books produced any. Which meant they had to be in the locked drawer.

"You might have provided a key," I muttered to my absent patron.

"I think he did," said Matthew.

Matthew stood by the hearth. He'd put the candle on the mantel and now held a wooden box. Inside lay a jeweled pin—a beautiful little bauble of silver and sapphires suitable to decorate a lady's stomacher. At least, it might have been taken for a mere bauble until one realized its straight pin resembled a tiny rapier and had surprisingly keen edges. I lifted the decoration, feeling something between wonder and a pang. Until recently, I had owned a similar bauble, one that had helped save my life.

"He knew," I said. "He knew this might happen."

"I expect when you're Mr. Tinderflint, you get ready for this sort of thing." Matthew did not sound impressed.

I ignored this and returned to the desk. I stuck the little

blade into the narrow space between drawer and desk, sliding it along until it clicked against the latch of the lock. I batted at the latch, once, twice, harder. There was a small click, and the lock's tongue snapped sideways. I slid the drawer open to see a stack of foolscap, several untrimmed quills, bricks of indigo and ink bottles, and a penknife, but no letters. I squeezed my lips shut around any further exclamation and made myself think. I picked up the stack of writing paper and saw nothing. Nothing under the quills, nothing among the penknives or empty ink bottles or sticks of sealing wax. No sign of a false bottom to the drawer, not even when I plied my pin to the corners.

"What about the top?" Matthew came up beside me. With a bit of wrestling, I pulled the drawer from its rails and slipped my hand into the narrow space left behind. At the very back, my groping fingers brushed against paper. I scrabbled and pulled gently, coming up with a folded page that had been stuck to the top of the space with sealing wax. I laid this on the desk and reached in again.

In all, I retrieved four letters from Mr. Tinderflint's desk.

"'Walpole.'" I read the name aloud on the first letter. "'Townshend,' 'Southerly,' and 'Sunderland.'" I swallowed. These were the men who ran the kingdom. Who ran the prince and, some said, the king. Mr. Walpole's letter was the heaviest, I noticed.

Unlike grand ladies, maids are allowed pockets in their skirts. I tucked the letters away before I could be tempted to try Mr. Tinderflint's trick with blade and candle flame to find out just what these missives contained.

"There it is, then," said Matthew. "We're done."

"We should go," I told him, but I did not move.

"We should," he agreed, but also did not move.

"We have run more than enough risks tonight."

"And you've found what you were sent for. We have no excuse to look about anymore."

"It would be rude, to say the least," I acknowledged.

"And it might indicate we did not entirely trust all we've been told," he added gently. "By Tinderflint or by anyone else."

On the way here, I'd told Matthew about what had happened in the Tower. Afterward, softly, with many stumbles and much backtracking, I'd told him what I'd come to suspect when I'd lied to my father.

I bit my lip and nodded once. In accord, we turned our backs on each other and set about searching the room.

It was not possible that this place was Mr. Tinderflint's home. This was a meeting place for conspirators. Someone did sometimes spend the night, for there was a broad cot with quilts and pillows and a nightstand beside it with a washbasin on top and a chamber pot (thankfully, clean) underneath. There was a trunk as well, which was not locked. At first it looked to hold nothing more than a few pairs of breeches and some plain shirts and stockings, all of them far too small for my patron. But as I lifted the shirts away, I found another box beneath. Inside that was a pair of pistols, complete with powder horn, a pouch of lead shot, ramrod, and wadding. There was also a leather satchel, which proved to hold a tinderbox, candles, a knife, a pouch with a handful of shillings and pence inside, and, most unexpectedly, a roll of cordage and iron hooks that proved to be a rope ladder.

Whomever Mr. Tinderflint hosted in this room, he believed they might have to leave in something of a hurry, and possibly from an awkward position, such as the rooftop.

"I don't think there's anything here," I called to Matthew as I shut the trunk. I was relieved. I didn't like the fact that we were searching Mr. Tinderflint's rooms, even if it was only a bolthole. "We can go."

But all Matthew said in answer was "Peggy."

There is a lightheaded feeling that comes with the presentiment of danger or doom. It came over me now as I turned toward Matthew. He waited beside the nightstand and gazed into his hands. A fine chain dangled across his fingers, and it glittered gold in the candlelight.

I moved to his side in order to see what so captivated his attention. Matthew cradled a golden locket in his palm. Inside, there was a painted miniature—a portrait of a dark-haired woman. The artist had caught her open smile and the tilt to her head that made her look both merry and knowing. In the other half of the locket lay a curling lock of black hair.

My ears were ringing. My thoughts clamored and shouted, but I could not hear them. I refused to hear them.

A gold ring had been threaded onto the locket's chain.

My hand trembled as I reached to pick it up off Matthew's palm. I turned it over. Slowly. Because I was afraid of what I would see. Because memory had already tried to warn me of what it was.

It was a signet ring, very plain, really, except for being gold. The surface was carved with two intertwined letters: a J and an E.

I knew this ring. My hand remembered the weight and the touch of it. When I had been small, I could fit two of my fingers through it and would hold them up so my mother could laugh. My father wore the ring's twin on a chain around his neck and had somehow, he said, kept it safe through all his years in France, in the Bastille, in the marshes with the Sandfords.

Mr. Tinderflint had my mother's ring. That merry, smiling dark-haired woman in the miniature was Elizabeth Fitzroy. I was eight when she died, but I had not forgotten her face, or her scent of lavender and chamomile, or this ring.

"Wh . . . ?" I choked. "Where did you find this?"

Matthew nodded toward the nightstand. There was a drawer and it was open. There was a box in the drawer and that was open too.

Mr. Tinderflint had my mother's ring, and her portrait, and a lock of her hair, and he kept them at his bedside. There was one very obvious reason a man might keep such tokens in a place where they would not be found even if his own house was searched by his many enemies.

"He . . . he . . . loved her, from a distance. It must have

been from a distance." It was not possible that Mr. Tinder-flint had carried on an assignation with my mother.

It was not possible because my mother would never do such a thing with such a man, especially not while her husband, my father, was away in service. Even if she suspected my father of trading information to anyone who could pay. Even if those suspicions were why she'd used Mrs. Oglethorpe to have him arrested. Jonathan Fitzroy was *her husband*. Other women might do such things. But not my mother, and not with Mr. Tinderflint: old, scheming, rich, untrustworthy, grossly fat, spy and master of spies . . .

She signed her letters Mrs. Tinderflint.

The next thing I knew, I was bent over the washbasin, violently ill.

"Oh, Lord, Peggy." Matthew was there, pushing my braid back from my face, rubbing my shoulders. "It's all right, it's all right."

"It is not all right!" I shouted over the foul taste of my bile. "It cannot possibly be all right! He must have robbed her when she died! He robbed my mother! He robbed me! He lied! He . . . he . . ."

I dissolved into an entirely useless and incoherent storm of tears. Because it was impossible that my mother had made a lover of Mr. Tinderflint. It had to be impossible, because a woman who had a lover . . . might also have a child by him.

Mr. Tinderflint had brought me into his web of spies and

schemes because I was the daughter of Jonathan and Elizabeth Fitzroy, as well as the entirely ignorant and accidental relation of a mass of important Jacobites. He had not, could never have, sought me out because I was the natural daughter of Hugh Thurlow Flintcross Gainsford, Earl Tierney.

CHAPTER TWENTY-SIX

IN WHICH AN ILL-TIMED EVENT OCCURS IN BED,
WITH UNMITIGATED DISASTER TO FOLLOW.

Matthew held me until I was able to stop crying, mostly. He then left me alone while he ran downstairs with a basin to fetch some cool water. I spent an eternity staring at my mother's portrait and ring, trying to believe that the most reasonable explanation for their presence here was that Mr. Tinderflint had stolen them.

He might have spoken tenderly of how much he admired my mother, what an astounding woman she was, of her skills and her intelligence. What of it? That was not him speaking like a man in love. He was a master reminiscing about a valued servant, nothing more. His unprecedented rage at being accused of her murder was because such accusations wounded his aristocratic honor. Any man would respond thus. He had known about me because he kept track of the lives of his spies, and because he was careful, and because it was his business. There was no affinity between us beyond what he had told me from the beginning—that he hoped I had inherited my parents' skills.

She signed her letters *Mrs. Tinderflint.*

No. My mother had not spied against my father. That was a lie Mrs. Oglethorpe told. My mother had not played the lover with Mr. Tinderflint to pass his secrets to the Old Fury. That was not why Lord Lynnfield and Mrs. Oglethorpe had let Sebastian and Sophy lead me to the enciphered letter, which he would accept in perfect trust from my hand.

I knew the truth. The truth was that Mother had fooled Mrs. Oglethorpe so thoroughly that when she came to me, the Old Fury thought she was saving the daughter of a friend. She did not realize my mother had been her cleverest enemy. For their part, the Sandfords had pressed the betrothal because they wanted me safe under their control to use against their banker Uncle Pierpont and keep him in line, or possibly against Jonathan Fitzroy, should he make an appearance. Their plan was not, was never, to use me against Mr. Tinderflint because I was his . . . his . . .

Daughter.

Because I wasn't. I couldn't be.

By the time Matthew returned, I'd dissolved into tears again. He found a rag so I could bathe my face. He uncorked the bottle on the mantel and poured out some of the dark wine to help wash the bitterness from my mouth.

I wrapped my arms around him so tightly, it might have

seemed I meant to press him into my heart and hold him there. He kissed me to help ease my confusion and despair. He laid me back onto the bed, so that we might embrace and kiss and murmur all the things that lovers say when they're alone. We touched and kissed and were both unable and unwilling to stop.

Then it happened. It happened so swiftly and softly I was not able to muster even token resistance: I fell asleep.

I feel I should perhaps apologize to the more worldly among my readers who might have been expecting some coy lines about rising early from my couch much changed, or finding that the maiden's innocent blush had drained from my cheeks. It was not so. The changes that came over me when I woke in Matthew's arms were caused solely by an abrupt plummet into terror, because gray daylight now pressed against the greasy windowpanes and I was not in my right bed.

Matthew stared at me, his eyes wide, his face ashen. "Don't panic," he advised.

"Don't talk nonsense!" I shouted back as I scrambled off the bed and ran to the door. I grabbed the handle to throw it open and cursed as I remembered I'd so intelligently locked the door when we came in. So intent was I on getting myself out, I paid no attention to whether Matthew followed me or not.

I barreled into the coffeehouse, which was empty.

"Help!" I cried. "Help!"

An enormously fat woman heaved herself out of the doorway, knuckling her eyes. "What the hell's that about?" she mumbled.

"I need a coach, a chair, anything. I have to get to St. James, now!"

She blinked and looked me up and down.

"And you've got the money to pay for it, I suppose?"

That was the moment I remembered my maid's costume.

"Of course I have!" I slapped my purse down onto the counter. Unfortunately, Matthew rushed through the door just then and came right up behind me.

The proprietress looked at Matthew and at me. She snickered, but she also shrugged. "Well, since you're paying, I'll see what can be done." She heaved herself back through the doorway, shouting for somebody named either "Tommy" or "You lazy sod!"

I faced Matthew. "No one has missed me yet," I told him firmly. "It's too early. We can be back in time and no one will notice one more maid slipping into the palace."

"Yes," agreed Matthew. "All will be well."

It was a year before the battered cart pulled up in front of the Cocoa Tree. It was a century before we made our way from the crooked streets filled with milkmaids, scissor grinders, ragpickers, and laborers trudging past with hods and shovels into the wider, straighter, cleaner avenues around the palace.

As soon as I spotted the red brick tower over the

gatehouse, I shouted at our slouching driver to stop. I scrambled down from my place on the boards and pressed some coins into his hand. "You're to take the gentleman to Great Queen Street," I said.

My rough appearance was at odds with my educated accents. This caused enough confusion for the driver that first he blinked, and then he bit the coin, testing whether it was genuine.

"Are you sure?" called Matthew to me from the back of the cart. "I could—"

"What? What on earth could having you with me possibly do now?"

He swallowed his reply and instead fished in his pocket. "Peggy . . ." He held out something that glittered in the cold sunlight. It was the locket and ring, of course. I closed my hand around the jewelry, and my throat around my anger and tears. I had important things to do. I would take part in no more violent displays today.

As it turned out, I was entirely mistaken.

Slipping back into the palace proved an almost trivial matter. I yanked my hair free from my cap so it straggled across my face. With my features thus obscured, I made my way across the courtyard at a trot, like a maid late for her post, which I certainly was. Inside, I joined the flow of scullions and washerwomen making their way through the back stairs.

I was a fair way up the steps before I took note of how

so many servants, in livery and out of it, stood in knots on the landings and in the narrow back corridors, talking in low voices. Once I did notice this, my ears pricked up of their own accord and I began to understand the murmur of their conversations.

". . . looks bad, don't it?"

". . . says that fancy man-midwife wouldn't touch her, for all he's English . . ."

". . . already dead . . ."

I stopped in my tracks.

"Who's dead?" I cried. "What's happened?"

Three of them turned to stare at me—a lady's maid, a page, and a footman. They drew themselves up when they saw my cap, loose hair, and rumpled skirts.

"The little prince, o' course," said the page. "Her Highness was taken to bed after the drawing room last night an' it's been a disaster since. Where you been that you ain't heard?"

I snatched at my skirt and bolted up the stairs.

Desperation has been said to clear the mind, and it did mine now. I was able to make my way to the princess's gallery with only one false turn. There were yeomen and footmen on guard, and an entire crowd outside the antechamber. I shouldered my way through them all and shoved the doors open before anyone had a chance to stop me. The antechamber was nearly as crowded as the gallery, with persons of all ranks and distinction. I ignored them and charged through to the inner threshold. The footman there recognized me and, with a wary glance at his companion, opened the second set of doors.

The drawing room beyond was empty, except for Mrs. Howard and Molly Lepell, who stood in hushed conversation. They both whirled around as I ran forward.

"Dear heavens, Peggy, where have you been!" cried Molly. "Everyone was searching for you all last night." Her voice was hoarse; her face was strained.

"I was . . . I was out, on business. I must . . . I have to . . ." I made to run forward.

But Mrs. Howard caught my shoulders. "No, Margaret. Don't. You shouldn't even be here."

"Quite right, Mrs. Howard." The door to the bed-chamber flew open and we all dropped instantly into our curtsies as the Prince of Wales strode toward us. "She should *not* be here."

The next thing I knew, His Royal Highness had clamped one great hand about my arm and was dragging me toward the antechamber. Mrs. Howard and Molly stared in shock and bewilderment and did not move an inch. The footmen stared as well, but they opened the doors.

"Out!" bellowed the prince to the assemblage in the antechamber. "Out, all of you!"

He was hurting me. His voice shook with rage. The persons murmured and bowed and the footmen threw open the doors and started herding them all out. Prince George did not let go of me until the doors were shut in both directions.

The slam of the doors was still reverberating when His Royal Highness whirled me around to face him and grabbed both my shoulders.

"You little *slut!*" he shouted in German, each word accompanied by a violent shake. "She trusted you! I trusted you! We allow you the run of our home and the friendship of our daughter, and this—*this*—is how you repay us!"

I tried to drop into a curtsy. I couldn't. He wouldn't let go. "Please, Your Highness, there is an explanation . . ."

"Explain! Explain how you were cavorting with your man while . . ." He choked on the words. "My son is dead," he whispered, his voice cold and sharp as winter steel. "My wife is broken almost past endurance, and you have the gall to come here with your *explanations.*" He pulled me closer. He smelled of sweat and brandy and the sour, sweet odor that comes from fear. "You will get out of my house," he hissed. "You and that sneaking cousin of yours, you will never enter here again!"

He shoved me away. I stumbled and my heel caught my skirt and I fell. The prince did not move. The footmen who had witnessed the scene did not move. I couldn't breathe. My arm hurt. I crawled to my knees and made myself stand. Trembling, I curtsied.

I heard the prince curse me and turn on his heel to snap his orders to the footmen as he marched away.

I straightened and stared, numb with disbelief, at the men by the door. One of them smirked. The other had a look of something close to pity. He was the one who opened the door for me.

The crowd might have been cleared from the antechamber, but the gallery outside was still brimming with the great and the near great. They had all heard the Prince of Wales shouting at me. Those who understood German had heard him order me out of the palace.

Some of them looked bewildered. Some of them smiled. A very few of them drew back so I would not touch them as I passed.

I made my way back to my own rooms only through a combination of blind luck and habit. I certainly was not watching my way. My heart hammered. My arm ached. I stumbled and stumbled again.

While I had spent my night thinking my mother had been unfaithful with Mr. Tinderflint, the prince thought I'd been having a tryst with Matthew. The princess must have thought the same. Her babe, the little prince, was dead. My mistress, who had been so kind to me, was ill, maybe dying, and they thought I'd abandoned my post for the sake of the lowest form of assignation.

I had reached my door. I could see it, but I couldn't make myself open it. I couldn't raise my arm.

"Peggy?" It was Olivia. She had come up behind me and I

hadn't even noticed. Molly was there too, I realized distract-edly. "Come along, Peggy—let's get you inside."

Olivia opened the door, and she and Molly moved me gently forward.

"Miss!" cried Libby at once. "Where have you been! You were sent for and—"

"She knows, Libby," said Molly quietly. "You should go now."

"Yes, miss."

I didn't see Libby leave. I couldn't turn my head. I blindly groped for the nearest hand. It was Olivia's.

"Here, Peggy, sit down," she murmured.

I ignored this. "What happened?" I cried. "Tell me what happened!"

"Not until you sit down." My cousin pushed me onto the stool. "Molly knows the whole of it, don't you, Molly?"

Molly first went to the door and shot home the bolt. I was so cold. Isolde nosed about my slippers, whining with more than her usual concern.

"It was horrible, Peggy, the whole affair . . . terrible." Molly spoke at a whisper, her face as pale as I had ever seen it. Her cosmetics were streaked and smudged, and the dark circles under her eyes spoke eloquently of having been awake all the night. "The princess's labors began after she left the drawing room. You know Their Highnesses had brought in a notable midwife, a German?" I nodded. "Well, there were some among the bedchamber ladies who wanted an English physician instead of a German woman, and both were sum-moned." Her face turned whiter. "But none could agree who should go to her. All fell to arguing, and there is the princess screaming in her pains, and the prince holding her hand."

"He was there!" I cried, shocked. There was normally no room for any man other than a physician or a priest in a birth-ing chamber.

"He never left her side. There were I don't know how many persons all arguing with Her Highness in favor of the Englishman, but the prince was bellowing for the German, and the princess was crying out, probably for the German but nobody could understand her. The Englishman was so offended by someone else even having been considered to at-tend her that he stomped off, and they wasted all sorts of time trying to persuade him to come back." She paused and touched her throat. "You can't imagine the confusion. There's the prince yelling orders in German and bad French, and no one can properly understand." She paused again. "Her High-ness called for you, Peg."

"Why? I know nothing about birthing . . ."

"You speak English and French *and* German well," said Olivia quietly. "They needed someone who could make all things understood."

"There are others, surely . . ."

"But you were the one who was wanted," said Olivia. "And you weren't there."

No. Quite right. I was not there. I had promised Her Royal Highness I would be, and I had failed.

"Maybe if the babe had lived, it would not be quite so bad," said Molly. "But after all the struggles . . . no one can say what caused it, of course, but . . ."

Stillborn. She didn't have to say it. The babe had been stillborn. And I had been wanted and I was not there. I closed my eyes. I tried to feel something beyond the numbing confusion. Anger rose to the surface first.

"Who was it who told them I was with Matthew?" I demanded. "It was the Howe, wasn't it? She came back and she told them . . ."

Olivia laid her hand on my arm. "No, Peggy. It wasn't Sophy this time. No one's seen her. It was Lady Portland."

Lady Portland was Princess Anne's governess, the one who had never liked me, even before I saddled her particular corner of the household with a flock of spoiled dogs. With her cold and scornful glances, she had promised to do me an injury if she could. I'd ignored her, as careless as Mary Bellenden, because I thought she had no power over me.

But in the end, it didn't matter who had tattled about where I was. My reputation rested on how well the princess believed I performed my duties, and the princess believed she had proof of indifference and betrayal. Therefore, I was dismissed. I was alone. I was just Margaret Preston Fitzroy once again.

Just Margaret Preston Fitzroy, who might well be the illegitimate daughter of an earl. Just Margaret, whose supposed father might be selling France's secrets to England, as well as England's secrets to France.

Just Margaret, who happened to know that Great Britain faced invasion from the Pretender and his allies.

Just Margaret, for whom one single fact was abundantly plain—she was now in more trouble than she had ever been in the whole of her eventful career.

CHAPTER TWENTY-SEVEN

IN WHICH CONFUSIONS OVER
THE MOTIVES OF MEN MAY BE SHOWN
TO DRIVE OUR HEROINE TO EXTREMES.

No one came to see us leave. Libby, stunned as I had ever seen her, said she would pack the rest of our things and see them delivered safely. Molly promised to help. But no one came close once Olivia and I walked out into the yard, not even Molly or Mrs. Howard. Especially not Libby, who must now decide what to do for her living.

Plenty of persons did watch us from the safety of windows and doorways. Despite their distance, I felt the currents of gossip swirling about as Olivia and I climbed into our coach.

I wasn't surprised, nor did I blame them. With the calamity of the royal birth so close on the heels of Mr. Tinderflint's arrest, I also would have stayed away, if given the choice. And I would have talked. I would have talked endlessly.

I did give Libby a letter to put into Mrs. Howard's hands. Addressed to Her Royal Highness, it was as abject and sincere an apology as I was capable of composing. It also contained the genuine, although unprovable, explanation for my absence. The princess would surely have any number of sardonic words to say about it, assuming she read it.

"It will work out," said Olivia as she latched the coach door and the driver touched up the horses. "We will make it right."

I didn't answer her, not then, nor all the long, weary drive back to my father's house. I could barely manage to respond to Isolde when she crawled out of her traveling basket and began nosing about under things looking for her biscuits.

Father met us at the house steps and helped me down from the coach. He held his questions until we got inside, but once the door closed behind us, he turned loose the flood.

I shook them all off.

"Olivia will tell you," I said as I pushed Isolde's basket into her hands. "I need to be alone."

Suiting actions to words, I retreated upstairs. I locked my door, lay down full length on my bed, and didn't move.

How long this lasted, I don't know, but it was some hours. Olivia knocked and called once. Father knocked and called some time after that. I lay on the bed and blinked at the lace canopy. It is possible that I slept, but I do not remember. If thoughts passed through my empty mind, I cannot recall them.

A third knock sounded. "Peggy? Please, won't you come out? Everyone is worried about you."

It was Matthew. I closed my eyes. They'd sent for Matthew to use against me.

And it worked. Of course it worked. When had I ever been able to tell him no? I got up from the bed, undid the lock, and opened the door.

He'd left the academy in such a hurry, he hadn't taken time to pull on his coat. He stood there in his paint-stained shirtsleeves, stray locks of dark red hair straggling about his ears and cheeks. I thought he would try to reach out to me, but he didn't. We just met each other's gazes in silence for a long moment, each on our own side of the threshold.

I stepped back and turned to let him follow me into the room if he chose. He understood the gesture, accepted it, and closed the door behind himself. We stood there, and it was maddeningly awkward. While it might be true we had been alone under many odd circumstances, it had never been in my personal chamber, in my father's house, with my father downstairs. It was, in fact, as improper a situation as could be imagined. The first and last rule of behavior for an unmarried young lady is to never, under any circumstances, be alone in a room with any man who might even vaguely be considered a potential paramour.

I sat in the chair by the window, which was about as

far away as I could get from him and still be in the room. Matthew didn't move. "Please sit down," I said.

Matthew perched on the very edge of a plain wooden chair by the hearth. Under other circumstances, I might have smiled to see my bold gallant turn so suddenly puppyish.

When he spoke, his voice and words were entirely those of the man I loved. "Tell me how I can help, Peggy Mostly."

I rubbed my hands together. When was the last time I had felt warm? I considered crossing the room in order to better collapse into his arms. But I didn't move. And yet, neither could I stand this distance. I had to do something.

"Tell me about your mother," I said distractedly. "We've never talked about her. Does she yet live?"

Matthew chuckled, just a little. "The day my mother dies is the day the devil shows up with a shovel to knock her over the head. And even then she'd probably just grab it out of his hands and slap the horns off his scalp."

"Matthew!"

"I'm sorry, but it's true. You've never met a woman made of sterner stuff. She's about this tall." He held his hand by his chin. "And not one of us ever dares talk back in her presence. Her house is neat as a pin, her children know their place, and my father adores her. It also happens that we're all so terrified of her that we'd sooner emigrate to the colonies than face her down. Oh, and she's only got one eye."

"Now you're making things up."

"I am not. There was a runaway horse in front of my father's shop one day, and my little brother bolted out to see.

She snatched him back just before he could be trampled, but one of the horses kicked up a cobble and it slammed against her right eye. She lay insensible for two days. My father was out of his mind. He tried everything he knew but nothing helped. Then, on the third day, she just woke up as if nothing had happened and got back to her work." He paused. "My brother says she didn't actually lose the eye. He says it flew up to Heaven and now she's got the same view as God and the angels and that's why you can't ever fool her."

"I think I'd like your mother."

"I'm glad. She'd like you." He smiled the smile that never failed to set my heart racing. I had felt dead, or as good as, but it seemed all I had to do was meet Matthew's gaze and I not only lived, but I wanted to keep on living.

"You need to come downstairs, Peggy Mostly," he said. "Olivia's driving us all to distraction. She's started planning how we'll break into the Tower and smuggle Mr. Tinderflint out through the water gate."

"Actually," called Olivia's voice, "she's on the other side of this door listening to your private conversation. Can I come in? Otherwise I'm going to drop this blessedly heavy tray and Isolde's going to eat all the food I've brought. Oh, and Uncle Fitzroy's going to lose what hold he's got on his patience and come up here with a meat cleaver or something."

I laughed and Matthew laughed, because what else was to be done? I got up and opened the door. Olivia, accompanied by an imperious and vocal Isolde, marched into the room carrying a silver tray loaded with roast beef and bread and a pitcher of small beer, not to mention all the necessary dishes, napkins, and cutlery. My cousin deposited the tray on the spindle-leg table, which wobbled under the weight.

"You"—she slapped beef on bread and handed it to me —"eat that. You," she said to Matthew, "tell me what happened when you went to the Cocoa Tree. You"—she dropped a large lump of beef on the floor beside the door, which she had, incidentally, left open a crack—"tell us if anyone comes." Isolde plumped herself down and began to feast on that good English beef as fiercely as any wolf on its kill. "Now, I don't suppose, of course, that you two really—"

"No!" cried Matthew at the same time I cried, "What do you take me for?"

"A girl with breath in her body and eyes in her head," Olivia replied calmly as she settled on the bed with her own plate of food. "If that wasn't what kept you away all night, then what was it?"

I bit my lip. My spell of solitude in combination with Matthew's presence had been enough for sense and spirit to reassert themselves. Heaven knows I did not want them. My sense and spirit seemed to do little more than drive me from one disaster to the next. At the same time, if I simply refused to tell her, Olivia would niggle and nag and harp and press until I shouted the truth from the rooftops.

Fortunately, at that moment, my cousin didn't care which of us talked, as long as somebody did. So while I nibbled beef and bread, Matthew did his best to explain all I had told him about my conversation with Mr. Tinderflint in the Tower. Then he told her about the bolthole room and what we had found there.

We came to the locket and the ring and I waited for Olivia's exclamations. I hoped for her to assemble one of her mad chains of dramatic logic, because it would be another way to not believe.

Instead, my cousin burst out laughing.

"Oh!" She held her sides. "Oh, oh, oh, you two! You imbeciles!"

"What?" I demanded. "What else could it mean when a man keeps a woman's tokens beside his bed!"

"Good heavens, Peggy, Mr. Tinderflint doesn't even *like* women!"

"What?"

"I mean, he likes women, clearly. He likes you and me and the princess. He probably liked your mother well enough, but not *like* as in like to take to bed." I must have looked very confused, because Olivia shook her head at me. "Didn't you ever find it strange that he's not married? That he has no children? He's one of *those* men, the ones who prefer men."

Matthew turned his face away, quickly. I wasn't supposed to know what Olivia was talking about, of course, but everyone did, if only to know it was a sin and a crime. I also wasn't supposed to know that there were any number of men at the court devoted to that particular sin and crime. I'd played cards with more than a few of them and was always glad to do so. They were much more polite, at least with us maids, than the sort generally reckoned to be morally upright.

But she was right. I never had thought Mr. Tinderflint might be one of them. Now I seized the idea.

"But what of the rest of it?" I asked her. "What of Father, and the money?" What of the letters and Mrs. Oglethorpe's lies?

Olivia glanced toward the doorway. "Peg. I've made a discovery. I know that I should have told you before, but . . ."

Outside, the floorboards creaked. Isolde leapt to her feet, barking her tiny heart out. "Peg," called my father. "Would you please call off your hound?"

Olivia blanched. Matthew slapped his hand over his mouth to stifle a curse. I swallowed all similar feeling and went to get Isolde. I set her, and a bit of bread sopped in beef juice, under my napkin on my lap. Thus freed from all danger of attack, Father pushed the door open.

"Olivia and Matthew told me something of what happened." He entered the room to drop a kiss on my forehead. "I am truly sorry, Peg. I just wanted to be certain you were all right. All of you." It was not my imagination that told me he spoke these last words to Olivia.

He did not, I noticed, launch into any conventional railings about my disgrace or lost honor. Not that I had any honor, really. In that, I seemed to be but once more following the family tradition.

How was I going to tell him about the ring and locket? He couldn't know, could he?

The nausea that had overtaken me in Mr. Tinderflint's rooms threatened again, and my stomach cramped painfully. While I might have been somewhat recovered, I still lacked the strength to keep the worst of my thoughts at bay. It was common knowledge that men sometimes killed their wives when they found them unfaithful. What if Mrs. Oglethorpe had been a little bit right? What if my mother had been murdered and Mrs. Oglethorpe had just been mistaken about whose hand had done the deed?

It was impossible, of course. Father had been in the Bastille at the time. At least, he said he had. Except that if he was really selling secrets to both Hanoverians and Jacobites, that tale of arrest and imprisonment might have been another lie. He might have been having himself and his contraband smuggled back and forth across the channel and—

Smuggled. My thoughts halted in their tracks. *Smuggled.*

I looked again at the rich, tasteful furnishings of my room. I looked at my father. He'd changed from his coachman's costume and once more wore the lace and velvet of a prosperous gentleman.

"Are you all right, Peg?" Father asked. "You've gone white as that dog of yours."

I swallowed hard. "I'm better," I told him honestly. "'All right' may take a while yet."

"I understand."

I met his gaze but couldn't hold it. My emotions were too raw and my doubts too grave for me to keep that much control.

Father sighed. "I must go out for an hour or two," he said. "There are people I need to speak to, if they'll still speak to me." He paused until he was sure he had our attention. "If things are as bad as they look—if there really is an invasion coming—we may all need to quickly get ourselves to safety. That includes you, Matthew. I want to have arrangements in place." He paused again and laid his hand on my shoulder. "No arguments, Peg," he said. "I've seen war and you haven't. I will not leave you in the path of it."

"I'm not arguing," I told him. "I've got no arguments left in me. Only, please, don't vanish again."

He smiled. "I'll do my best, as long as you promise you'll still be here when I get back."

I promised, and he bowed to us all and left us there. We waited, each of us examining the mantelpiece, the remains of the beef on the tray, the way the napkin in my lap shifted as Isolde underneath tried to find a more comfortable place to curl up. We, in fact, looked at anything and everything except one another, until we heard the door close downstairs.

Olivia sprang up and ran to the window. I heard the thud of horses' hooves against the dirt road. "He's gone," she said.

"You think he was using the Sandfords' smuggling men to get secrets out of France, don't you?" said Matthew.

How very well my sweetheart had come to know me. "Or into it, yes. I think . . . it's possible he might be a double agent, in the pay of both sides."

I waited for them to contradict me. Matthew's face went

hard and grim and he folded his arms. I could not guess his thoughts in that moment and found I did not want to. Olivia, for her part, grew as grave as I have ever seen her.

"Dear heavens, Peggy," she breathed. "I'm sorry. You just found him again, too."

"Wait," said Matthew. "Olivia, before this, you said you'd made a discovery. What was it?"

But my cousin only shook her head. "I'll explain afterward. If Peggy's right, then there's going to be nothing to tell."

I was not happy about this answer, but time was short in the extreme. Father had gifted us with only a brace of hours, and there were plans to make. Carefully. Quietly. We could not forget that this was his house and the servants were in his employ. I didn't even have Libby to call upon here.

"What will you do?" asked Matthew with remarkable calm. "There are still Mr. Tinderflint's letters, on top of everything else. Will you send them?"

"I will, but not to Mr. Townshend or anybody else." I took a deep breath. "I'm going to send them to Mrs. Oglethorpe. It will be a sign of good faith when I ask her to help me escape my father's clutches."

CHAPTER TWENTY-EIGHT

IN WHICH OUR HEROINE MAKES
HER ESCAPE, BUT NOT QUITE UNDER
THE CIRCUMSTANCES SHE PLANNED.

As I made my bold declaration, I steeled myself for a lengthy exchange, most probably involving attempts on the parts of both Olivia and Matthew to ascertain the current health of my mental faculties.

Much to my surprise, however, Olivia's first question dealt entirely with practical matters.

"Is there time to get the Oglethorpe a message? Uncle Fitzroy said he'd be gone only an hour or two. He tends to be overly optimistic about such things, but considering the circumstances, I don't think he'll leave you alone for long."

"Not on purpose, anyway," added Matthew. "Can a message wait until tomorrow?"

Were they agreeing with me? Shock robbed me of my voice for a good long moment. But at last, I was able to force both mind and mouth into action. "There's no knowing what plans Father will have made by tomorrow." We also couldn't know what plans the Oglethorpes and the Sandfords already had in place. Allowing those to advance undisturbed did not seem at all prudent. "We must make our move tonight."

"So you're going to escape under the nose of a double agent?" Matthew cocked his head toward us. "With the help of a woman he's declared to be his enemy?"

"Not ideal circumstances, I admit." I dug into my desk drawer for pen, ink, and paper. I also pulled the paper Mrs. Oglethorpe had given me out of the bottom of my reticule. "Matthew, I think we may need to call on some of that experience you've gained helping in your father's apothecary shop . . ."

A gleam showed in his gray eyes. "You're about to ask me if I can mix a sleeping draft, aren't you?"

I smiled over my shoulder at him. "However did you guess, Mr. Reade?"

Matthew's pause was a long one and caused me all sorts of misgivings. He drew a deep breath. "I will do this under one condition: whatever we learn, wherever it may lead, at the first opportunity, word goes back to Their Royal Highnesses, and no one else."

"If I can—" I began, but Matthew cut me off.

"No. That is what will happen. They are the only ones whose loyalties we can be sure of."

"They're loyal to themselves," said Olivia.

"And to their children. Exactly," said Matthew. "We

know that. It's almost the only thing we do know. Do I have a promise? From you both?"

I nodded my agreement and Olivia sighed and said, "Very well—we promise, and we'd better get started."

I am pleased to be able to report that once committed to the task at hand, we three proved remarkably efficient. Matthew at once took himself off to the nearest apothecary's shop to have the recipe for his father's strongest sleeping draft made up. Olivia and I set ourselves to writing a suitably hysterical letter for Mrs. Oglethorpe.

We detailed certain threatening and entirely fictitious things my patron had said when I supposedly confronted him with the lies he'd told about my mother's life. We further declared that when my father learned I had lost my valuable position with the Hanoverians, he flew into a towering rage.

"'And now I fear for my very life!'" Olivia said. "Is that an *a* or an *e*?" She pointed. "Peggy, your handwriting hasn't gotten any better."

"I write with perfect clarity. And isn't fearing for my life coming on a bit strong?"

Olivia turned toward me, eyebrows raised to their limit. I put up my hands. "You're right. I should not even have brought it up." I wrote what I was told, being sure to add extra flourishes to the *e*'s.

From there, we went on to detail my complete conversion to the Jacobite cause and to say that I had been entrusted with several letters by my patron, which I now enclosed because I didn't know what else to do with them, and I was certain that she, Mrs. Oglethorpe, would be a better judge of what they contained. The Old Fury had already demonstrated that she believed me to be a little fool. This action would in no way strain her credulity.

Our letter concluded with my begging her to send some trusted person to my aid, for my father was even now making arrangements to spirit me away to I knew not where.

This last was as close to the truth as we came in the entire narrative.

When Matthew returned, we proudly showed him our effort. As he read it, he frowned, and I felt all manner of second thoughts rise to the surface. Olivia visibly gathered herself to answer whatever objections he might have as to the tone and content of our missive. But Matthew just went over to the water pitcher, dipped his fingers in, and shook out the droplets over the paper.

"Tears," he said. Then he carefully ran his thumb across several words to smudge them lightly and shook one large blot of ink from my quill. "Distress." He also crumpled one edge of the paper. "Uncertainty."

There are, it seems, many advantages to involving an artist when committing any sort of fraud to paper.

Once these additions were dry, I folded the missive around Mr. Tinderflint's letters.

"I still say we should read them first," muttered Olivia.

"This is not the time to find out how bad we are at unsealing letters," I told her as I set my own seal to the packet. "You should have thought to give it some practice."

"You should have thought to give us an extra s'en day before letting slip this level of disaster," she answered righteously. "I would have been perfect by then."

I ignored this and wrote "Mrs. Righthandwall" on the packet, making sure my hand shook. It did not take a great deal of effort. Then I handed the packet to Matthew.

"Are you sure about this?" he asked.

I nodded. This was no longer merely about spies and thrones and invasions. This was about me—that same Margaret Fitzroy who had learned too much and not enough and had unwittingly claimed attention for so many busy persons. This was about finding out the truth of who I was and where I came from, so that no one—be he Jacobite, Hanoverian, or Holy Roman Emperor—would ever again be able to use my name and family against me.

One glance at Matthew was enough to show me he understood all this and more. His own hand was entirely steady as he took the packet and stowed it safely away.

Despite Matthew's and Olivia's cogent reasoning on the subject, I admit to being surprised when Father returned after only two and a half hours. Darkness had settled in by then, and the clock had chimed half nine. He stumped into the parlor somewhat mud-spattered and quite rumpled, and without bothering to remove his spurs or boots. I sat by the fire, pretending to read. Isolde sat at my feet, pretending to be a civilized creature. Being so overfed on roast beef that she could barely move contributed greatly to the success of this performance.

I got to my feet and made my curtsy as Father came in. He grunted, trudged past me, and threw himself down into a chair.

"That," I remarked, "does not sound like your business met with a successful conclusion."

"No." He swept his hat off and tossed it across to the sofa. "At least, not entirely. Everybody's watching to see which way the wind blows. Is this supper?" He eyed the loaded tray on the marquetry table.

"Certainly. Let me fix you a plate while you take off your boots."

That drew a tired chuckle. "Going to be my civilizing influence, are you, Peg?"

"I was always told it is maiden's chief function." I laid beef on bread and cut a large slice of ripe golden cheese. We'd told the cook that no dinner would be required and instead brought into the parlor the remains of the roast beef and bread that had played such a central part in my own revival. Cook, torn between being angry that her talents were not being more regularly employed and concerned that her charges might be going without adequate nourishment, sent up a large wedge of cheese, some pickles, and a walnut cake to complete the collation. She'd also refilled the pitcher of beer.

My hand had been shaking rather more than it should

have when I'd poured Matthew's sleeping draft into the beer. It shook again now that I poured the beer from the pitcher into a tankard. I hoped I had angled myself properly to keep Father from seeing.

"Your mother," he said, "assured me maiden's chief function was keeping man from believing all the mighty things he said about himself."

"And how is that different?"

Father barked out another laugh. I wished I hadn't started joking. I didn't want to laugh with him or be in any way comfortable. What I was about to do would be much easier if he remained surly or even growled an insult. As it was, he took the food and drink I held out and set them on the table at his elbow. He had, I noticed, taken off his boots.

By way of being companionable, I helped myself to walnut cake I did not want. At Olivia's advising I had already placed a tankard full of beer by my own chair, so that it would not look strange when I did not pour myself any fresh.

"Where's our Mr. Reade?" Father mumbled around a large mouthful of beef and bread.

"He had to go back to the academy. He's still an apprentice, after all."

"Yes, of course. He's a good fellow. Steady in the face of . . . well, us. I like him."

"I'm glad."

"Will Olivia be joining us?" Father gestured toward the door with his food.

"She's upstairs, writing to her mother. I thought we should let her be." In truth, she was packing for our separate clandestine departures. Leaving her this task had caused me a certain amount of consternation. I knew how Olivia packed. However, I could not both be there, loading hand luggage, and here, drugging my father.

I poked my fork into my cake. "Have you heard anything from Aunt Pierpont yet?"

Father shook his head and took a bite of cheese. The tankard remained untouched on the table. I did not stare at it, exactly, but I did take a certain uneasy notice. "I've written her people in Colchester. If all is well, we'll hear from them tomorrow or the next day."

"And if it isn't?" I poked my cake again.

"I'll think of something else." He paused and bit into one of the pickles. "Are you going to eat that cake, Peg, or dismember it?"

I set the cake aside and picked up my tankard. Although my throat actively rebelled against the action, I forced myself to take a swallow. Had Father drunk anything while my eyes were riveted on my plate? I could not tell.

"You don't really believe Aunt Pierpont's involved with the Jacobites?" I said, hoping any tension in my voice would be thought to come from the subject, rather than the strain of not staring at his tankard.

"Two weeks ago, I would have laughed at the idea." Father bit into a fresh slice of bread. "Now I cannot say what she might be involved in." He picked up his tankard. My breath stopped. He stared moodily at the contents. "I've begun to think I've been wrong about everything from the start."

"Yes," I whispered. "I understand."

"I rather imagine you do." He set the tankard down. I suppressed an urge to scream. "I would change things if I could."

"So would I."

"And Tierney would as well, I expect." The corner of his mouth twitched. "So here we all are, wishing things were different, but with no way to make that difference. Should we curse fate? Or blame our own frail selves for our faults?"

"I could not begin to say," I answered, which was surprisingly close to the truth.

"No. Neither can I."

A dozen tensions and contradictions knotted themselves up inside me. I did not want this comfortable, sympathetic conversation. I was angry and I was frightened and I doubted myself as badly as I doubted this man sitting with me.

"If . . ." I began hesitantly, "if I asked you where you went tonight, would you tell me?"

"I might," he said. "But then I might be lying about it all again. That's what worries you, isn't it?"

The question hit me hard, but not so hard as his eyes as they looked at me, and through me.

"Should I deny it?" I answered back.

"I'd rather you didn't." He shook his head. "I could list a

few names, some of which are genuine. Some are cant names of certain low persons involved in making sure . . . things . . . get where they're meant to go."

"Smugglers."

He shrugged. "Almost everyone smuggles something now and again, Peg. It's one of the truths of life if you're a sailor or a carter. The only question is what you personally decide you'll take on and what you won't."

I made no answer. I understood better than I wanted to.

Father didn't seem to notice. "I'm not going to tell you these names, though, because neither of us knows what will happen next, and the less you know, the less you can give away."

"I'm not a spy anymore," I reminded him.

"Of course not," he said softly. "But not everyone is going to take your word on that."

He was still looking through me, waiting for me to make some answer. I wanted to, but my wit had for once deserted me. Father shrugged.

"Welladay. I suppose there's nothing for it in the end but to trust each other." He contemplated the tankard again and lifted it to his mouth. Then lowered it. "And since we're trusting, you might tell me what it is I'm drinking here, Peg."

CHAPTER TWENTY-NINE

IN WHICH OUR HEROINE FINDS SOME LITTLE
OPPORTUNITY TO MEDITATE UPON OLD SAYINGS
REGARDING FRYING PANS AND FIRES.

I should perhaps have been violently shocked at this question and its implicit revelation that I had entirely failed to dupe my father. As it was, I felt only a certain weary acceptance.

"It's a sleeping draft," I told him. "A strong one."

He nodded, sniffed, and nodded again. "I would have chosen an emetic myself. Nothing so distracts a man as vomiting his guts out for a few hours, and it leaves him less suspicious afterward." He swirled the tankard gently. "Can I ask why?"

"Can I ask how you've become so suddenly wealthy, sir?" I replied. My voice was hoarse. I was glad I'd put my plate down, because I otherwise would have dropped it.

"And please, don't try any more tales about money left with friends."

His mouth twitched. "Oh, Peg, you are so very like your mother. I should have . . ." He sighed. I did not permit my gaze to waver. If he was readying yet another lie, I wanted to see his face.

"I stole it," he said.

"What?"

He smiled at my slack jaw and furrowed brow. "The idea came to me when you were still sleeping, after we'd pulled ourselves out of the Thames and were safe. I watched you, you know. I saw what a fine lady you were, and here I returned all but a pauper. I couldn't help thinking about all that silver coin Sir Oliver had been hiding in his warehouse, and how it would now be sitting there with barely any guard."

"You stole a barrel of silver?"

He smiled with becoming modesty. "Ten of them, actually. I was able to borrow a very stout cart. And d'you know, I think the Crown should pay the harbor watchmen better. Far too easy to bribe them."

"Mr. Tinderflint helped you, didn't he?"

"Actually, he knows nothing about it. That money, you see, technically belongs to the Crown, and I didn't wish to create any further awkwardness for my daughter's friend."

Friend. The word twisted around all my suspicions and squeezed. I shook this off, but only because a separate, slow realization had crept into my thoughts. "Olivia found you out, didn't she?" A smugglers' tunnel full of stolen silver. My cousin, with her love of all things theatrical, must have been in ecstasies.

"I swore her to secrecy. But apparently, since the funeral, your cousin's been searching the house from top to bottom. Remind me not to leave any more trapdoors open when she's about. "

"Ah. That was a serious mistake on your part."

"So I understand." He sighed again. "Well, what now, Peg? I'm assuming you've already made plans of your own?" He hoisted the doctored tankard again.

I looked away. I sat in silence for a long moment to let my swirling thoughts settle. Then I told him. It did not take long, since he'd already heard most of what had passed between myself and the Old Fury when she and I were last together.

When I finished, he nodded thoughtfully. "A good idea. It has every chance of success."

"You . . . you're not going to try to talk us out of it?"

He smiled. "Actually, I was planning on going along with it. It's the best plan I've heard in the past few days, and that includes any number I've come up with myself." I quite honestly didn't know whether to be flattered or appalled by this statement. Was there ever such a father as mine? I had no time to decide, because my father lifted his tankard to his mouth and swallowed the entire contents in a single draft.

"You . . . I . . . you didn't have to drink that," I stammered. "It was only to keep you from interfering."

"Verisimilitude," he said as he slapped the tankard down. "You might be quizzed about your preparations. You need to be able to say you saw me take the whole of your potion." He belched.

Pride threatened. "I am an accomplished liar, you know."

"I do, but you'll be doing enough of that. Trust me, it's better if you can tell plenty of truths among the lies. But it would probably be useful if you spoke a word on my behalf to Olivia." He gave a prodigious yawn. "Now, I seem to be mightily tired and should get myself upstairs. Verisimilitude," he added as he got to his feet, and he staggered a moment before he crossed to me. He kissed my cheek and murmured in my ear, "Good luck, Pretty Peggy-O."

I watched him leave, regret and fear together closing around my thoughts.

Staying awake while an entire household around you is preparing for sleep is no mean feat. I'm not at all sure I could have managed it without Olivia. She was full of ideas as to how to arrange my traveling box, Isolde's basket, and my clothing. We even had a long argument about whether to take me out the front door or try the smugglers' tunnel now that I told her I knew that Father was using it as his private bank vault.

I did exact a promise that when Matthew came to get her, she would leave by the servants' entrance. Someone belonging to the Oglethorpe might stay to watch the house. If it appeared we knew too much about my father's secrets, it might destroy the façade of naiveté I was counting on to help protect me in Mrs. Oglethorpe's company.

Olivia was mollified by being allowed to change back into her Orlando Preston costume. Our plan, such as it was, was for Olivia and Matthew to ride to Godalming, the town nearest the Oglethorpes' home of Westbrook. There, they would take rooms at an inn. We would then find some way to establish contact with one another, and I would pass to them all I learned from the Oglethorpes.

This was a far less specific course of action than I was happy with, but it was the best any of us could do.

Matthew returned once. He brought the satchel he'd retrieved from Mr. Tinderflint's bolthole. I reasoned that my patron kept those rooms stocked for his spies, and so I was perfectly justified in making use of what he left there.

Matthew also brought a letter written in a firm and feminine hand. It was sealed with plain blue wax and admirably brief.

The coach will be harnessed by grays. Three of the clock.
E.O.

"How did she seem? What did you make of her?" demanded Olivia, but Matthew just shook his head.

"It seems Mrs. Oglethorpe does not see mere messengers. The letters were taken in to her, the reply was brought out, and I was told to hurry off. Oh, and I was given a shilling for my pains." He produced the coin. "I think it's genuine."

After that, there was nothing to do but wait. I'm afraid I made rather a poor job of it. Between my jumping at shadows and Isolde's insistence on checking each cubby and corner for either biscuits or threats, I resembled nothing so much as a complete near hysteric by the time we carried my trunk down to the front hall.

"Don't worry," whispered Olivia. "The more flustered you look, the more she'll believe your conversion to be genuine. Good luck." She kissed my cheek. "Matthew and I will be at Godalming tomorrow at the latest." Matthew was not with us anymore. He had left to hire a cart and horses for the journey. Coming from the family he did, Matthew had learned to drive a team but not to ride. Because Uncle Pierpont's beliefs about education for girls had not extended toward familiarity with managing equines, Olivia could do neither.

"You will remember to leave a message for Father?" I asked in a final burst of nerves. If I ever saw Aunt Pierpont again, I would have to apologize for never taking her attacks seriously.

"You may depend on it."

I grabbed the handle of my distressingly heavy trunk with one hand and dragged it out the front door. Isolde's basket swung on my other arm, much to my puppy's distress.

At this hour, no light showed in any window. The rutted road remained empty and silent. There was neither sight nor sound of any coach, harnessed by grays or otherwise.

Had it been a ruse? No. That was not possible. What could be the purpose of leaving me standing like a jilted girl looking for her suitor? I tried to compose myself to patience, but that lasted only a handful of heartbeats.

If she wasn't here, what was Mrs. Oglethorpe doing? I glanced back toward the house. The only light showing was in Olivia's window. Of course my cousin was keeping watch. I bit my lip. What if that light had made the Old Fury suspicious? What if she thought it was my father?

A shadow moved beyond the house's corner. It was gone in an instant. I reached into the basket where Isolde dozed and rubbed her ears until she stirred.

Then I heard it—the soft thump of hooves and the creak and jingle of an approaching coach. I couldn't see it clearly, but it seemed to be that same small black conveyance I had seen before, and the horses were indeed matched grays.

The coach came to a halt, and the door swung slowly open.

"It's all right, Margaret," said a voice behind my shoulder. "You're safe now."

Before I could scream, a gloved hand clapped over my mouth. I was turned firmly to see a woman's sharp face peering out from under the hood of a quite ordinary traveling cloak.

"Mrs. Oglethorpe," I mumbled against the glove.

She nodded and grabbed my arm to hustle me across to the coach. She did take her hand off my mouth. This enabled me to squeak.

"My things . . ."

"Yes, yes." She signaled to the boy at the back of the coach but did not pause in the process of bundling me inside. The boy jumped down to grab my box and toss it up to the driver. I had barely found my seat before Mrs. Oglethorpe pounded on the coach ceiling. "Drive on!"

There was a crack of a whip and a shout and the coach lurched into motion. I grabbed the railing as we bounced across the ruts, gathering speed.

"I'm sorry for startling you, Margaret." Mrs. Oglethorpe lowered her hood. At least, I supposed that was what she did. There was no light in the carriage and the curtains were drawn, so I had to struggle to make out even the suggestion of motion. "I had to be certain you were not watched."

"Of course," I said, or tried to, for the violent motion of our speeding coach caused my teeth to chatter and clack. Isolde poked her head out of her basket and uttered several sharp yips of complaint.

"I . . . ah . . ." What did one ask at this point in a desperate escape? "I . . . ouch . . . Is it far to Godalming?"

"Oh, Peggy, I'm sorry. We're not going to Godalming."

Her words slammed against me, knocking me backwards in my seat. If I had been standing, I would have staggered, perhaps even fallen.

"I . . . but . . . you said . . . that you would take me to your house."

"I know I did, and I am sorry. Had your letter come yesterday, we would have still gone to my home. But things have proceeded too fast and there is far too much that requires my presence. No. We must go at once to Bidmarsh."

"Bidmarsh? Where is that?"

"You don't know?" Genuine surprise filled her voice. "Bidmarsh is the home of Baron Lynnfield."

~ ❦ ~

CHAPTER THIRTY

IN WHICH OUR HEROINE FINDS THAT
ONE MAY BE CONFINED TO MORE
PLACES THAN JUST THE TOWER.

We arrived at Bidmarsh House in the last gray light of evening. We had traveled all night and throughout the next day, stopping only to change horses and to purchase such refreshment as could be eaten out of hand in a fast-moving carriage.

I had fully intended to spend my time in the coach with Mrs. Oglethorpe making light conversation and, incidentally, discovering as much about her and her plans that I could. After she revealed our true destination, however, it was a long time before I was able to say anything at all. My thoughts had become fixed on a single point and could not be shifted.

How on earth had I been so terribly, terribly stupid?

I told myself I had faced far worse situations and gotten out of them. This time, for instance, no one was pointing a pistol or sword at me. The coach houses where we stopped to change horses would be filled with disinterested parties who would respond to a scream or a cry for help. I'd stashed a purse of coins in Isolde's traveling basket, so I was not without means if I needed to make an escape while we were still on the road.

Despite these preparations, I kept my seat during that mad ride. Because if I did try to run, what then? Would I creep home to go to whatever hiding place my father chose and wait for the coming invasion to play itself out?

No. My hand was dealt. I must play it through.

The mansion housing those I feared most looked quite normal. I had conjured vague images of a ruined abbey or cavernous Norman fortress where I would be greeted by hooded monks or masked men. I could blame these fanciful images on my association with Olivia, but that would not be entirely fair or truthful.

In point of fact, Bidmarsh House proved to be a sound edifice of pale brick shaped like a squared-off letter U. A small, neat court nestled between its two projecting arms. It looked like recent construction to me, although I was given to understand from Mrs. Oglethorpe—who evidently felt that an unbroken stream of small talk was the best way to keep me calm and in good spirits—that there had been a manor house here since the Middle Ages. At least, I think that's what she said. I had stopped listening to her at some point. I fear this was rude of me, and possibly a little incautious, but

I was still too amazed and alarmed by my predicament, not to mention the constant jolting and tipping of the coach, to pay much heed to her attempts at soothing the daughter of her "best and dearest friend."

Mrs. Oglethorpe had stepped down from the coach after me, and now she took my arm. "I understand this is difficult for you, Margaret, truly I do." She sounded so much like Mr. Tinderflint as she said this that I'm afraid I stared. "But you must trust me. I would not have brought you here if it were not the best and safest place for you to be."

I nodded and let her lead me inside. If my hand stole beneath my cloak to touch my sapphire straight pin—at the ready on my stomacher—I can hardly be blamed.

Our arrival had evidently been anticipated. A butler directed a pair of porters to take my box while he led us through the house. It was indeed modern inside, with the current fashions in marble and blue paint, not to mention curving foyers and staircases, all well represented. The paintings on the walls of the first-floor gallery were a jumble of ancestors and landscapes. I wished Matthew were here to comment on them and say whether they were any good.

In truth, I just wished Matthew were here.

The second-floor corridors were lined with painted wood and green silk. We passed several white doors but nowhere did we meet a single Sandford, much less a Lord or Lady Lynnfield. Mrs. Oglethorpe appeared entirely unconcerned by this lack of attention from any host or hostess.

Indeed, she moved through the hallways as comfortably as if the house were her own. Certainly the servants obeyed her as if she were their mistress.

We reached a closed door at the very end of the long corridor. Mrs. Oglethorpe pushed it open to reveal a small, tidy bedroom.

"Here is where you will stay, Margaret." She directed the men to bring my box inside. She used her candle to light the fresh one that stood on the table by the door. "I will send Hannah up with some supper on a tray. She can help you with your unpacking. We will speak more about your position here and how we may help each other in the morning. Is there anything that you need?"

Training and etiquette came to my aid. I curtsied. "Thank you, Mrs. Oglethorpe. I'm sure I shall do very well."

She left me then and closed the door behind her. I set Isolde's basket down beside the bed. My puppy scrambled out from under her blanket and plopped onto the small carpet. I ignored her, listening instead for a most particular noise. I was not disappointed, for a moment later, I detected the click and scrape of a key turning in the lock.

I ran to the door and checked the keyhole, although I did not truly expect Mrs. Oglethorpe to be so careless as to leave the key in the lock. In this I was also not disappointed.

My status as prisoner confirmed, I hurried to my box and fumbled with my own keys and locks. I dug under my clothing for the leather satchel Matthew had retrieved from Mr. Tinderflint's bolthole. I hesitated, looking about for a place to conceal this most important item. A soft creaking sounded from the floorboards outside, telling me I was out of time. I resorted at once to the most obvious measure and stuffed the satchel underneath the bolsters.

There was a knock, which I acknowledged. The key turned and a maid, whom I presumed to be Hannah, entered. She was a woman of hard musculature and a rectangular face. Her eyes, by contrast, were large and round, giving her a look like a rabbit startled out of some unpleasant meditation. She had with her a tray of stew and fresh bread, a country cheese, a jam tart, and a carafe of red wine. She set these on the round table that waited under the window and advised me to eat while the food was still hot.

The room was provided with a slat-backed chair. I sat and picked up my spoon. Isolde decided, most unexpectedly, that investigating the maid's shoes and hems, and afterward the rest of the room, was more important than receiving a share of my supper.

I was oddly glad of this. Given how I had left my father, it was perhaps natural that thoughts of poison and sleeping powders crossed my mind. I dismissed these, in part because I was genuinely hungry and in part because I was already locked in. Proceeding to drug me seemed a bit much, even for a cautious spy. Mrs. Oglethorpe was, after all, doing her best to convince me she was my friend as she had been my mother's.

I broke the bread, spread the cheese, and ate my supper. It was all excellent.

While I ate, I looked out the darkened window. The glass provided a remarkably clear reflection of Hannah's movements. She was spare and thorough. She laid out my few, plain dresses to smooth down before she hung them on their pegs in the room's small closet. She unfolded and refolded my chemises and stockings and shook out my stays before laying them in the room's dressing table. This was surely to prevent creasing. It had, of course, nothing to do with the possibility of shaking out anything I might have concealed among my clothing, such as letters or picklocks or anything of that kind.

It was difficult to avoid wincing every time she walked past the bed and the bolsters.

At last my trunk was empty and Hannah seemed satisfied with what she had found, or had not found. I polished off my dinner without noticing myself to be more than ordinarily tired. A little less so, in fact, because my nerves were very much on edge. Nonetheless, I let Hannah help me into my nightclothes and cap and then into bed.

She took the room's one candle with her as she left.

I waited and I listened. The key turned in the lock. The candle's light moved away from the door. The darkness was complete.

I slipped my hand under my bolsters and pulled out my satchel. I rolled toward the wall, straining to hear any sound of approach from the corridor outside. All I heard was the wind rushing beneath the eaves. I didn't like it. It sounded too much like the rising of floodwaters.

I forced myself to dismiss this thought. I had work to

do. Firstly, I had to hide the contents of my satchel more securely. I pulled back the window draperies to allow in what little light the moon afforded, and considered my accommodations. Isolde was more than ready to help, of course, nosing into each corner and scrabbling at the baseboards. I hoped Bidmarsh's mice were very small.

The difficult question when seeking to conceal any item in a strange house is how diligent are the servants? A slovenly maid is a spy's best ally. She does not turn mattresses regularly or air pillows and bolsters, let alone move the rugs to sweep underneath them, so any items concealed beneath these articles remain safe and secure. I could not, however, picture Lord Lynnfield permitting any such useful creatures in his establishment.

The spare candles and tinderbox went into the bottom of my work basket. If discovered, I could say they were a precaution against dim coach-house rooms. I bundled my spare clothes onto a shelf in the very bottom of the closet where I could deny ever having seen them at all. As they were a laborer's breeches, smock, and stockings, this would not be as far-fetched as one might think.

If anyone happened upon the rope ladder, however, explanations would prove far more difficult. I cast about helplessly for a long minute. The bed was comfortable but lacked a canopy that I could have secreted it on top of. The closet was shallow, and adding a rope ladder to the roll of old clothes would make that previously innocuous bundle decidedly suspicious. There was no hearth, and so no convenient chimney to tuck anything up. I wondered if I was going to have to risk lighting one of the candles to better assess the room.

Isolde whimpered.

"Izzy, where are you?" I whispered exasperatedly.

She answered with a tiny growl from under the armchair.

"Izzy, come out of there."

She did, triumphantly and with several threads hanging out of her mouth. Clearly, I had just been saved from a dangerous piece of loose fabric. She shook and sneezed and waited for her praise.

I gave it, rather more fulsomely than I had intended. "You clever, clever girl!"

That armchair was the room's one luxury, being covered in fabric, sprung, and well padded. As carefully and quietly as I could, I tipped it onto its back. There was burlap underneath, but the scissors in my work basket were sharp, and I quickly slit the seam at the edge, just far enough that I could slide my ladder inside.

Izzy wagged her bottom and nosed my hand.

"Yes, now, you guard that carefully," I murmured to her as I righted the chair.

It was then I heard the footsteps.

They were quick and light, a scant pattering against the floorboards. I froze in place and held my breath. I also grabbed up Isolde so that she might not make any undue sound.

The footsteps tapped up to my door. A light flickered

through the crack underneath. Stealthily, the knob was turned. My heart stopped. My straight pin was not on hand, but the scissors in my basket were.

Then a second pair of footsteps sounded. These came, I thought, from the other end of the hall. It is not so easy to track movement by sound as playwrights and poets would have us believe. But my doorknob stilled and those steps moved away.

"Well, Izzy," I breathed. "What do you make of that?" Isolde growled. "I agree."

I waited quietly, holding Izzy in my arms, but Bidmarsh House seemed to be admirably and frustratingly supplied with thick walls. Strain my ears as I might, I could make out no further noises. My window looked out from the rear of the house rather than the front. I peered out of it anyway, remembering to keep behind the curtain. The moon had risen, but with the wind-blown clouds cluttering the sky, its light was neither bright nor certain. As far as I could tell, however, the lawns and the flat land beyond appeared empty of movement.

Izzy growled again, and squirmed. I heard a new noise as well, and sprang back from the window. It was a hesitant rustling of thick skirts, accompanied by an equally hesitant scraping and groping. Next came a soft whimpering that reminded me very much of Izzy when she was uneasy.

"There!" cried a woman's voice, too high and harried to recognize. "Catch her!"

There followed the slap of running feet and a woman's scream, accompanied by a flurry of thumps and struggles. Izzy barked as loudly as her tiny lungs allowed. I grabbed the doorknob unthinkingly, but froze. Did I want them to know I was awake? Light flickered beyond the door and someone moaned. Then, within the space of a few heartbeats, all sound of struggle ceased. I bit my lip and laid my hand over Izzy's head to muffle her barks. While my dog most ungraciously attempted to gnaw my finger-ends, I backed away from the door.

There was the sound of something heavy being dragged. Then there was silence. There was silence for a very long time.

CHAPTER THIRTY-ONE

IN WHICH FRESH INTRODUCTIONS ARE
MADE AND A BREAKFAST PROVIDED, WHICH
PROVES TO BE GENEROUS AND UNNERVING.

My next several hours were divided between pacing and hesitation. I crossed from the door to the window and back again, straining eyes and ears to detect some additional sound or action. I knelt and peered at the keyhole, even though I already knew my jailers had not been so careless as to leave the key in place. Time and again, I considered unearthing my candle and starting out from my prison of a room by means of the rope ladder and the window.

I fed Izzy half my little stock of biscuits in an effort to keep her quiet.

No new noises came. In fact, the night remained absolutely still, except for me and my awareness that there was some woman or girl in this house who should not have been, or who did not want to be.

It can't be Olivia, I told myself over and over again. *It cannot possibly be Olivia.*

They would have had to break into Father's house, where Father lay in a drugged sleep. Or they would have had to catch up with Olivia on the road, going in the obvious, but entirely wrong, direction with Matthew.

It could not be Olivia. But as dark and cold leeched into my impatient self, another thought occurred to me. It could be Aunt Pierpont. My naive aunt might have tried to divest herself of any last incriminating papers by handing them over to the Jacobites and begging them to leave her and her daughter alone. Given how soon they all said they expected their plans to come to fruition, they might not have wanted to risk leaving so foolish a woman at liberty.

Any sympathy I might have harbored toward these people and their cause was driven away entirely by the idea that they might have confined my harmless, nervous aunt.

But I could not go out to discover the truth, no matter how badly I wanted to. I knew nothing of the house. I had no idea who might be awake and watching. I could not risk it.

Not yet.

I peered out the window at the empty gardens. The silhouette of a single church steeple stood out sharply against the brightening sky. A profound awareness of how very alone I was stole over me. No one who meant me any good knew I was here. No one would know if I was made to disappear forever into the November marshes.

It was too much. I curled up on the bed. Isolde, with much scrabbling and circling, managed to make herself comfortable in the hollow near my stomach. I clutched her tightly and tried not to be afraid.

I must have slept at some point, for I did eventually sit up on my bed in the full light of morning, stiff as a board and cold to the bone. Someone was knocking at the door.

I found I had enough presence of mind left to scramble beneath my covers before I called out my permission to enter. The maid from the night before came in with candles and a chocolate pot. She did not, I noticed, have to pause to unlock the door. Which meant either she'd already done so or someone else had unlocked it earlier.

This was not a comforting thought.

Frost ferns decorated my window, and my prison room lacked any sort of fireplace. I'd brought with me only two shawls and one pair of slippers, and they felt entirely too thin for the circumstances. The candle Hannah carried provided no relief. My extreme desire to find the breakfast room, where it was surely warmer, almost drowned out my worries as to what, and whom, I would find when I reached it.

As it happened, I was not the first person to arrive at breakfast, not by a long chalk. Bidmarsh's pleasant, pale green dining room with its long painted table and commodious sideboard was already well filled with talk, activity, and a variety of persons, both male and female.

Among them waited Lord Lynnfield and his younger brother.

I had known they must be here. This, after all, was their house. I had thought myself ready for it, but as I reached the room's threshold and saw both Sebastian and Julius, I froze.

Lord Lynnfield rose politely from his place at the head of the table and bowed. Sebastian, who stood at the sideboard next to a round-faced gentleman in clerical garb, straightened from his slouch. His hand spasmed so severely that the piece of cake he held broke apart and its crumbs rained to the floor.

Mrs. Oglethorpe, seated at the foot of the table, did not appear to notice anything amiss with her hosts. Nor did she wait, as normal courtesy would have dictated, for either of them to speak.

"Ah! Here at last is our guest of honor!" Mrs. Oglethorpe came to take my arm. "Now, my dear, what can have so disconcerted you? We are all friends here."

I swallowed. "Yes, of course," I croaked. "I was simply startled. Since he did not come to greet us last night, I had thought Lord Lynnfield was away from home."

"So we were," replied Lynnfield calmly. "Detained on a matter of business, as it happens. We only arrived very late last night."

Late last night? Before or after the disturbance outside my door? I racked my brain. Had I heard a man's voice in the commotion? Certainly some of the steps had been heavy enough to belong to a man. *It can't have been Olivia*, I told myself again. *Oh, please, Heaven above me, don't let Olivia have done anything so foolish as to get caught by Lynnfield.*

And not Aunt Pierpont, either. I don't know what I'd do if they hurt Aunt Pierpont. I almost had to stifle a laugh. While I was praying, was there anybody else I should make sure of?

Besides Matthew, who might very well have died before he let anyone lay hands on Olivia.

I blessed my stars for my courtier's training, for it was only this that enabled me to keep my features composed as Mrs. Oglethorpe led me farther into the room.

"Now, Miss Fitzroy, do let me make you known to our dear friend Dr. Atterbury." The clerical gentleman standing at the sideboard bowed in acknowledgment of this introduction. To my shock, I realized I had seen him at several of the princess's levees. "And my daughter Anne." Miss Anne Oglethorpe did not rise from her place at the table. At least as old as Princess Caroline, Miss Olgethorpe strongly resembled her mother, particularly about her neck, which was inordinately long and stiff, and her sharp nose. She did possess a fine head of dark hair and wide-set brown eyes to balance these prominent features. Those eyes watched me with the sort of keen discernment that would have done credit to Sophy Howe.

"And of course," Mrs. Oglethorpe went on, "you are well acquainted with our excellent Lord Lynnfield and his brother."

"Very well. Yes." I met Julius's assessing gaze. "Although,"

I added, careful to sound both bemused and fluttery, "I wonder if they are surprised to find me here on such terms."

"Not at all," Lynnfield replied. "The only uncertainty was when you'd arrive. I did not think you would precede us."

To my surprise it was Sebastian who answered next, and his answer was a loud and dismissive snort. "Oh, for God's sake, Julius!"

"Sebastian!" cried Mrs. Oglethorpe. "Do not blaspheme!"

Sebastian ignored her. "Surely you didn't expect the old snake and her daughters to change their spots just because you've declared for the same side! Why, someone might think she gave a damn about either one of us!" He aimed a vicious kick at the bit of the seed cake he'd dropped and stomped out of the room.

We all stared after him. Not one of us moved. The clerical gentleman, Dr. Atterbury, cleared his throat.

"For shame, Mrs. Oglethorpe," he murmured. "Here we are, keeping Miss Fitzroy standing and talking, when she is clearly faint with hunger." He gestured to the battalion of covered porcelain dishes that crowded the sideboard. "What can I help you to, Miss Fitzroy?"

The thought of food was actively sickening, but I forced that feeling to one side, along with all misapprehensions about my current company. I needed to eat. Firstly, to maintain strength of body and mind. Secondly, because the process of choosing breakfast would keep me from having to make polite conversation while I marshaled something approaching rational thought.

Dr. Atterbury solicitously helped me to fish, muffins, and a thick slice of fruit cake, accompanied by a cup of strong coffee.

Once again, the food proved to be excellent. Mrs. Oglethorpe presided over the table without reference to Lord Lynnfield, who resumed his seat at its head. While we ate, she chatted calmly and casually with Dr. Atterbury and Miss Anne Oglethorpe about what I guessed to be local news and mutual acquaintances.

Lord Lynnfield, naturally, watched me. It took all my training to keep my hands steady as I wielded fork and knife to cut the fillet of sole in lemon sauce and to butter the freshly baked muffins. I was so fixed on navigating my breakfast and concealing any hint of genuine feeling that I barely noticed that Mrs. Oglethorpe had paused in her chatter.

"You seem a bit pale and quiet this morning, Miss Fitzroy. I trust you slept well?"

"Very well, thank you, madame," I answered, grateful that established courtesy provided the set form of answer. The spy in me, however, decided that this was not quite enough. "My room is extremely comfortable. Although . . ."

"Although?" Lynnfield barked. As sharp as the single word was, the glance he received in answer from Mrs. Oglethorpe was sharper.

"I'm afraid my puppy, Isolde, finds the change unnerving."

I smiled and lowered my eyes. The edge to Lord Lynnfield's inquiry gave me the answer I sought. Whatever had happened last night, Lynnfield knew about it, and it worried him. He was a man who liked to be in control, and that control had slipped. "The poor thing woke up at some time during the night, and I had quite a time getting her settled again. I am, however, certain she will soon grow used to her new surroundings."

"Yes indeed," agreed Dr. Atterbury, smiling. "Young things of all sorts are highly adaptable."

"No doubt." Lynnfield's reply and countenance were bland, but he climbed to his feet. "I'm afraid I must beg a word in private with you, Mrs. Oglethorpe," he said.

"And with Miss Fitzroy as well, I imagine." Mrs. Oglethorpe cast me a positively conspiratorial glance.

"If she has no objection."

I had a thousand objections and would cheerfully have listed them. Unfortunately, this did not seem like an opportune moment. Instead, I wiped my mouth and fingers on my napkin and stood obediently.

"Perhaps once our business is concluded, Anne can show you the grounds." Mrs. Oglethorpe smiled. "Unless, of course, it's too cold for you?"

"Oh, you needn't be concerned about me," I murmured. "I am quite used to going abroad in all weathers."

"Ah, yes." Miss Anne Oglethorpe smiled. "We've heard how the German bitch loves the out-of-doors."

The hard word was dropped so casually, I started as if it were a china cup let fall. Mrs. Oglethorpe did not seem to notice anything, however. She just turned smoothly and left the room, with Lynnfield striding behind her. I was left to follow along.

CHAPTER THIRTY-TWO

IN WHICH A COLD WALK PROVIDES
OUR HEROINE WITH CERTAIN UNSETTLING
REVELATIONS AND AN UNINSPIRING VIEW.

The library of Bidmarsh House would have moved Olivia to raptures. It was a broad room with soaring ceilings. Shelves lined its walls, and those shelves were entirely lined with books. Comfort had not in any way been neglected, as there were several plump armchairs and sofas scattered about, as well as a broad writing desk.

Of course Lord Lynnfield locked the doors. Mrs. Oglethorpe settled herself onto the sofa nearest the fire. "Well, Julius, what is it you wish to say?"

He smiled and folded his hands behind his back.

"I merely wished for the opportunity to welcome Miss Fitzroy into my house." I thought I detected a slight emphasis on the possessive pronoun. "And to inquire whether her journey here was comfortable."

I took some time in answering. I wanted to be sure my gaze and hands would stay steady before I spoke. I might play the fool for Mrs. Oglethorpe, but that disguise would not serve me in front of Lynnfield, who had seen me much closer to my true self. "The drive was difficult, and I regret the necessity of having made it. However, I am here, and I mean to stay as long as I am welcome."

"Well spoken, Margaret," said Mrs. Oglethorpe with warm approval.

Lord Lynnfield, though, shook his head. "I admit to a certain disappointment. I really did think I'd found in you someone more creative, and more loyal to her own. Still." He shrugged. "Perhaps now I'll have a chance to begin again with you. That also might have its advantages." As he spoke, he bestowed on me one more long and thoughtful look. It traveled up my body and down again, carefully weighing and assessing all that I wore and all that I was.

Mrs. Oglethorpe smiled to see this close regard. I suppressed the urge to run to find the nearest basin of fresh water to wash the oily touch of Lynnfield's gaze off my skin.

"But that's for later," said Lord Lynnfield. "What we need to know now is how successful our plans have been thus far."

Mrs. Oglethorpe's fond smile turned into a grin of absolute triumph. "Margaret, perhaps you will do me the favor of telling Lord Lynnfield where you last spoke to Tierney."

"In his cell in the Tower of London." I couldn't keep the catch out of my voice as I spoke.

Lynnfield was in no way impressed. "She could be lying," he said to Mrs. Oglethorpe. "She's better at it than you might think, and none of us would find her out for several days."

"True," I replied calmly. "But you might also ask yourself whether I would be here, with you, if I had anywhere else to go."

Another man might have smiled in amusement at this, but in my experience, there were no other men like Lord Lynnfield. "No, you would not."

"Perhaps you should inform Julius what happened to you in that Tower cell?" Mrs. Oglethorpe prompted. I'm afraid I rather started at this question. In response, I received another of her benign smiles, which were truly beginning to grate on my nerves. "It's all right. We've already heard the story. At least, I have."

There was danger underneath the confident and honeyed tones of those words. I was on display here in more ways than one. The Old Fury was demonstrating her talents and her resources to the doubting Lord Lynnfield. She was also warning me that if I strayed from what she believed she knew, there would be consequences.

As I spun my tale, I wondered: Did Mr. Tinderflint know she would find out about my visit to the Tower and our conversation? He must have. This was why he'd wanted us to be heard quarreling—not because word would get to the palace, but because word would get to the Old Fury.

I would have a great deal to say to my patron when we both emerged from our respective difficulties.

If there was one aspect of Lord Lynnfield's character that held steady, it was his respect for an accomplished game-ster, even when he lost. "You are to be congratulated, Mrs. Oglethorpe." He bowed. "I did not believe she could be turned."

Mrs. Oglethorpe inclined her head regally. "I think we may now safely say I have fulfilled my end of our bargain."

"Have no fear. I will do as I promised. Provided she be-haves with discretion and compliance, Miss Fitzroy is our welcome guest." He smiled that bland and terrible smile. "Now that you are here, under my roof, Miss Fitzroy, you will find that the rules of engagement are somewhat different. We are not a court or a coffee society. There is no going back, no cheating the conclusion. You have made yourself depen-dent on me, and you will conduct yourself accordingly. Is that understood?"

I should have shown submission, but to acknowledge myself beholden to Julius Sandford was beyond me. "I know how this game is played, my lord. You even once suggested I might teach you a few refinements."

I instantly regretted these words because they bought me another long look of assessment. "Yes, and you may be sure we will speak further on that point, once I have cleared up some trifling business with our good Dr. Atterbury and my brother. Good morning to you both."

He took his leave. My knees trembled suddenly and I sat down. I should have picked somewhere other than the sofa that was also occupied by Mrs. Oglethorpe. She reached out and patted my hand, and I had to resist the urge to yank myself away.

"I know—he can be most unsettling. It is his way. You will soon become accustomed to it."

But I would never become accustomed to Lord Lynnfield. Not even if my only other option was to drown myself in the marshes. This, however, was not a suitable reply. "That letter, the enciphered one that trapped Mr. . . . . Lord Tierney. That was your doing?" I twisted my fingers in my lap. "Was it genuine?"

Mrs. Oglethorpe frowned, and for a moment I feared I had gone too far. "It was genuine in that it genuinely used the Great Cipher of the French Court, which should keep the German's code masters busy for some time. It has never yet been broken."

"Then it was all a trap," I murmured.

"Tierney was one of the few men who could have brought our plans to a halt," said Mrs. Oglethorpe. "He had to be gotten out of the way. It was all a fairly simple matter to orchestrate. Sebastian led you to the library and placed the letter for you to find. You gave it to Tierney, and he took it into his possession. Lord Lynnfield whispered to the German princeling, who by this time was more than willing to hear what he had to say, and all was done."

But even as all these pieces fell into place, I remembered

Sophy's parting words: *Find me when you know the favor I've done you.* One did not speak of favors to someone falling into a trap. "What was Sophy Howe's part?"

Mrs. Oglethorpe shook her head. "Poor Miss Howe. Such wasted talents. I do hope she weathers the coming storm."

I had intended to ask the Old Fury how she'd induced Sophy to change her mind about Lord Lynnfield, but I bit the question back. "Sophy left the palace before I did."

"Yes. Lord Lynnfield warned her away."

"Has he said she might marry Sebastian?" I ventured, but Mrs. Oglethorpe only gave a small shrug.

"Sebastian, as I think I intimated, has been a disappointment." Her mouth pressed into a thin line. "Sometimes it is best to tell him what he wants to hear and deal with the consequences later."

I stared. I couldn't help it. Why was she talking about Sebastian this way? Who was this woman? What right had she to run this house? Why did Lord Lynnfield permit it?

Mrs. Oglethorpe, however, did not choose to give me the leisure to contemplate these highly interesting questions.

"Now," she said briskly. "As you can imagine, our business requires a great deal of careful correspondence. My eyes are not what they should be anymore, and I was hoping you'd oblige me by writing to my dictation." She gestured toward the desk that waited by the French doors.

"Of course. I'd be glad to." I settled myself at the neat, practical desk. There, I found paper, quills, and ink at the ready. I tried to compose myself to patience as I trimmed the first quill. This would, if nothing else, keep me out of Lord Lynnfield's way. It also might provide me with information I could pass on to Matthew and Olivia when they found me. If they found me.

A wave of loneliness passed over me. Where were Matthew and Olivia now? Had they reached Godalming yet? How long would it be before they realized I was not there?

What had Olivia said in the letter she left for my father?

Mrs. Oglethorpe proved to be a harsh taskmistress. She dictated quickly and expected me to keep up. Her letters, addressed to a wealth of correspondents from all parts of England and Scotland, were filled with references to "our friends" and "our business."

It wasn't until the third thoroughly ambiguous letter that I realized what she was doing. This was not an old woman with tired eyes dictating her business. This was my enemy creating a stack of letters in my handwriting. These letters could then be produced the moment any person needed to be convinced that I, Margaret Fitzroy, was a secret Jacobite. I wasn't signing any of them, that was true, but such forgery would be the work of a moment.

I was assisting in my own blackmail, and there was not a thing I could do, save to smile and keep writing.

We worked until one of the clock. By then, my hand had begun to cramp. Ink stained my fingers and spattered my sleeves. Libby would have fits, assuming I ever saw Libby again. Mrs.

Oglethorpe, however, appeared as fresh and alert as she had when we'd begun. So fresh was she, in fact, that she ordered the footman to bring us a cold collation by way of nuncheon so that I might keep writing and reading for her.

This had the effect of keeping me under her eye in this one room and prevented me from wandering off to discover anything about the house or join in any unauthorized conversation.

Exactly as the hour struck three, the library door opened and Miss Anne Oglethorpe sailed in.

"How is this, Mother!" she cried heartily, in order, I suspect, to disguise how false her merry tone sounded. "You haven't kept Miss Fitzroy at work all this time?"

Mrs. Oglethorpe laughed, to all appearances highly amused by her daughter's impetuousness. I found myself wondering if these two had at any time played in Drury Lane, so expert were they at staging scenes.

Well, they were not the only ones who knew their lines. "I'm glad to be of some use," I said. "It's all been such a shock, and, well, I have no idea what my future is to be now."

Anne Oglethorpe beamed. "Oh, there's plenty of time to decide that, Margaret."

I made a show of hesitation. "And yet your mother . . . Mrs. Oglethorpe . . . said our *business* was moving along more quickly than anticipated?"

"Why should that matter?" Miss Oglethorpe waved her hand, a gesture that rivaled any of Mary Bellenden's for carelessness. "Once we are successful, we will be better positioned than ever to help you to a good future. Unless you think something's bound to go wrong?" She cocked her head toward me.

"I'm sure I could not say. I know so very little of the . . . the . . . business."

"Oh?" She arched a carefully plucked brow in her mother's direction. "An oversight, surely. But we'll speak of it later. I insist you come along with me. You were promised a tour of the grounds, and I've already sent the maid for our cloaks and bonnets, and your dog."

I made my curtsy to Mrs. Oglethorpe and obediently followed her daughter. At least this would get me out of the library, even though I was still quite unmistakably under guard.

Miss Anne Oglethorpe might have been a hardened veteran of the Jacobite cause, but the moment she saw little Isolde trotting downstairs at the maid's heels, she became a simple and simpering country girl.

"How precious!" She clapped her hands. "What a darling! Does she know her name? Here, Isolde! Here, darling! Come see your Auntie Anne!"

"You'll do better if you give her this." I fished a bit of biscuit out of the reticule the maid had also thought to bring.

Miss Oglethorpe held up the biscuit for Isolde. Born courtier that she was, my puppy responded by jumping up and attempting to balance on her hind legs, and promptly falling over. Which brought on another bout of laughing and cooing, earning her the biscuit. I smiled and Miss Oglethorpe smiled, and I swear upon my life Isolde smiled. At least, she pricked up her ears, in case any more biscuits might be forthcoming.

From this felicitous beginning, the tour proceeded in all outward signs of conviviality. The Bidmarsh gardens proved to be strictly conventional. Even Isolde had difficulty finding things of interest as she nosed about. There was the wide lawn, turned brown and white by frost. The rectangular flower beds were quite bare except for rosebushes wrapped in burlap. A thick grove of poplars and elms was already stripped bare of leaves by the frigid wind that blew off the marsh. The orchard looked out of place in the otherwise empty landscape, and I imagined the trees to be huddling together for warmth.

Miss Oglethorpe did not seem discommoded by the cold or the wind. She led me down the straight gravel path to the garden wall at a leisurely pace. It was at the gate that my breath was finally well and truly taken away. Because out there lay the vastness of the Great Romney Marsh.

People speak of London's streets as bleak. But the melancholy of the meanest alleyway was nothing compared to the view of the Romney Marsh in November. There was no color in this whole world except for the hard blue sky overhead. To the west, the land stretched out brown and gray and white all the way to the black line of the horizon. The only visible building was the church I'd seen the night before, keeping its proud and solitary watch over the empty countryside.

To the south, the ground sloped toward a great black lake with a hunched brown island in its center. Several boats lay beached on the gravelly bank. Shelves of gray ice had formed about the shore and the island, all decorated with white ribbons of early snow.

"I hope you're not contemplating a stroll, Miss Fitzroy," said Miss Oglethorpe cozily. "That smooth-looking ground" —she gestured toward the west—"is a maze of water, channels, creeks, and quicksands. Those who don't know their way are in very grave peril indeed."

"What about there?" I pointed toward the island. "Surely that's a pleasant place for a day's excursion? A picnic, perhaps?"

I'd meant it as a joke, considering my hands were all but blue with cold as it was. But when Miss Oglethorpe answered, she had a knowing gleam in her dark eyes. "Ah! Now, there's a very special place. We will be housing our . . . extra guests there as they come to us."

"Guests from France?" I murmured.

"Of course from France. And Spain as well."

As she spoke, Miss Oglethorpe's drawn face glowed with an inner light. There was nothing soft or elevated in her rapture. It was sharp as frost or any smile of Lord Lynnfield's. Anne Oglethorpe gazed at that lake, those small boats, and that bare brown island, and she saw victory.

"Is *he* coming as well?" I made myself ask softly. "The King over the Water?"

Miss Oglethorpe's fiery expression dimmed just a little. "Not here. He'll be greeted by our friends in the north. That will keep the German prince's attention focused there while our allies in England rise and walk toward London."

And there it was. All the plans hinted at in those letters I'd written this morning. Now I knew them. And now I would never be allowed to leave this place.

"The country around here is very open," I ventured. "I would think any . . . guests . . . would be seen arriving and would be stopped."

Miss Oglethorpe shrugged. "If they are stopped, the troops our king brings to the north will be more than enough to succeed, and of course London will be all in confusion."

"How is that?"

She smiled. "Because the false prince will be dead. And with his father still away in Hanover, who will there be to lead the German allies?"

CHAPTER THIRTY-THREE

IN WHICH A REUNION OF SORTS IS ACHIEVED.

It never ceases to amaze me how difficult it is to hear one's own fears spoken aloud. I could see the prince as if he stood before me now — saw him bowing to his wife, saw him patting his daughter indulgently on her head, saw him sick with rage at the death of his son.

Saw him stretched out on the ground, blood on his chest, his eyes open and staring.

I cast my gaze about quickly, searching for something to distract me from this ominous vision. It was then that I noticed that Isolde was no longer nosing about the base of the wall where she had been a moment before.

My first reaction was annoyance, but then I remembered I was meant to be playing the nervous child in front of these would-be assassins. In service of this illusion, I clapped my hands together. "Oh! Oh! Miss Oglethorpe! Isolde! Wherever has she gone!"

Miss Oglethorpe tore her gaze away from the island to see my open-mouthed distress. "Dear me, Miss Fitzroy, you would think we're in a wilderness!" She laughed. "Your puppy can't have gotten far. You take the gardens." She pointed. "I'll look out that way." She set off through the knee-high brown grasses toward the lake. "Here, Isolde! Here, girl!"

I hurried back into the garden's safer confines. I was worried, and annoyed at my worry. I should never have brought the blasted dog. Indeed, I would not have except that I'd thought she would suit the nervous character I had adopted.

"Isolde! Izzy!"

I saw an unmistakable flash of pure white bounding away in the direction of the grove I'd noted earlier. I muttered an oath as I set off after her as quickly as skirts and half boots permitted. By the time I reached the trees, Isolde had darted between them. Then I saw another movement.

Isolde was not alone. A man peered out from behind the nearest tree trunk and ducked back again just as quickly.

My breath caught in my throat, and I glanced behind me. In the distance, I saw that Miss Oglethorpe had reached the boats beached on the lake's gravelly shore and was paying no attention to us. Cautiously, I slid into the grove's shadows. I did not have my straight pin immediately to hand, but my boots were sturdy enough that I could deliver a good kick if that proved necessary.

The grove was an old one, and its trees crowded so

closely together that the space beneath them was filled with permanent twilight. Isolde was leaping up and down, trying to snatch a tidbit held out for her by a man in a dirty smock.

I drew on my best expression of haughty outrage and, despite the unevenness of the frozen ground, attempted to sail up to the stranger. The man grinned saucily at my approach and, as he had no hat brim to tug in salute, touched his knuckle to his forehead. A hoe rested carelessly across his shoulders, but if he was really a gardener for Bidmarsh House, I was the Queen of Sheba. Now that my eyes had adjusted to the shade, I saw that he was younger than he'd first appeared. He was also unshaven and unwashed, and his hair was nothing so much as a black tangle on his head. His gray eyes stood out, strangely bright in his grimy face.

His gray eyes.

I stared. I stared and I forgot to breathe.

Matthew—for it was Matthew—let Isolde catch the bit of cake he held.

The sight of his beloved, if somewhat poorly disguised, countenance raised but one response in me. "What in Heaven's name are you *doing!*"

Matthew just grinned his saucy grin and touched his forehead again. "Making sure you're all right," he breathed. He held out a scrap of paper I was sure hadn't been half so grubby before he got his hands on it. I snatched it away and stuffed it up my sleeve.

"Note's from some devilish French-lookin' chap wi' a

nephew, a fancy fellow all in blue. Said I was to have extra if I give it to Pretty Peggy-O. Oh, he's a sly one. Made certain inquiries on the road, he did. Kept some people from goin' too far astray."

Clearly, Matthew had been much contaminated by his association with Olivia. Further, his attempt at a working-man's accent was truly atrocious and I would tell him so later, when I had my breath back, for between his appearance and his news, he had taken it quite away. Olivia was here! And my father. They were well and together, all of them. They were still free and they knew where I was. My heart soared for the simple fact that I was not alone.

There were, unfortunately, two sides to that particular state of being.

"Miss Fitzroy!" called Miss Oglethorpe, and her voice was much closer than it should have been. "Miss Fitzroy!"

I snatched up Isolde and whirled around, endeavoring to put myself between Matthew and the rapidly approaching Oglethorpe.

"Oh, look, Miss Oglethorpe, I have her!" I cried happily as I hurried forward.

But Miss Oglethorpe wasn't looking at me, or Isolde. She was staring at the grove's deeper shadows. "Who was that?" she demanded.

"One of the gardeners." I had to force the words out through a throat that was attempting to clamp shut. But as I turned to follow her narrowed gaze, my breath returned in a rush. Matthew had vanished as if he'd never been. "He had Isolde." I held my wriggling dog up a little higher, in case Miss Oglethorpe had missed her.

She hadn't. Nor, apparently, had she missed a decent look at my greasy messenger. "He was none of ours. What did he want? What did he say?"

"He said nothing." Fortunately for me, a blank and confused expression was entirely appropriate to the moment. "Nothing of any import. He had Isolde, and I—"

I was not permitted to get any further. "This is extremely bad, Miss Fitzroy. What on *earth* were you thinking?" She grabbed my arm. "We must get you back to the house."

It was indeed bad. In fact, it was disastrous, although Miss Oglethorpe and I probably wouldn't agree as to the reason why. If this woman, her mother, or—Heaven help me —Lord Lynnfield realized I had just met with a confederate, it was all up and I'd be lucky to live through the rest of the day.

I had only one choice.

"Oh, no . . ." I panted. "Oh, no, Miss Oglethorpe! Could I have been followed? I was so careful. I . . . I . . ."

I burst into tears. Or at least plentiful sobs with my hand over my eyes, which I hoped was close enough.

"Hold your noise! We've no time for it!"

Anne Oglethorpe, it transpired, could keep up an impressive turn of speed for a woman in skirts and corsets. Even Isolde was out of breath by the time we burst into the library.

"Anne! What is the meaning of this!" snapped Mrs. Oglethorpe, who had been deep in conference with Lynnfield and his cleric.

"Miss Fitzroy has been found out," announced the younger Oglethorpe.

"It's all my fault!" I wailed. "Isolde was lost in the garden . . . There was a man . . . I thought he was a gardener . . . I . . ."

"He was not one of our people," said Miss Oglethorpe. "He was a stranger, and a rough one."

Mrs. Oglethorpe turned to Lord Lynnfield. "Julius, could he have been one of your men?"

Lynnfield shook his head. "My orders were that they should keep to their quarters during the day. I'll turn them out now, though. Have them search the grounds."

"Do so," agreed Mrs. Oglethorpe. "Could you lend one or two to Dr. Atterbury? Sir, I must beg a favor of you to go into the village. If people are asking questions about Miss Fitzroy, we must know of it at once."

Dr. Atterbury bowed. "I am entirely at your service, Mrs. Oglethorpe."

As I listened to all this decisive action, panic spread through my limbs. The paper I concealed in my sleeve burned my forearm as if it were a live coal. "I'm so sorry, Mrs. Oglethorpe." I meant it, too.

"It is not your fault." Mrs. Oglethorpe glowered at her eldest daughter. "I warned you she would be watched! How could you have let this happen!"

Miss Oglethorpe, however, was not in the least intimidated. "I had thought that with such a great gathering of Lord Lynnfield's men, at *least* his gardens would be safe."

"You may be sure I will be quizzing my men closely about this, Miss Oglethorpe." Lord Lynnfield looked directly at me as he said this. "A serious error in judgment has been made by someone. If that person is any of mine, they will be properly punished."

It was impossible not to hear the promise of murder under those words.

I must have blanched, because Mrs. Oglethorpe said kindly, "I think, Miss Fitzroy, you'd better return to your room."

"Yes, thank you."

While I made my curtsy and turned away, Lord Lynnfield took up one of the candles from the mantelpiece and lit it from the fire. "I'll see her up."

This was hardly a proper arrangement, never mind a comfortable one. But as neither of the Oglethorpe ladies raised any objections, I could not voice mine. I gathered Isolde more firmly into my arms and followed Lord Lynnfield out.

He said nothing as we traversed the corridor to the grand entranceway. He said nothing as we mounted the curving stair and turned down the narrower but still grand hallway that led to my little room.

Lynnfield drew a ring of keys out of his pocket, sorted through them, found the correct one, unlocked my door, and stood back.

"Thank you." The words were hoarse because my mouth had gone completely dry.

"There is still time to change your mind, Miss Fitzroy," he answered coolly. "I would suggest you use it." He handed me the candle. "I'd also suggest you keep your curtains drawn. It would be a shame for someone to be able to look in and see all your business."

I took the candle, rather impressed with how little my hand shook, and walked past him into the room.

The room was quite dark. Someone—I assumed the maid—had already closed the draperies. The door shut. Isolde wriggled in my arms, yipping in fury and distress. I set her down at the same time I heard the sound I was truly beginning to loathe and fear: the key in the lock.

Isolde ran to the door, barking her little heart out. Despite the shadows filling my room, it took only a single instant to see what so disturbed her. The candle's light, though faint, was more than enough to show me that the small space beside the door was occupied by Sebastian Sandford.

And I was locked in with him.

CHAPTER THIRTY-FOUR

I<small>N</small> <small>WHICH</small> O<small>UR</small> H<small>EROINE</small> <small>LEARNS</small>

<small>AN</small> <small>UNCOMFORTABLE</small> <small>FACT</small> <small>REGARDING</small>

<small>FAMILY</small> <small>TREES,</small> <small>MAKES</small> <small>A</small> <small>MOST</small> <small>DANGEROUS</small>

<small>BARGAIN,</small> <small>AND</small> <small>EATS</small> <small>SUPPER.</small>

My jaw fell open. I am uncertain whether I meant to curse, exclaim, or simply scream. Sebastian held one finger to his lips and then pointed at the door.

I shut my mouth. We both stood quite still until we heard Lord Lynnfield's footsteps thud away down the hall.

At last, Sebastian nodded. "I hope you'll excuse the liberty, Miss Fitzroy. I'm sure you'll agree it's high time we had a few words."

"I might." I set my candle down carefully. I also touched my stomacher to make sure of my sapphire pin. "I would, however, like to know how you think you're going to get out now that we're locked in together."

He smiled sagely and fished a key out of his pocket. "I

came prepared. Now." He slid the key back into his waist-coat. "Where is she?"

"Who?"

"Miss Howe." Sebastian stepped forward. He wanted to make me retreat, but my back was already against the wall. "What has your fat puppet master done with her?"

Finally, a question I could answer honestly. "If Lord Tierney has had any doings with Sophy, he told me nothing about them."

"Come, come, Miss Fitzroy," Sebastian sneered. "You can do better than that. In fact, you'll have to. Otherwise, I'll inform my brother that it was your artist you met out there among the elms."

He'd been watching me, and in so doing he'd managed to see more than anyone else. Because he was Sebastian Sand-ford, constantly overlooked, yet as dangerous and clever as the rest.

But worse than his words was the gleam in Sebastian's eye.

"Got you," he whispered. "That was a guess, but I was right. Your people are here."

I had to pull myself together, and quickly. I could say not one word to betray the others. "What do you want?" I asked.

"What I said. I want to know where Sophy is and that she's all right. After that . . ." He shrugged. "We'll take it as it comes."

My mind was reeling. I never would have believed it

possible, but Sophy Howe had not fallen in love alone. Sebastian had fallen with her. I didn't know whether to laugh or cry.

"I take it you don't believe she just went home?"

"She'd never leave voluntarily without sending me word."

He certainly believed this, but I had no way to tell if the belief was well founded. "Why did you come away without her, then?"

"What was I supposed to do? Stay in the palace, waiting for the princess's pet spy to say she saw me carrying Jacobite letters?"

If you really cared, yes. But then, Sebastian's courage had never been as strong as his sense of self-preservation. "Agreeing to play the courier at the masquerade was not your most well-considered move."

"I was set up for the job," he said. "Just as you have been," he added. "My brother made promises. He lies as easily as breathing, but I thought I could . . . that it would be better for all concerned if I did what he wanted."

He'd thought his obedience would keep Sophy safe. He knew exactly how dangerous Lord Lynnfield was and how few choices were left open to those who opposed him. Sebastian thought he could avoid the worst by walking along with his eyes open. Just like I had.

I met Sebastian's sharp blue gaze, and I hated him and I pitied him. I also for the first time saw how this shallow, untrustworthy, violent man might just be my way out.

"I'll need that key," I told him.

"Why?"

"Because I really don't know what's happened to Sophy, and I won't be able to find out if I'm locked in here." I held out my hand.

He stared at my open palm. "*That* stupid, Miss Fitzroy, I am not."

I made myself sigh and roll my eyes. "Do you really want to risk your own neck sneaking about after dark? Or be the one your brother catches going through drawers and letters looking for clues?" I did not even consider telling him there was a woman prisoner in this house. I knew what happened when this man got angry. A mad bull in a china shop would do less damage than Sebastian with his temper unleashed.

Sebastian's face twisted into an expression of serious reluctance. Despite this, he pressed the key into my palm.

"There, now." He folded his arms. "We are both entirely dependent on each other's silence."

"So it would seem," I agreed.

"Don't presume too much on it, Miss Fitzroy. If I fall, you will come with me. You may have fooled the Old Fury, but Julius's mind is nowhere near as fixed in your favor."

"I had noticed, thank you." And considering the insinuating and covetous nature of some of Lynnfield's remarks, that was actually something of a comfort. "Now, you'd best get out of here, before someone takes it into their head to check up on me."

"I would gladly, except you've got my key."

I blushed. Sebastian snickered, and I had to control the urge to stomp on his toes as I crossed to the door. I was just putting the key into the lock when another thought occurred to me.

"Who is Mrs. Oglethorpe to your family?" I said. "Why does your brother give her the run of his house? He certainly doesn't trust her." *Or share her fervor regarding the Pretender's rightful place in the world.*

Sebastian grinned. "If this is a sample of your vaunted powers of observation, Miss Fitzroy, I can't say I think much of them. Most people see the resemblance right away, particularly around the eyes."

I whirled around. He opened his eyes so wide as to be ridiculous and leaned in toward me. "Look," he whispered. "Look closely, Miss Fitzroy."

"No," I breathed. Mrs. Oglethorpe's features had indeed stirred feelings of recognition in me, and Sebastian's bright blue eyes and high cheekbones had always been his most noteworthy attributes. Well, aside from his cruelty, violence, and lack of any moral scruple. Now that it was laid before me, it was impossible not to see the family resemblance on every level.

Sebastian smiled again, and here too he resembled Mrs. Oglethorpe in the smug triumph of his expression. "You thought my brother and I call each other bastards as a figure of speech. I assure you, in our case, the appellation is quite literal."

"It was supposed to be James the Second she had a child with," I said weakly.

Sebastian shrugged. "I'm sure she would have had the opportunity arisen. Unfortunately, my father was the best she could do. He needed heirs and didn't want to be bothered with a wife. He always said women got in the way of serious business." His voice faltered and I found myself wondering if he was thinking of Sophy. "He legally acknowledged us and she didn't have to, which suited them both, and that's all there is to it."

I swallowed. "I suppose our betrothal finally makes some sort of sense."

"Yes." Sebastian's tone was so bland, he sounded terrifyingly like his brother. "She did mean to unite her secret family with that of her dearest friend. She's ludicrously sentimental in that way."

I wondered what Mrs. Oglethorpe would do if she knew my mother might have had a liaison with Mr. . . .

I couldn't finish the thought. I was upset enough. If I rehearsed those particular suspicions now, I might be sick again, or simply faint. There was no time for either.

I finished unlocking the door and stepped back. Sebastian held himself still, listening for a time. Only when he was satisfied with the level of silence outside did he slip through the door, leaving me finally and truly alone.

I locked the door and, as quickly as I could, stuffed the key into Isolde's basket. Ignoring her protests, I yanked the note Matthew had passed me from my sleeve.

The handwriting was cramped and the ink was cheap and pale, but eventually I made out:

The church. After moonrise.

I held the paper up to my candle's flame and let it burn.

I shall one day write a book of advice: *A Young Spy's Guide*. In it, I shall take pains to point out that a spy is by necessity a busy individual and must therefore find an opportunity every day to list the tasks required of her and organize them in order of priority. For example, my list at the end of my first day at Bidmarsh House might read:

1) *Discover the true identity of the whimpering woman (who has replaced the veiled mourner in the pantheon of mysterious persons in Peggy Fitzroy's existence).*

2) *Find dates and times for scheduled invasion and assassination attempts, preferably in a nonenciphered form.*

3) *Accomplish 1 and 2 in time to sneak out of the house after dark to make rendezvous with loved ones and co-conspirators.*

4) *Swear faithfully to Our Heavenly Father to never, ever, ever again fall asleep or giggle during services if only Sebastian succeeds in keeping his mouth shut.*

5) *Survive.*

The Young Spy may also at any time be called upon to sit down at the dinner table and conduct herself in such a manner that hosts, enemies, and jailers, in whatever combination, do not suspect she has any priorities at all.

At first, this was helped by dinner being a grim and silent affair. Whatever had been discovered on the grounds, no one was willing to speak of it where the servants could hear. As the desultory removes proceeded, I had far too much time to consider how little information I had and how much I needed. Unfortunately, silence, however wide and gaping, is a contradictory thing in that it provides very few conversational openings. Indeed, the only intelligence I gained during that interminable meal came when Dr. Atterbury returned, blowing on his hands and gulping down the glass of wine Mrs. Oglethorpe directed the butler to give him.

The good cleric informed us that no one at the White Hart had overheard any strangers asking about Bidmarsh House, the Oglethorpes, or one Margaret Fitzroy. Indeed, no one had seen any travelers of any sort passing through the village during the whole day.

Lord Lynnfield remarked coolly that this only proved that whoever had followed me wasn't fool enough to put up at the public house. In this we were in agreement, although I could hardly say so. As it was, I had to stuff my mouth with venison to cover my relief.

There was one other piece of good news. Although he scowled at every dish laid in front of him and snorted each time any person did venture some remark, Sebastian did, in fact, keep his mouth shut.

Given Dr. Atterbury's failure to uncover anything in

the village, I was not surprised when Mrs. Oglethorpe suggested I take myself up to my room directly after dinner. I agreed with what I hoped was nervous and subdued obedience. Once more locked in by the dutiful Hannah, Isolde and I proceeded to curl up together in the armchair and nap.

There was no question but that it was going to be another long night.

As I was certain I would be, I was eventually roused by Hannah, who had brought in my allotted candle and a clean nightdress. I let myself be changed and wished a good night. Hannah closed the door, taking the candle with her as usual. As soon as I saw the light move away, I scrambled from my bed. And I waited.

Despite my nap, I was tired. It had been a long day, and I yearned to remain in bed with the covers pulled up about my ears. This was where my time in waiting once again came to my aid, in that I was used to days that could measure twenty hours out of twenty-four. Compared to flirting and deliberately losing at cards with the French ambassador for six hours straight, a little late-night trespass would be nothing at all.

But before I attempted to make my way to the church, I would do all I could to find some sign of my fellow prisoner. In this I was determined. Quite apart from any bargain I'd made with Sebastian, I would not leave anyone to the nonexistent mercies of Lord Lynnfield, especially when that someone might be my aunt.

My only clock was the moon. I stood at the edge of the

window and peered out carefully from behind the draperies, watching that waning orb inch its way up the vault of the sky. The house had fallen silent around me. The only movement I could detect came from the gardens outside, in the form of torch lights proceeding slowly across the lawn.

Those had to be Lord Lynnfield's men. I counted six lights, then eight.

When I lifted my eyes to the horizon, I could see the church standing black and tall in the moonlight. It looked impossibly distant. When I remembered all Anne Oglethorpe had said about the dangers of the marshland, it seemed impossible I should reach its sanctuary at all. I reminded myself repeatedly that Matthew had come to me. There must be a road through those marshes. Somewhere. That Lynnfield's men would surely be patrolling that road as well as the grounds was something I would deal with when I had to.

I turned away from the window and the unsettling scene beyond. It was time for me to set to work.

My room was pitch black. Because of the men on patrol outside, I did not dare open the draperies, much less light one of my precious candles. I groped about, wincing at every scrape and sound I made. I retrieved the rope ladder from its hiding place underneath my chair and stowed it with the candles and tinderbox in my leather satchel, because one never knew where one might end up on such an eventful evening as I had planned. Isolde followed me, wagging and snuffling, showing every sign of enjoying this new game.

At last, I pulled out the breeches, smock shirt, and stockings I'd hidden in the closet. As painful as this additional delay was, I had to change clothes. I knew from hard experience that attempting any act of stealth in skirts came very close to physical impossibility.

I stuck my straight pin into the breeches seam at my hip where a man might hang a sword and pulled down my smock's hem to hide it. I checked the window again and saw no more lights in the garden. Judging that the way was as clear as it could be, I lit one of my candles and retrieved the key from where I'd hidden it in Isolde's basket.

Isolde whined and pawed at my boots.

"Secrets, Izzy," I whispered, trying to step around her.

She whined again as my toe nudged her. Then she growled meaningfully and nipped at one of my breeches' laces.

"Secrets!" I hissed. In answer, she growled again and scrabbled at my heels.

I bit my lip. I couldn't have her setting up a howl behind me while I was trying to sneak through the house. At the same time, who knew what would happen to the pair of us out in the darkness?

Isolde growled again, as if to demonstrate both her innate ferocity and her willingness to make trouble. I rolled my eyes.

"This is why spies in general do not keep pets." I scooped Isolde up with my free hand and put her, and a biscuit, into my satchel. "Secrets!"

She made no sound but settled into the bottom of the bag. Praying we did not both come to regret this sudden soft-ness of head and heart, I turned the key in the lock, put my hand on the doorknob, prayed, and pulled.

The door came silently open and I stepped out into the dead black corridor.

CHAPTER THIRTY-FIVE

IN WHICH A NUMBER OF NEW THINGS
ARE FOUND IN THE DARKNESS.

We are informed by writers of dramas and romances that there are two places to confine a female prisoner in any great house: the attics and the cellars. Given the possibility that this particular prisoner had been brought into the house by means of a tunnel—such as, I was reliably informed, smugglers routinely employed—I decided to begin with the cellars.

I had made my way through a dark house with nefarious intent before. But during that previous attempt, the house had been empty. This house was filled with an unknown number of persons, any of whom might be light sleepers or even wide-awake. It also had armed men patrolling the grounds who might have orders to reconnoiter the house at regular intervals.

That other time, I'd had Matthew with me. I wished I had him with me now, although, I must confess, what I wished for even more was a lantern. As I picked my way down the grand curving staircase, the candle in my hand flickered badly from the drafts and my own movement. The wax was softening in my grip, and some had dripped onto my fingers.

But this was far from the worst of my circumstances. I was utterly exposed here. If anyone came upon me now, I had nowhere to hide and no way to explain. But I also had no choice. This was the only stair I knew in Bidmarsh House, and I had no time to search for some safer alternative.

The marble foyer was cold as a tomb. My breath steamed in the feeble candlelight. I stood in the center of the vestibule, turning slowly, and then I saw it—the green baize door that was, in so many grand houses, the portal to those nether regions occupied by the servants.

Surely, surely, surely such a door was not kept locked. Surely it must be left open in case of some summons after dark. I probably shouldn't have thought of that. A sleepy servant stumbling through the kitchens because the master rang for milk and brandy could end my investigations just as surely as Lord Lynnfield's armed men.

I reached for the handle and I pulled. The door silently swung back, but my relief was momentary. Light flickered outside one of the foyer's grand windows. My heart slammed against my ribs and I darted through the baize door. My candle flickered wildly and more hot wax spattered onto my fingertips.

I also nearly toppled down the staircase in front of me.

I slapped my hand against the wall and stumbled back, bumping hard against the door I'd just come through. Isolde whined uneasily in my satchel. I stood on that top stair for a moment, trying to recover breath and nerve. No one came. No one tugged at the door at my back and no light showed below me. I swallowed and started down these new stairs.

They did not go down very far, and I quickly found myself in a narrow corridor lined with closed doors. I ignored them and moved cautiously forward.

Someone was snoring.

My breath stopped. I told myself I could not freeze—I could not even hesitate. I had to keep moving toward the open doorway, even though each step felt as though it must surely be my last.

I crossed the threshold and found myself in the kitchens. The snoring was fainter here, but still sounded to me like the rumble of approaching thunder. I raised my candle with my trembling hand and made out the long board tables, the counters, all the great pots and similar utensils laid out for the coming day's work. The place smelled of fresh food and old slops and was filled with a cold that was unrelieved by the carefully banked coals in the hearth.

There were, however, candles waiting on the mantel, prudently and efficiently set into holders by diligent servants whom I surely had to remember to thank later. I helped myself to one such candleholder. Service to the Crown did not require me to burn my fingers, especially if it meant I would drop my only source of light.

The snoring faltered. I bit my lip and tasted blood. My hand shook so badly, I almost put my old candle out before I had the fresh one lit.

Isolde whined again.

Something creaked. Something scrabbled behind the walls. The snoring faltered again and Isolde stirred restlessly.

I made myself ignore all of these noises and concentrate on the room. No fewer than four doors led out of this cavernous kitchen. One, I could see, opened onto the gardens. The next . . . I was halfway across the floor before the stench told me that way was the scullery.

The third opened onto yet another stair. This one was flagstone and smelled of damp and dirt. I slipped inside and started down. My boot soles slapped against the stone and the sound echoed off the walls. I ducked the trailing cobwebs that hung from the walls and ceilings. My hands were all but numb from fear and cold. I could no longer hear the snoring, but the scrabbling was getting louder. Something squeaked, and for a change it wasn't Isolde or me. The Bidmarsh rats were awake and at play in the cellars down below.

I don't know quite what I expected of a smugglers' cellar. The ceiling was low enough that I had to duck beneath the ancient beams. The floor was dirt and the atmosphere smelled cold, dank, and unwholesome.

There were doors in the left-hand wall. Wooden and

banded with iron, they reminded me most unpleasantly of the doors in the Tower. No one had wasted money on locks down here. These doors were barred with broad wooden beams, and there were a lot of them.

Fighting indecision, and a not unjustified fear of lurking, horrible, unnaturally huge rats, I reached into my satchel and lifted Isolde out. She wriggled anxiously in my hand as I set her down.

"Come on, girl," I whispered. "There's somebody here. They might have cake. Come on."

I pushed her forward. She looked at me, puzzled, and turned in a circle three or four times, growling at the dark, but instead of moving forward, she backed up until her rump pressed against my boots.

I straightened, pressing my hand against my mouth to keep my exclamations of despair silent. I told myself it had been a poor bet from the beginning and I could not blame Isolde. But even as I reached for her, the pup leapt to her feet, put her nose to the floor, and scampered ahead, all the way to the door farthest from the stair.

I followed, hoping against all hope. These were probably the longest odds I'd play all night, but what other help did I have? When I reached the door, Isolde was scrabbling at the crack beneath it, trying to dig herself an entrance.

From the other side, I heard a heavy rustling and a low moan.

"Who is that?" I whispered at the lock.

The moan cut off short, only to be followed by more indistinct shuffling.

"I'm a friend," I said. "I promise. Who is there?"

"Margaret?" said the woman on the other side. "Good Lord, Margaret Fitzroy—is that you?"

I licked my dry lips. "Yes, Sophy. It's me."

It seemed I wasn't going to need my rope ladder after all.

CHAPTER THIRTY-SIX

In which Our Heroine is once again
forced to reevaluate the utility
of corsets and small dogs.

The bar was unwieldy and had to be slid out of two iron brackets. I swore and strained and made far too much noise, all of which set Isolde yipping at a dangerous volume.

Eventually, however, I did manage to get the door open. The chamber on the other side was about the size of my bedroom upstairs and contained a large number of wooden boxes and kegs.

It also contained Sophy Howe.

She sat propped up against a pile of corded chests. She'd been bound hand and foot. Her face and dress were smeared with dirt and probably worse than dirt, and her hair was in straggling disarray. She shrank back from my meager candlelight, blinking hard.

I hated Sophy Howe, and she returned the sentiment. I had in the past amused myself by imagining her in various uncomfortable and embarrassing situations. But not like this. Never like this.

I could not even smile when Isolde bounded in to scrabble around her skirts, looking for biscuits.

"Please tell me you brought something more useful for an escape than this creature."

I had to give Sophy her due. Filthy, imprisoned, and tightly bound, she still raised her chin defiantly.

Her familiar contempt broke my paralysis. "Fortunately, yes." I dropped to my knees beside her and set my candle on the nearest keg. "Give me your hands." I pulled out my straight pin.

Sophy's hands had been tied behind her, and she wriggled around until she had her back to me. The ropes were stout, and her slender, white wrists were badly chafed. I winced in sympathy and set to work.

"How did this happen?" I asked as I picked and sawed at the rough hemp.

She was silent for so long, I thought she wasn't going to answer at all. When she did speak, the words came out in a harsh whisper. "I believed I was deceiving Lord Lynnfield. He told me that once Sebastian and I were both here in Bidmarsh, we could be married and wait out what was to come in safety. He . . ." She stopped and I heard her swallow. I suspected tears. I kept my eyes on the rope in front of me. I was less than halfway through it. I cursed myself for not remembering a proper knife. What was the point in experience with such things if it was not properly applied?

"It was a trap, of course. I knew it when I agreed. I thought if I could just get to Sebastian, I could convince him . . ." She stopped again. "You thought the same, didn't you? You thought, *Since I know it's a trap, I will be able to get out before it's sprung.*"

"I'd be lying if I said no," I muttered.

I expected a witty rejoinder, but Sophy had other things on her mind. "Have you seen Sebastian? Is he all right?"

"Yes. He's worried about you." I sat back on my heels. "Pull your wrists apart. See if you can break the rope."

"He doesn't know," she declared as she struggled to separate her wrists. "Ow! That hurts."

"No, he doesn't, and yes, I know. Try again."

Sophy gritted her teeth and tried a second time. This time the rope snapped. She gasped with the pain as she slowly brought her arms around to a more natural position. She looked at her raw, bleeding wrists and at once grasped the essentials of her situation.

"Will it scar, do you think?"

"Mine didn't," I assured her as I moved to her feet. "Matthew has a recipe for an excellent medicinal salve. I'll have him copy it out for you."

I shoved her filthy skirts aside and started sawing vigorously at the ropes that held her ankles. *Should I have done these first?* Then she could have at least run, if someone came upon us suddenly.

But run where?

"I was trying to help, you know," said Sophy with a startling amount of belligerence, considering the circumstances.

"How? By getting Lord Tierney arrested?" Isolde had grown bored with these events and was delving into corners. This was taking too long. I should have shut the door. I should have hidden the bar. I stabbed at the rope.

"Lynnfield and the Oglethorpe woman had two letters to be delivered at the masquerade. One was genuine, with plans to assassinate the prince and how it should be timed for best effect to support the coming invasion. The other looked similar but was just a dummy to ensnare Lord Tierney. The information it contained was false, so even if the code was broken, no real plans would be compromised. Sebastian was meant to hide the dummy at the masquerade, because . . ."

"Because they knew I would follow him."

"And find the dummy letter to give to Tierney, exactly. You have always been predictable in these matters."

I gritted my teeth and kept sawing at the abominably thick ropes. "You should consider carefully before insulting the one setting you free, you know."

Sophy sniffed. "Sebastian knew there were two letters. I convinced him to help me lay hands on the other. I told him we would profit if we had copies of them both. We could either sell them later or use them as evidence against his brother and the Oglethorpe, if things didn't go as they planned."

Forgery and blackmail, two of Sophy's specialties. Three, if you counted seduction. I had no doubt she'd worked all her wiles on Sebastian to get him to play along.

The rope parted another fraction of an inch. I really had to get Mr. Tinderflint to tell me the name of his jeweler. The man did excellent work.

"After that, it was simply a matter of putting the genuine letter into the hidey hole where you would find it, instead of the false one they meant you to have."

My hands stilled. Had she said the *genuine* letter?

"That was why you were in the palace library. You were swapping the letters."

"Sebastian would not do it, so I had to."

That explained why Sebastian had taken the front ways rather than the back stairs. I had been meant to follow him. While I was busy cursing myself once more for a fool, I realized something else. This meant I had given the genuine letter, with the real assassination plans, to Mr. Tinderflint. That was the letter that had been taken from Mr. Tinderflint and was now in the hands of assorted agents of the Crown and, most likely, that legendary code breaker Mr. Willis.

"That was why Sebastian came to my door during the masque," I said slowly. "He wanted to get me away so he could search my rooms, or have them searched, for the genuine letter."

"He did not agree with my plan but in the end was not able to do much about it." She paused. "He was terribly angry, which ought to please you."

So Sophy had, in fact, been playing a double game. Quietly, using her own methods, she'd managed to get the real information about the planned assassination to the prince and his people.

"He thought Julius would find out I had switched the letters. He thought I would be in danger." Sophy's voice filled with bitter pride. "What a time for him to be right and for me to ignore it."

I took a moment to appreciate the irony inherent in the fact that Sophy's plans had worked out rather better than mine. Until, that is, she had decided to emulate the rest of us and disregard Sebastian's understanding of his own family.

"Why are you down here?" I asked her as I resumed sawing at her ropes.

"I was in the attics. They threatened me with rather dire consequences if I attempted to reach Sebastian." She swallowed. "They meant it."

She'd been trying to reach her lover when she'd been caught outside my door. That made a good deal of sense. What did not make sense was that she'd been left alive. This thought felt like a blade against my ribs. I told myself it didn't matter. I had to keep working.

"Well," I murmured, "you did ask me to come find you when I understood what kind of favor you'd done me."

"I had hoped you'd work it out sooner than this."

"I'm slow—you've often pointed this out."

"I'm proven right again. How thrilling."

The rope snapped. I scrambled to my feet and held out my hand. Sophy took it and let me help to pull her upright. But as soon as I let go, she staggered and fell hard against me, almost slamming the both of us, and the candle, to the floor.

She hissed. "I don't think I can walk."

Isolde made my answer for me. She barked and ran out into the main cellar area.

"No!" I gasped. Then I heard them. Footsteps. Heavy footsteps running across the floor above. Voices shouting.

"Lie down!" I ordered Sophy as I snatched up the candle. Overhead a door scraped open. I swung our cell door shut and, in the same motion, pressed myself against the wall and blew my candle out. The darkness was instant and absolute.

Boots thudded against dirt outside our door. I clutched the straight pin in my cold and sweating hand.

"I'll check the tunnel. You and you, come with me." It was Lord Lynnfield's voice and he was not alone. What surely must have been a whole army worth of footsteps raced past us.

"I'll check on the girl," called Mrs. Oglethorpe after him.

The sounds of running faded. *She means me; she means me up in my room,* I prayed frantically, but to no effect. Light appeared around the edges of our cell door. Our unbarred cell door.

That door swung slowly back and light spilled into the room. I had just enough time to see that Sophy had, for once, done as she was told and stretched out on the dirt floor, before the door cut off my view.

"Now it's you?" Sophy croaked.

"Who else has been here?" Eleanor Oglethorpe stepped, I supposed, across the threshold. She had a light with her. I could see the flickering glow of her candles around the edge of the door, but concealed as I was by oak and iron, it was all I could see.

Sophy managed a credible snort. My sister maid of honor might not have a scruple in her body, but she did not lack for nerve. "They didn't leave a card," she said coldly.

I couldn't see what was happening. There was a rustling of cloth, and the light dipped. Sophy squeaked.

"Who else? Was it Sebastian?"

Before Sophy could frame her answer, my world was shattered by a tiny, angry yip.

Oh, Isolde.

More rustling and abrupt movement of the light. A shriek from Mrs. Oglethorpe. An outraged bark. A heartbeat to hope Isolde had drawn blood.

"Where is she?" cried Mrs. Oglethorpe. "Where?"

In answer, I kicked the door back. Mrs. Oglethorpe jumped, stumbled over Sophy, and toppled to the floor.

I dived down on top of her, grabbing at flailing arms and rolling us over. I was vaguely aware of Sophy struggling to grab the candelabra and get out of the way at the same time.

Isolde yipped and Mrs. Oglethorpe screamed and I twisted, coming up straddled across her body with my hand gripping one of hers and my knee pinning down the other.

Oh, yes, and with my very sharp straight pin pressed against her long, skinny neck.

"Not a sound," I breathed. "Not one. Sophy, get up." Isolde growled. "Secrets," I told her, and she silenced.

I didn't look away. I couldn't. The Old Fury went still, but her mind was at least as sharp as my little pin. She'd be looking for some trick—any trick—to try.

She began by testing my resolve. "You wouldn't dare," she spat. "You haven't the nerve."

I felt myself smile. "I am the daughter of Elizabeth Fitzroy." My voice was as steady as stone and ice. "You are trying to bring war to my country, and you would use me and my family to do it. You imprisoned and abused a colleague. You threatened the lives of me and mine." I dug the tip of my pin a little farther into her skin. "Think on all this, madame, and then tell yourself again what Elizabeth Fitzroy's daughter will not do." Mrs. Oglethorpe didn't answer. My smile stretched, and it was not at all a pleasant feeling. "Sophy, get the rope and find a gag."

As it transpires, tying up an uncooperative person is more difficult than cutting a cooperative one free, especially when you have not been able to make advance preparation. Fortunately, Sophy had recovered enough of her strength to be of some help.

"Margaret, stop this," the Old Fury commanded as we

wrenched her hands behind her and wrapped the lengths of severed rope around her wrists. "Remember your mother. Remember I am the one who is your friend."

"My mother was never your friend." Once again, all those years of being confined in corsets and ribbons were proving unexpectedly useful. Both Sophy and I were rather good with knots. "She betrayed you a hundred times to the Hanoverians."

It was rewarding to watch the Old Fury flush scarlet, but not quite as rewarding as grabbing her skinny ankles so Sophy could wind another length of rope around them. "Elizabeth Pierpont never betrayed me."

"Perhaps not, but Mrs. Jonathan Fitzroy did." I let myself smile. "She completely took you in."

"Your father and Lord Tierney have taken you in, foolish child! You—"

I stuffed the scrap of cloth Sophy had torn from her skirt into Mrs. Oglethorpe's mouth. I should have done that first.

I meant for us to bar her in. I'm sure I also meant to leave her with some clever parting words. Why should she be the only one who got to make a dramatic exit? All these plans, however, were entirely wiped away by the sound of heavy thuds and muffled curses.

I grabbed Sophy with one hand and Isolde with the other and ran out into the cellar. Or rather, I ran and Sophy stumbled.

There was just enough light to see the staircase. There were sounds behind us—men running, raised voices. I dragged

Sophy up the stairs and we all but fell into the kitchen. Sophy banged into my back. She was in skirts and had been tied up for Heaven knew how long. I was in breeches and boots and could move much faster.

I hated Sophy Howe.

Lord Lynnfield was behind us. I could leave her and make my own escape.

I hated myself for thinking this.

I yanked Sophy hard across the kitchen, through the garden door, and up the three steps into the open air. Sophy gasped and moaned and Isolde wriggled and growled and I dragged them both into the bitter cold and dark.

"Sebastian!" she cried, or tried to. She also tried to pull away.

"No!" I yanked her back, and at that moment, at least, I was the stronger of us. With all the breath in my body, I hauled her through the kitchen gardens and across the dead and frozen lawn, away from the house, toward the wall, toward the lake and the marsh, where we could hide in the tall grasses. Where we could wait until the searchers passed us by, and from there make our way to the church. Matthew and my father would wait for us. They'd make Olivia wait. They'd be there with a coach or a cart, or horses, or something. The moon had risen hours ago; now it was well past its zenith. It didn't matter. They'd be there. They would.

The garden opened in front of us. There were more shouts, but none close. I charged through the gate. Sophy wailed. Isolde wriggled and scrabbled, and I almost lost hold of them both. The lake stretched before us, black and still, its ice shelves shining in what little moonlight remained.

A figure rose from between the boats at the lake's edge. I skidded to a halt.

"I thought you might come this way."

Lord Lynnfield raised his sword.

CHAPTER THIRTY-SEVEN

WHEREIN THERE IS MORE THAN ONE ENDING.

Lord Lynnfield, I noticed, favored a cutlass. No dainty court rapier for him. He was a serious man with serious business. I measured the shrinking distance between us as he advanced. On my own I would have run, but Sophy was already staggering and whimpering as I pushed us both back. She had reached her limit.

"Sebastian!" she cried again.

Much to my shock, there came an answer. "Sophy!" Someone jerked Sophy out of my grip. "What's happened?" demanded Sebastian.

This, I decided, was one of those rare moments Mr. Tinderflint had mentioned when the truth would serve best. "Your brother had her trussed up in the cellar," I told

Sebastian. "We're lucky she's not dead." I paused. "Why aren't you dead, Sophy?"

"You're a liar!" Sebastian growled.

"No! It's the truth!" announced Sophy. I couldn't see what she did then. I didn't dare take my eyes off Lynnfield. He'd reached the edge of the gravel, and now he waded through the grass. I should run, before he got any closer. Alone. Sophy had Sebastian. I could leave them to each other's tender care and run.

Run out into the marsh, with its channels and quicksands and its gang of Lynnfield's smuggling men.

Isolde trotted up to me from wherever she'd been and whined questioningly. I ignored her.

"He promised you two could marry, didn't he?" I said to Sebastian, wherever he was behind me. "He said he'd remain a bachelor and that you'd be his heir. All you had to do was lie low and not do anything stupid until the invasion played out. But Sophy worked out their plan and they had to try to silence her." I paused again. "Why did you leave her alive?" I asked Lynnfield this time. "Come to that, why am I alive?"

"Why waste the bait?" Lynnfield shrugged. Fewer than three yards separated us now. "There were still others to rope in."

"You filthy bastard!" Sebastian finally stepped into my line of sight. His fists were clenched; he was breathing hard. I suspected he meant to put himself between Lynnfield's cutlass and Sophy, which was surprisingly gallant of him.

Lynnfield made a strangled sound. "Stop being ridiculous, Sebastian. It's already a cock-up. Even if I was dead, do you think the Hanoverians would ever hand you the title now? Our mother has enough letters to convict us both, and she'll use them. If she's still alive, that is. Have you left her alive, Miss Fitzroy?" The note of hope in this question set my skin crawling.

I didn't bother to answer. He was stalling, holding us here until his men arrived. How many men did he have? How close were they? There was no way to tell and no way to find out.

"He's going to kill us now," I said. "That was the plan all along. To get us out here and make us vanish in the marsh. That way, even if things went wrong, there'd be no witnesses to his role in the conspiracy. You, me, and Sophy, we'd all be dead and gone."

Sebastian turned to me, trying to see my face. He was wavering, uncertain which enemy to believe.

"She's lying, you idiot." Lynnfield sighed. "We only have to keep things quiet until the landing!"

"I never changed sides," I reminded him.

Lord Lynnfield ran, cat quick, straight for his brother's back.

I tackled Sebastian sideways and we all went down in a heap together with Sophy. There was cursing and flailing and roaring, and something hard slammed against my waist.

With a wordless roar, Sebastian shook himself free

of our writhing mass. Lynnfield was on his feet. His blade gleamed in the moonlight. Sebastian leapt at him, head down, arms out. Lynnfield swung the cutlass, but the blow missed. Sebastian hit him dead center and they collapsed, rolling, kicking, cursing. Sebastian came up on top and Lynnfield dealt him a blow to the chin that snapped his head around. They rolled over again.

"Sebastian!" screamed Sophy. I got hold of her by the sleeve and dragged her to her feet. I looked about us, searching for torches, waiting for shouts, trying to decide which way to run.

Cursing, struggling, tumbling, the Sandfords rolled down the hill toward the lake. They shouted and they swore and they ordered each other to stop.

They rolled out onto the lake's black ice.

Sophy ripped herself from my hands and stumbled down the slope, still trying to scream. I ran after her. Isolde was barking somewhere. I kept after Sophy, swearing and crying, with no thought in my head except to try to get her back from the lake's edge. I all but stumbled over Lynnfield's cutlass where it lay like a fallen branch on the gravel. I scooped it up with numbed fingers.

"Stop it, you idiot! We'll both drown!" screamed Lynnfield.

He was on his knees on the ice with Sebastian in front of him. Sebastian roared and somehow found enough purchase to fling himself forward.

"See you in hell!" Sebastian grabbed his brother's wrists. "See you in hell!"

"Sebastian, stop!" shrieked Sophy.

But Sebastian was too far gone in his own rage. He twisted and swung himself around, sliding on the ice, swinging his brother's prone body out toward the black and open waters. Lynnfield screamed again and slid to the ice shelf's ragged edge, and over.

There was barely any splash. He was just gone. Swallowed by darkness.

There was a moment of silence, broken only by the sound of harsh panting. Sebastian turned his head toward the shore, and me, and Sophy.

He laughed. He threw back his head and flung his fists to the sky. "Yes! You goddamned bastard! I got you! I beat you!"

Then he leapt to his feet.

There was an ugly sound, like glass breaking, only slower and much, much louder. Sophy screamed.

We all stared at the ice and saw the crack form. Sebastian leapt sideways, slipped, and slammed down. The shelf under him crumbled.

Sophy lunged forward, too fast and too hard for me to keep hold of. She all but fell down the bank and I threw myself after her. Sebastian sprawled on the ice. I couldn't tell if he was sliding toward the waters or if the waters were advancing beneath the fragile ice to claim him.

Sophy was on the ice now too, on her stomach, struggling

toward him. He scrambled to reach her, but there was no purchase for him. They were screaming to each other, incoherent words of love and desperation. The ice was under me too, and I was flat on my belly, like they were, trying to scrabble forward and somehow catch hold of Sophy's hems.

There was the smack of flesh against flesh. Another cry, different this time, for it was hope and triumph. Sebastian had hold of Sophy's wounded wrist. She went still a moment. I grabbed her skirts and used them to haul myself far enough forward that I could grab her waist.

"Hold on, you idiots!" I bellowed. "Hold still!"

I don't know if Sebastian struggled. I don't know if he squeezed Sophy's wounds too hard, or if he was too heavy, or if his brother reached up from the black depths to haul him down. I couldn't see. All I knew was that Sophy screamed, and I felt her weight shift and his weight slip.

Sebastian screamed, and that scream ended in a horrible choking, and in the next heartbeat, that choking ended too.

Sophy tried to fling herself forward. I held on and rolled, and rolled again. The ice cracked. Sophy struggled. I rolled again and cried and prayed.

I felt gravel under my back, against my cheek.

I stopped. Sophy was on top of me, wailing out her grief, screaming Sebastian's name to the entirely indifferent sky.

She was very heavy.

Someone was running toward us. With the last of my energies, I shoved Sophy to the side and struggled to my feet.

Whoever it was, whatever their orders, I would meet them standing. I would not be humiliated at the last by dying tangled in Sophy Howe's skirts. I raised my hands. I raised my head.

I looked into Matthew's wide, frightened gray eyes.

I fainted dead away.

CHAPTER THIRTY-EIGHT

BY WAY OF AN EPILOGUE, IN WHICH
ALL IS REVEALED — AT LEAST,
ALL THAT'S LEFT.

It was a long, cold, maddened coach ride back to London. My father all but killed the horses he'd stolen from the Lynnfield stables. Sophy didn't stop weeping the entire way. How Olivia resisted the urge to slap her, I am not sure. My only excuse was exhaustion. That, and the fact that Matthew wouldn't let go of my hands for a single instant.

It seems that the three of them were the direct cause of Lynnfield's men failing to put a stop to the altercation at the lakeside. When I missed the rendezvous at the church, Father and Olivia had both become convinced that something was horribly wrong, such as my having been found out. The only solution was to make use of Father's extensive knowledge of the area and come look for me at once. They found the alarm had been raised, concluded I was the cause, and set about an impromptu rescue attempt. This, in the end, necessitated incapacitating any number of ruffians.

Matthew declined to correct any of these particulars. I made a note to have a word with him on the subject as soon as we were alone. He did venture that Father might not be the best role model for my impressionable cousin.

Despite Father's best efforts, we were not entirely in time to stop all of the assassination plans. One person, a Mr. Freeman by name, did escape the net flung by the palace guard. This Freeman got one shot off at Prince George from an empty box in the Drury Lane theater. That shot sailed over the prince's shoulder and hit a defenseless wall, causing some small damage to the plasterwork. In what must be taken as a bad sign for the Jacobite cause, Mr. Freeman was promptly tackled by an irate mob and barely escaped with his life.

All witnesses agreed that throughout the entire incident, the prince conducted himself with a soldier's courage as well as royal dignity, and public opinion in his favor swelled. Princess Caroline was by then recovered enough from her own tragedy to stand and greet him when he returned to the palace. Their tender reunion was recounted by the papers in great detail.

When I made my own return to the palace, Princess Caroline remained seated and showed few signs of tenderness. She did, however, shake her head a great deal as I recounted what happened at Bidmarsh House.

When I asked her if I could take the winter off from waiting, she agreed.

Sophy Howe also went home for the winter. This time her arrival could be verified, for Molly Lepell received letters almost daily complaining about how very dull everything was and that nobody in her home county had any head for cards.

According to the papers, the brothers Sandford had died in a tragic accident. There was one account in particular of Sebastian losing his life trying to pull his noble brother from the lake that I suspect might have been contributed by Sophy herself. Olivia read it aloud to me over breakfast. She tried to make me laugh at it. She failed.

The noted artist Mr. James Thornhill tried to cancel the articles of apprenticeship for the troublesome and frequently absent Matthew Reade, as well as to demand payment for unfulfilled years of service. But the academy's students and masters rebelled in such numbers that Mr. Thornhill was forced to relent. I suspect there might also have been a quiet word sent from the palace, but I have no direct proof of this.

Father tendered his official resignation to whoever within the depths of government took such things. He said he was growing too old for adventures and wanted time to smoke and think and take his leisure. I expected this to last perhaps as long as a month.

I was two solid weeks in bed recovering from a fever brought on by exposure to ice and falling damps. During my illness, Olivia, who remained infuriatingly healthy, took it upon herself to spoil Isolde until she really did forget every single command I'd ever taught her.

Also during this time, an enormous bundle of letters arrived from Colchester. They were filled with Aunt Pierpont's profuse apologies if she had caused any worry, as well as a long and detailed account of how the local mail coach had been beset by highwaymen, all of whom escaped and were even now being pursued across the countryside.

I found myself wondering exactly who those highwaymen had been, and which lake they had dropped my aunt's papers into and whether the medallion had gone with them.

Mr. Tinderflint, having been released from the Tower without fuss or apologies, sent us all gold-edged invitations to a dinner to be held at Tierney Manor as soon as I was *quite* recovered. My card mentioned that Mr. Reade had also received an invitation.

Two days before the suggested date, I made a trip to that august residence on my own. My patron's door was answered by a slim footman in the plainest possible livery. He evidenced no surprise at all to see a solitary maiden on his master's doorstep and conducted me into a demure yellow and cream morning room with a fire blazing in the broad hearth.

I sat on a comfortable sofa and clutched my reticule, which contained, among other things, what would ordinarily be a month's supply of handkerchiefs.

My patron was not long in arriving. He carefully slid

the doors shut behind him before making his bow. He had restored himself to his customary magnificence, from gilded buckles to sparkling rings to full-bottomed wig.

"How are you, Peggy, my dear?" he inquired as I stood to make my curtsy.

"Better, thank you."

"Please sit, please sit." Mr. Tinderflint gestured toward the sofa. "You're pale. You should not be up yet. I've instructed my man to make up some chocolate, as I know you don't care for tea . . ." His words trailed away. "Has something new happened?"

"No, not new. I . . ." I coughed into my handkerchief. Why was I even here? What did this matter? Surely now that the Sandfords could no longer trouble me, I could just set about being happy.

Mr. Tinderflint also coughed. "As you know by now, Her Royal Highness has been fully informed—yes, fully—as to the names of all those responsible for uncovering the assassination plot. She has been fulsome in her praise of you, and she expressed to me privately—yes, quite privately—that she hopes you will choose eventually to return to the palace. Apparently Princess Anne misses you terribly."

"As does Lady Portland, I'm sure," I murmured. "Is there any word of the Oglethorpes?"

"They appear to have abandoned their house at Godalming for the time being. Most likely they have gone abroad to join the rest of the family in Paris." He paused. "You did magnificently, Peggy. I could not have hoped for half so much when we set out on this path together."

I dropped my gaze, my emotions a tangled knot inside me. I could still change my mind and remain silent. I could simply choose not to know and continue to behave as if my family consisted of Father and Olivia and—perhaps one day in the very distant future, if all went unexpectedly well— Matthew.

But it would not last and I knew that. Secrets rotted certainty. Sooner or later, they would break through.

I reached into my reticule. I pulled out the gold chain and locket and the signet ring, and laid them on the coffee table. Mr. Tinderflint looked at them. His face betrayed not the smallest sign of upset.

"I found these in your room above the Cocoa Tree," I said. "We . . . I . . . searched it. I confess to that, and I am not sorry."

Mr. Tinderflint gently touched the locket with the tips of his fingers. "I wondered if you might," he breathed. "I did not know whether to hope you had, or had not. I know . . . I know I should have spoken to you before, but the truth of the matter is, I did not know how to begin."

"When did you become lovers?"

Mr. Tinderflint's head jerked up with a great quivering of chins. "Lovers? Oh, dear heavens, Peggy, Peggy, no, no! No, never . . . that is to say, no—Elizabeth, your mother, was not my lover!"

All my anger reared up inside me. I meant to begin

shouting at him, to say I would no longer tolerate his lies. I had done too much, suffered and dared too much, for him to treat me like his child protégé any longer.

"My love was your grandmother."

My jaw dropped.

Fortunately, Mr. Tinderflint wasn't looking at me at that moment. He had taken the ring and locket into his hands and was turning them over, slowly and carefully.

"You've only met your grandfather's second wife, of course," he said. "The first Mrs. Pierpont was a very different woman. She . . ." Memory dimmed Mr. Tinderflint's gaze and softened his voice. "They made a very poor match, and I was, you may imagine, much younger and, shall we say, a far different figure of a man." He shifted his weight. The chair creaked in answer. "We met at court. She was already married to Pierpont, who was clearly her inferior in every way, and she was very unhappy. I was rather enthralled with the idea of an intrigue with such a woman and . . ." He paused again and closed his hand around the locket. "Peggy, I should have told you. I wanted to tell you. But there were so many dangers and so much I might yet have to do that could fall upon your head. I wanted to preserve that last measure of distance between us."

The paralysis caused by his words was complete. Even my tongue refused to move. He was babbling, falling into his habit of embellishment and repetition. He'd never say what was necessary, and I could no longer stand the delays. "There was a child. That's why Uncle Pierpont hated my mother, even though she was his older sister. He found out somehow she was illegitimate."

Mr. Tinderflint nodded. "Your mother, Elizabeth Amelia Pierpont, was my natural daughter by Elizabeth Margaret Pierpont. You, Peggy, are my granddaughter."

I stood, slowly. I have no idea what expression showed upon my face, but I believe that I may have, for once in my life, successfully loomed. I can say with confidence, and some pride, that Mr. Tinderflint, who could kill a man with his bare hands and not flinch at the deed, shrank back.

"You knew when we met. You *knew* who I was."

"Yes." For a brief moment, I gained some slight, and most unmaidenly, satisfaction in the fact that he seemed genuinely afraid of what I might do next. "I would have spoken sooner . . . yes, yes, well, I might have spoken much sooner, but your mother asked me to keep the secret."

I waited.

"She knew the scandal of her true birth would make things even more difficult for you," he told me. "With your father gone, there were already rumors concerning your legitimacy."

I knew about those. I had grown up hearing them. "And when she died? You left me in that house with a man you *knew* to be a traitor!" Left me in danger of Sandfords and Oglethorpes and every other overly ambitious Jacobite slinking about the streets.

"I did, and I did it for the very same reasons I kept my silence for so long. I truly, truly believed that after he lost his business the first time, your uncle was done with the Jacobites. Indeed, he might have been, were it not for the Sandfords and Oglethorpes insisting he take up their cause again." Mr. Tinderflint made some effort to straighten himself. "That was why I sought you out. I heard the Old Fury meant to press the engagement. It was a step too far. I would have intervened even had . . . other necessities not made it convenient."

"You knew I was your granddaughter when you decided to use me to flush out the palace conspirators. You sent me into danger, knowing!"

"Yes. I did. Just as I quite deliberately endangered Lady Francesca before you, and Elizabeth—my only daughter—before you both." He lifted his eyes to mine, and both gaze and words were perfectly steady. "This is who I am, Peggy. This is what I have given my life over to. Perhaps you can understand now why I might have hesitated at taking on any part of the care of an eight-year-old child."

I had no answer for this. Except, perhaps, one.

"Does my father know?"

"I don't know. I never asked him, and Elizabeth never confided that point to me."

"I'm going to tell him."

"I would expect nothing less. You should perhaps do it before our dinner. I dislike having secrets around the table. It impedes the flow of good conversation."

What was I to do? I'd come here with no plan, no genuine expectation. I sneezed. I wiped my nose. I stared at the fire. I waited for more outrage to arrive, or at least an appropriate storm of tears. I waited for something, anything.

Anything other than this obscure and not entirely comfortable sort of relief. After all, I had at last achieved my goal, hadn't I? I knew the truth of myself and my family. No one could wield their secrets against me again. At least, not easily.

I looked up at the very fat, somewhat ridiculous, shrewd, dangerous, sad man in front of me. The man who was my friend, my patron, my chief goad and troublemaker, and my grandfather.

Who had almost gotten me, my cousin, and my father killed. Who played at kings and thrones and lied whenever he felt the need. Who set me loose to become a spy and troublemaker in my own right. Who made it possible for me to meet Matthew and assorted lords, kings, and princesses, and to try my worth against the whole world.

And win.

Who was now watching me anxiously, waiting for whatever I might choose to say or do.

"I think," I said slowly, "this is going to be a very interesting dinner party."

SARAH ZETTEL is an award-winning science fiction, fantasy, romance, and mystery writer and the author of the American Fairy trilogy and the Palace of Spies trilogy. She is married to a rocket scientist and has a cat named Buffy the Vermin Slayer. Visit her at **www.sarahzettel.com**.